RJ WHELDRAKE

*To Alan —
Wishing you all the
best for a great read!
Martin (RJ)*

A TRICK OF THE LIGHT

Copyright © 2023 RJ Wheldrake. All rights reserved

No part of this publication may be reproduced, distributed, or transmitted in any form or by any means, including photocopying, recording, or other electronic or mechanical methods, without the prior written permission of the publisher, except in the case of brief quotations embodied in reviews and certain other non-commercial uses permitted by copyright law.

ISBN: 9798391660705

For Linda

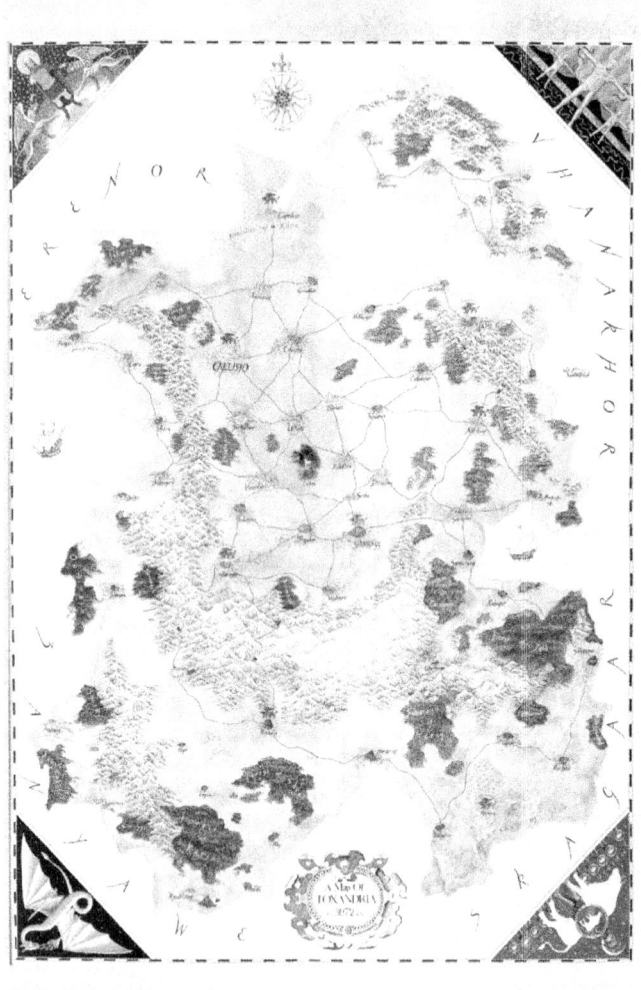

A Map of the island of Eudora in the Hierarchy of Vhanakhor

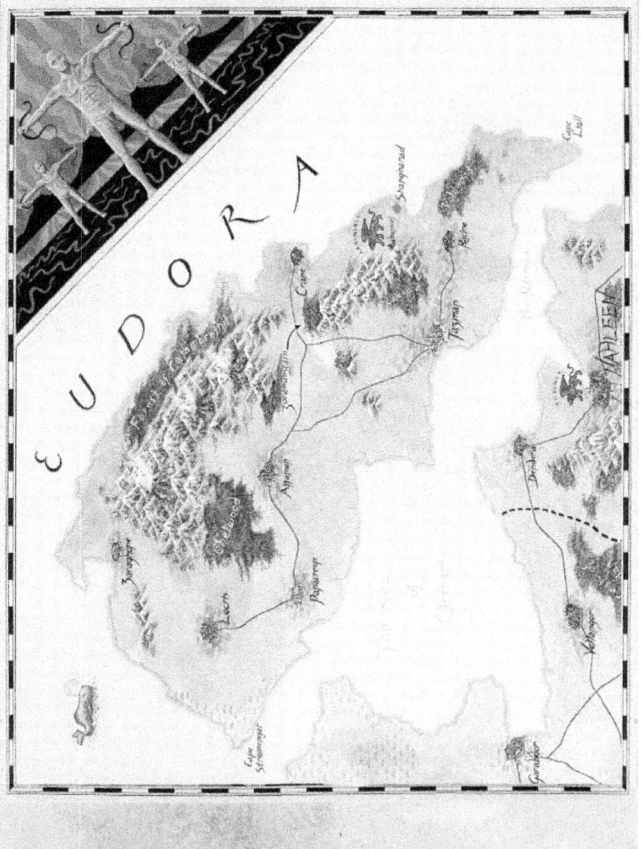

The Exiles' Lament

Beneath that sun, that cruel unblinking eye,
We toilers in these foreign fields of dust
Oppressed beneath the furnace of the sky
By alien heat, by ceaseless labours crushed.
We flinch beneath the fury of the lash
And groan and turn our faces from the rage
Of our tormentors. Blood and ash
The price of failure or the bitter cage.
Iron's bite on that enfeebled wrist
Or neck or ankle where the fetter chafes
Dare not to raise our eyes or yet the fist
Somnambulists by day, we living wraiths
Seek solace in the respite of the night,
Where darkling may our restless spirits roam
On breezes borne, soft airs for souls in flight
To waft us o'er the verdant vales of home
Cool waters bathe our insubstantial feet
When we alight beside those blessed streams
Despite these dismal wages of defeat
The foeman has no strength to still our dreams.

Prologue

Two gods paced upon the strand. It was a warm but hazy day, with a vague and pale horizon. The distant cry of gulls and the quiet susurrus of lapping waves on coral sand was in their ears. High above, the white disc of the sun showed through the haze.
'This is *the* beach, you know?' observed Tio after a while.
'*The* beach?' enquired his brother, Yuzanid with a sidelong glance.
'It was here that our mother encountered Tetheos long ago. Just here'.
The two paused and glanced around them, casting their gaze to the low dunes and rocky headland beyond.
'And there endeavoured to press his suit upon her', replied Yuzanid. 'The god of the sea upon the goddess of the earth. You are right'.
'Indeed, although I doubt that such a union would have borne fruit, even had she consented to it'.
'Why so?'
'There is such a thing as fundamental incompatibility, brother. You will see it once, if you give thought to it. I believe poets have spilt much ink over it during the course of the ages'.
Yuzanid's face reddened, stung by this condescension.
'Your poets'.
'Yours too, although you are perhaps temperamentally disinclined to notice them. I know your interests lie elsewhere', noted Tio, airily waving a hand. 'War, death, destruction – that kind of thing'.
'Oh, please', scoffed Yuzanid. 'Spare me your hypocrisy. I suppose your own followers do not wield sword and fire with *your* name on their lips as they cut down mine'.

'The harvest of war', mused Tio. 'It is inevitable, I suppose, but I do not embrace it to my heart as you do, and I do not insist upon it in those who follow me as a holy duty of theirs. Rather, it is a regrettable necessity'.

'Hah!' laughed Yuzanid scornfully. 'You should listen to yourself!'

'Perhaps I make fewer demands of my followers than you do. Perhaps I am more indulgent of their frailties than you'.

'If you mean that I expect their whole-hearted and unwavering devotion to me, then yes. So is my strength increased and yours diminished, I might add'.

Tio's countenance was now enlivened by a half-smile.

'You make great demands upon them, do you not? You require them to give up their lives to you before nature's appointed hour and to take the lives of their fellows, that you may prematurely embrace their souls to your being'.

'I do not deny that I demand their complete commitment', agreed Yuzanid. 'Nor do I discourage them from magnifying the value of their earthly existence. They are as complete in me as yours are in you'.

'Of course, but when one makes such stringent demands of your earthy flock, it must be all the more galling when they fall short of their obligations, must it not?'

'To what do you refer?' demanded Yuzanid suspiciously, narrowing his eyes.

'I think you know to what I refer', answered Tio with a nod.

Chapter One

Stilli lay perfectly at ease amongst the long grasses and watched with a languorous eye as the clouds passed overhead. It was at times like these when it was possible to feel at one with the world, to feel a perfect unity of earth and heavens beneath and above. The faintest of breezes stirred the nodding seedheads around her. Towards the distant mountains the cry of a ghost buzzard came faintly to her ear, but that was all. The earth and heavens were mute, stilled in the summer heat, as though they held their collective breath and waited. But for what? What did they await? Stilli frowned and flicked away a strand of dark hair that the breeze had blown around her face. The sun emerged from behind a cloud, and her pupils constricted amongst pools of pale blue that darkened to indigo at their edges. She blinked and reminded herself that her mother would scold her for exposing her pale skin to this brutal assault.

'Do you wish to be thought a common farm hand or a country wench burnt berry-brown in the fields? Is that your aspiration? How then shall we marry you to a young man of befitting station?'

This warning held little power to trouble Stilli, because although she had already celebrated her seventeenth name-day, the prospect of marriage seemed a remote contingency. She was small for her age, and while she was uncommonly fair of face, the flower of womanhood had yet to rise appreciably in her form. Perhaps when her breasts and her hips resembled those of her contemporaries, she would begin to feel the heat of those animal passions and the desire to lie with a man.

Perhaps. She had wondered what it would be like, with the various young men of her acquaintance, turning the idea in her mind for close inspection, as one might turn a curious object in the hand, but the imagining of it had yet to bring a connected resolve to accomplish it.

Besides, it was doubtful whether a candidate matching her mother's exacting requirements for her spouse would ever stray within the spotlight of her scrutiny. Living, as they did, on the fringes of the world, the pool of eligible young men was necessarily a small one. She was idly considering some of these potential suitors when a faint tickle on her forearm recalled a mind whose attention was no more than tenuously engaged. The moment summoned her. She stirred and flapped vaguely at the spot and the tickle vanished. Another moment and it returned. Sitting up now, Stilli waved her arms to shoo away the fly that had settled upon her. After a few seconds, it returned, this time to her knee. Although not – so far as she could see – of the stinging variety, the creature seemed intent on palpating the skin there, raising and lowering its mouth parts purposefully. Stilli raised her hand, brought it stealthily close and prepared to swat the creature with lethal force. Closer, closer. Now! The hand swept down, and the fly darted away so that the hand slapped only her skin. She cursed and frowned, but the scowl gradually faded as a wry smile took its place. She wondered at the speed of the fly's reactions. What would it be like to be so swift to act?

Stilli mused in consideration of this notion, contravening yet another of her mother's regulations: *Don't spend your time daydreaming. You will be thought an unserious, frivolous person*. It was at that point that a faint cry intruded upon her thoughts.

Turning her head, she saw that a small figure was making its way along the path towards her, labouring

rather as the gradient of the hill began to take its toll. This was evidently Manda, one of the younger house servants.
'Miss Stilitha', she called at intervals, becoming increasingly breathless. 'There is post', she gasped at last, standing before Stilli, hand on hips. 'At the house. From Tazman. Madam requests...'
'I shall come, then', interrupted Stilli, getting to her feet whilst brushing seeds and stray strands of grass from her frock.
As the pair made their way down the grassy hill and through the orange orchard, by way of the place where the drystone wall was broken down, Stilli frowned once more. A letter had been expected for several weeks from the College of Priests in Tazman, the chief city of Vhanakhor. Although correspondence from the capital was commonplace enough, it was unlikely that her mother would have summoned her unless it were of particular significance. For this reason, it must surely be from the college. A sinking feeling came into her stomach as she emerged from the orchard and out into the lane that led to the gates of the big house. Tall hedges loomed over her on either side as she passed through, leaving her companion to close the gates behind her. The broad steps leading up to the front door were still under maintenance, so her path necessarily led her through the rose garden and in through the side door, to where her family were gathered in her father's office. Her mother, tall and stately with her iron-grey hair, favoured her with a nod.
'He has been sent for', she announced, forestalling Stilli's enquiry even as her lips parted. 'From the bone-acre'.
'Ah', replied Stilli with a nod of her own.
Her stepbrother, Middo, stood by the fireplace, apparently lost in his own thoughts. A familiar glint of

irritation had disclosed itself in his eye as Stilli made her entrance, but he made no sign of greeting that might bring his usual contempt for her to utterance. Instead, that eye, followed by Stilli's, found its way to his father's desk, where the letter lay upon a silver tray.

"*For att. The Reverend A.T. Zandravo, Zoramanstarn, Crane,*" declared the direction in the elegant flowing hand of the chancery clerk.

Stilli's father, Andax, would reach his sixtieth year in just a few months, and so, in accordance with the law, he would be required to relinquish his earthly existence and seek the embrace of the Lord. It was the word of the divine Yuzanid that all mortals must acknowledge and obey. There were circumstances, however, when the College of Priests might countenance an extension, after prayer, detailed consideration and upon certain applications to the divinity, certain indications of a favourable response. Priests whose talents were exceptionally useful to the wider community of the realm might be favoured by such an extension. An acquaintance of the family, renowned as a surgeon in distant Tazman, had been granted a number of such marks of official recognition. Father, for his part, had allowed himself to conceive that his undoubted efficiency as an administrator might see his own request favoured through the approval of the priesthood. The long-awaited response now lay within that small rectangular enclosure, exercising a grim fascination over those gathered there.

The clock, Father's pride and joy, measured the passage of the seconds solemnly from the mantelpiece, and a bee buzzed impotently at the window that looked out over the garden. Mother's eyes were cast down, her face pale. Middo bit his nails and then snatched his hand savagely away when he sensed Stilli's gaze upon him. He had a high opinion of his own dignity. He must show no sign of human frailty, of course, no taint of any unworthy emotion, and anxiety was surely to be categorised as such. The distant whickering of a horse, the crunch of wheels on gravel, preceded Father's arrival, and suddenly he was amongst them, shrugging off the official robe, running his hand over that bald pate where the blue tattoos writhed.

'Well?' he enquired.

Mother's look, a significant glance, was enough to draw his attention to the ominous letter, one that had the capacity to alter all their lives and to confirm the termination of his own. He picked it up, reached for the paper knife and presently drew out the single sheet of folded paper it contained, crossing to the window where the light was better, his back presented to his family. After a few moments, the paper came down and he turned, pursing his lips and nodding slowly before proclaiming the verdict.

'Request denied', he uttered in a voice that had a curiously strained quality, quite unlike the smooth, confident tone Stilli was used to. Nevertheless, few might read their own death sentence with perfect equanimity, she supposed. A thrill of sympathetic horror traversed her scalp, and her mouth was suddenly dry.

Mother crossed to him and placed her hand upon his shoulder, looking into his face.

'What? This is outrageous!', cried Middo, taking the letter from his father's hand and reading it for himself. 'You must appeal'.

'There is no appeal against the word of God, as you well know', Andax informed him coldly. 'Naturally, I accept the verdict gladly'.

And well he should, reflected Stilli glumly, given that it fell to Andax to impose the "Sixty" in his own domain. Few enough of the villagers and the out-dwellers in the region beyond reached that age, given the twin scourges of hardship and disease, but those so distinguished were destined to feel the bite of the inevitable "blade of reunion" that lay in the drawer in her father's desk. With that knife he opened the veins of the faithful and stilled their hearts, so that their spirits might be reunited with the eternal community of souls. There, on the bloodstone before the bone-acre, they were stretched, and their life's essence leached into the earth around as the community looked on.

'Now, will you please excuse me', continued Father, nodding meaningfully towards the door, 'for I must pray'.

'Of course, come on', beckoned Mother, suddenly matter of fact, dutiful, as she ushered Middo and Stilli out into the corridor beyond. 'We must all of us go to our rooms and reflect on the wisdom of God and the sanctity of reunion. I shall have you summoned for dinner'.

But that's three hours away, objected Stilli under her breath, although the thought could never be expressed vocally. She was not a pious girl, and whereas public prayer was a necessary burden, private prayer was a practice with which she rarely persevered. By its nature it could not be monitored or controlled, although the outward appearance thereof must be assumed. Stilli's private thoughts were rarely to be confined by the familiar prayers and mental exercises that so many of the faithful found a comfort to their minds. On this occasion, it was easy enough to dwell on the faith, even if it were only the final bloody expression of it. Everyone knew that a priest must wield the knife upon himself at the end of his days, must drive the cold steel between his own ribs to still the beating heart within. She knew it, had often thought of it, even, but the grim vision of it behind her eyes caused a cold shudder to pass through her as she lay face down, arms outstretched upon her bedroom floor in the posture that prayer required of her. She turned her head sideways and bit her lip as the dread vision of her father pushing the knife home swelled and flared within her mind.

'It is not fair', she heard from her stepbrother's room next door, where Middo was making his dissatisfaction known to his mother. 'Father has done so much to improve this parish. Look at the yields. Look at the numbers. You may tell me that the envy of our neighbours has nothing to do with this contemptible stain upon our family's honour, but you will tell me in vain. There are voices hostile to us in Tazman, and their words have not gone unheard in certain quarters. You may be sure of that'.

'In what way is our honour impugned?' asked Stilli's mother patiently. 'I see no stain'.

'Then you are blind, Mother. Blind!' cried Middo, his voice trembling with outrage. 'Everyone knows that Father applied for this extension, and everyone will soon know that his very reasonable request has been slapped down. Some will say that his request must be seen as impudence and presumption, that it derived from a most improper *grifdenzail*, scandalous in a priest. *Grifdenzail*, Mother. A serious accusation. To cling to this earthly life in defiance of scripture is to offend against God. I grieve for his reputation – and for ours'.

Middo's grief, reflected Stilli, was chiefly for his own prospects. It had been he who had importuned Father to submit his plea, this because the completion of Father's sixtieth year came the day before his own eighteenth name-day, this because Father's death before his own coming of age would disbar him from entering into his rightful inheritance as priest of the parish. Of course, a person of such tender years could not hope to take on those onerous responsibilities unassisted. He could, however, work under the nominal supervision of the deacon, the sub-priest, until such time as he was judged experienced enough to shoulder those burdens alone. It was to that which Middo aspired, and it was those hopes that Father's disappointment had dashed. One day, a single unlucky day, came between Middo and the consummation of his desires.

'Your father's reputation is secure in every quarter where it matters', Mother told him after a pause during which she doubtless considered that Middo's concern for his father's reputation had been less than evident when he had pressed him to petition the college.

'I shall certainly strike down any fellow who speaks ill of him', blustered Middo. 'But now what are we to do? You know that my own claim becomes invalid. You well know that pompous ass on the other side of the hill will be importuning the college as soon as he hears of this. You know he has long coveted The Hedges'.

The old house, Stilli's home, was so named because of the high thorn hedges that encircled it on all sides and had once, in centuries past, protected it from livestock rustlers. Now they served simply to preserve the privacy of the dwellers within, in what was widely acknowledged to be the finest residence in that part of the province. Few other priest halls could boast stained glass in their windows, marble-flagged floors and architectural embellishments in the Ahrvhoni style of the last century. It was surely a prize to be coveted, and Father's death would certainly bring with it a flurry of applications from those desiring to succeed to his position.

Ingridex, the pompous ass Middo to whom referred, was sure to be amongst them. Well-connected in the region, and with a cousin in the chancery, he was ideally situated for pressing his own claim. Stilli's heart sank at the prospect. Like all who dwelt there, she had hoped that her father's request might have been favourably received. The prospect of her brother's rise to prominence was not one that she could contemplate with relish, but it was surely preferable to being summarily ejected from the only home she had ever known.

'If only your brother...' began Mother, before a squall of fury from Middo cut her short.

'If only, Mother, if only! Why do you persist in persecuting me with his name. Why do I feel that you only ever cared for him and for him alone?'

This was entirely typical of Middo, who, to a remarkable degree, combined self-pity with a profound indifference to the feelings of others. Mother's mention of Corriden, Stilli's older stepbrother, caused her to feel hot tears spring in her eyes. Corriden was everything that Middo was not – brave, honest and devoted to the welfare of others – but he had died the previous year of blood poisoning, having suffered an apparently trivial cut from a rusty knife. Stilli's faith taught her that she must not regret the death of those who made that inevitable journey to Yuzanid's embrace, even when that journey might be thought premature. Nevertheless, she missed him terribly, the only other sibling who had survived the perils of early childhood.

Chapter Two

After the initial shock of the college's response, life continued in its usual way. Father must necessarily continue with his duties as the remaining days of his life ebbed away, and Mother was engaged in a constant round of visiting in the region. The college had been petitioned, but the likelihood was that the family must soon leave The Hedges and seek alternative accommodation appropriate to their station. She must consult with her friends and clients, if this was to be managed effectively. For this reason, Mother was frequently absent from the house, and since Stilli's governess had been laid low with a crippling arthritis these last few weeks, the girl found herself largely unsupervised. She was meant to work at her samplers or at the loom that occupied much of one half of her room, but these activities gave her little satisfaction. Instead, at the risk of invoking the displeasure of Smeeton, the house steward, she took advantage of these last days of summer by venturing out more frequently than usual into the world beyond, taking with her a sketchbook and her pencils.
'I have borrowed a few things from the pantry, Smeeton', she told him one morning, when the sound of Mother's departing carriage had faded in the forecourt. 'So you may not fear that I shall starve. And I shall walk out Galsanmide way with my sketchbook. Perhaps I shall meet Tye and his sister there'.
This last remark had effectively quelled Smeeton's objection, and he closed his mouth, contenting himself with a few muttered comments about her loom standing

idle and her mother blaming him if any harm might befall her in her absence.

She and Tye, the son of one of the better local families, had long been friends and he would certainly ensure her safety should he be present and should any threat arise. Although a person of extraordinary simplicity, he was a sturdy young man with an earnest, open face and a long-standing devotion to Stilli. Not that she faced any danger in her locality. To offend against the person of the priest's daughter would bring with it swift and painful retribution. For this reason, the villagers treated her with a wary respect. Private conversations inevitably stuttered to a halt as she approached, resuming only once she had passed, having received whatever signs of respect were due in the circumstances.

Stilli barely noticed such things. They were simply the inevitable attributes of her status, part of the familiar furniture of life. She whistled now as she strode cheerfully past the forge, where Lalak the smith hammered at a horseshoe, and turned along the lane that led to the mere at the edge of the village.

You should not whistle, her mother's well-remembered voice nagged from some corner of her mind. *It shows an unbecoming levity in a person of your status.*

'Nor should you take those monstrous strides', she said aloud, in an affectation of that voice. 'Do you wish to be taken for a soldier, girl? Small steps, you should take, in a manner that creates the impression of a graceful flow'.

She grinned, another prohibited behaviour, and crammed her straw hat more firmly on her head as a warm gust blew around the end of the last outlying barn. It was a splendid day, the last in August, and the scrubby hills, merging into forest in their higher regions, reflected in the mere like a vast polished mirror, where puffy white clouds, barely ruffled by a single ripple, floated below their counterparts high above. Soon, she passed Galsanmide, the pretty hamlet with meadows by the tumbling stream, but it was the first of those hills beyond that were her objective, the hill that offered an elevated view of her village that she intended to sketch. She did not meet her friends, nor had she expected to, but her mention of Galsanmide and the *possibility* of meeting her friends there had made it unnecessary for her to lie to Smeeton.

'Why is it that Stilitha is allowed such licence, Mother?' Middo had objected on more than one occasion. 'She does not work, she does not study, she does not apply herself to the cultivation of female accomplishments. All she does is wander the hills and lanes like a vagrant, and you do nothing to stop her. When will you insist that she grows up?'

Such bouts of fraternal peevishness could usually be relied upon to bring about some temporary restraint on her liberty, some temporary increase in her mother's vigilance. In truth, it seemed that Mother's desire that her daughter should grow to be a dutiful young lady in the traditional mould was hardly more keenly felt than her determination to insist upon it. Hence, Middo's dissatisfaction. Nor could her father be prevailed upon to enforce this regime. He left such matters to Mother. His relationship with his daughter, as with all in his family, was a distant one, marked by none of the overt signs of affection that typically distinguish familial relations. There were no hugs and kisses, so far as Stilli could remember, and any physical contact between her parents, beyond those notional ones in the privacy of the marriage bed, were so rare as to be particularly prominent in her memory.

After half an hour or so, Stilli had reached her favourite perch on the saddle of high land between the rich valley of her village and the poorer lands beyond where the Drumogari dwelt. The Drumogari were foreigners, slaves faithful to their own false god and utterly despised by the true believers all around. They had been settled there since the last great war against the distant Empire of Erenor, more than thirty years previously, and some of them still conversed amongst themselves in a tongue unintelligible to civilised men. From this elevated position, Stilli could look down upon their meagre fields and pastures, the tumbled thatch roofs of their sprawling village. The settlement exercised a strange fascination for her, and she often went there to gaze upon the homes of these strange, foreign people.

'They are like insects, not human beings at all', Middo had once assured her when she spoke of it. 'They preferred our dominion here to dying for their own false god in battle. They do not deserve to live. If it were in my power, I should dispatch the lot of them to the glory of Yuzanid. Their existence is an offence in his eyes'.

'Then it is as well that it is not in your power', Father had countered in those calm, measured tones. 'Nor will it be until you have reached an age and a level of maturity consistent with the rule of men. The warm bodies of living men are needed to repair the roads and the bridges, to labour in our own fields when hands are short and the need pressing. Sure, they are lesser men, but they are men nevertheless, and they have a place in God's system of authority, beneath the faithful but above the beast'.

Middo and some of his equally odious friends took pleasure in stealing their property and in raping their women, whenever the fancy took them – and this often enough. It was quite legal to slay a Drumogaros, although not strictly honourable, and to do so might bring about the jealous disapproval of the church and its authorities. However, a Drumogaros who took exception to the rape of his wife or daughter, and one who chose to express his annoyance by way of raising his voice or hand, was likely to pay for it with his life.

'How can a man of Vhanakhor respect a creature who places his own worthless life above honour?' Middo would ask when defending such conduct to his father. 'Besides, for one of them to strike a member of the faithful or to utter impious words is to place themselves beyond the protection of the law, is it not?'

'It is', Father had been obliged to agree. 'But I wish you would not exult in it so. It demeans you. Besides, there is always the House of the Mares. Why don't you take your pleasure there, like the other young stallions of the area?'

This thought, entering Stilli's mind as she gazed around her from that high vantage point, caused her to shade her eyes and squint sunwards. There, towards the Crane road, a distant scatter of squat white buildings, huddled around a somewhat larger and higher edifice, stood at the head of the low valley, almost hidden beyond the stands of cypresses and a curve in the road. This was the House of the Mares of which Father had spoken, and the circumstances of its use exercised a grim fascination for her. All the Drumogari girls of marriageable age were obliged to spend a year there, where they satisfied the carnal desires of the young Vhanakhori men of the region, the "stallions." Naturally, this was a source of great resentment amongst the Drumogari men, who were necessarily excluded from this arrangement, and from the Drumogari community in general, whose periodic uprisings, occasioned by this and other grievances, required to be bloodily supressed. Girl babies arising from such congress might be retained or destroyed by their community, according to their whim, but boy babies were taken away to be brought up as soldiers for the faith, in the nurseries and boarding schools attached to the military academies.

The full heat of the day was soon upon Stilli, but despite her fair skin, she was never greatly troubled by it. Her mother's anxieties were misplaced, since the sun, however fierce at its zenith, seemed to have no power to leave its mark upon her. Nevertheless, she found a shady spot amongst the roots of an old holm oak and leant her back against its gnarled grey bark. Here, whilst the cicadas chirruped around her, she surveyed a great sweep of the hills and vales of that part of the province. Away somewhere to the right, beyond the distant purple ridge, lay the ocean, and to her left stood the rising ramparts, ridge upon fading ridge of the high mountains, the great curving spine of the island of Eudora that was her home. When the air was clear, it was possible to discern the shape of Mount Zayat, the nearest of the active volcanoes for which the land was renowned. Stilli had sketched out the rough outlines of her view, one she had addressed on many previous occasions, when a young woman arrived at her side.
'Yonder tree's too big', she grunted.
'Did I seek your opinion?' asked Stilli without turning, nevertheless applying an eraser to this area.
'Better', conceded the young woman when Stilli had made this correction.
Her name was Radda, a squarish, thickset figure with a broad face and a single, united eyebrow that surmounted small dark eyes. She was a Drumogaros from the settlement below, habitually to be found herding her goats thereabouts or gathering brushwood from the edges of the forest on the slopes above. She had served her time in the House of the Mares, although her residence there had perhaps seen fewer outrages upon her person than some of her comelier fellows had

endured. Still, the getting of a girl child there showed that at least one stallion had coupled with her. The child had died or been destroyed, it appeared, although Radda could not be brought to speak of it. Stilli knew these things because she had known the Drumogari woman for several months now, had enjoyed many conversations with her there on the fringe of both their worlds. At first, those encounters had been markedly wary on both sides. Radda had every reason to fear the daughter of a Vhanakhori priest, and Stilli, for her part, had heard much of the hatred and resentment the Drumogari felt for their betters.

'Don't you ever tire of drawing that?' asked Radda, settling herself at Stilli's side and chewing on a grass stalk. 'You must have drawn it a hundred times'.

'I should paint it if I had paints', Stilli told her with a sidelong glance. 'My friend's mother has some that she brought from Nahleen. Made in the Empire, she says. Little cakes of dried colour they are, all in a metal pan. If one applies water to them, they melt and the brush can collect the colour'.

'I know what paints are. The best paints in the world were made in Callisto, or so they say', remarked Radda. 'Not that I would ever have set eyes on them, my family being from labouring stock as they are. Great leveller, poverty, see? When you have nothing, you have nothing wherever you go. Here or in the Empire, it's all the same to me. It's a very portable thing, poverty'.

'You don't yearn to be in the Empire, then?' asked Stilli, curious to explore a topic that had previously seemed too awkward to discuss.

'You'd think I wouldn't, after what I just said, wouldn't you? But I do', shrugged Radda, her eyes momentarily downcast. 'We all do. And I was born right here, so I've never even set eyes on it. Although, I don't know why I'm telling the likes of you'.

'Why do you say that?' asked Stilli, her brow clouding, setting her pencil aside. She felt that a significant moment had arrived in her rather unsuitable relationship with this woman, an opening of minds, and although this brought with it a certain trepidation, there was a strange excitement, too.

'You don't know? You really don't know?' Radda asked, shaking her head slowly.

'Well yes, I suppose you mean the difference in our status', conceded Stilli frankly. 'But you should know by now that it doesn't mean a fig to me. I look at you and I do not see an inferior being, as many would prompt me to. I do not see a creature whose existence may be judged an offence to God. I see a familiar companion, that is all'.

Radda laughed suddenly, her head cast back in a manner that would certainly have scandalised Mother had Stilli attempted to emulate it.

'Well, I suppose I should rejoice in it', she managed at last, wiping a tear from her eye. 'You honour me, so you do. A companion, indeed. I suppose you almost allowed the word "friend" to slip from your lips just then', she noted dryly.

Stilli felt the blood flush hotly in her cheeks.

'I did not mean...' she began.

'I know you meant nothing by it', pronounced Radda, punching Stilli lightly on the shoulder, 'innocent creature that you are. I suppose you think my folks would be glad to see me passing the time of day with you, too. The enemy, you are, see? You and all your people. The enemy, and our God's not too keen on the likes of yours, either. At least if I were in the Empire, I could be dirt poor without the heavens getting involved in the matter. At least those rich folks looking down their noses on me there would be praying to the same god. It adds an extra layer, if you take my meaning.

Gods, I mean. Gods give folks the holy thumbs-up for their more brutal urges and cheer them on when they do the most wicked things. Your folks could smite me down as soon as look at me, you know? With no recourse to law, no justice at all. There – in the Empire, I mean – the law would have a say in it, and they do say we're all equal before the law in *that* land, rich and poor alike'.

'Well, I'm sure it all sounds very nice, in theory at least', sniffed Stilli, thinking that this seemed an odd way of going about things.

Surely the application of the law must reflect social station, the most basic of human categorisation? She wondered if Radda hadn't acquired a rather romanticised notion of the "old country."

'Not that I'd know about it,' conceded Radda, perhaps divining these thoughts. 'Not that I know anything other than this place,' she continued, gesturing towards her own valley, where a group of men could distantly be discerned, tiny ant-like figures gathered about a cart. 'There are plenty that do, though, the older folks. They remember it and they keep it alive in their hearts'.

'The Empire?'

'Aye, the Empire, although soon enough they'll all be in the ground, I suppose, and what then will we be?'

Stilli could not answer this question, and so she only bit her lip, staring out across the distant mountains, now rather wishing that their conversation had not taken this direction.

'She never uses them anyway', she said after a while, when a companionable silence had settled upon them.

'What?'

'The paints. She never uses them. Perhaps she conceives them to be somehow impious, coming from the Empire as they do'.

'Perhaps she's just plain lazy', observed Radda. 'I don't doubt you'd use them. I'm sure you'd paint right well with them'.

'Well, I should like the chance to try at least', agreed Stilli with a nod.

At that moment, a fly alighted upon her page. She flapped a hand at it, whereupon it flew up and alighted once more. A determined fly. A twinge of irritation caused Stilli to raise her hand once more, but this time there was something different. She felt momentarily dizzy, and as the fly sprang upwards it was as though time slowed down. She could clearly see the motions through the air of its individual wings, glinting as they sparked reflected sunlight. She could clearly see her own hand descending to meet it with implacable force. Surely, were it to continue on this trajectory, it would squash the creature upon her drawing. Seeing this, she began to clench her fingers so that her fist closed around her quarry in a perfectly timed interception. There was something momentarily odd about her vision, a yellowish tinge at the fringes. No matter. She squeezed tight, and the fly died. A sense of weariness came upon her and awareness that Radda was regarding her curiously.

'I am death to flies', laughed Stilli, turning her face to her friend and dropping the remains of her victim at her side.

'That you are', agreed Radda. 'And to more besides, I swear, with reactions like that'.

Stilli reflected upon this incident a week or so later, when she attended her governess's passing ceremony. The woman had given up her battle with the crippling arthritis that had disabled her and had chosen to go to the knife a full two years before the "Sixty." In truth, Stilli felt little grief, although she had known Sister

Dahria for eighteen months. She charitably supposed that the woman's impatience and irascibility in Stilli's presence derived from her condition and not from any deficiency in her pupil's desire for learning, nor indeed the faults within her character. Sister Dahria had been quick to find such fault, possessing a remarkable ability to detect a "tone" in Stilli's voice, even when there was none there. The sharp and peevish tone in her own voice, when addressing Stilli, was strikingly different to the one she employed when conversing with her parents. Sister Dahria's mind sprang lightning fast to the expression of censure, whereas praise, grudgingly conceded, appeared to oppress that same mind with a sense of having endured defeat. Stilli's needlework was judged inept, her ability at the loom wanted attention to detail and she seemed quite unable to commit to her mind the essential passages of scripture that a gentlewoman should know as well as she knew her own name. In short, Stilli was a disappointment to her, a most unrewarding pupil. Accordingly, that pupil could not find it within her to mourn as she watched the woman go to her death.

It was an overcast day, one that promised the first of the September downpours that generally soaked the valley as autumn approached, and a few hundred or so of the people of the region were crowded within the courtyard of the temple to bear witness. High walls surrounded the enclosure on all sides, and to the further end stood the temple itself, a sturdy cylinder of stone pierced by narrow windows, surmounted by a fretwork of carved stone that incorporated interwoven serpents, the eternal symbol of Yuzanid. The flagpole that emerged from the high platform at its crown supported a long serpent banner of scarlet silk, a slender tube that rippled out splendidly in any breeze. The air was almost completely still and it hung flaccid. Its open mouth was stiffened with wire, and this clanked vaguely against the pole. On the roof of the encircling portico beneath, a number of acolytes stood ready with long trumpets to sound the lengthy, mournful notes that accompanied a passing. They directed their attention, at that moment, to the sacrificial stone that stood before the temple at the highest point of the enclosure, the Temenos as it was called. There stood Father, the deacon and various of the local officials whose presence the occasion required, including the registrar and the criers, official mourners whose shrill voices would accompany the song of the trumpets.

'Do stop fidgeting, dear', scolded Stilli's mother, speaking sotto voce from the side of her mouth. 'Did Sister Dahria teach you nothing of deportment?'

Stilli furrowed her brow, feeling that such criticism was out of place in the circumstances, reflecting upon the poor woman before them as much as on her unsatisfactory pupil. For there was Sister Dahria, emerging from the high temple portal after the final rituals of cleansing, the crowd drawing back as she approached the altar. Her steps were halting, and she was supported on either side by her daughter and her son-in-law. Her face was pale, and it was clear from her manner that she had drunk of the poppy milk. Certainly, she seemed perfectly content to be led to the side of the altar and to climb the three broad steps that gave access to its platform. Here, Father embraced her and observed as his assistants helped her gently into position on the altar stone, before beginning the prayers that ritual required.

Stilli always felt a little awkward and ashamed on these occasions. Her father was a fine administrator, as all acknowledged, and his care for his flock ensured that all in spiritual difficulty would receive a sympathetic hearing. However, he was no orator, and the familiar words of the "petition for souls," "the recommendation" and "the committal" were uttered in a low drone, with many a stutter and more than one hesitation, quite inconsistent with his undoubted powers of memory. Nor was his figure one to command admiration when seen naked, as age-old tradition required. He was not a tall man, and since he was prone to corpulence, his person was best observed clothed. Standing naked as God had made him, with all about privately making humorous comparisons between the size of his belly and his private parts, he was bound to excite ridicule, had it not been for the extreme severity of the circumstances. Sure, the writhing blue tattoos that encompassed the whole of his flesh added some dignity to the spectacle, but in general it was one that caused Stilli some discomfort. It caused discomfort to Middo, too, to judge from the expression on his face. He stood to the side of the altar with the other *dedicati*, half a dozen young men destined for the priesthood when they came of age and who were presently undergoing the initial stages of their long training.

'I wish you would at least attempt to drive that contempt from your face!' murmured Stilli under her breath as the prayers continued.

Father's voice was quite inadequate to reach the furthest edges of the crowd, but most understood the responses perfectly well and could readily tell when these were required of them from the behaviour of those standing closer to the altar. The language of the faith was incomprehensible to many of those present, illiterate in any tongue, but the general meaning was well known to all and the cadences of the prayers were pleasantly familiar, comforting to their ear.

It was the tiny tickle of a fly alighting on Stilli's forearm that recalled her mind to the occasion when her reactions had seemed supernaturally fast. The sensation that had accompanied it and the recollection of her hand closing around its tiny body were imprinted on her memory with a strange vividness. She swiped at it now, in the hope that she could repeat that feat, but her movement was clumsy and slow, the fly correspondingly nimble. Why? What had been different?

The low murmur of the crowd recalled her attention to the ceremony. The prayers had ended with the "farewell," and Father was now turning to receive the sacrificial knife from the deacon, a man whose rigid demeanour and spare, wiry physique made a stark contrast with his superior's. Sister Dahria lay stretched upon the slab, wearing a plain white shift, her throat stretched open by the rounded stone beneath her neck, placed there for exactly that purpose. Father reached for the curved, wickedly sharp knife, the blade two fingers' breadth wide, fumbled and dropped it with a clatter to the platform.

'Oh, husband!' gasped Mother at Stilli's side, her hand flying to her mouth.

A few faces turned to them, but most were directed to the altar, and a muttering grew in the crowd. This was most inauspicious, most unlucky, and it took Father's fierce gaze, directed amongst them, to reduce them once more to a sullen silence. The knife, once picked up, must be purified and re-dedicated, a process that involved more prayer, more arcane symbols drawn in the air and a solemn procession to the temple, where holy water could be sprinkled upon it. It was a most awkward delay. Stilli, despite her general indifference to Sister Dahria's passing, nevertheless felt the keenest sympathy for her present predicament. Lying upon the cold stone with the poppy milk gradually fading from her mind and body was a most unenviable situation. Still, she neither stirred nor cried out, and the ceremony was presently under way once more.

Pray do not mishandle this, cautioned Stilli inwardly as her father finally made the fatal cut. Bright blood leapt and then poured into the channels around the stone as Sister Dahria surrendered her earthly existence. It ran into the covered drain around the altar from which it would be absorbed by the earth beneath them. Her spirit had departed and would be embraced by the wider community of the dead in due course.

Stilli sighed with relief and made Yuzanid's sign before her breast, the "S" shape of the serpent, conscious that most of those present were doing likewise. It was over, and the lifeless body would be conveyed to the bone-acre. There, in that palisaded enclosure on the low hill above the village, Sister Dahria's mortal remains would be placed on a high wooden platform and left there until the crows and the vultures cleaned the flesh from her bones.

'And what then?' she remembered asking Mother when she was quite small. 'What when the birds have eaten their fill?'

'Do you see yonder mound, a hill upon a hill? Within that mound is the bone hall, and that is where the bones of our people are gathered for all time, to watch over us and keep us safe'.

'And do they – keep us safe, I mean?'

'Of course they do', answered Mother's mouth.

'We shall see', said her eyes.

Chapter Three

It was necessary that Stilli should have a new tutor or governess, now that Sister Dahria had gone to Yuzanid's embrace. Accordingly, the word had been put out that there was such a vacancy within the household. Accordingly, Father began to take a belated interest in his daughter's education. He had merely a few weeks to live when he summoned Stilli to his study to judge the extent of the task that faced the next incumbent of that post. Naturally, she was required to bring with her the best of her samplers and some of the cloth that she had woven on her loom, although there was little enough of this. Likewise, there were her copybooks to be examined and her knowledge of scripture to be assessed. This entailed her recitation of various passages from the holy book, the Mindoriad, and from the forty-nine ordinances: God's inflexible rules for the conduct of mankind that governed his behaviour in this world. "Shall worship me and none other or shall suffer death," was the first of these. "Or shall suffer death," was how many of them ended, with a severe finality that priests usually accompanied by glaring about them meaningfully, whenever their duties required that they should recite them. There was a special significance in the word "suffer," too. Those who transgressed against the forty-nine ordinances might experience a great deal of suffering on the road to that death. Sister Darhia's death had been benign and consensual, the "little path" as it was called. Those found guilty of criminal offences may be obliged to travel the "bitter path" in its various forms or even the "fiery path," the contemplation of which caused Stilli a special dread, but for reasons she was unable to define.

'I see', said her father, taking off his spectacles when Stilli had completed her halting recitation of various of these ordinances. 'So you believe that the theft of a chicken should merit the loss of a finger but that of rooster a thumb. Is that the case?'

Stilli, who had been required to stand before her father's desk for the better part of an hour by now, frowned and consulted her memory.

'I do not know', she admitted when Father leant back in his chair and sighed.

Stilli wondered if his sudden interest in her, after years of apparent indifference, stemmed from a growing sense of his own mortality as the days of his remaining span dwindled. Perhaps, also, he was conscious of his indifferent performance at Sister Dahria's passing and wished to mend his reputation with his family by showing a new paternal zeal. Middo had likewise found his conduct and behaviour under new scrutiny, particularly with regard to the outward signs of respect he owed to his mother.

'I know little of the needle, nor of the loom', Father admitted as Stilli's examination continued. 'But I have sought your mother's opinion, and she tells me that your work is of indifferent quality, motivated by no great enthusiasm or indeed by any corresponding desire for improvement. I find that your grasp of scripture is but a tenuous one and that you can demonstrate no evident familiarity with the work of the prophets or of sacred poetry'.

He shook his head slowly and ran his hands over those plump tattooed cheeks. 'Where *do* your talents lie, daughter? It appears that your family and your governess have been singularly unable to discover them'.

'I have this, Father', said Stilli with some trepidation, pulling out a sketchbook from beneath the pile of her samplers and copybooks on the edge of his desk.

Her father replaced his spectacles on his nose and flipped through the pages without comment for some time, occasionally turning the book or peering close to pick out the finer detail of her drawings.

'I see', he sniffed. 'I accept that drawing is a recognised accomplishment for young ladies. I have no eye for this, but my instinct tells me that you have some facility for it. Your choice of subject helps to place in context your brother's complaint that you endlessly roam the countryside, when you should be attending to your studies'.

'Yes, Father, although I venture to protest that "endlessly" overstates the case, if you will forgive me. But yes, certainly that is where I find my pleasure', she added with a nod.

'And yet pleasure and duty are to be set in balance, are they not?' observed Father. 'And I fear that the balance is lamentably skewed in your case'.

He sighed once more, toyed idly with his spectacles and then suddenly smiled, a phenomenon so rare as to fill his daughter with consternation and a curious warmth about her heart.

'I suppose your next tutor or governess must take up the burden that I shall soon set down', he said. 'And I am conscious that there are things that must be said to you as my end approaches. Perhaps you would summon your mother', he added, indicating the door.

Moments later, Mother stood at Stilli's side, and Father came from around his desk to take her hand. Together, they each reached forward to take one of Stilli's, so that they made a circle, causing Stilli such a tumult of confusion she could barely breathe. She was used to the warm pressure of Mother's hand on hers but certainly not of Father's. What was happening to her? She looked anxiously from face to face, finding only kindliness and concern there.

'You will not remember this, Stilitha', said her mother. 'But we three stood like this many years ago, when you were very small...'

'And when we adopted you as our own', added Father, causing Stilli's heart to race within her. She felt that she might faint, and her legs felt suddenly weak beneath her. 'And now, as my end draws near, I felt that we should share this with you'.

'What...? How...?'

'Sit down, child', soothed Mother, pulling out a chair as the momentary circle dissolved.

She knelt at Stilli's side and Father retreated to stand watchfully by his desk, tugging absently at the sleeve of his robe in a distracted manner quite at variance with his usual self-possession.

'It is a simple enough story to tell', Mother continued. 'I had a maidservant, a good and dutiful woman whom I valued highly. She had a young daughter but was otherwise alone in the city as a captive brought there after war. When that maidservant became fatally ill, I promised her that I would look after that girl and raise her as my own. She died, and I did as I had promised. When my first husband died a short time later, I married your father, here, and he was gracious enough to embrace the adoption, accepting you as his own'.

Father inclined his head. A flush had risen in Mother's cheeks as she recounted these events, and a tear came to her eye that she was obliged to dash away with the back of her hand. Mother was rarely to be observed in the grip of strong emotion, and this, after Father's unexpected smile, reinforced Stilli's strong sense of having entered unknown territory. Nor did Mother appear to be able to meet Father's eye when she looked up at last – a circumstance that might normally have been found troubling but one that was now swallowed up in the overwhelming shock of the moment.

'There', she said in voice with a distinct quaver. 'We have told you, as is our duty, and you must deal with it as you will. Do, pray, return to your room and consider what you have learned'.

And then she was gone, hurrying from the room.

It was hardly necessary for Mother to make such a recommendation, and indeed Stilli was greatly preoccupied with such a consideration in the coming days, whether within her room or without. Persistent rain curbed her wandering in the countryside beyond, where the community looked anxiously at the heavens and their crops, waiting for the moment when the harvest should be brought in. Such concerns were the province of the common folk, of course, those whose labours brought food to the tables of the priestly class. Stilli was barely conscious of such practical circumstances, although her father's duties obliged him to understand them very well indeed. It was strange to reflect that he was not, in fact, her father, that the aspects of her own character or physique which she sought in vain to see in his were simply not there to be discovered. The same was true of her mother, although in this case, by what could only be coincidence, there was a marked physical similarity. Her mother's slender stature, the iron-grey hair that had once been raven black and the structure of her face had always struck Stilli as the prototype for her own, so it was surprising to learn that they were not, that her own physical characteristics derived from another, one wholly unknown to her. It was this person, the person who had brought her into the world, who now became the focus of Stilli's inner mind. Even Middo noticed when the family sat down to dine together.

'What is wrong with Stilitha, Mother?' he asked when Stilli's sightless gaze had been fixed on a section of the wall behind his head for a prolonged period. 'She seems even more distracted than usual. Do you suppose she will ever acquire the skills to enter society?'

'Certainly, she is given to abstract thought', her mother had declared. 'And certainly, we seek in vain to detect it in her brother'.

Middo had flushed, suspecting a slight.

'If you mean that I am a man of action, *will* be a man of action, then you are correct. My swordsmanship is second to none in this valley'.

'Amongst your age and rank', supplied Father, dabbing his lip with a serviette whilst a servant reached in to take his plate.

'Amongst any age and rank in due course, I promise you', countered Middo, a fierce glint in his eye. 'When I come of age...'

This train of thought could not be brought to conclusion, since all present knew that Middo came of age on the day that succeeded his father's death, and a silence fell upon the company.

'Well', said Mother brightly after a while. 'I am told by those who know these things that the winds will presently drive away this rain, that the harvest may be gathered in, in fact'.

Stilli cared little for the harvest at that moment. She cared only for the new status that her parents' revelation had imposed upon her and for the nature of her true mother.

'I am and will always be your mother', Mother told her when Stilli had gone in search of a private conversation with her. 'And I would not have you think that anything has occurred to change that. Naturally, you wish to

know something of your birthmother, and I will tell you that her name was Yahli, if that helps you. She looked remarkably like you. That is all I will tell you, however, since I do not wish you to dwell upon it. In order to thrive in our station, we must demonstrate strength of mind, and I hope that you will discipline yours accordingly. Your father wished to share this with you before his passing, as part of his setting his affairs in order'.
'You would not have told me, then, if he had not insisted upon it?'
'I do not see what you have gained from it', Mother had said from her place sitting at her dressing table. Stilli's view of her face was reflected in the mirror set there, a fine silvered glass one such as few houses in the region could boast. The face reflected showed what Stilli interpreted as a certain impatience, a certain evasiveness.
'I have gained knowledge of the truth'.
'Then be assured that ignorance is often infinitely preferable. Life will teach you that'.
'Perhaps, but it has yet to do so', answered Stilli doggedly. 'And I wish to know more of my birthmother. 'Her name will not suffice. You must tell me'.
'I will thank you not to compel me to that or any other course here in my own house. I think you forget yourself, daughter, and I think that our conversation is at an end'.
'Very well', said Stilli, turning upon her heel.
'And Stilitha', added Mother, recalling her as she drew open the door. 'You would be well to keep this to yourself'.
'Of course, Mother; I am not a fool', replied Stilli, rolling her eyes in a manner that, in any other context, would have earned her the severest of censure.

It had not occurred to her for an instant that she might share her new status with anyone else. Middo was Father's true son, from his first marriage. Were he to hear of Stilli's origins, he would certainly rejoice to learn that his stepsister was not only a stepsister but a stepsister of base origin. How he would crow to find that the blood of a common serving girl muddied her veins, whereas his had the distinction of noble ancestry as far back as the written pedigree could show. It would surely lead to a lamentable alteration in a relationship that was already marked by jealousy and ill-feeling on his part.

Accordingly, Stilli was obliged to carry the burden of this news alone, though it ached about her heart and oppressed her mind with a baleful severity whenever she laid her head upon the pillow. But she could not conceal this oppression from the world at large. Her friends were quick to comment on the dark rings about her eyes when she went walking with them one fine afternoon as the harvest was being brought in.

Mother's prediction had proved correct, and the wheat and the barley stood swaying golden beneath the September sun, awaiting scythe and sickle. All other activities were set aside as the village people took their familiar places in the fields, male and female alike. Even the little children were found roles, and their laughter rang out amongst the swish of the scythe and the creak and rattle of the hay wagon.

'I confess I have not been sleeping well', admitted Stilli in answer to her friend Tolly's enquiry as they walked side-by-side along the main street of the village.

Tolonia, universally called Tolly, except by her parents, had been joined by her twin brother, Tye. The latter had fallen a little way behind in order to admire an acquaintance's new coat, but now he caught up with them, looking earnestly from face to face in order that he might be admitted to their conversation.

'I was saying that Stilli's complexion seems unusually wan', said Tolly, whose own face was presently disfigured by various spots and pustules that puberty so often brings with it. 'She seems quite without colour, without the healthy glow of youth, indeed. Does something trouble you, my dear?' she asked.

'It will pass, no doubt', sighed Stilli, keen to move the conversation on to fresh pastures and reflecting that her own complexion, pale as it was, had at least the virtue of clarity. 'But is that a new bonnet you wear today?' she asked in return.

She knew perfectly well that Tolly's sun bonnet was not new, was one of many she possessed, but that the application of new ribbons to the rim had caused it to appear so. Tolly's family, the extensive clan of the Marcuzii, were far richer than Stilli's and dwelt in the great house at the further edge of the village, owning much of the best farmland thereabouts. It was their tenants who were now to be discerned labouring in the fields to the side of the road and beyond the cottages at the roadside.

'She has more bonnets than I have teeth', declared Tye, showing many of these last named in a broad grin as his sister's disapproving eye fell upon him.

'And if I were a man, I should certainly part you from some of them', retorted Tolly, 'if you propose to accuse me of vanity'.

Stilli worked hard to discipline her mouth so that it should not likewise shape itself into a smile. Tye was a simple, cheerful soul, the despair of his father. Tolly had evidently garnered all the brains for herself when the two of them shared the womb, leaving Tye with all the natural charm and amiability for his portion. Tolly's lot in life was that of a gentlewoman when she reached her majority, whereas Tye would enter upon a rich inheritance, one that brought with it responsibilities far beyond his intellectual capacity to grasp.

'I would not dare', answered Tye, shrinking before her frown. 'I, er...'

Stilli watched with amusement as his face disclosed the passage of various thoughts, none of which gave rise to the witty response he evidently hoped to supply.

'Look! There's an eagle, up beyond the temple', he cried instead, rescued by circumstances. 'It has a snake in its talons. See!'

His pointing hand, his excited capering, caused various heads to turn in the street and in the adjacent fields. Indeed, an eagle bearing a snake was an auspicious omen.

'Oh no, it is just a stick', he conceded as the stick fell to earth.

'Tye, Tye, I despair of you', clucked Tolly as they approached the open area before the inn, where the common folk held their festivals. 'When will you ever learn to comport yourself with a proper dignity?'

'Never, I suppose', conceded Tye sadly, scratching at the back of his head beneath his hat. His eye found Stilli's – as it often did, given that he was quite unable to conceal his evident admiration for her – and she allowed the corners of her mouth to twitch upwards in response.

'Is that Pyresion I see?' wondered Tolly aloud, twirling her parasol as they drew near to the inn. 'I believe it is. How downcast he looks'.

'I suppose he has every reason to feel downcast', observed Stilli.

Pyresion was that year's Green King. Chosen after the previous year's harvest, he had enjoyed twelve months of leisure and indulgence, reigning notionally over the common people to the extent that they were obliged to furnish him with as much food and drink as he desired. Likewise, he was entitled to bed those girls of the village whose charms recommended them to him, and they, for their part, were required to regard this as an honour. The offspring of such sacred unions were recognised as being especially favoured by the heavens. They might, in their turn, follow the sacred path that their father had marked out. In short, the Green King enjoyed a year of honour and luxury, but those privileges came at the highest of prices. The Green King represented the living bounty of the earth, and in due course he must replenish that bounty with his own blood. When the harvest was safely home, he must go to the knife and the stone. This, as fate would have it, was the last of the official duties that Stilli's father would be required to undertake before his own inevitable submission to the steel. Once the sacrifice was made, and the Green King had given up his life for his community, his blood would be gathered and a little supplied to each of the families in the community. Mixed with water it would be sprinkled on their fields to prepare the earth for when the next sowing began. It was an ancient, hallowed tradition, one that was practiced in most faithful communities across the realm, thereby ensuring the continued benevolence of the earth beneath them.

'Does he ignore us?' asked Tolly in outraged tones when the young man failed to respond to her respectful nod in his direction. 'Truly, his official status is an exalted one, but...'

'He is drunk, my dear', murmured Stilli, nodding towards the cider flagon at his side. 'As well he might be. No one expects *him* to lay to with the scythe'.

Pyresion was a handsome young man in his middle twenties. His figure and his countenance were such that Stilli had sometimes wondered what it would feel like to be subject to his attentions. Not that this would ever happen, since the priestly class fell beyond his remit.

'Well indeed, he's going to bleed', observed Tye, pleased with this fortunate conjunction of words. He continued. 'Yes indeed. He's going to bleed. To bleed, to bleed. Perhaps there is a song in that'.

'There most certainly is not', hissed Tolly. 'And it is most indelicate of you to say it'.

'He didn't hear', objected Tye peevishly, 'so I don't know what I did wrong'.

'It is impious!'

Stilli spared only half an ear for the sibling disagreement that ensued, because at that moment a long file of Drumogari fieldhands appeared around the corner by the carpenter's house, led by a hard-faced overseer in a cart and with a brute bearing a lash bringing up the rear to encourage the laggards. The people from beyond the hill were required to supplement the labours of their betters when necessary, and at harvest time they were often to be seen working in the fields next to free men. Stilli noted, to her disquiet, that the file included her friend Radda. Despite herself, her step faltered, and she felt a flush rise in her cheeks as her companions moved onwards, quite oblivious to it all. Radda trudged between an elderly woman and a young man with a look of settled resentment on his face and a shock of dark hair. Her friend bore a sickle in one hand and a basket in the other, and for one dreadful moment her eye met Stilli's. Recognition sparked there and Stilli felt her mouth fall open. But then the moment was gone. Radda's own eyes were suddenly directed to the dusty road and the sullen file moved past, silent except for the clatter of the cart and the curses of the overseer.

In retrospect, Stilla supposed that it was the shock of this unexpected encounter that brought about the strange phenomenon that next occurred. Everything seemed to slow down around her. The movements of the Drumogari labourers proceeded with a sudden balletic grace. She felt light-headed and a thin buzzing began in her ears, through which the harsh voice of the overseer became a strangely distorted extended roar. The periphery of her vision was tinged with yellow, and she was filled with a sense of an unfamiliar latent power, as though she were a coiled spring, ready to unleash its sudden energy.

And then it was gone.

She gasped, and the world continued on its way.

'Stilli?' called Tolly over her shoulder. 'Do keep up'.

When she returned home, still somewhat disconcerted by her strange experience, Stilli found that her new tutor had arrived. Father was busy with his duties at the temple, and so Mother was entertaining him in the parlour at the front of the house. Drinks had been brought and stood steaming on a small table between them, filling the air with the scent of lemon.

'Stilitha', announced Mother as they both rose from their seats. 'I am glad to introduce you to Mr Bondorin, who I have engaged as your new tutor. Mr Bondorin comes highly recommended by friends of mine in Tazman, in fact, and his credentials lead me to believe that you should get on together very well. Mr Bondorin is from Radagar, which is a city in the distant south, in the Kingdom of Skagaar, as you will recall, but he has lived in our country for many years and is well acquainted with all spheres of learning, both sacred and secular'.

'Delighted', murmured Bondorin, tilting somewhat from the waist. 'I look forward to working with you and with assisting you in treading the path of knowledge'.

The glint in Mother's eye showed that she had little opinion of her stepdaughter's readiness to advance along that path, but Stilli was oblivious to this, her attention entirely taken up by the newcomer.

Bondorin was quite exceptionally tall and thin. In addition, he was by far the oldest man that Stilli had ever seen, given that almost no one was permitted to live more than sixty years. As a foreigner, he was evidently not subject to that law. The lines on his face, the mottled skin upon his gnarled old hands, suggested that those deep-sunk eyes had seen the passage of many more years. Nevertheless, the smooth, decisive manner of his movements suggested no diminution of vigour, and his eyes held a spark of lively intelligence, a spark that hinted at a wry amusement for the world around him.

'The flesh is aged, you are thinking', observed the newcomer accurately enough. He tapped his head whilst Stilli blushed, and added, 'But the brain is a nimble limb indeed, as you shall see'. He turned his head towards Mother. 'As you *both* shall see in due course, and I make no doubt that we shall get on famously, Miss Stilitha and I'.

Whilst Stilli resented the imposition of any regime of learning upon her, she could not but feel somewhat encouraged by the circumstances of this first encounter. Her first meeting with Sister Dahria had seen that woman adopt a posture of imperious disdain as soon as her Mother had withdrawn from the room, apparently taking with her the necessity for common civility. The governess had surveyed her new charge with a cold eye, as though Stilli's education were some unpleasant and unrewarding duty that she must shoulder for the common good. Nothing in their future relationship had suggested that Sister Dahria had ever been brought to revise that opinion. With Bondorin, though, it was quite different from the outset. There had been much talk of texts, much scrutiny of samplers and copy books, during which the new tutor had affected to see promise, and finally, whilst Mother's attention was distracted with gathering up her books, he spared her a glance that could only be described as conspiratorial, so roguish was the twinkle in his eye. Naturally, this intrigued Stilli, prompting her to wonder if this new regime might cause the accumulation of knowledge to become less oppressive to her mind.

Before Bondorin could do more than establish himself in the house and take some small first steps in gauging the extent of the task ahead of him, more pressing matters rose to prominence in the family.

The day of Father's death arrived. It was incumbent on all of his family to discipline their minds and to remind themselves that he was passing into the certain embrace of God, and that this embrace, because of his priestly status, might be enjoyed far more quickly than ordinary mortals, who must wait patiently to advance through the circles of admission that surrounded godhead. Nevertheless, Stilli felt sure that she would miss his steady, reassuring presence in the household. He was not a person to inspire affection. Indeed, his face was usually set in an attitude that discouraged such tokens of affection in others. Although that person could not be described as radiating kindness, neither did it practice cruelty, except in the necessary cruelties that his duties required of him. His most admirable quality was a conscientious efficiency, but his bravery had never been tested, and it was this that caused his family some anxiety as they gathered in the temple temenos to bear witness to his passing.

The whole of the community gathered with them, grave beneath a steady rain as Father completed his final ceremony, standing naked before the altar and raising a snake, a writhing fire asp, in each outstretched arm. His face, tilted to the heavens, streamed with rain so that he blinked as his mouth moved with the final bidding prayer. The congregation murmured its sombre response and father relinquished the asps into the hands of the acolytes on either side of him, who dutifully returned the creatures to their baskets. Then, with no more than a nod and a significant glance for his family, he paced towards the temple doors at the head of a procession of clergy and acolytes from the surrounding region. Within those doors, swung shut now with a grim finality, Father would be offered the fatal knife and drive it into his own heart. The deacon, his trusted subordinate of many years would certainly be there to guide and add strength to the hand, should Father's resolve fail. It would be deeply shameful if this were to occur, of course, and Stilli squeezed Mother's hand as they stood at the forefront of the assembly.

Despite her best intentions, a tremor came into her jaw and a tear to her eye, but the blessed rain concealed it, and she mastered herself as the minutes passed. The altar before them was still adorned with wilting flowers, battered by the falling rain. These were from the ceremony a few days previously in which the Green King had been dispatched once more into the earth to work his magic on the land.

This particular Green King had gone stoically enough, although some showed fear or reluctance at the end, and a very few, shamefully resisting their fate, called out pitifully and required manhandling and securing to the altar. Those long months of bliss they had enjoyed must finally be paid for. For the four young men who were his attendants during that year, the King's passing was one that brought relief as well as sadness. They had accompanied him in his carousing throughout those joyful seasons, but they were his guardians as well as his companions. Should the King repent of his hard bargain with death, should he attempt to abscond into the hills, those friends would be required to take his place. Such was the implacable law of the land.

Stilli reflected on these musings as the dismal rain splashed on the cobbled court around her, and the temple doors swung open once more. Heads covered now, through devotion rather than through any recognition of the rain, the procession retraced its steps to the altar with Father's body carried on a bier. There would be more prayers, more recitations from scripture and the trumpets would call out what was at once their lament and their exhortation to joy in the hearts of his congregation. At last, the procession paused before Mother, Middo and Stilli so that they may look upon their father's body and make their final signs of respect. Stilli saw Mother's eyes move to the deacon's. *Did he die well?* was their question.

The deacon made an almost imperceptible nod, but there was a look of falsity there that caused Stilli's heart to sink within her. She bit her lip and fiddled absently with her fingers as the bier was borne up once more and carried out through the gate that led to the bone-acre on its looming hill.

It is over, she murmured under her breath. *Over at last.*

Chapter Four

It seemed that a new chapter in her life had begun. The celebrations attendant upon Middo's name-day and his consequent majority took place the next day, when Father's body was barely cold upon its high wooden platform, when the crows had barely so much as pecked at his eyes. Consciousness of this gave the celebrations a certain forced quality so far as Mother and daughter were concerned, but this scarcely seemed a burden upon Middo's mind. There was a fierce exultation in his face as he drank with his friends and danced with the young noblewomen of the locality in the marquee that had been erected in the garden. Musicians were on hand, brought at significant expense from Crane, the provincial capital, together with expensive foodstuffs and the colourful bunting with which the marquee was adorned.

'It is a great thing to set aside childish preoccupations and step over the threshold of manhood', observed Bondorin, appearing at Stilli's side in a manner so sudden as to cause her to start. 'But you must forgive me for breaking your train of thought,' he added.

Together they gazed upon Middo as he passed by with Tolly upon his arm, bobbing and dipping with the stately motions of the pavane. His head was newly shaven in the manner that all adult males dedicated to the priesthood must adopt, and somewhere beneath his clothing the first of the priestly tattoos had been applied. 'And what sort of man do you suppose he will be?' asked her tutor, raising a glass of elderflower wine to his lips. 'I barely know him'.

'I am sure he will do very well', asserted Stilli in a confident tone designed to defeat any attempt by Bondorin to detect enmity in their relationship. Indeed, she rather resented such an impertinent enquiry, and her brows knitted, despite herself.

'I beg forgiveness', replied Bondorin archly, surveying her inner mind in a manner that was already beginning to seem uncanny to her, 'if my enquiry gave any appearance of an opinion to the contrary. Nothing could be further from my mind, indeed, and the assurance of your answer places the matter beyond all reasonable doubt'.

Stilli blushed and cast her eyes down to the lacework on her best frock, wondering whether she could ever preserve any secrets from this strange man.

There was plenty of opportunity for Stilli to answer this question for herself during the next few weeks as life began to settle into what she must come to recognise as its familiar course. Mother bore her father's loss with the public stoicism that her station obliged in her, wearing the black garments that all associated with mourning and daubing her cheeks with the ashes from the fire. Within the home, Stilli frequently found her in moments of private reflection, when thoughts of Father might presumably be occupying her mind, and once, when clearing items from his office, she was to be seen momentarily standing there with unshed tears in her eyes. She never spoke of it. Mother's mind was closed to Stilli, as it had always been, and there was never to be community of grief between them.

For herself, she missed Father's presence in the house, the little ways he had that were as much a part of her life as the house itself, but it was hard to feel any but the mildest pangs of grief. He had been a remote figure who had shown little sign of any reciprocal affection when, as a small child, she had been so bold as to embrace him. She had learned, soon enough, that such impulsive advances were unwelcome, and now it was easy to seek refuge in the religious certainty that Father was in a better place, where he might come to find union with the divine in due course.

To her shame, the grief most oppressive to her mind was the one she felt for the house in which they dwelt. It was only a matter of time before notification had arrived from Tazman that Father's replacement had been appointed, bringing with it their necessary eviction in due course. Mother had secured a new house on the other side of the village, one that might be their temporary refuge, until such time as Stilli had achieved her own majority and a husband could be found for her. These prospects caused Stilli considerable apprehension as the days passed by.

'My understanding is that it was your pleasure to roam the countryside hereabouts and enjoy the clear air, the exercise, the stimulating landscapes to be observed there', remarked Bondorin one morning after breakfast, when her lessons were to begin.

He crossed to the window to look out past the high hedges to where the shoulders of the tree-clad hills to the south could be observed.

'And it is an uncommonly fine morning, is it not?' he continued, turning to her, head tilted and with a knowing smile upon his face. 'What say you we take out our schoolroom to yonder hill and conduct our lessons there?'

Stilli's heart leapt within her.

'I should like that', she answered, eyes wide. 'But what of...?'

'Your mother? Never fear, I have solicited her approval already. Those with a grasp of etymology will know that the word "education" means "leading out," in this and many other languages besides. You may take these books in a satchel', he instructed, indicating a selection from those that lay before her, 'a piece of board to serve you as a desk, some writing materials and I shall see that the kitchen does not suffer us to starve'.

Thus equipped, Stilli and her tutor ventured forth into the countryside, where the autumn ploughing was well under way, making their way along paths and byways that led ever upward, through the common lands where the village folk grazed their beasts and at last to the fringes of the woods and hills. All the while, Bondorin regaled her with poetry, much of which was quite unfamiliar to her ear, and with a detailed commentary on the plants and trees they passed.

'This tree, the wild olive, is the ancestor of those we cultivate today. See how small its fruits are? And they would be bitter, should you eat them. Human husbandry has rendered it more amenable, more yielding and of a greater treasure, a delight to the palette, a source of light, a salve, a lubricant and many other uses besides. How we have tamed Nature and placed it at our service at last!'

'And yet Nature is not our servant', objected Stilli when they sat upon a convenient hummock and looked back across the hedgerows down towards the village. 'And she may withdraw her bounty, should we fall from favour. The harvest fails from time to time, does it not? And the beasts that serve us are stricken with pest or murrain. Such tribulations surely remind us that the fields and the pastures yield up our livelihood only because it pleases the earth and our god that they should do so. It is not our birth-right'.

'Indeed', nodded Bondorin, taking a bite from an apple. 'In this country it is judged to be in the nature of a bargain. Your people placate the earth and the heavens alike, giving tokens of your gratitude and devotion in return for their continued benevolence, their continuing provision of the produce that sustains you'.

'Of course', agreed Stilli, unwrapping bread and cheese from within the cloth they had been wrapped in. 'How else are we to explain the Green King and those other sacrifices we must occasionally make when the favour of the heavens and of the earth is withdrawn? All know this. It is our faith'. She frowned. 'I'm surprised that you should raise it'.

'I do not seek to question it' he answered. 'I have learned that certain questions are best not asked, especially in this country. I seek only to discuss and to examine, because to do so is to gain further knowledge, as we might gain further knowledge of a flower through a close examination of its constituent parts'.

'Does your own god not drive the hard bargain that ours does?' asked Stilli, reflecting that her wondering frowns escaped her tutor's censure in a way that set him apart from either Mother or Sister Dahria.

Bondorin did not answer for some time, instead staring at the distant mountains, chewing abstractedly, as though wondering whether to share a confidence.

'He does not', murmured Bondorin at last. Then, turning to Stilli, he fixed her with a gaze of great intensity. 'Tell me, Stilli. What do you know of your mother's origins?'

'Why do you ask?' demanded Stilli evasively, resenting Bondorin's intrusion into a field of particular sensitivity for her.

Mother could never be brought to discuss the time before she married Father. Besides, she now knew that this person was not her mother at all, and consequently she preferred not to speak of it, for fear that the circumstance might disclose itself in her countenance or in her bearing. All she knew, and this from occasional snippets let slip by her father, was that Mother was an Erenori of noble birth, married, along with others of her class, into the priesthood as part of the provisions of the Treaty of 3938.

'Why do you evade my question?' he pressed. 'Such evasion is itself instructive, suggesting an uneasy mind'. Stung by this assessment, Stilli sullenly told her tutor what little she knew, finishing with, '...although I'm sure I don't know how telling you this advances my education'.

'You may be surprised. I may be able to add to your knowledge', announced Bondorin with a grin, throwing the apple core into a hedge. 'I was in Tazman when your mother sailed in with the Imperial embassy when the peace of that name was agreed, seventeen years ago. There were a dozen such young ladies of noble birth, each to be exchanged with a matching dozen Vhanakhori maidens of the priestly caste. She was, I should say, the fairest of them all, and the eye of Vindex, High Priest of the great temple of Draganach, soon fell upon her'.

'How do you know this?' interrupted Stilli, feeling a sudden engorgement in her throat and a prickle across her scalp. It was as though Bondorin recounted some children's fantasy tale.

'I know this because I was there, as I have said', said Bondorin patiently. 'I was an observer with the Imperial embassy. Do you wish me to continue?'

'Do, please', replied Stilli, earnestly, all suspicion set aside. She leant forward and placed an encouraging hand upon his forearm.

'Vindex, the person you may regard as your step-uncle, was in a position of power and influence within the state. Besides, his own wife had recently died in childbirth. It was not difficult for him to secure your mother for his own. We might expect that love would struggle to establish itself within such a marriage of state, the seeds of affection cast upon such stony ground, but grow they did. It was as though two worlds collided, that of the god Tio, he who your people abhor, and of his divine sibling Yuzanid, who receives your boundless devotions. Despite this, despite the enmity of their two peoples, your mother, Rosania Thandora Tanatiel, for I shall dignify her with her full name, and the High Priest Vindex fell deeply in love'.

Bondorin stood up now, his eyes unfocussed as though searching his memory to recite some ancient work of poetry.

'It was the kind of all-consuming love that shuts out the world beyond and makes of each moment together a crystallised jewel of contentment. The world looked on amazed that the grim priest, whose duties required that he should deal in death from day to day, should find such pleasure in this most vivid expression of life's bounty. Many murmured that he whose mind should dwell on the eternal verities were focused instead on the momentary, the ephemeral. Within a year, they had a daughter, the perfect physical manifestation of their perfect love for each other'.

'Do please go on', urged Stilli, eyes wide when Bondorin paused and the look of vicarious joy faded from his face. 'You say that my mother had a daughter of her own!'

'I have heard it said that the heavens are jealous', he sighed. 'That too much pleasure and good fortune in one life attract their envy and their displeasure. It is hard to resist the notion that these two were so fated'.

'Why so?' demanded Stilli, her brow creased once more. 'Why so?'

Bondorin sighed deeply now and passed a hand across his scalp, where a thin growth of white hair yet remained.

'I should not have begun this story', he lamented with an apologetic glance. 'I really should not. I shall only be the bearer of distress'.

'Nonsense, Mr Bondorin', urged Stilli, standing to take both of his bony arms in her hands. 'I insist that you do'.

'Have you heard of the Golden Child, Stilli?' he asked gravely, inclining his head towards her.

'I have', gasped Stilli, in whose breast a gathering anxiety caused her heart to beat with a sudden furious intensity. She shook her head. 'No. You will not tell me...'

'Then you will know that every five years, your people make their greatest sacrifice to their god. You will know that a child is selected by lot from amongst the highest echelons of the priestly caste...'

'I do not wish to hear', cried Stilli, placing her hands over her ears but hearing nevertheless.

'And that doomed child is thrown into the fire in the belly of the great brass serpent who stands in the forecourt of the holiest of holies, the famous temple of Draganach on the sacred mount in Tazman. By sacrificing their dearest possessions do the priests of your god demonstrate the boundless extent of their love for him. So it has always been, and when your mother's child was three years old...'

'No, no, no!' moaned Stilli, shaking her head and closing her eyes.

'The lot fell for her'.

'Why do you tell me this?' protested Stilli, tears starting in her eyes.

Bondorin continued, his own eyes remaining strangely unfocussed, as though those grim events played themselves out before his inner vision.

'And the child was adorned with gold, as tradition demanded, and a golden diadem placed upon her head, and she perished in the flame. And Yuzanid was satisfied, the bargain with his people fulfilled'.

Stilli felt the hot tears on her cheek now, and she dashed them fiercely away as a sudden realisation dawned upon her.

She was the replacement for that Golden Child.

Upon the completion of that dreadful sacrifice her mother had seized upon the opportunity to take another daughter for her own. The trauma and the loss her mother must have suffered were barely to be contemplated. It was little wonder that she could never be induced to discuss those days in Tazman before her removal to this place. How those events must haunt her dreams!

'A dark bargain indeed', continued Bondorin softly, his eyes upon Stilli's face in a quiet, considering manner.

He knew. He knew that she was adopted, that she was the replacement her mother had found for the child that had perished in the flames.

'Oh yes, I know', murmured Bondorin, as though her thoughts paraded themselves before him. 'But you need not fear that I shall disclose your secret to others. It is a secret that Rosania Thandora Zandravo guards within her heart – and one that may someday destroy her'.

He placed a gentle hand to her cheek to wipe away a tear.

'Forgive me, child', he soothed. 'There is knowledge that is a dawning in the heart, and then there is knowledge that is a burden to the soul. I am sorry to have brought you the latter, but it was necessary, as you shall see some day. I mean no harm by it. Nor is it the whole story'.

'Then you must tell me it!' Stilli insisted when she could master her voice once more.

'I may not', said Bondorin regretfully. 'It is not the time'.

To have given up a child to the flames of Draganach was surely a sacrifice that even the faithful must contemplate with dread, but Mother was of another faith entirely, and so the loss must have been doubly traumatic. Surely Stilli, although of a similar age, could never have replaced that doomed child. Surely this explained the haunted look that sometimes came into Mother's eyes when she looked upon her adopted daughter. She was remembering the daughter that Yuzanid had taken from her for his own.

It soon became clear that Middo disapproved of Stilli's new tutor. He resented the manner of Bondorin's teaching methods, observing that they were very much in accord with Stilli's own preferences and so much to be deplored, seeing also that they brought about a remarkable improvement in her learning. Within weeks, she was confidently reciting at dinner the words of the Dargiriad, that great epic poem, in addition to discussing natural philosophy and poetry with her mother in a manner that showed real pleasure and accordingly won her real praise.

'I must say, you are much improved', Mother declared, clapping her hands when Stilli sat down after her recitation one evening. You must allow she is improved, Middo', she added, turning to her stepson.

'I allow nothing', grunted Middo, cutting savagely at his meat. 'I have not time for profane nonsense of that kind. Only poetry of the sacred kind brings joy to my heart and glorifies our god. I suppose my own accomplishments are unworthy of note in my father's house'.

Colour rose in Mother's cheeks as he said this, and once she might have admonished him for the surly gracelessness of his reply. The relationship between them was necessarily changed by his majority, however, and by the death of her husband.

'You will soon have ample opportunity to lavish praise upon your favourite', he continued. 'For I shall be away from here. I am to attend a course at the military academy in Crane. My swordsmanship has come to the attention of a visiting master, who made the necessary recommendation. I shall be there until the end of the month'.

He smiled, in that odious way he had, one that disclosed private enjoyment of another's discomfiture.

'I rejoice to hear it', said Mother, concealing her irritation that her stepson had made no previous mention of this, had asked no permission of her.

'Of course you do, Mother. I shall go far in this world, you shall see', he answered with a particularly cold glance for Stilli, to show that she – by comparison – was doomed by her sex to go nowhere and to achieve nothing.

The object of his scorn merely shrugged. There was nothing to be said.

'So what's he like, your new tutor?' asked Radda a few days later when Stilli sat with her in their habitual meeting place, looking down upon both their separate worlds.

'He is a vast improvement on Sister Dahria, I swear', admitted Stilli, making the serpent sign before her, pencil in hand, having spoken ill of the dead. 'And with him I do not find myself confined to the house. He is very happy to be outside and knows everything there is to know about every tree or plant you care to name. He is a very learned fellow, I am sure'.

'Pah!' spat the charcoal-burner's boy Mull, who had joined them and was lying on his back while regarding the clouds pass high overhead. 'What use is learning?

What use are books to anyone? I never read a book and I never need to, neither'.

It was likely enough that Mull would never need to trouble his head over the world of literature. He and his family lived a nomadic life in the woods that clothed the mountain flanks in this part of the island of Eudora. They felled the smaller saplings there and burned them beneath mounds of peat and soil to make the charcoal that iron-makers needed for their work, carrying it down to the towns from time to time in vast baskets almost as big as themselves. The work and the mysteries thereof were transmitted along the generations. On a still day such as this, a thin thread of smoke from high in the hills disclosed the site of their present encampment.

Stilli and Radda exchanged humorous glances over his recumbent form.

'Well perhaps your head is filled up already. Perhaps there is no room for any more of the world in there', suggested Radda. 'I wouldn't turn a book away, were one to come my way. Books are too good for the likes of me and mine, though. If your people find them amongst us, they burn them, saying they are heretical or heathen, or such like. Either way, they burn them. My old Aunt Ara had some once, but now they are gone and we have nothing to read'.

These remarks were directed to Stilli, whose cheeks burned suddenly hot with the implication.

'I regret it extremely', she asserted. 'I should never have allowed it, had I had a say in it at all, which I don't, owing to my being a girl and a young one at that. If only the world attended to my views, you would still have your books, I assure you'.

'You are not like the others of your kind', laughed Mull, turning onto his side. 'Haughty, they are. Think they own the world under our feet and the heavens above it'.

The distinctive smoky smell that always clung to the boy came into Stilli's nostrils on the faintest of breezes that stirred the grasses around them. He was not unattractive, she decided, with his dark eyes and his close-cropped curly hair. He was habitually unwashed, however, and his ragged clothes showed the evidence of a great deal of mending, and that with indifferent skill. She wrinkled her nose and turned her attention to the blank page of her sketchbook, one on which her pencil had yet to make its mark.
'And what were they, those books?' she asked.
'You wouldn't have taken anything from them, I suppose', answered Radda, looking to where one of her goats cropped the grass a short way away, the bell around its neck clanking gently with its movements. 'Written in Cantrophene, they were, the ancient speech of my people in the old country. My aunt could read it a little, but mostly she just liked looking at it. Said it reminded her of home, she did'.
'Oh', muttered Stilli, conscious once more of being amongst Radda's oppressors.
'It had pictures in it, though, pictures of ancient heroes with swords riding horses and such like', she sighed. 'I liked those, and Mother had taught me some of the words, too. Just a few. I probably couldn't even remember them now'.
'When did she die? Your aunt, I mean?' asked Stilli, despairing of her purely notional drawing now and setting down her pencil.
'A couple of years since', Radda shrugged. 'When there was that blue fever'.
'A great leveller, fever', opined Mull, throwing small stones at the yellow fungus that clung to a nearby rotten log. 'It doesn't much care whether you're slave or free, Drumogari or Vhanakhori. Even-handed it is. No

respecter of rank, neither. Like you', he added with a gesture for Stilli.

'You make me sound like a disease', laughed Stilli, causing Mull to grin in return.

'By which I mean you don't much care for rank, or you wouldn't be here talking to the likes of us'.

'That's right', agreed Radda with a glance for the distant roofs of Stilli's village. 'There are folks who would certainly take a dim view of this acquaintance, on your side and on mine. I've told you this before and yet here we are'.

'I don't care', shrugged Stilli, feeling as she often did, that she didn't fit naturally within her world. Now, at least, she had a reason to ascribe to this notion. The fact that she was the daughter of a lowly servant was never far from the forefront of her mind. Perhaps she, too, had been a captive, a Drumogaros. "Erenori," that was what they called themselves, the conquered people taken out of their empire and carried away to this land to labour for those who had vanquished them.

'What is that smoke I see?' asked Stilli, in order to move the subject away from one uncongenial to her. 'Out yonder, beyond those barns and byres'.

'That is the house of Lumania Trimandrios', answered Radda, shading her eyes and frowning. 'The Steward and his men burnt it down earlier today because her son, Axilo, raised his hand against them, struck one, they say. Pitched him on his back, the fat bastard'.

She spat contemptuously on the ground in front of her to express her opinion of this exchange.

'Silly fellow!' laughed Mull. 'I suppose they have hanged him for it'.

'I'm sure they would if they could lay hands on him', nodded Radda with a glance for Stilli, who felt a new pang of despondency. 'But they can't, seeing as he's run away. They had to content themselves with burning

down the house and beating his poor mother to death. There'll be trouble if they catch him'.
'He will hang for it then?' asked Stilli, feeling that she must make some comment.
'I assure you he'll be crying out to be hanged by the time they've finished with him', noted Radda grimly. 'And your brother was with them, they do say'.

It was entirely possible that Middo had been involved in the incident, mused Stilli as she made her way back down the hill in readiness for her afternoon lessons. The oppression of his social inferiors was a delight to his soul, and his contact with them frequently brought duty and inclination into the closest of alignments. His training would certainly involve working with the Steward whose duties encompassed the oversight of the Drumogari. He was employed to discipline their community and summon them to whatever labours their betters required of them. Stilli well knew that her friendship with Mull and Radda invited the censure of her peers, should any learn of it, and yet she continued to pursue it, feeling a strange affinity with their world, a strange disassociation from her own. Her visits to the hill, her regular encounters with Radda and her more occasional ones with Mull were ones that she must necessarily keep secret. She felt that her heart was increasingly burdened with secrets and that these must one day disclose themselves upon her countenance.

Chapter Five

'Now there is a face that has seen its share of woe', laughed Bondorin when she encountered him on the front steps of the house, causing her a new twinge of anxiety on this account.

He turned and she pursued him along towards the study as he talked of the cow with two heads that had been born in a neighbouring village and other strange natural phenomena he had heard of. When the door was closed, however, he looked about him in a conspiratorial manner and grinned.

'Your mother is with friends today, is she not?' he asked, and then, when Stilli nodded. 'And I believe the Steward rejoices in your brother's company'.

'So, I have heard'.

'Aha! I had planned to require you to write out sections of improving literature, adapted to the ready comprehension of the female mind, as your brother recommended when last I saw him, but another idea presents itself to me'.

'It does?' Stilli enquired, knitting her brows and regarding him suspiciously.

'It does', Bondorin nodded, reaching behind a curtain and bringing out two swords. 'Certainly, it does'.

'Surely you don't propose to teach me... that', she objected, gesturing at the weapons as Bondorin turned one to present it to her hand, setting the other on her desk.

'Why not?' he asked as she cautiously enfolded the grip in her hand, trying the weight and the balance of it.

'Because it is not a female accomplishment', Stilli explained. 'And Mother would certainly dismiss you if she learned that you were training me to be a warrior'.

'A warrior!' laughed Bondorin. 'Such stuff! Nothing could be further from my thoughts. And yet to learn the steps and the moves we employ in swordplay is a most valuable exercise for mind and body. It encourages the eye to be more discerning, the movements of sinews and limbs to be directed with a surpassing elegance and grace. However', he frowned, 'if you fear your brother's disapproval, and you are no doubt correct to do so, perhaps the idea was ill-conceived'.

Stilli turned the sword in her hand, making the light glint on the brass work of the basket hilt, and looked along the blade, straight and true.

'What manner of sword is this?' she asked. 'I have not seen soldiers carry them. Theirs are generally wider in the blade, with a simple cross shape, in fact'.

'Indeed, such are the weapons a man generally bears in battle, the kind that your brother daily trains to employ for when he is summoned to the banners, as one day he must be. Such a weapon, wielded with the muscular force that a strong man can bring to bear, is a powerful thing indeed, but this, my dear, is equally deadly in its own way. It delivers no great weight in the cut, but the thrust is very potent'.

He tilted his head to one side and regarded her quizzically.

'But I can see that I weary you', he noted. 'It was a mere whim, a foolish fancy to think that a gentle maiden such as yourself might wish to associate herself with the steely toys of manhood'.

He reached to take the sword from her, but she twitched her hand aside.

'No', she said. 'If Middo disapproves, then surely it is my pleasure to embrace it. I'm sure you may teach me a very little'.

'Well, if you insist', laughed Bondorin, as though it were Stilli who had conceived of the scheme. 'There is a place at the very end of the garden where we may practise, out of sight. There is no need to excite the displeasure of your family until such time as circumstances may bring about their forbidding it'.

'Or, as a friend tells me, *what the head don't know, the heart don't grieve over*', murmured Stilli, feeling a growing excitement, a growing determination to push at the boundaries that confined her.

The swords, it appeared, were called rapiers and were of the kind employed by swordsmen in Bondorin's native Skagaar, where the nobles were famously resentful of a slight and much given to duelling as a consequence. Stilli's sword was well-adapted to her size, and she soon learned the parries, the feints and the lunges that were the basic repertoire of the swordsman, practising these beneath the boughs of the peach trees in the garden whenever her mother's or Middo's absence from the house gave opportunity. Fortunately, there were many such opportunities, and as September gave way to October, Bondorin professed himself content with her progress.

'I will not say you are a natural, nor that your motions are the most elegant, but you have a sound instinct for a move – and the directing mind is the most deadly limb of all, as the masters of this art acknowledge', Bondorin told her as they sat eating lunch one day with their backs pressed to the gnarled trunk of the holm oak that stood huge amongst the surrounding peaches.

'Swiftness of thought and action is truly the wellspring of victory', he continued.

'I'm sure you are right', agreed Stilli. 'Not that I shall ever be required to demonstrate those things in earnest, I suppose'.

'Perhaps not', conceded Bondorin. 'Although no one truly knows what the future holds in store for them', he added with a significant glance.

'Tell me, Stilli. Have you given much thought to *time*, to the notion of *time* as a concept, I mean?'

'I have given much thought to it', answered Stilli. 'Every day brings me closer to the day when I must quit this place, my home. Every hour and every minute are steps along that path. I shall hate it. I know I shall. That fateful letter from Tazman must surely soon arrive, and then my world shall end'.

'I think not', soothed Bondorin, toying idly with the hilt of his rapier. 'The world has a larger place for you, and everyone must someday emerge from behind their mother's skirts, even you, Stilitha Zandravo'.

'I know. I must grow up', conceded Stilli glumly. 'But I do not welcome it'.

A fly passed between them, and without thinking, Stilli snatched at it. In a way that no longer surprised her, time seemed to slow to a trickle, and the vague yellow tinge on the fringes of her vision hinted at the imminence of a faint. Her fingers darted out to seize the fly as its wings beat the air balletically. And then she gasped. Time continued at its habitual pace. Bondorin held the fly between two fingers.

'How did you do that?' she demanded.

'In the same way that you did', he answered with a wry smile. 'Time is my servant, as it is yours'.

'I don't understand', gasped Stilli. 'I thought it was only myself...'

Bondorin took Stilli's hand and placed it gently to his breast, where she could feel the beads of the necklace he always wore beneath his shirt.

'Do you feel my heartbeat, Stilli?'

'I do', she admitted. 'But why...?'

'Every creature in this world has its allotted span', he interrupted, releasing her hand. 'Our hearts may beat more than two billion times whilst we walk the earth, whereas that of a mouse may beat four hundred times as many in its short span. Each creature has its unvarying pulse, and it is that which governs its perception of time. The mouse may live only two years, but its relationship with time is very different to ours. Its life seems as long to that creature as ours do to us. To such a creature it seems that we move with ponderous slowness, as though moving in treacle. To the fly, as you see, our movements are slower still'.

'Then how did you catch it? How can I catch it?'

'Consider this tree', continued Bondorin, placing his hand on the gnarled bark between them. 'If it had a heartbeat at all, it would be vast and almost incomprehensibly slow, perhaps a single one in each of our passing months, but the tree lives very slowly by comparison. This one is already more than four hundred years old. The earth beneath our feet, if it may be considered a living entity at all, lives so slowly that it may barely be aware of our existence upon its surface. The first of our race's footprints on the primordial strand, until today, a mere blink in the eye of eternity. It is the *pace* of life that is important, and all the living things in creation have their pace and their span accordingly'.

'I ask you again', insisted Stilli, knitting her brow and bridling at this evasion. 'How do we do it? How are we able to slow time to suit our own needs as we did just now?'

'We adjust our pace, Stilli', nodded Bondorin. 'We call upon that which we sense is there for us, and we adjust the pace of our lives to fit the circumstances. You adjusted the pace of your life to that of the fly, faster still than the fly, I should say, and so you were able to match its speed and its movement. It is a skill so rare – so special – as to be considered miraculous. You can do this at will, Stilli, if I am not mistaken. You have only to learn to turn your mind to it, to reach within for it, and you may equal or even surpass the pace of any creature'.

'Miraculous!' Stilli gasped, her mouth falling open whilst fixing Bondorin with an incredulous glare. 'Can this be true?'

'True, indeed, and you began to be aware of this power the moment I stepped into your world, some little while ago. But I should warn you, for reasons I cannot now disclose to you, that you should use this ability but sparingly – and for no frivolous purpose. The ability is limited in duration and may not be used once more when its vital essence within you is expended. You will find that you can use it only on a few occasions and then no more. It should certainly not be expended in the killing of flies, Stilli'.

Bondorin laughed and shook his head, mimicking her furrowed brow and slack jaw.

'There will come a time when such a rare ability may be of vital importance to you. For now, as I have mentioned, you should not disclose it to others'.

'What are you saying?' Stilli asked, regarding him quizzically.

'I am saying only this. If others were to remark upon this... talent, or be told of it, you might be considered a sorceress in some quarters. You should not mention it to a living soul. To do so might invite those who feel threatened by it to seek to destroy you. You know the fate of those found guilty of sorcery'.

'I do', admitted Stilli, swallowing hard, the pyre coming into her mind. The fate of sorcerers was to be burned.

'What does it mean?' she asked. 'Catching flies offers no great advantage in life, I suppose'.
Bondorin laughed and regarded her with a wry look, reaching across to tousle her hair.
'Does it not? Not yet, I may allow, but you will surely see great advantage if you consider. And consider you must'.

The fateful letter arrived. The new priest had finally been appointed and would arrive with his entourage in the first week of November. At least some small solace might be found in the fact that their intolerable neighbour, Ingridex, had been disappointed and that a stranger, an appointee from Tazman, was to take Father's place instead.
Nevertheless, the news inevitably threw the household into turmoil. Mother's already intermittent oversight of her daughter's education became more tenuous still, as she was required to supervise the removal of their possessions to their new house on the eastern edge of the village. This was a much smaller property, comparatively cramped and cast into shade by a vast row of tall cedars. The sun barely penetrated into Stilli's new room until late in the afternoon. For days, she was much engaged in helping Mother with the carts of furniture and all the necessary baggage of a household that must be conveyed along the half a mile or so of streets between the two properties. She would be sad to leave the house that was the only one she had ever known, and the future held little in prospect to cheer her. Mother had identified a number of young men in neighbouring properties who might be considered a match for her when she came of age, but these brought no leap of joy in her heart when she looked upon them. One, a lad called Canda, was of a noble family that had fallen on hard times, and although circumstances

offered little alternative, the young man evidently resented the possibility of marriage to a girl of a less exalted bloodline. Given that he was unable to conceal his disdain, it seemed unlikely that any relationship would flourish between them.

Another, rather unfortunately, was Tye, whose family were enticingly wealthy but whose name held none of the lustre of the Zandravids of Tazman. Tye was much taken with Stilli, and she had known him for as long as she could remember. Although she made no criticism of his character, he would surely make a dull companion, untroubled as he was by learning, wit or the first inkling of what might constitute a stimulating conversation.

Consequently, Stilli's marital destiny remained unsettled, and the last days of her life at The Hedges ebbed like some doleful tide. She had come to enjoy her swordplay with her tutor, and since the new property lacked any significant grounds, it was likely that her removal there must necessarily see an end to that exercise. It seemed almost miraculous that her untroubled weeks of training in the orchard should not have come to the attention of her family. Fortunately, Bondorin seemed to have Smeeton in his thrall, and so the house steward had pointedly averted his gaze on those few occasions when he might have spied them in the corridors with weapons inadequately concealed beneath coats or cloaks. Nor had Myal the groundsman thought it necessary to mention the various episodes of swordplay he must certainly have witnessed whilst he swept leaves or trimmed the great hedges. It was inevitable, however, as Stilli spent her last few days in her dear home, that this must come to an end. And come to an end it did, with remarkable suddenness.

Middo had returned from the first week of his military training, much inflated with a sense of his own worth, and strolled into the garden one afternoon in late October to be confronted by the alarming sight of his sister fencing with her tutor.

'Hey, hey, hey!' he called, standing hand on hips at the entrance to the little orchard. 'What have we here? Does Master Bondorin propose to make a man of you?'

'I do not', answered Bondorin, lowering his sword and allowing it to dangle at his side. 'Although what makes a man is a concept that not all may sensibly comprehend'.

Stilli dropped her own rapier with a dull clatter to the hard earth beneath and felt the colour rise in her cheeks. 'I'm not sure that I don't resent your implication', snarled Middo, flexing his gloved hands and placing one meaningfully on the hilt of the great sword that hung in its scabbard at his left side. 'And I had not heard that swordplay was part of the curriculum you taught. My mother may likewise be surprised to hear it. Besides, that puny hat pin is not a sword. *This* is a sword'.

So saying, he drew his own from its scabbard with a fine ringing swish and brandished it across his chest.

'Perhaps we should try a few passes to see if my own skills might be increased through your tutelage'.

'Perhaps we should', agreed Bondorin, grinning, with a bow. 'It would be my pleasure'.

Stilli was well aware that no good could come of this. She did not wish to see Bondorin defeated, possibly injured, but neither was the prospect of Middo's humiliation to be countenanced, except for the momentary delight it would bring to her heart. The prospect of his taking revenge, and the manner of his taking it, filled her with dread. She clasped her hands to her face as the two combatants circled each other warily, observing each other's movements through narrowed eyes as the sun slanted down through the branches.

Middo struck first, a scything downward diagonal blow that must surely have cut Bondorin in half had it found its mark. It did not. Bondorin stepped back, adjusted his balance and guided Middo's sword harmlessly aside with his own blade. Another attack came, and then another, faster and faster, Middo cursing and roaring as he hacked and slashed at his opponent, sometimes stepping forward with a vicious darting thrust. It seemed that Bondorin wove a mesh of glinting metal about him, the movement of his body and blade a blur of purposeful activity, the orchard ringing with the clash of steel on steel.

Middo's curses became more profane, his breath more laboured as the moments passed and he stepped back, lowering his sword to mop his brow with the forearm of his free arm.

'Not bad, old man', he grunted, 'but in a moment your defence shall break. Good fortune will only take you so far, and when...'

He did not complete this sentence, instead bringing up his blade in a vicious and unheralded swipe that he hoped might take Bondorin by surprise.

Bondorin, whose own demeanour was one of unruffled amusement, seemed barely to have broken sweat. He merely stepped aside and eased the blow away with contemptuous ease. Middo's movements became more desperate, more clumsy as his endurance diminished and his rage increased. Sudden realisation struck Stilli, with a shock that caused an electric thrill to traverse her scalp. Bondorin's movements were preternaturally fast. He had said that he shared her apparent ability to adjust the passage of time to suit her own needs – and this was what he was evidently doing. He was toying with Middo now, making the occasional lunge or probing attack, which obliged his opponent to duck or to dodge, all the time wearing a complacent smile upon his face.

At last, the bout came to its inevitable conclusion. With a roar, Middo hurled himself at Bondorin, his sword whirling about him. Bondorin stepped forward, knee bent and braced, allowing Middo's full weight to strike it. Unbalanced, pivoting suddenly over this immovable obstacle, Middo crashed heavily to the ground, dropping his weapon and striking his head hard against the trunk of the tree. Rolling over, eyes unfocused, he lay there gasping whilst Stilli rushed to his side.

'Middo!' she cried, and then glancing sidelong at Bondorin. 'What have you done?!'

Blood trickled across Middo's bald pate, where the first of his cranial tattoos had recently been applied. He touched his scalp gingerly and brought his hand down to regard the blood with vague, bleary eyes.

'You show promise but have much to learn, young man', laughed Bondorin, brandishing his sword in the air before him before sliding it into his scabbard. Then to Stilli, he said, 'Do not be apprehensive, my dear. I warrant his skull is hard enough to withstand a little knock or two. Besides, it is a small price to learn humility, as he will doubtless acknowledge in due course'.

Stilli could only stare, her gaze passing from Bondorin's face to Middo's. It seemed most unlikely that Middo would ever thank Bondorin for teaching him humility and quite certain that he would resent the attempt.

'Miss Stilitha'.

Smeeton's call from the kitchen steps summoned Stilli from her shocked reverie.

'Miss Stilitha, your Mother requires you urgently', Smeeton continued, out of sight from behind a row of cypresses that separated the orchard from the formal parts of the garden.

With a wide-eyed glance for Bondorin and her stunned recumbent brother, she turned and hurried to the house, where Smeeton's countenance showed evidence of severe concern.

In the study, calming her breathing, she found herself confronted by her mother and a short, plump gentleman with an unhealthily mottled face and a sheaf of papers in his hand.
'Stilitha', said Mother, whose own face wore an expression of grave suspicion. "Allow me to introduce you to Mr Bondorin'.
'Delighted', announced the newcomer, whereas Stilli could only stifle a gasp and make what might generously be described as a curtsey. She exchanged a puzzled glance with her parent.
'Mr Bondorin, I say', repeated Mother, a significant tone in her voice. 'He has presented his references and credentials, all of which seem impeccable'.
'Then who...?' began Stilli, twitching her head in the direction of the garden, making plain her enquiry.
'Exactly', nodded Mother. 'We appear to have two gentlemen of this name'.
'Well indeed', objected the newcomer, finding his voice now. 'I assure you I am the legitimate owner of that title. Had not I been taken ill, seriously ill, I might add, I should certainly have been with you months ago. I take it you did not receive my letter, then? I wrote on several occasions when I received no reply to my first'.
'No', said Mother slowly. 'We did not. Stilitha, perhaps you would fetch the other gentleman'.
Stilli's heart was racing as she hurried back through the house to the garden, but when she arrived there it was to find only Middo, sitting up and rubbing his head ruefully. The enigmatic tutor was nowhere to be seen.

Chapter Six

It was raining in Tazman when Zanidas came in from the morning sacrifice, and the temenos of the Great Temple was thrashed by drifting veils of it. The wretched attendants had hurried for the refuge of the columned portico that surrounded this space as soon as the goat had been despatched to Yuzanid, the most routine of blood tributes. Within moments, the creature's blood had dissipated in the rain flow and its body had been carried away for the subsequent inspection of its liver and the necessary reading of the auspices.

Such matters were not amongst Zanidas' concerns. In the antechamber to his apartments, he handed the sacred knife to his servant and took a towel from another, drying himself vigorously for a few moments whilst his mind turned to the necessary appointments of the day to come.

To begin with, there was breakfast and then the first of many meetings with staff and subordinates, before the hour he had set aside for himself to read and to reflect. Last month's earthquake, which had destroyed a number of buildings in the poorer quarters of the city and toppled a statue on the portico of this very temple, was to be the first item on the agenda of the Council of Hierarchs. For this reason, all the hierarchs had journeyed from the outlying provinces in Eudora and the mainland opposite to consult with their peers and to seek divine guidance in the chief temples of the realm. The prospect of this filled Zanidas with gloom, as it always did. It was only strictly necessary for him to attend personally to the views of his fellow hierarchs twice a year, but he was not a natural politician, and the advancing years had made him increasingly deaf, increasingly impatient of criticism or opposition.

Advancing years be damned! he muttered curtly to himself as these thoughts presented themselves to his mind.

His mouth pursed peevishly as he pulled on his official robes, slapping away the overly solicitous hand of the cleric whose duty it was to assist him in this matter.

He knew, though, that his advancing years could not so lightly be dismissed. He had already lived seventy-three of them, having annually sought and won divine approval in recognition of his indispensability to the state. He was well aware of the grumbling amongst the council that accompanied each granting of the additional year. That grumbling would surely one day culminate in a refusal, a humiliation that he could not endure. The possibility that his own mortality might be raised as "any other business" in the coming meeting was not one that he could contemplate with an easy mind. Death, forever at his shoulder these last thirteen years, must claim his own at last. Accordingly, he must then drive home the fatal blade and seek the embrace of his Lord.

'Damn your clumsy fat fingers', he grumbled as the Clerk of the Robe fumbled to fasten his sandals. 'I trust breakfast is on the table, hmm? Breakfast? Yes?'

The official, a short, oleaginous young man with a generous paunch, owed his exalted post to the influence of well-placed relatives rather than through any noticeable virtues of his own. He nodded, stood and indicated the various chains and trinkets of office laid out on the table by the door.

'After I have eaten, dolt!' spat Zanidas. 'I don't suppose you will wish to be wiping egg off my finery. Good Lord, how long have you been at this?'

'A week, your worship', answered the Clerk meekly, his fat cheeks shining with the ample breakfast he had recently consumed whilst his master was standing naked, killing goats in the rain.

Consciousness of this caused Zanidas a new twinge of irritation, but he only knitted his brow, shot the little man a poisonous glance and swept through into the breakfast room, where his Steward of the Table awaited him.

The Steward had served the Supreme Hierarch for many years and knew his master's manners well. Judging the mood with his usual penetrating insight, he remained mute, head bowed, bringing forth the various drinks and foodstuffs with the silent efficiency that Zanidas found soothing to his soul.

Zanidas ate sparingly this morning, his rheumy eyes fixed on nothing in particular, his gaze turned inward. It was likely enough that the Interdict would be discussed, given that Yuzanid's continuing displeasure was undoubtedly to be detected in this last shaking of the earth. He must be prepared for this, must have to hand the necessary records and documentation if he was to be required to explain the persistence of this intolerable stain upon his long reign.

'Thirteen years. I know. Thirteen damned years and we're no closer now than we ever were', observed Zanidas later when he entertained his nephew, Marshal of the Faith, General Azimandro in his private study. The Clerk had been permitted to drape his master with the official gold chains and ornaments of his office, but the gold diadem with its intertwined serpents irritated his brow and remained in its velvet-lined box until the official business of the day began.

'There are some who observe that the beginning of the nation's woes coincided with the first of your pious petitions', said Azimandro, referring to the life extensions that had enabled Zanidas to arrive in this present state of decrepitude.

'Well they're damned fools, then', snapped Zanidas. 'Stromengar happened the day *before* my first deferral.

Cape Stromengar was the rocky western extremity of Eudora, and it was on these brutal iron-bound shores and headlands, verged inland with swamps, that the greatest armada ever to set sail from Tazman had come to grief. Of four hundred and nineteen ships, only eighty-two had survived. The rest had been dashed on the rocks by a wholly unseasonal gale, taking more than sixty-five thousand soldiers and mariners to their watery deaths. It was one of the grimmest days in Vhanakhori history, and the hand of a vengeful god was surely to be discerned there. Subsequent years had seen a steady succession of plagues, famines, earthquakes and volcanic eruptions, in addition to various other military reverses. It was called the Interdict, the suspension of Yuzanid's favour, and none knew for certain what had brought it about.

Blood sacrifices designed to appease the heavens had been made throughout the realm since then. From one end of the realm to the other, every sizeable settlement had been required to furnish a life, but there were many who observed that Yuzanid had already drunk his fill from the cup of souls, that the twenty thousand oarsmen, sailors and marines of the fleet were more than sufficient to pay down the debt of sin. However, the identification of that original sin remained an urgent preoccupation of those who held the highest offices in the realm.

Azimandro smiled, impervious to his uncle's petulance, armoured in the knowledge that he was the bright hope of the nation, the great paladin of the realm. He kept to himself the objection that his uncle's first *application* had certainly been made *before* the fleet was wrecked and that the divinity's anger might conceivably have been incurred even before its approval by council.

'It matters not', he said smoothly in response to his uncle's protestations. 'As you well know, it has always seemed unlikely to scholars that God would be enraged to such an extent by so slight a transgression. Besides, all the auspices indicated his fulsome approval of your petition'.

'So it did', agreed Zanidas, rubbing the back of his head, where the interlinked blue tattoos were now dulled and blurred by age. 'Anyone who consults the records can see for themselves. And besides, all our pieties and devotions have been exactly in order, exactly as our Lord requires of us'.

He glanced up from the files he had been perusing and regarded his nephew approvingly. Tall and muscular, General Azimandro was a fine-looking man in the prime of life. The nature of his tattoos and their absence from the left side of his head marked him as a *divancus*, a priest soldier. He was, in fact, the chief of the Hierarchy's soldiers, the Scourge of the Infidel and the Hammer of God. He was the bright hope of his nation, and Zanidas regarded him complacently as the man stretched himself languorously before the small fire that burned in the grate, flexing the powerful muscles in his bare arms.

'So we know that our Lord is angry with us, but he declines to inform us of the nature of his resentment, requiring instead that we should determine this for ourselves'.

'Indeed', agreed Zanidas with a sigh. 'That would appear to be the case'.

As on many previous occasions, this analysis reminded him irresistibly of his first wife and came with such force into his mind that he was obliged to bite his lip and clench his fists. The unflattering comparison was not one that could be concealed from Yuzanid, and it caused Zanidas a pang of shocked guilt so intense he found that his hands were shaking. Surely, when the business of the day was over, he must mortify his flesh and purify his mind. It would be necessary for him to take the fire asp from its basket and press it to his breast; the agony that the creature's bite occasioned was highly pleasing to God, a sure mark of devotion. Lesser mortals were prone to dying from the fire asp's bite, but priests were gradually inured to its venom, at first in dilute form, applied to small ritual cuts in the skin from the time of their first novitiation, and becoming progressively more concentrated until they could endure the fiery bite itself.

'The coming enterprise must be considered in the light of it', continued Azimandro. 'It would be folly to proceed without the mandate of heaven, would it not?'

A new fleet was being assembled in Tazman's naval harbour, readied for a fresh descent upon the infidel coastlands, now that the recent truce was soon due to expire. Already, more than a hundred vessels had been constructed or taken there, including several dozen powerful galleys. Stromengar hung heavy in the minds of the Hierarchy, however, and there were many who counselled that to set forth with such an armament would be to court fresh disaster – unless clear signs were evident that Yuzanid's favour might be anticipated.

'Of course', agreed Zanidas, 'my meeting with my fellows this afternoon will doubtless discuss this, doubtless propose ways in which we may further propitiate our Lord'.

'I hope you are successful', replied Azimandro, turning to face him now so that Zanidas must necessarily admire the taut musculature of his broad chest.

The plain baldric of his sword belt passed across that bronzed and tattooed expanse. There was nothing showy about Azimandro, unless one counted his magnificent physique. His only concession to ornament was the single ring he wore upon the finger of his left hand, one that was reputed to have been blessed by Yuzanid himself in centuries past and had been handed down from father to son, from generation to generation. It was believed to bestow upon the wearer the power to inspire a petrifying dread in his foes. Zanidas rather doubted that any supernatural enhancement was necessary in this respect. From the toes of his booted feet to the crown of his smooth pate, Azimandro was a terrifying prospect, marked here and there with the pale and puckered scars of battle.

'This one', murmured Zanidas, gesturing at one of the welts that traversed his side above his nephew's belt, a long jagged curve. 'Remind me how you acquired that one'.

'A pike thrust from a rebel', grunted Azimandro with a wry grin. 'When I was putting down that revolt in Tandanan, last fall. You may be sure that he paid the price. He and all the others'.

'I don't doubt it'.

Zanidas recalled, with a shudder, the very sanguinary manner in which Azimandro had quelled the revolt, with fire and the sword. It was said that the roads around that city were lined with impalements and crucifixions for miles in every direction.

'But I tire of fighting desperate peasants, uncle', said Azimandro, crossing to Zanidas' desk and idly stirring the papers that lay there with a fingertip, as though he resented the power of bureaucracy to curb his liberty of action. 'I am wasted here. The army I have raised and trained chafes in its confinement. I long to lead those men into battle against our true foes. Those lickspittle degenerates in the Empire fear us now, and I long to add substance to those fears. Yuzanid fills me with a bitter hatred of his enemies. Allow me to smite them, and I shall lay waste their coastlands like holy fire, send them to hell in their shrieking myriads'.

Azimandro clenched his huge fist before him to make plain the sincerity of these words, and his face was momentarily transfigured with his fierce passion.

'I do not doubt your commitment for a moment', coughed Zanidas, intimidated despite his exalted status and determined that none of this dismay should reveal itself upon his countenance.

He straightened himself to his full height, which was not very considerable now that arthritis had bent his back, and placed a hand on Azimandro's smooth-oiled bicep. 'Be patient, nephew. This that I hold here is the strong arm of our Lord, and it shall serve its holy purpose, I promise you', he assured, looking up into the man's smouldering eyes, where a murderous glint was clearly to be discerned. 'We await a sign, that is all, and then you shall have your war, if Yuzanid wills it'.

'Like a drawn bow, the army cannot be held in such readiness for long, uncle', grunted Azimandro, who appeared to expect that such auspicious "signs" might be detected to suit his own convenience. 'I urge you to find your *signs* with the utmost dispatch. The campaigning season will be upon us in May, and there remains much to set in place before then'.

I know when the campaigning season begins, you oaf, Zanidas wanted to say, but the words remained unspoken, could never be uttered. Besides, the man had already turned on his heel and was gone, slamming the door thunderously behind him, as though to underline the elemental nature of his power.

'We simply *must* find the reason for the Interdict', the Supreme Hierarch muttered to himself, shuffling the papers distractedly.

It was at that moment, oppressed by that debilitating sense of hopelessness and confusion that so often visited him these days, that Zanidas felt a sudden faintness, a sudden light-headedness, that caused him to sway and grab at the edge of the desk. The part of him still capable of rational thought wondered if he was having a stroke, whether indeed Yuzanid himself intervened to revoke the privilege of this latest additional year. Within a second or so it was over, the blur fled from his vision, and he was left only with a sense of wet congestion in his nose.

Before he could reach for his kerchief, a single drop of blood fell from his nostril and onto the page before him. It fell with a splash onto a record of human sacrifices that had taken place in the city for the previous fifty years or so. Having dabbed at his nose, Zanidas now made to remove the drop from the parchment, but he paused with the cloth a finger's breadth away. With a sense of gathering excitement in his breast, he placed his spectacles on his nose and leaned close to study the entry the drop obscured. He then carefully dabbed and wiped the blood away to reveal the entry for the sacrifice type and the location.

'Draganach. Aramantha Zandravo', he read aloud. 'Midsummer Day 3942'.

He looked up, lips moving silently. Thirteen years ago. The year of Stromengar. The year the great fleet had been destroyed – and with it the nation's hopes. What did this mean?

'My Lord?' breathed Zanidas, finding speech at last and glancing around him distractedly. 'Was that you? Is this a sign, an indication?'

Surely it was. Zanidas threw himself face down on the hard floor and spread his arms wide, murmuring the prayers of submission and making his gratitude plain. He was quite sure now that the passing dizziness had announced the presence of God in that blessed space, and that God had shown him the way forward at last. His attention had been drawn to the Golden Child for 3942, the child that had been consumed in the bronze belly of Draganch. Something had evidently been amiss with that most important devotion of all. He knew now where his investigations must begin, and he thanked Yuzanid with all his heart.

'It appears that our Lord has manifested himself through the agency of our Supreme Hierarch's nose', observed the Hierarch of Nahleen to his assistant when they proceeded to his quarters later that afternoon.

'You amaze me!' said this assistant, the Preceptor, Taradon, knitting his brows as they passed along a cloister where the skulls of recent sacrifices grinned out at intervals from atop their wooden poles. 'He chooses to forsake the usual agencies, I take it. The liver of the beast, the birds in the heavens, the falling of stars; all these he has forsaken in order to prefer Zanidas' nose?'

'So it would appear', agreed the Hierarch, whose name was Garrol and who held the second-highest post in the state.

He was an exceptionally tall man, spare of limb and with a permanent stoop caused by the necessity of conversing with those of more moderate height. Taradon, whose height was barely moderate and who walked with a limp, occasioned by a childhood accident, regarded his superior sidelong.

'You reject this "communication," then?' he asked as various servants stepped aside to let them pass, bowing low and making the sign before them.

'I do not. Not yet at least. His Worship was most passionate in his description of the divine visitation, speaking with an animation such as I cannot recall in him for many years. His eyes positively blazed, I tell you. There was no mistaking his sincerity. I suppose all of us there were impressed. I suppose our Lord may signal his desires to us in any manner he chooses'.

'I see,' Taradon responded, nodding to the servants who drew open the doors to the outer vestibule of the peacock palace. 'What is proposed? I trust the council was obliged to deliberate'.

'Certainly we did', sighed Garrol wearily, 'and that deliberation resulted in a lamentable increase in my burdens'.

'I grieve to hear it'.

'Your grief will know no bounds when you hear that I am to lead an investigation into the Golden Child of 3942, and that I am assigning you to be its functional head. This is deemed extremely urgent, and so I have assured Zanidas that we shall begin immediately', Garrol announced, allowing himself a thin smile and a sidelong glance to observe the dismay in his subordinate's face. 'By which I mean *you* will begin immediately'.

'But my retreat!' Taradon implored, his pace faltering as they entered the reception hall of his master's quarters. Taradon had planned a prayer retreat in a valley of extraordinary beauty amidst the mountains south of Nahleen, in order that he might combine pious reflection with his passion for ornithology. His superior had already found cause to postpone this on several occasions, and now his long-cherished plans receded still further into the unknowable future. Taradon's long, intelligent face, with those deep sunk dark eyes, wore an expression of dismay.

'You said that...' he continued to protest, before Garrol's raised hand cut him short.

'Never mind what I said', snapped the Hierarch. 'The Lord's work is the reason for our existence, is it not? And the Lord's work presently requires you to conduct this investigation with all possible dispatch'.

Shrugging off his outer red robe, he slumped into a chair and beckoned for a servant to bring wine.

'All files and records are open to you. You may show my seal as required, if authority is required of you. All persons of interest are to be interviewed, chastened or detained at your pleasure. Likewise, you may detach any of the secretariat you deem essential to your purpose. I shall require your report on my desk within the week. Is that clear?'

'Forgive me, your worship', stammered Taradon, feeling that he was being swept away with events like a rainswept leaf in a gutter, spreading his hands wide before him. 'I'm not sure...'

'Never mind what you're not sure of', sniffed Garrol, taking a sip from his goblet. 'It's very simple. Assume as a starting point that there was something amiss with the Golden Child sacrifice of 3942. I doubt I need to remind you of the paramount importance of these things, for goodness's sake! Find out what went wrong. That's it. Have I made myself plain?'

'You have, your worship', answered Taradon with a bow.

'Good. Then get on with it', Garrol ordered, glancing at his goblet and making a wry face. 'And what is this piss? Is this what passes in this city for wine nowadays?'

The common people of Vhanakhor were wont to grumble at the cost of sustaining the vast bureaucracy that existed to ensure the smooth running of the machinery of state. However, it was to Taradon's advantage that the teeming armies of officials in the palaces and temples made quite sure that no aspect of the nation's life passed unrecorded. No part of this life received more attention than the administration of the faith. Every ceremony, every sacrifice, from the humblest offering of doves to the acrobats and dancers who perished at the culmination of the annual games, required their entry into the records.

The Golden Children, in recognition of their significance, required more than most. Armed with the authority of the Hierarch of Nahleen, it was perfectly straightforward for Taradon to present himself to the temple hall of records and demand to be shown the documents in question. For this sacrifice to be the cause of such divine discontent, there must certainly have been some significant irregularity in the manner of its conduct.

Taradon sat in the chilly office to the rear of the hall and wrapped his garments more tightly around him as he ran his finger down the lists that had been brought out for him. It was not hard to find. Beneath the yellow glow of an oil lamp, he quickly noted down the essential circumstances of the sacrifice.

Presiding, he read, adjusting his glasses and peering closer. *AH-HPZ V. Zandravo*.

AH meant "Assistant Hierarch," while HP denoted the "High Priest" of the temple of Draganach. The name Zandravo was familiar to him, a clan long established in the Tazman establishment, but the initial told him nothing. Nevertheless, he noted it down. It was surprising that Zanidas, the Supreme Hierarch, had not presided, but it was conceivable that illness or some other pressing cause had intervened to prevent it.

Having frowned and returned his gaze to the book of records, he moved his finger along the line of the faded entry to see the name of the child whose life had been given up to Yuzanid. *Zandravo*, he read, absently tapping the page with his forefinger. 'Hmm', he then murmured aloud. 'Another Zandravo. Aramantha Zandravo. Interesting'.

The Zandravids were a large clan, of course, with branches in many cities and provinces of the realm, so perhaps the coincidence was not a great one. Nevertheless, Taradon's interest was piqued. He looked further up the page to see that V. Zandravo had officiated at no other sacrifices of this nature. R. Zanidas, the present Supreme Hierarch, had performed this function in the previous ten years, and before that, T. Balliorzes, his predecessor, had done so until the top of the page brought the list to a close. Nor did V. Zandravo's name appear elsewhere in the list. This was evidently a line of enquiry to pursue.

The custodian of the Draganach temple was a large, slow-moving man with an expression of weary resignation in his features, as though every moment that the day brought forth brought closer the inevitable collapse of the order he strove to maintain in his little corner of the world.

In truth, Draganach's temple was a large responsibility, and the damage caused by the recent earthquake had caused him a great deal of concern. Documents from various architects, surveyors and building contractors were strewn across his desk as a servant showed The Reverend Preceptor, T.C. Taradon, into his presence.

'What is this?! Did I not say I was to be undisturbed!' he protested, his gaze directed at the anxious servant, whose face was pale with distress.

'Please, do not blame your servant', soothed Taradon, pulling up a chair opposite the custodian's desk without invitation, causing the man further dismay.

He brandished a document and a seal ring, tossing these onto the desk before him.

'The man yielded before my authority, as must you', he continued. 'Here it is. I trust you will not seek to impede my investigation'.

'Investigation, what investigation?' the custodian asked brusquely, his brow furrowed.

'Read, man, read', instructed Taradon wearily.

The custodian read for some moments, sniffed and then leaned forward to replace the emblems of authority in Taradon's outstretched hand.

'High authority indeed', he conceded. 'May I offer you a drink? I usually favour a herbal infusion at…'

'Thank you, but no', replied Taradon with a tight smile. 'I come here in search of answers only, and you would oblige me if you were to tell me what you know of Vindex Zandravo, he who officiated in the sacrifice in question'.

'Zandravo, yes I knew Zandravo', acknowledged the custodian, his eyes momentarily clouded by recollection. 'We were in the seminary together. He did very well for himself, far outstripped all of us in that intake'.

'Became the High Priest of this temple, actually', observed Taradon, bringing out his notebook. 'Although only very briefly, it appears'.

'Well, yes. He was appointed to this post, as you have established. A very brilliant man, a very gifted man, as everyone agreed, although naturally there were some who were envious of his rapid ascent. I suppose there always are, human nature being as it is, when an individual seems so blessed by nature and by fortune. There were those who whispered that he might have become Supreme Hierarch in his turn, but his death – his untimely death, I should say – naturally frustrated any ambitions he might have nurtured'.

'I see. And he died very shortly after the event in question, according to my information. The records are mute regarding the circumstances, however. I have only a bald statement of his demise, with date and location. Can I ask you to elaborate on this, to flesh out the details for me. I trust there was no hint of foul play?'

'Oh no, none at all', answered the custodian, blushing as though personally accused of such wrongdoing. 'I'm afraid he suffered a kind of seizure. It's hard not to connect it with the pressure the poor man found himself under'.

'Do go on', encouraged Taradon, leaning forward in his chair a little despite his determination to maintain a professional impassivity.

'Well, it was a rather surprising and tragic coincidence. The Supreme Patriarch was indisposed, so that the High Priest must deputise for him, and most unfortunately the lot had fallen to claim his own daughter, you see'.

Taradon's eyebrows twitched upwards. He stroked his chin.

'Then Zandravo was obliged to sacrifice his own daughter?'

'He was, I'm afraid. Our love for our creator knows no limits, none at all, but that must have been a most painful expression of his commitment to our Lord'.

'Indeed it must', agreed Taradon with feeling. 'And his death ensued soon after?'

'It did. I knew him well, he and his family. He was never a man given to levity, I should say, but the change in him following from that day was most pronounced. All commented on it. And then he was found collapsed, frothing at the mouth after some kind of fit. There were those who murmured of suicide, although no conclusive evidence was found to sustain it. Certainly, his wife always adamantly denied it, knowing, of course, that suicide invalidates inheritance and that his property would be forfeit to the state'.

Taradon nodded thoughtfully whilst the custodian continued with a tedious summation of the lamentable legal circumstances that an official's suicide must occasion. Finally, he raised a finger to still his host's flow.

'His wife; I imagine she must likewise have been distraught, although no more than those others obliged to supply a Golden Child, I suppose'.

'Certainly, she was. And she was not originally of our faith, of course, which may have added materially to her distress'.

'She was not?' Taradon asked, tilting his head on one side. 'How curious. Do tell me more'.

The custodian described how Rosania Thandora Tanatiel had been amongst the noble hostages exchanged at the end of the Four Years War in 3938. She had been a high-born Erenori from a distinguished family, and Vindex Zandravo had taken her to wife. It was their only child who had nourished the fires of Draganach that day.

'Some say that by making that marriage, Zandravo set aside his ambitions to be Supreme Hierarch. I counselled him against it, as did many, but he was blinded by love and behaved in a wholly irrational manner'.

'Innumerable promising careers have foundered upon that very rock', agreed Taradon, whose own marriage owed nothing to sentiment and everything to expediency. 'But you will agree that we have a quite remarkable set of circumstances around this particularly significant sacrifice. Were you there present that day?'

'I was', nodded the custodian. 'I stood with him on that high platform and observed as he pitched the little girl into the serpent's open mouth. I have been honoured in that manner on several occasions during the last decade, although it does, as you might imagine, require considerable fortitude and a rather intense state of prayer'.

'I imagine it must', shuddered Taradon, whose necessary attendance at human sacrifices had been at a considerable distance and who had privately found his own faith put to the severest of tests by this most extreme expression of devotion. 'But we are asked to discover what circumstance might have led to our Lord's severe displeasure. As one present on that day, can you think of anything that might have been so deeply offensive to Yuzanid's eye?'

'I cannot', admitted the custodian, having frozen into immobility for several pensive moments. 'I really cannot. Everything was strictly in accordance with protocol, so far as I can recall, and Zandravo was a stickler for protocol, of course. Even in a body of men addicted to such things, he stood out as one constitutionally unable to deviate from order or tradition. No. It is out of the question'.

Taradon nodded and both men lapsed into silence for a moment.

'Tell me of the family. Tell me of the household', suggested Taradon at last.

Chapter Seven

Waid had once been steward of the Zandravo household, but now he was almost blind and approaching his Sixty, living with his daughter in a small house in one of the poorer streets uphill from the commercial port. It took Taradon the better part of the following day to consult with various record offices, the census and the ward rolls before finally tracking him down. It was a cold day, but despite this, they were required to meet in a narrow, unheated room, little better than a passage, furnished with two chairs. Waid was almost incapacitated with shame at being unable to accommodate his visitor in more comfort. It appeared, however, that the recent earthquake had rendered the main reception room uninhabitable, and its ceiling was presently supported by an arrangement of wooden props.
'And how long did you serve the family?' asked Taradon, gratefully accepting a warming cup of spiced tea from Waid's daughter, a thin, narrow-faced woman in her early forties, who appeared to regard their visitor with superstitious awe. He pulled his cloak more tightly around him and then cradled the cup in both hands.
'Eh? Oh, the better part of twenty years, I should think', replied Waid, whose hearing was little better than his vision, having had the question repeated for him twice. 'Never a big household, mind you. No pretensions, you see, Mistress Rosania and Master Vindex. They liked to keep things simple, so they did, and that Master Vindex, he was a true holy man, if I ever saw one, forever in his private chapel he was, laid out on that floor, filling the

air around him with those sacred words, hour after hour'.

'I see', nodded Taradon, having heard details of the household's make-up. 'And how did your master and mistress get on? Did they always seem to agree? I ask this because your mistress was a foreigner, an infidel in fact, and it might be supposed that a man as pious as your master might find such a circumstance oppressive to his mind'.

'Oh, never in life!' laughed Waid, once he had been brought to understand the question. 'I never seen a more devoted couple. Whatever errors she had in her faith, whatever mismatches in their devotions, you might say, never seemed to trouble them at all. It seemed they could keep that kind of thing in a separate box, if you take my meaning. No, you only had to look at them when they were together to see that they were in love. We all remarked on it, wondered at it in fact, because who'd have thought it would have worked? When she came back to the house, we all thought, there's a comely foreign piece to warm his bed, quite the prettiest thing you ever saw...'

A distant look came into Waid's eyes as he remembered this vision, and a wistful smile enlivened his grey countenance.

'Oh yes,' he continued eventually. 'But even if Master Vindex's first intent was simply in the carnal line, if you'll forgive me for saying so, well soon enough she won his heart. The victor was enthralled by the vanquished, if we are to look at it in a wider context, you might say. Anyways, they were in love, sure enough, and when that child came along...'

Waid's discourse faltered at this point, and the smile fled from his face.

Taradon leaned forward, delighted that Waid had arrived at this juncture without the need for any prompting from himself.
'The child?'
'Well, the lot fell for her, as I suppose you know', resumed Waid, looking up, his eyes filmed over with tears. 'A cruel, cruel thing, if you ask me, and I'm as God-fearing as the next man. Yuzanid tests our faith to the limit, doesn't he? And he teases out the faults in our hearts through his demands on us'.
'Naturally, they were distraught when they heard', suggested Taradon when Waid fell silent once more.
'Well yes. More than distraught, I'd say. She was such a sweetheart, that little girl. I suppose you can't blame our dear Lord for wanting her for his own. It was more than we could bear to see our mistress and our master weep so. He tried to conceal it, bless him, but there are some matters too great for the heart and the countenance to conceal, as they say. And it was a desperate bad time for the household, too, that whole year, so it was'.
'I grieve to hear it', murmured Taradon, setting down his cup. 'In what manner, pray?'
'Oh, Mistress's handmaid, she died in the getting out of a child, she did, and there weren't no father around either. She had a little girl of her own about the same age as young Aramantha, that being Master and Mistress's daughter, I should say'.
'I see,' replied Taradon, now feeling a strange sense that he approached the core of the mystery, that he stood on the threshold of some vital disclosure. 'And I suppose the poor child was put out to the care of a relative... after the death of her mother, I mean'.
'No, not at all, sir. The two little girls were always playmates, being of an age and like two peas in a pod, too. Like sisters they were, and Mistress were not so

proud she wouldn't let Miss Aramantha play with the servant's kin'.

'Yes, but what happened to her?' pressed Taradon, oblivious now to the chill in the air. 'What happened to this servant's child?'

'They adopted her as their own, so they did'.

'They did?' Taradon pressed, drying his lip with his sleeve and setting down the cup on the wooden box that served as a table beside him.

'They did, although I believe it was something in the nature of an informal arrangement, you understand. I'm not sure it was ever given the full dignity of the law, papers signed and all that. Stilitha, her name was, our poor Yahli's little girl'.

'Aha! Then this was not brought before a magistrate?'

'No, sir, it was not. Not to my knowledge anyways'.

'I see', nodded Taradon. 'And what happened on the day of the sacrifice, the Golden Child? Doubtless it was very upsetting for all concerned'.

'It was', agreed Waid, having had the question repeated three times. 'Certainly it was. More than upsetting. *Upsetting* doesn't even come close to it. Master and Mistress left the house on the day after and went to stay with my master's brother, out of the city, to seek the support of family, they said, and we never saw them again. Never. Not so much as a *how-do-you-do?* Of course, they made sure we were well looked after, being such fine and considerate beings as they were, but soon the house was sold, and then everything came to an end. It was the end of our world, you see, when little Miss Aramantha went to the fire, bless her'.

Waid's eyes filled with tears once more, which he wiped away with the back of his hand.

'Master died soon after, of course, as you may have heard, from grief, some say, but we never heard from Mistress ever after'.

'So they took the little servant girl with her, I imagine'.
'Stilitha? Oh yes. That they did. Such a sweet little thing, she was'.
A silence fell between them, punctuated only by the sounds of Waid's bronchitic wheezing and of water dripping from the ceiling.
'Well, there you are', announced Waid at last. 'Is there anything else you need to know?'
'No. I think I have the full picture now', said Taradon, getting to his feet. 'I thank you for your indulgence of me, and I shall certainly see if the ward officers can do anything to assist you in your...' he glanced around at the wretched space, '... predicament'.

The custodian of Draganach's temple was surprised and alarmed to find himself summoned to an audience with the Supreme Patriarch himself. The fact that the hour was late and his dinner half-eaten only contributed further to his state of agitation. The messenger, made haughty by the high office of his employer, had merely tossed the summons onto the table before him and regarded him with an imperious eye whilst the custodian wiped greasy fingers on the napkin that lay across his ample paunch. He picked up the document and held it to the light of the oil lamps that dangled from their brass stand.
'I, er...' the custodian began, his own eye darting from the plate to his visitor, whose posture stiffened.
'Immediately', he snapped.
'Yes. Of course', murmured the custodian, setting down his napkin.

Minutes later, he found himself standing before a bench in the Supreme Hierarch's palace, in that chamber where investigations were conducted prior to prosecution and trial. Paintings on the ceiling and on the walls showed episodes from scripture in the style of the previous century. The artist was a rather famous one, but the name eluded the custodian and his mind now darted anxiously between groping for this irrelevant fact and searching his own conscience for faults that might condemn him. Sure, a painstaking analysis of the books might reveal certain irregularities, but his lifestyle was hardly opulent enough for this summons to indicate an investigation for corruption. Or was it? The custodian found that he was sweating profusely as he was shown in.

The faces that looked back at him across the polished expanse of the bench were those of the Supreme Hierarch himself, the Hierarch of Nahleen, the Marshall Azimandro and, he noted with relief, the Preceptor, Taradon, Nahleen's assistant. Perhaps this summons related to their recent interview? Nor were they attired formally in a manner that might suggest an investigation into his own activities. Certainly, the air of contained anticipation in all of their faces suggested a resumption of that earlier conversation. He felt himself relax, the queasiness in his stomach abate.

'I have informed His High Worship of our discussion yesterday', stated Taradon, once the necessary formalities had been concluded, 'and he has asked that you be brought to this place today in order that further questions may be put to you'.

'You say that you were present at the Golden Child of 3942?' began the Supreme Patriarch, having consulted his notes and set his spectacles on the bridge of his long, purple-veined nose.

'I was', agreed the custodian, feeling a warm sense of relief that his own recent conduct seemed not to be the focus of interest, and an earnest desire to be of assistance, accordingly.

'And you were familiar with both of the little girls?' asked Taradon after various other details of the sacrifice had been discussed.

'I would not claim to know them well', answered the custodian. 'But I was present in their household on a number of occasions, and I certainly knew them by sight'.

'So you would have noticed if the girl intended to be the subject of the sacrifice was substituted for the other?'

Suddenly, the custodian was painfully aware of the weight of four piercing glances upon him. A cold prickle of horror traversed his scalp. That was what this was about, then – the shocking and impious substitution of the rightful sacrifice, surely a grievous offence in the eyes of God, one so grievous he uttered an involuntary gasp at the thought of it.

'Yes', agreed the Hierarch of Nahleen, perceiving his shock. 'It is a matter of the utmost import that we must investigate. If the wrong sacrifice was made on that fateful day, the various signs of divine displeasure visited upon this nation in recent years may be placed in their proper context'.

'I ask you again', persisted Taradon, leaning forward in his seat. 'Could it have escaped your notice that the wrong girl was brought to sacrifice?'

'I don't know', stammered the custodian. 'It never occurred to me... to any of us. I mean, the two girls were of an age, a stature... Besides, as you know, she was heavily made-up, draped with costumes of cloth and gold, wearing that ornate headdress as they always do. I suppose it could have happened. I mean...'

'*Could have* does not mean *did*', interrupted the Supreme Hierarch, taking his spectacles off and gesturing with them vaguely. 'Circumstantial evidence supports that theory, the immediate withdrawal of the family to new premises, leaving their domestic staff behind, but we need more than that. Think hard, sir. Turn your mind to that day, that moment as the girl approached the edge of the platform, ready to be reunited with her maker. Picture it in your mind. Is there anything in that image that raises the possibility that you looked upon the servant girl and not upon the true and rightful sacrifice?'

The custodian directed his eyes down and cast his mind back to that far-distant moment. He saw the vast crowd assembled far below, the city and the distant blue sea beyond the high walls of the temple temenos. In his nostrils was the scent of incense and of the acrid smoke that rose from the gaping jaws of the great bronze serpent below them. It was a chilly day, but the heat that rose from there beat on his cheeks and made the stone platform warm beneath his feet. Around him, various other clerics were chanting, swinging censers, heads bowed as the High Priest Vindex led the little girl forward. His own face was concealed beneath the gold mask that the officiating priest must wear on this occasion, but the eyes that peered out from it were dark pits of grief, and his voice shook as he muttered the invocations that preceded the moment of committal. The little girl's face was painted with white and gold, her lips cherry red and her eyes outlined with kohl. She showed no fear. Her eyes seemed glazed, and her gait, as she moved forward, showed that the poppy milk swam in her veins. Gold jewellery glinted at her ankles, wrists and around her tiny neck. In her hand she bore the small posy of flowers that was one of the inevitable tokens of this array. She stepped forward to the edge of the platform, and a great wailing cry rose up from the masses beneath. The rising crescendo of pipes and drums reached its culmination, and the priest pushed her forward. Her small body fell, death reached up to claim her, and the posy flew from her hand. From her left hand.

The custodian gasped, placed his hand to his mouth, and his head jerked upward, until he met Taradon's gaze.

'What? What did you see?'

'She held the posy in her left hand'.

'And?'

Suddenly all behind the bench stiffened in anticipation.

'Aramantha was right-handed'.

'She was?' pressed the Supreme Hierarch. 'Are you sure of this?'

'I am', insisted the custodian. 'I clearly recall stooping to take little Aramantha's hand, one day, when she was pretending to introduce me to her dolls. It was her right hand I shook, and I swear it was her dominant one. And the other little girl was with her. Rosania, her stepmother by that time, mentioned then that she should extend her right hand, as was traditional, rather than the left that was natural to her'.

The members of the tribunal exchanged glances and muttered to each other behind their hands, before finally returning their attention to the custodian.

'Thank you for your assistance. You may go', instructed the Supreme Hierarch, and then, even as the custodian was backing away gratefully towards the door. 'That's it, then. That is surely it. Yuzanid be praised. He has spoken at last. Now we may act to set right this monstrous crime'.

'It may have been coincidence', ventured Taradon, although reluctant to oppose the Supreme Hierarch's enthusiastic conviction. 'Surely, this is not conclusive evidence'.

'The child is always offered the posy. We may expect that they reach for it in the hand that is natural for them. It is all the evidence I need!' snapped the Supreme Hierarch, the fierce glint in his eyes sufficient to quench any further intimations of doubt amongst his companions. 'Our Maker has spoken, and we have heard his voice. Now we must take decisive action'.

'In what manner?' The Hierarch of Nahleen asked, raising an elegant eyebrow.

'I'm surprised that I must spell it out', snarled the Supreme Hierarch. 'Yuzanid will doubtless exact vengeance from that execrable Vindex. I shudder to think what eternal torment his wretched soul must endure. However, there is no reason to assume that this... Rosania is not still amongst the living, she and her daughter'.

'The girl would be at least sixteen by now', supplied Taradon, 'perhaps already seventeen'.

'Indeed' concurred the Hierarch. 'Well every passing day that she exists on this earth is an offence against our Lord. She should have died long ago, as Yuzanid desired', he noted, turning to Azimandro, who had sat silently until this point. 'Hunt them down. Take as many men as you need. Taradon will consult with the records, establish their location and you will bring them back here. The mother shall certainly die a very painful death in expiation of her sin, but Aramantha must embrace the fate that Yuzanid had declared for her. She shall fall into the fire at last. We must make it so. It is no more than our duty in the sight of God. Perhaps then the mandate of heaven shall be restored to us. Perhaps then your great fleet may set sail at last to smite the infidel once more'.

After Taradon had been shown out of his dwelling, Waid had sat for some moments in silence, stroking the rasping grey stubble on his chin. It was only for a very few moments because his daughter, who had been listening on the further side of a door, stepped in and regarded him with every sign of anxiety, hands on hips.

'Well?' she said, when Waid only regarded her, eyes clouded with thought.

'Well, what?' he asked at last.

'You know what', the woman said. 'Mistress Rosania's in trouble if you ask me. Is that not what you took from that fellow...'

'Reverend Preceptor Taradon'.

'Him'. she nodded. 'If he and the likes of him are sniffing around after Mistress Rosania there might be trouble for her'.

'What kind of trouble?'

'I don't know. I don't care, neither. I suppose it was in your mind also, or you wouldn't have told the Reverend you didn't know where Mistress Rosania now resides'.

'I suppose you're right', conceded Waid with a slow nod, getting to his feet. 'You usually are, as I am reminded daily'.

'With good cause', laughed the woman. 'Then what are we to do? She needs to know there's folks in high places sniffing around'.

'I don't know'. Waid frowned and rubbed the back of his neck, ruefully. 'Crane's a fair long way from here. Trouble will reach her before any word of ours'.

'What about young Tebi? He's on the posts. If he can't avail himself of a few post horses once in a while to oblige his uncle, I don't know who can. He could be there by tomorrow e'en, I should think'.

'Do you think he would?'

'I know he would', insisted the woman. 'He lived under this very roof long enough when your brother died. He owes us'.

'He does', nodded Waid, pressing his lips together. 'Bring me paper and pen, and you can help me write a note'.

Chapter Eight

It was a cold afternoon, but the fire in the grate of the best room did something to drive the chill from the air as Stilli endured her mother's morning reception. The wind was in the east, and for this reason the occasional stronger gust caused a little puff of woodsmoke to escape from the chimney into the room. This was one of many reasons to regret the move from The Hedges, but this afternoon at least, Stilli had other, more immediate causes for regret. Foremost amongst these was the necessity of entertaining Dar Hierena Hortixia Mardaxa, the leading aristocrat and landowner in those parts, widow of the previous Hierarch of Crane. She had been in the area visiting her second cousin, Irizoni, mother of Tolly and Tye. Naturally, having become aware of the reduction of Stilli's family's circumstances consequent upon their removal from The Hedges, Hortixia had thought it incumbent on her to call in to commiserate with Andax's widow, both with regard to the passing of her husband and the material reduction in her comfort. Now, she sat in the best chair, next to the fire, and brushed crumbs from her lap, having eaten a prodigious quantity of lemon cake and drunk a fair quantity of the local spirit, this without showing any signs of inebriation, unless one counted the occasional hiccup. Her ample frame suggested more than a passing acquaintance with cake, and her conversation, by dint of frequent reiteration, flowed with an easy confidence and persistence.

'It is only when the wind is in the east', observed Mother anxiously, when Hortixia wafted a little smoke away and reached for a handkerchief.

'Well, perhaps, but this room suffers from an inconvenient aspect, you must admit', sniffed Hortixia, glancing around censoriously. 'North-facing as it is, and I regret that you must endure it. How you must miss the commodious environs of your previous residence. I trust that you have not suffered any consequent diminution in your social standing. You will note that I am not too proud to associate myself with a worthy family that has suffered loss of rank and income and where blame may not be attached to them, but I don't doubt there are others less sensible of that distinction'.

'We do very well, thank you', replied Mother a little stiffly, having exchanged a weary glance with her good friend Irizoni. 'And naturally, we applaud your sentiments and humbly embrace your indulgence'.

'Well, if my presence here today may serve as a mark of distinction, I trust others may look kindly upon you in their turn, regardless of your origins'.

Stilli, whose mind had wandered somewhat in recent minutes, found her attention engaged once more. Mother had lived in that country so long now that she had never heard any to comment upon her Erenori heritage, or indeed of the faint trace of a foreign accent that yet remained in her speech. Her husband's rank had armoured her against the necessity of hearing such comment, but his death had inevitably withdrawn that protection. Might Mother now face the hostility of those who recalled that she was a stranger in their midst and had once worshipped Tio, that strange foreign devil?

Tolly's wry expression recalled her from this train of thought. She had evidently enjoyed these last remarks and was setting them aside in her memory, in order to tease Stilli with them later.

The conversation moved on to Hortixia's own house and the difficulty she had in engaging servants who were not either lazy or insolent, or both. Stilli's new bodice had been laced too tightly and she felt the awkward constriction of it under her arms. Her dress, although a splendid tone of blue, was torn in one place at the hem, and she must keep her legs still in order that this should not be disclosed to the company. Glancing up from her lap, she found that Hortixia's grandson, Lamo, was gazing upon her. He had done this for so long now that she wondered if he had suffered some form of seizure. His small, dull eyes showed no expression, unless mere resignation and contempt could be detected there. His rank was so exalted that she could not possibly be considered as a potential marriage partner for him, but perhaps he sought to make plain his conviction of this without recourse to mere words. Stilli suppressed a shudder at the prospect of marriage to anyone. Her coming of age was only months away, and she supposed that it was inevitable that something must be done to find her a suitable partner.

A wholly unsuitable partner, in all respects but that of her personal enrichment, was one Tye Marcuzi, who sat next to Lamo, gazing out of the window with every sign of absorption. Perhaps a cat could be discerned in the garden, or a raptor above the distant hill. He was a perfectly charming young man, but the buttons on his waistcoat had been fastened incorrectly and such heedless incompetence affected every aspect of his conduct, much to the despair of his parents. Now he turned to fix his own attention on Stilli, and the smile that spread across his face was one of simple pleasure and devotion. Devotion. Tye was evidently very much in love with Stilli, a circumstance that brought her a mixture of emotions. On one level, it would have taken a harder heart than Stilli's, a heart of stony impermeability, in fact, to have remained unmoved by the unfeigned admiration in his eyes when he looked upon her. For her part, she had a real liking for the young man. However, it was impossible to conceive of circumstances in which a marriage between them could be considered a union of equals, given his very considerable intellectual shortcomings. Sure, his speech was pretty enough and his diction likewise, but he was barely able to write his own name, and his grasp of the world around him was little removed from that of a seven-year-old's.

Nevertheless, she rewarded him with an answering smile before her elders' conversation moved into the uncongenial territory of her own education, and her attention must necessarily be recalled there.

'Extraordinary. I never heard of such a thing!' exclaimed Hortixia when told of the bogus Bondorin, the strange interloper who had taken charge of Stilli's education for so long a period.

'You had no idea he was an imposter?' she demanded, raising an eyebrow. 'I swear an imposter never slips past my defences. I have a shrewd eye for such fellows, as any who know me will declare; none shrewder, I say. How on earth did you permit yourself to be deceived in this manner?'

Mother blushed profusely at this, as did Irizoni, whose daughter Tolly had thought to mention it, and who now had the decency to allow regret to visit her countenance. Her eyes met Stilli's for a moment, who in turn twitched her own upward in a tiny gesture of exasperation.

'And he taught Stilitha to fight with swords', added Tye, cutting across Hortixia's expressions of surprise and reflections upon her own sagacity.

Perhaps he expected this disclosure to prompt cries of general admiration. Instead, the gathering fell silent and all eyes turned to Stilli, who felt herself quail beneath the weight of their undivided attention.

'As part of a general programme of physical exercise, I should think', ventured Irizoni when Mother's mouth fell open, and she seemed momentarily at a loss to respond.

'Well, yes. Exactly so', said Mother with a grateful glance for her friend. 'I'm sure he meant no impropriety by it'.

'What he intended and what he accomplished could scarcely be further apart, as you must acknowledge', declared Hortixia. 'I swear I never heard of such a thing amongst persons of our station. Stilitha, dear', she added, returning her piercing gaze to Stilli. 'Did it not occur to you that your tutor made improper demands upon your attention?'

'It did not', admitted Stilli. 'He was a very plausible gentleman, and I cannot believe his motives were at all ignoble'.

'The innocence of youth, you see', huffed Hortixia, leaning towards Mother and Irizoni. 'How charmingly naive, as one so typically expects from persons of her tender years. Hence the heavy burden of responsibility we all must bear for guarding their welfare in these troubled times'.

Mother, whose guarding was evidently thought to be insufficient, showed that she understood this comment through a further reddening of her cheeks.

'His references were impeccable', she muttered, toying distractedly with the necklace at her breast. 'Everything exactly in order'.

'And where is your son?" asked Hortixia after a moment in which she merely frowned and pursed her lips. 'I imagine he must be disappointed not to be able to join us on this occasion'.

'I'm sure he is most downcast', agreed Mother, glad of this change of subject, although even here, her own duty as a mother might be open to criticism. 'He is with the Steward dealing with some difficulty with the Drumogari in the neighbouring valley, I understand'.

'I have heard that he is a very zealous young man', nodded Hortixia. 'And I'm sure you will agree that it is incumbent on all of us to remind those people of their status and their duty. Let not indulgence be mistaken for weakness when a proper harshness may from time to time be necessary'.

'I'm sure Middo can be relied upon in that respect', observed Irizoni. 'He is a young man very conscious of his responsibility'.

'And very willing to supply harshness, proper or otherwise', supplied Stilli under her breath.

'Their harvest failed, you see', offered Tye, beaming about him, having delivered this insight. 'Because they were obliged to assist with our own harvest, and then it rained for days and theirs was spoiled. They are very hungry, it appears, and accordingly they are resentful'.

'Then it is surely Yuzanid's verdict upon them', declared Hortixia, making the sign before her. 'Do they persist in their blasphemous devotions, do you suppose? I trust a few judicious hangings will persuade them of the error of their ways'.

Hortixia's eyes, which had darted about with a fine, imperious confidence, now showed momentary disquiet as she recalled that her hostess had once, long ago, been accustomed to make blasphemous devotions of her own.

'Not that the faith does not embrace those who genuinely repent and see that error, of course. That much is accepted by all reasonable persons', she continued.

Afterwards, when Hortixia had been driven away in her carriage, with its three attendants and its four fine black horses, Stilli stood in the forecourt with Tye and twisted a strand of her hair pensively around her finger. Tolly had already departed with Irizoni, and Mother had business with the house steward to attend to.

'Would you care to go riding later this afternoon?' asked Tye, moved by the association of ideas and images as the clatter and creak of the carriage died away. 'Tolly has a lesson with her tutor, but the gentleman assures me that my own education is as complete as he can make it, and so I find myself at liberty. I could bring, Merli', he added, turning his hat in his hands earnestly before him, mentioning one of more tractable mares in the family's extensive stable. 'I swear she adores you'.

'Perhaps she does', conceded Stilli, stooping to examine the tear in her hem. 'But you know me for a timid rider, and besides, I had thought to take a walk to Rin Hill to clear my head'.

'Perhaps I may accompany you, then', persisted Tye. 'The crest of that hill may place you in danger of the Drumogari people who live beyond. I should be glad to offer you my protection. I might bring my sword, perhaps, and then we shall see who dares to offend my dear Stilli. What say you?'

His whole face radiated enthusiasm now.

Stilli had heard from Tolly that Tye's swordplay placed no one in danger but himself, and so she suppressed a smile, accordingly.

'I walk there often', she said. 'And I find no danger. None at all'.

'I am well aware that you go there often', ventured Tye, looking somewhat crestfallen but with a knowing glint in his eye. 'I have followed you, on occasion, in case you should need protection, and once, from behind a tree, I saw you talking with some people. Well, on a number of occasions, now that I think of it'.

'How dare you follow me!' cried Stilli. 'How presumptuous of you! How thoroughly underhand. May a girl have no privacy, no life of her own?'

'It was a Drumogari girl I saw you with', he continued doggedly. 'And another boy I could not place. There are folks who might say you put yourself in danger by so doing. Not that you need worry, though. I look out for you. You may be sure of it'.

'I know you do, Tye', soothed Stilli, very alarmed now, very conscious that her friend was a most unreliable custodian of her secrets. The likelihood that he might mention his acquaintance with Radda and Mull was a very real one, particularly if conversation drifted towards discussion of the Drumogari people.

'You must never mention this to anyone', she told him sternly. 'There are those who might disapprove of my association with such people, no matter how harmless. Never. Do you understand me?'

She stepped closer to Tye and gripped his upper arm with surprising force, if the upward movement of his eyebrows was any indication. 'Can I rely upon you?'

'You can always rely on me, Stilli. You know that', he replied, eyes shining with sincerity. She had known that he would say this, just as she had known that it would bring her no reassurance whatsoever.

'And how is your new tutor?' asked Radda when they met later that afternoon. 'I mean, how do you get along?' Radda was late in arriving that day, and Stilli had sat alone for some time with her coat folded beneath her, scanning the distant hedgerows for any signs that Tye, her unwelcome guardian, might be observing her from there. At last, when she had almost given up hope that Radda would arrive, when she had concluded that the girl must be attending to more pressing business of her own, she saw the distant stocky figure of her friend approaching along the rutted track that led up from her village.

'He is a tutor in the traditional mode, I should say', answered Stilli, now that they were both settled as comfortably as a windy autumn day would allow. 'Very attentive to my handwriting and to my familiarity with those traditional texts that persons of my station must commit to heart. At least he has nothing to say about my loom or my samplers. But those texts, oh dear, those texts! You would find it all very tedious, no doubt'.

'I'm not sure I would. I have my own words to learn', shrugged Radda, seated on a ragged blanket and regarding Stilli seriously through a curtain of breeze-blown dark hair. 'But I rejoice in them. Not that there are any texts to learn from, seeing as how your folks root them out and burn them if they find them, you will forgive me for reminding you. We aren't allowed our own books, and yet we keep the word alive up here, see', she explained, tapping the side of her broad forehead to emphasise this point. 'The steward and his foreman can't root them out from here, unless they chop off our heads first. This is our last refuge, so it is, our final fortress, and we pass the word on from one to another over the years. I reckon there'd be chapters and chapters of it, maybe whole books up there, if I had the skill to write it down'.

'Perhaps, you would tell me some', suggested Stilli, intrigued by this notion.

'Oh, I'm sure you wouldn't want…' grumbled Radda, casting her gaze down.

'I do! Honestly, I do. Please tell me some of what your people carry in their heads'.

'And in their hearts', added Radda, 'because there we keep the old country alive', she sighed. 'I suppose I could tell you a little of the Ardoriad, the tale of the noble youth Ardorios and his doomed love for the water nymph Antofia'.

'Do, please', insisted Stilli, clapping her hands. 'I should like that'.

'Well, it begins in a forest', sighed Radda, looking around as if she feared being overheard. 'Although not like the hot, dry forests here in Eudora. The forests in my country are cool and damp, with deer and crags of tumbled stone and great meres where the water birds gather'.

A distance came into Radda's eyes as she spoke, and her voice changed as she spoke the words that were not her own, the phrases and the lines tumbling from her lips with an eloquence that was strange to her and that carried Stilli with her to a far southern land beyond the sea. There were great deeds to be described, a wholly unlikely romance between beings of earth and water, where each lover pledged to give up their native element, exchanged these through the intervention of powerful magic, fought those who opposed them with magic, fire and sword and finally endured exile, lost and alone, the water nymph wandering a parched desert, the youth condemned to whisper his loss in the brooks and freshets of the endless green forest.

When Radda finished, Stilli found that she had been wholly absorbed in the tale, utterly oblivious to her surroundings and that her cheeks were wet with tears.

'That was wonderful', she said through a throat that was strangely constricted.

'They are not my words', answered Radda. 'Although I'm glad you liked them. They're the words of Parmenio, a poet who lived many years ago. But when we hear his story, we are reminded of our god and of the cool forests of our far country'.

'But you have never been there', observed Stilli. 'You were born here, in Eudora'.

'Even so', said Radda with a wry smile, 'it is my country and my soul resides there, wherever my body may be'.

'And your god', continued Stilli. 'He who makes his presence felt within that story, he who intervenes to guide those lovers' course, does he not make the same fierce bargain with your people? Does he not demand your blood and the giving up of your lives, as well as your obedience?'

'Tio. Let us name him, shall we, since I don't think you'll condemn me for it. No, Tio doesn't ask that we pitch our daughters into Draganach's fiery belly or open our veins when we have lived three score years. It is Tio's to number our days, but he doesn't ask that we step in before him, to cut them short of our own accord', she laughed, shaking her head. 'How strange to us are the ways of you folk who worship Yuzanid'.

'I do not count myself amongst them', said Stilli simply. Her eyes opened wide after these words had left her mouth, and that mouth remained open as though more words may yet emerge. She found that Radda's gaze was fixed upon her, and a long silence passed between them. Radda toyed with a dry stick whilst Stilli's mind reeled beneath the import of the words she had uttered. In that moment, she had alienated herself from the world she had grown up in and associated herself with another. To repudiate Yuzanid was to place herself beyond the protection of her community and to excite the hostility of all who embraced that faith. She could die a horrible death, should she injudiciously make those feelings plain to society at large. Everyone knew the fate of apostates. Her mind filled with images of the fire and the flaying knife, and she thought for a moment that she might faint.

'Don't worry', Radda assured her, placing a hand on her forearm and squeezing. 'I shan't tell anyone'.

It was a great relief to Stilli that she encountered no one to whom she must speak on her journey home, none for whom politeness required that she should acknowledge with more than a nod and a smile. Mother was in the garden, discussing something with the gardener. Accordingly, it was easy enough to make her way to her room without being invited to account for the pallor of her countenance or the uneasiness in her eye. Only Smeeton, encountering her in the corridor, had set eyes upon her. He had made his dutiful twitch of a bow, but his wondering gaze, as she hurried past, thankfully brought with it no requirement for explanation.

Once within the privacy of her room, she threw herself face down upon the bed and buried her face in the pillow. What did it mean? There was no crime greater in the eyes of God than to renounce *Him*. Then *why* had she done it? She examined her conscience, and this organ assured her that she was perfectly sincere. In fact, upon reflection, she could see now that her devotions had only been of the most superficial kind. In public they must necessarily be consistent with her station, but in private they had been of a most perfunctory kind, wholly without genuine piety. The realisation grew within her that she had never worshipped Yuzanid at all, and now that this conviction gathered in her breast, the reasons for it crowded in upon her.

'It is wrong!' she murmured, turning over and frowning at the ceiling. 'Surely, it is wrong that men and women must be slain to satiate a god's greed for blood and souls. Well, he shall not have mine'.

She bit her lip as she made this resolve and knitted her brows. What was this sudden apotheosis, and what had prompted it? Could it really be that Radda's tale had freed the logjam of her doubt, releasing the pent-up tide of scepticism and resentment that had grown within her and that could be contained no more. She felt that she had crossed a deep chasm between her old, familiar world and an entirely new one, lit by the dawn of her awakening conscience. And yet, whilst the light of realisation brought new glory to her mind, like a window thrown open on a spring morning, so were the shadows therein cast into sharper and darker relief. It was said that Yuzanid could peer into all men's hearts and measure their love for him, or their indifference, or indeed their enmity. Stilli shuddered. Was that jealous god looking down upon her now, considering how best she may be punished for her rejection of him?

'Everything is surpassingly strange to me', she said aloud, sitting up and running her hands through her hair distractedly. 'First Bondorin, and those odd episodes with time... and now this. What does it mean?' She wondered if she was losing her mind. Some spoke of hysteria and strange imaginings amongst girls of her age as they made that difficult transition between childhood and adulthood. Could it be that she was afflicted in this manner? No. Nothing could have been more real to her than that moment on Rin Hill, when the scales had fallen from her eyes and she had looked upon the world anew. Did infidelity swim in her veins? She crossed to look down from her window, to where her mother still moved amongst the roses, with her basket, pruning and cutting the season's final blooms. Mother was Erenori. Perhaps her own birthmother, the servant Yahli, was likewise of that nation, a follower of Tio. Tio, that false alien god, as all in her own community declared. Reviled in this land, even as he was lauded in that far empire, nourished by the ascending prayers of millions in their distant fields and teeming cities. Perhaps her adoptive mother had also continued secretly in her adherence to him, as Stilli might do now. Perhaps she had presented the appearance of devotion for all these years whilst privately nurturing that other god in her heart. Did Erenori blood, if it ran in Stilli's veins at all, necessarily carry that faith with it? If thus, it might also explain her strange fascination with those people beyond the hill.

Her mother looked up now, as though sensing Stilli's gaze upon her, and the daughter stepped back with a gasp, crossing to sit heavily upon her bed once more. This was no time for communication with Mother, or with anyone else for that matter. Only isolation and introspection might enable her to make sense of what was happening to her.

'The world is a closed book to me', she sighed. 'And I am powerless to turn the cover. Whatever will become of me?'

To her great consternation, it appeared that even sleep brought no respite to her troubled soul. For a long time, she struggled to sleep at all as the day's events played themselves out relentlessly across the forefront of her restless mind. And then, at last, when she did sleep, the form of a great golden lion came into her mind, one with splendid white wings upon its back. The lion did not speak or move, it merely stood there and challenged her by its mute presence, driving all other notions from her consciousness. The expression in the creature's eyes was strange, one that silently taunted her with a connection that she was at a loss to make, one that caused her to wake on several occasions and stare fixedly at the dark ceiling above her. When she closed her eyes, the lion remained there, but gradually it faded and, finally, dreamless sleep brought her grateful relief.

'Mother, I would be glad if you would tell me more of she who gave birth to me', announced Stilli the following morning when the woman who undoubtedly possessed so many answers to her daughter's questions was seated at the accounts in her study.

'That plasterer has charged me twice what he said he would', observed Mother, continuing her close scrutiny of the paper in front of her. 'Now that your father is gone, tradesmen think that a simple woman such as me will be oblivious to their chicanery. Pass me that writing paper, would you, dear?'

'Mother!' insisted Stilli, nevertheless doing as she was asked. 'You are being evasive, I declare!'

'Really, Stilli, this is not the time', murmured Mother without looking up, searching in a drawer for a quill.

'Then when *will* the time be?' pressed Stilli, stifling an impulsive stamp of her foot. 'Do please answer me. I have a right to know!'

'Do you? Do you really?' sighed Mother, pushing the paper aside. 'And in which statute is that entitlement defined? Must I consult the law books when I have many more pressing matters to address'.

'You know I am right', maintained Stilli, approaching closer to the desk and provocatively furrowing her brow. 'Why would a girl in my circumstances not wish to know more of the person that brought them into this world? Why will you not tell me? Must I assume that something shameful attaches to those circumstances?'

Now Mother looked up into Stilli's eyes, and she saw for the first time the weight of the years upon her, the lines on her brow and the dull greyness of her hair. It was not that she had been unaware of these things, of course. Nevertheless, consciousness of it had brushed lightly against the surface of her mind, along with all other familiar aspects of the world around her. Now the reality of her mother's appearance – her careworn features, the wrinkled folds beneath her chin – struck Stilli with sudden force, as did the certainty of her mortality. She felt a sharp pang of pity in her heart, and so the firm resolution she had brought with her into the room ebbed swiftly away.

'You must not', replied Mother, 'and you need not. Today is not the right time for this. You know that I am oppressed with the many duties that crowd in upon me now that your father has died. You know that...'

Her eyes filled with tears, and for an awful moment Stilli feared that her mother might weep. Stilli was quite able to complete the abandoned sentence that hung in the air, the one that described how much Mother missed him. But she mastered herself, straightened her back and regarded Stilli with a resolute gaze.

'But when, Mother?' persisted Stilli. 'When will you share these things with me?'

'The time will come, daughter', she said. 'The time will come'.

Chapter Nine

And come it did, with a suddenness that neither mother nor daughter could have predicted. Less than a week after that interview, Stilli's afternoon grammar lesson with her new tutor was interrupted by the entry of Smeeton into the room, begging Mr Bondorin's indulgence, but would he care to finish early today, as a result of unforeseen circumstances? Smeeton, and a mildly baffled tutor, had left the room before Mother came in, shutting the door carefully behind her, having first checked to see that the corridor was empty. She was dressed for travelling and immediately crossed to place her own worn cloak and a large blanket-wrapped bundle on Stilli's desk before her.
'Huh? Where are you going?' asked Stilli, eyes clouded with confusion. 'Has something happened? Is something wrong?'
Mother's cheeks were unusually flushed, and there was a startling air of agitation about her as she placed her hands on the desktop and leaned forward towards her daughter.
'Not entirely unexpected, but yes, it has occurred', answered Mother, adding to Stilli's gathering sense of dismay. Her mother was nothing if not self-possessed in all circumstances, and this new manifestation of her showed every indication that she was in the grip of fear. Could it really be?
'What? Tell me!' urged Stilli, standing up. 'What is happening? Are we in trouble?'
'We are', nodded Mother, grimly. 'I'm afraid to say that we are. There are things that I must tell you now that can be delayed no longer'.

She glanced hurriedly out of the window and then leaned forward across Stilli's desk, eyes shining with sincerity.

'I have lied to you, Stilli', she began, causing Stilli to catch her breath, so shocking was this frank and uncharacteristic announcement. 'You must believe that we did this for your own good, but your stepfather and I lied to you when we told you that you were the daughter of a servant. Your stepfather's was an unconscious lie. He knew no different, but mine was an entirely deliberate one'.

'What?!' Stilli exclaimed, gaping uncomprehendingly at her mother. A part of her, although not a prominent part, was surprised that Father should now be referred as 'stepfather' in defiance of all previous practice. 'Why? What do you mean?'

The words that Bondorin had spoken to her resonated in her mind now. She knew that Mother's own daughter had gone to the fire, but what did this new disclosure mean?

'Listen to me', continued Mother, coming around the desk to grasp Stilli by her upper arms and stare earnestly into her eyes. 'I did this for your own protection. *We* did this. Because a child cannot – could not – be entrusted with such a truth'.

'What truth?!'

'Listen, I say!' snapped Mother. 'And listen well. Your name is not Stilitha, it is Aramantha, and you are my true and dear child, the blessed fruit of my womb. Long ago, when I was brought to this country, your father Vindex, a high-ranking priest, took me for his own and we married...'

'Aramantha! Is that what you said?!' gasped Stilli. 'Aramantha!'

'Hear me out, child!' Mother chided, waving an impatient hand in front of Stilli. 'You were our first and only child. We loved you dearly, more dearly than I can ever express in mere words, but Yuzanid was jealous of our bliss, it appears, and he claimed you for his own. The lot fell for you'.

Stilli's eyes were wide now.

'The Golden Child!' she gasped.

'Yes, yes. You were to be the Golden Child when you were three years old. And your father, by law and tradition, must sacrifice that child, casting her into the flames in the brazen belly of Draganach. You know these tenets of the faith'.

'Then why am I still here?' demanded Stilli, shaking her head incredulously. 'How did I cheat that fate?'

'Because we suffered another child to go to the flames in order to spare our own', admitted Mother, her eyes rimmed with tears. 'And for that we are forever damned by this or any god. Yahli's child, she who was entrusted to my care, she whom I had promised to nurture as my own when the poor woman died, that child was very similar to you. Like two peas in a pod they said, all who knew you both'.

Mother's story was interspersed with sobs now, and Stilli stood back in horror, incapable of speech, incapable of doing more than clasping her hand to her mouth and shaking her head in mute incomprehension. To know that she was a replacement for a sacrificed child had been burdensome enough, but this shocking revelation was almost too overwhelming to bear.

'And we saw that the only way that you might be spared was if we sent poor Stilitha to the flames instead. Yes. That was her name, the name you have falsely borne all these years. The child Stilitha died that you may live'.

'No!' Stilli cried out, finding her voice once more as a cloying wave of guilt and revulsion passed through her, leaving her suddenly light-headed, nauseous. 'How could you?'

'You have not known what it is to feel a mother's love for her child', Mother told her, wiping her cheeks with the back of her hand, 'or you would not ask that question. It is a love so strong, so deep, so overwhelming that you would do anything – anything – in its service, though it cost you your immortal soul', she explained, placing her hands to Stilli's face, although her daughter flinched momentarily away. 'And it did, daughter. It cost me my soul, and that of your father, in this and all perpetuity. And the guilt, daughter. Can you even begin to imagine the guilt that has gnawed at the bitter remnant of that soul these last long thirteen years? Can you? I am consumed by it!'

These last words emerged as a hoarse roar of self-condemnation and caused a new convulsion, so vigorous that Stilli was obliged to help Mother to her chair, placing an arm around her trembling shoulders and feeling warm pity contending with shock for dominance in her heart.

Mother poured out her story in halting fragments: how they had fled from all who might suspect their subterfuge, setting up a new home far distant from their old, how the shock and the guilt had mortally oppressed her father, carrying him to an early death, how Andax had rescued her and the child at last, taking them into his own home upon the death of his brother and taking Mother to be his own bride.

'The lies. They eat you up at last, my dear child. They eat you up', she murmured, leaning her head on Stilli's shoulder.

'Then I am not Stilitha', said Stilli, 'if what you tell me is true, and I have no reason to doubt you. I have never...'

The words *seen you like this, embraced you in this way, heard your love for me so openly expressed* came to her mind but would not find utterance. Now Stilli could see the source of her mother's habitual reserve. Her love for her daughter was forever assailed by the dreadful guilt of having murdered another in her place, for that was what it certainly was.

Murder.

There was no sense here of religious obligation, of an all-consuming faith that must surpass all urgings of the human heart. She did not *believe*, as Stilli had indeed surmised. Stilli saw it now with blinding clarity. Like Stilli, she rejected Yuzanid, had always rejected him, and the outward profession of her faith in him was another dark lie that she must nourish in her soul.

'Enough of this', said Mother at last, drawing herself from Stilli's embrace and reaching for her handkerchief. 'Now, I have unburdened myself to you, and perhaps you may see something of the ponderous weight that I have borne for you all these years'.

She drew in a deep breath and made an effort to compose herself, dabbing at her nose. 'Truly, that weight had almost crushed me on occasion, as you may readily imagine. Every day, I have feared that my crime may be exposed at last and that I must suffer the inevitable consequence of it, in this world and the next. Every day, I have feared the hoofbeats of retribution on the road beyond our walls and the knock at the door that will signify the end of all things for me and for you'.

'What do you mean? Whatever do you mean?' Now it was Stilli's turn to take Mother's face gently and turn it to her own.

'I mean that my crime is detected. A messenger arrived just now to say that the authorities in Tazman are likely on their way even now to arrest us'.

'Arrest?! What do you mean?'

'You know what I mean, daughter. Yuzanid has been thwarted of his blood sacrifice for all these years, but he will take what is his rightful entitlement at last. If we do nothing now, you will go to Draganach. To the flames, my dear daughter, to the flames!'

'Oh my!' Stilli whimpered, her hand flying to her mouth once more and her eyes widening. 'How...?'

'We must get away from here, daughter. There is not a moment to lose. Nothing could be more grievous to the authorities than that they have failed their god in this way. They will exert every effort to catch us. Every fibre of the state's strength will be set forth in this, I do assure you. You may imagine that I have rehearsed this scenario in my head on countless occasions and have made preparations against it. There are addresses in Tazman that we may safely seek out, and we must go at once, even as Yuzanid's avenging forces set out to seize us. We shall travel by the rural byways rather than by the main road that they will certainly employ and so hope to avoid them'.

Mother was all steely resolution now, standing to open the bundle on Stilli's desk and spreading out its contents thereon.

'There is plenty of money for our immediate needs here', she said, lifting a heavy bag, 'and some clothes that you must wear'.

'But what about Middo?' asked Stilli, more from a sentiment that she ought to ask this question than through any feeling of genuine concern for his wellbeing.

'He is not implicated in this', said Mother. 'And I do not doubt that he will make his own way in this world. We must think of ourselves'.

Stilli nodded and looked askance at the worn male attire that confronted her there: a felt hat, a voluminous shirt, a leathern jerkin, knee stockings, breeches and a pair of stout brogues.

'Yes, we must disguise you as a boy', said Mother with a vague twitch of a smile. 'Set aside your dismay. It is good that your figure does not yet give it the lie to the casual observer, and I have made sure that the clothes are cut loosely. I have refreshed them from time to time as you have grown, you see'.

'But Mother!'

Stilli's hand darted instinctively to the dark curls that hung to her shoulder, and her eye fell gloomily upon the scissors that nestled next to the shoes.

'Yes. That must go'.

Mind dulled with shock, Stilli found herself seated before the small mirror at her desk, sitting mute, unresisting, as the scissors snipped busily around her head and tumbled tresses of hair gathered before her. Who was she now? Did that slow cascade signify the end of Stilitha and the beginning of Aramantha, the doomed child that had concealed herself within her unknowing frame all these years? Was she now that child, shrugging aside that subterfuge as a snake sheds its skin?

'You may call yourself whatever you wish. Your heart will know', Mother told her, as though divining these thoughts. 'Stilitha or Aramantha, whatever seems most true to you. Although, for now, you must adopt another name to suit your new status. I shall call you Khimelon, because the name, although a Vhanakhori one, has the meaning of "illusion" in my own land. That is where we must travel, daughter. We must travel to my own land, to the Empire. That is the only place where we shall be safe'.

She set the scissors down then, smoothing Stilli's hair with her hands into a style that might, perhaps, be adopted by a boy of her own age, amongst the middling people of the region.

'There, that must do', she said finally, picking up the mirror and holding it at various angles in order that her dismayed daughter may gaze astonished at her reflection. 'Oh, and there is this', she added, setting down the mirror and turning to reach for the last wrapped object that the bundle contained.

Stilli took it and pulled aside the cloth, gasping as her mother revealed her sword, together with its scabbard and the arrangement of leather straps and buckles that she guessed must enable it to be suspended conveniently at her side.

'Mother!' objected Stilli, eyes clouded. 'I can't!'

'Hush, daughter. Smeeton is coming with us, but he is no hand with a sword, and we may need protection on the road. Your previous tutor assured me that you were able to employ it with some skill'.

'You knew! You knew that Bondorin was teaching me'.

'I did. Now get dressed, child. There is not a moment to lose. Smeeton is readying a cart, even as we speak'.

Without further objection, carried along helplessly by this swirling current of circumstance, Stilli set down the sword, stripped herself of her familiar female attire and hesitantly arrayed herself in the strange garments of a boy. All the while, her mother fussed around her, helping her with the belt, with the buckles at her knee, adjusting the sword belt so that it hung neatly at her left side, perfectly balanced.

'There, let me see. That will have to do', she clucked, standing back to admire the strikingly pretty young man that her young daughter had suddenly become. 'Now you must learn to swear and to swagger, if the subterfuge is to be complete. You must unlearn the proper deportment for a lady that I have attempted to instil in you all these years and practise to look all folks boldly in the eye, unless they be superior in status to yourself, of course. There is much to learn indeed, if you are to pass as a boy. How I wish we had more time!'

No sooner had she uttered these words than there came the sound of horses and harnesses in the yard outside, accompanied by the harsh voices of men. Even at this remove, the sound of impatient official hammering on the front door could soon be heard. Mother darted to the window, looked out, saw soldiers in the livery of Tazman and stepped quickly back.

'That's it! So soon! So soon! What are we to do?!' she cried, momentarily paralysed with fear, her hands raised before her.

Stilli could only stare wide-eyed at her, heart thudding in her chest.

'Out through the back!' gasped Mother at last, seizing Stilli by the arm and pushing her through into the corridor, where the rear stairs gave access to the scullery. 'Smeeton may hold them for a few seconds'.

There was a panicked thundering down the stairs, past a startled maid, flattening herself to the wall, and to the threshold of the garden door, where Mother abruptly pulled her back. Stilli found herself suddenly face to pale face with the woman who had given her life, and her mouth was held in a hard line, doom lain bare in her eyes.

'Kiss me', she demanded, and Stilli did, the first she could remember for many years and all the more shocking for that, the brief pressure of her mother's lips on her own, so strange as to bring a leap of sudden fiery affection in her heart. Tears sprang in her eyes.

'What?!' Stilli stuttered, confusion seizing her mind in its paralysing grip. 'What are we...?!'

'You go', snapped Mother. 'Just go. Run, hide, get away from here. You know what to do. Go to the Empire, if you can'.

'But Mother, what about you?' cried Stilli plaintively, anguished beyond anything she had ever known.

'I'll come after you', she hissed, pushing Stilli down the step and along the path. 'Go!'

And then she turned and was gone, back into the house.

For a moment, Stilli looked after her, rooted to the spot, but then the sound of raised voices, a scream, breaking pottery, carried to her ear and she ran, instinct supplying what resolution could not.

It was a lie. Mother would not come after her.

She had known instantly, perceived it in the desperate gleam in her mother's eyes as she had turned away. She had gone to her death, gone to buy for her daughter a few precious moments of time, by which she may attempt to set a little distance between herself and her pursuers.

With laboured breath sobbing in her throat, Stilli dashed through the garden gate and into the quiet lane beyond, running at full pelt in the only direction that came naturally to her – to the hill. She held the inconvenient, clumsy, swinging sword with one hand and crammed the felt hat to her head with the other as she went, turning into the narrow path between two high-fenced market gardens that soon placed her out of sight of her own house.

Stilli was unused to running for her life, or indeed to running in any context. Accordingly, she was already panting hard when a familiar figure turned into the path from another way.

'Tye!' she gasped as he stepped instinctively aside to let her past, momentarily deceived by her disguise.

'Stilli?' he cried, his face transfigured by confusion. 'Is that you? Why are you dressed as a boy?'

'Yes, yes. It is I', panted Stilli, gripping his arm and regarding him wild-eyed. 'There are people chasing me, Tye. Bad people. That's why...' she explained, gesturing at her clothing and standing for a moment, taking deep breaths whilst he looked upon her bemused.

'Then I shall certainly stop them', he said grimly, reaching for the hilt of the knife at his belt. 'You may be sure of it. Why are...?'

'Not now, Tye. Not now', breathed Stilli, flapping hands about her face in a futile attempt to cool herself. 'Questions later. I just need to get to the hill'.

'Indeed? Then surely I shall convey you there in safety. Never fear, dear Stilli'.

'Well let us make haste, then', urged Stilli, beckoning for him to follow as they hurried along a way that led amongst a network of allotments and scattered small dwellings, finally opening onto the fields that gave access to the lower slopes of Rin Hill.

Stilli's mind was a whirl of emotions and thoughts, too numerous, too importunate to address with any clarity or control. Her body took charge, for want of any directing intelligence from her brain.

Some minutes later, when other pedestrians and an elderly man on horseback appeared upon the path, instinct insisted that she should slow to a walk and calm her breathing, in case such obvious hurry may single her out for attention.

Tye walked at her side with an easy stride, his smooth face wreathed in smiles, for this was an adventure he could never have anticipated. Having spent some time with a friend on the far side of the village, he had taken a somewhat circuitous homeward route, one that had the virtue of passing by Stilli's house, and now he was rewarded by joining her at the moment of some unlooked-for crisis. Surely, he could now prove his worth to her. Surely, the immediate future was full of promise.

Chapter Ten

By the time Stilli and Tye arrived at the top of Rin Hill, where the first outlying trees of the forest began, Stilli was red-faced and panting hard. Tye, whose tutor had accustomed him to a regime of hard physical training, when exercise of the mental kind had proved unrewarding, looked on in amusement as his friend clutched her sides. Taking off her unfamiliar hat, she turned to look down along the shoulder of the hill towards her village. There was as yet no sign of pursuit, she noted with relief.

'I can't see anybody actually following you', agreed Tye, scratching his head. 'Are you sure you are not mistaken? Oh, dear. You are very red', he laughed. 'I never saw you this red'.

This was the first time that any significant conversation had been possible between them since the beginning of their precipitate flight. More than that, though, it was the first time that Stilli had found leisure to reflect upon the circumstances that fate had imposed upon her, to order her thoughts and to make decisions other than what instinct prompted in her.

'Ladies are not supposed to run', she gasped, seating herself heavily on a familiar fallen log and looking in vain for Radda on the far downslope.

'And are you yet a lady, then?' teased Tye, continuing to delight in this unfamiliar entertainment. 'One would not think it from your garb – and see, you have a sword. Can I try your sword, please?'

'No, you cannot', grunted Stilli, taking a precautionary grip on its hilt.

'And you have cut your hair. What a shame. I was a great admirer of your hair'.

'Get off!' Stilli chastised, swiping at a questing hand and cramming the hat back on her head.

Stilli's breathing was easier now, and sparks of light no longer danced before her vision. She had to rid herself of her companion. She knew now that she must certainly journey to the Empire or die in the attempt, although she hardly knew where to begin. And brutal, agonising death surely awaited her should she be recaptured. She shuddered at this prospect, but more thoughts, namely those of Mother facing down her captors, suddenly assailed her mind with fresh force, causing her to sink her face into her hands and for new tears to start in her eyes. Mother was surely dead by now. Stilli knew it in her heart, and that heart swelled with a sudden unbearable incursion of grief so great she thought it must burst apart.

'Don't cry, Stilli', comforted Tye softly, the humour draining from his features.

He put his arm around her shoulders and drew her to him, making soothing noises and patting her gently. One part of her revolted against this unlooked-for advance upon her dignity, but the greater part found solace in his embrace and, after a while, she was able to curb her sobbing, able to exert some small control over her mind once more.

'I'll look after you', ventured Tye, squeezing her a little tighter. 'Everything will be alright, you will see'.

'No, it will not, Tye', she sniffed, twitching herself free of his embrace. 'You haven't the first idea. I have to go away, and I shall not come back'.

'Oh dear', he said as she gave back the handkerchief that he had lent her, rather soggy by now.

Handling it gingerly with thumb and forefinger, he dropped it on the log to his side. Then he looked out

towards his native village, an expression of steely resolve gradually settling in his countenance.
'Then I shall come with you, Stilli. It will be a great adventure', he resolved, waving his arm dismissively. 'I have finished with all this now. I am ready to step out into the world. With you, Stilli', he added with a warm sidelong glance.
The object of his affection sighed and cast her eyes upward, although a turn of her head concealed this from her uninvited companion.
'We have no money, no supplies, nothing at all that we need for any kind of journey, Tye. It is hopeless', she said, taking his hand. 'Truly, I am grateful that you wish to accompany me, but it is no use. I don't suppose I shall get very far before I starve to death or I am captured'.
She wondered, for a moment, if Tye might safely be sent down to his own home to fetch such essentials, but she was quickly obliged to set aside that notion. Were he to encounter those who searched for her, even a casual conversation might quickly prompt him to talk enthusiastically of his "adventure." The risk was too great. Tye would need to be indulged in his desire, at least for now. Besides, he was a well-built youth, and any rogues they met upon the road might think twice of attacking him, providing that he could be induced to keep his mouth shut.
But what road should she take?
Where should she go?
She tried hard to picture in her mind the map of Eudora that her first Bondorin had encouraged her to learn by heart. It was a hundred miles to Tazman and almost forty to Crane. It had to be presumed that both of those roads might now be too dangerous to travel, and perhaps also the smaller side roads. Mother's account of her daughter's importance to the authorities made it certain that vast resources must be committed to her

capture. She was the Golden Child, and she had cheated death. How they must fear the retribution of their god! Nothing could be more certain than that they would spare no effort to bring reality into accordance with intention. She felt quite sure of this.

Where should she go?

She supposed there must be other smaller ports or fishing villages along the northern coast of the island. Surely, they could not watch all of them. Perhaps she might persuade a passing trading vessel to take her on board and thereby find her way to the Empire at last. For the present, perhaps Radda and her family would take pity on her and give her a little food to take with her on her journey.

It was growing dark, and soon Stilli would have small chance of finding her way to Radda's house.

'Let us go, then', she said to Tye with a twitch of her head towards the Drumogari country. 'We shall go to my friend's house'.

'Down there?' asked Tye, following her gaze. 'The Drumogari live down there'.

His brow was creased with a wondering frown.

'They do not care for us, I think. I have heard it said that they nourish a dislike for us in their breasts. It would not be right'.

'I care not if it's right', snorted Stilli. 'Do you wish to accompany me, or not?'

'Oh, I do, I do', soothed Tye. 'I only wish to sound a cautionary note'.

On many occasions, Stilli had watched as her friend had herded her goats along the track that led around the shoulder of the hill on the Drumogari side, and she was almost certain that the distant low house, nearly lost in darkness now, was the one from which she had set out. With Tye following cheerfully in her footsteps, she hurried down a track made treacherous with mud and with the deeply implanted hoofprints of goats, holding on to the boy in support where the way was particularly difficult.

It was quite dark by the time they arrived before a deep-thatched, single-storeyed house, from which a thin column of smoke rose up until the chill breezes whipped it away. Searching the gloom, Stilli located the door and knocked timidly, holding her finger to her lips to enjoin silence upon her companion. She hardly dared consider what salutation Tye might have thought suitable as a greeting to the inhabitants of this place.

A murmur of vague conversation could be heard from inside, and then the door was pulled open a little, grating on the flat slab of stone that served as a threshold. A young woman's face was revealed in the gap, dimly lit by candlelight and bearing an expression of wary distrust.

'Who are you?' she demanded. 'We don't need no...'
'We mean no harm, I assure you', blurted Stilli. 'Is Radda there?'
'Radda!' called the woman, turning her head. 'Someone for you'.

After a few moments, the woman's hostile, suspicious face was replaced with Radda's, whose surprise was evidently very great after several moments of steady scrutiny.

'Stilli! Is that you? Why are you...?'
'I shall gladly explain if you will admit me', offered Stilli, glancing at Tye. 'And my friend here. He is quite harmless, I assure you'.
'Is he?' asked Radda in a tone that carried no conviction, but she nevertheless drew the door fully open and stood back in order that Stilli and her companion might enter, stooping to clear the low lintel. Inside, there was a single room with beds around the walls and a fire in the centre.

Smoke from this almost immediately began to sting Stilli's eyes, but for now she was oblivious to such things as she set eyes upon an elderly woman with her hair tied back in a headscarf. Apart from the ruddy glow of the fire, the only light was cast by several tallow candles set upon the table that occupied most of one side of the space. A meal was evidently in progress. There was a jug, a loaf of coarse brown bread on a platter and wooden bowls containing some steaming substance. The first woman stood next to the fire, having picked up an iron poker, which she now held in front of her meaningfully.
'Calm yourself, Reena', Radda laughed, before turning to the old woman. 'Mother, this is my friend, Stilli, although why she is dressed as a boy, I'm sure I can't guess. Doubtless, she will account for it when she's ready. As for this...'
Radda's eye fell upon Tye, who was looking around him with interest.
'Tye', he said brightly. 'Tye Marcuzio. Delighted to make your acquaintance'.
'Are you, indeed?' grunted the old woman. 'Delighted, he is! I wish I could say the feeling was mutual. What do you want with us?'
'They're Vhanakhori', warned Reena, edging towards her mother. 'Clear as clear can be. Careful what you say. Why should we trust these folks? They mean nothing but trouble for the likes of us'.
'Not Stilli', Radda assured her, face suddenly earnest. 'She's not as the others are, I assure you'.
'Perhaps not', sniffed the old woman, regarding Stilli with a piercing eye. 'Perhaps not, but let me be the judge of that. And perhaps you would care to answer my question'.
'Gladly!' answered Stilli, having swept off her hat upon a sudden impulse, feeling a warm sense of relief that she

might not immediately be ejected into the night. 'We come humbly in search of your indulgence'.
A snort of derision came from Reena, but the old woman merely raised her hand to quell her daughter, and Stilli rushed on to pour out her story.

'You were the Golden Child?' reflected the old woman, shaking her head, an hour or so later when Stilli's account was complete. 'It is scarcely credible'.
'Nevertheless, it is true', asserted Stilli, regarding her with fierce sincerity. 'And I *am* the Golden Child. I have cheated death, but death comes to claim me, at last'.
'And will claim us, too, Mother', warned Reena, whose suspicion of the newcomers had not abated. 'If they find her here with us, or discover that we helped them. Are you quite mad?'
'Hush, daughter', said the old woman, whose name, it appeared, was Maleg and who was what Radda referred to as the "cunning woman."
It was she that her people sought when assailed with illness, or for anything but the most straightforward childbirth.
'And what would you have of us?' she asked.
'As you see, we have nothing', answered Stilli, holding up her open hands.
'We have courage and a song in our hearts', declared Tye, thumping the table at which they now sat.
He beamed about him confidently.
There was a silence, during which the crackle of the fire and the sound of goats, from within the adjoining chamber, could be heard.
'Well, almost nothing', she conceded, having spared Tye a despairing glance. 'And I know your people owe mine nothing; how could they?' she said, glancing about her earnestly. 'But I would be grateful if, setting aside such

considerations, you could spare us a little food for our journey'.

'When we have little enough of our own!' scoffed Reena.

'You shall have some', nodded Maleg. 'As much as we can spare, and as much as you can carry. If the Hierarchy seek to kill you, if they perceive you to be such a threat, then we should rejoice that you yet live. These last thirteen years have not been prosperous ones for them, if what tales reach my ears are correct, and it may well be that they are right to blame the righteous anger of their god'.

She turned to her recalcitrant daughter.

'You are a fool if you can't see that it is in our people's interests to see this person evade her pursuers. Every dawn she lives to see is to spit afresh in Yuzanid's eye'.

'Mother!' admonished Radda and Reena together. 'To say that name...' added Reena, with a shudder.

Maleg poured more small beer into the chipped clay cups she had earlier set before her guests and smiled. The uneven light of fire and candle revealed a countenance with more lines than Stilli had ever seen. Surely, she must have exceeded the "sixty."

'I do not fear their god, daughters', she laughed. 'And neither should you, if you have any faith in our own. But what will you do, child?' she asked, turning suddenly upon Stilli. 'Where will you go?'

Stilli mentioned the vague notion she entertained of travelling to the north coast, of finding a ship.

'I wonder that your people don't all take that path and sail away', suggested Tye, causing her hosts to regard the boy incredulously.

'Well, there is this', snapped Reena, pulling back her dress from her shoulder and turning to reveal the mark of the serpent branded into her skin. 'The mark that we all must bear, we exiles in this place. To be found with this mark upon us, beyond our appointed lands, is to face instant death, if we are lucky, and blood sacrifice if we are not. Your people call it the "bitter path," and it is bitter indeed'.

She regarded her guests icily and let fall her dress.

'And then, if any of us are found missing when the rolls are called each morning, the rest of us are punished for it', added Radda.

She now turned her gaze to Stilli.

'You will recall I told you that Axilo Trimandrios fled into the wastes some weeks ago, yes?'

Stilli nodded, miserably.

'Well, as you know, they burnt his house down and they killed his mother. I will not describe to you how she died'.

Tye opened his mouth to speak, but Stilli dug her fingernails into his thigh and, after a reflective moment, he closed it again.

'That is why we do not flee', observed Maleg. 'We must bear our exile in this life and await the next for our reunion. Besides, there are no maps. It would be folly to seek the coast anywhere near Crane. You must give it a very wide berth. Nor do we do know the way to the coast to the north or the south of that town. None of us has ever travelled that road, and we know nothing of that land'.

'I have no choice', declared Stilli with a despairing shrug. 'I must try to find a way'.

'Mother, may I accompany her?' asked Radda suddenly, causing Stilli to turn upon her in surprise. 'I should like to see the land of my ancestors'.

'Radda, no!' cried Stilli. 'I would not ask such a thing…'

'You did not ask', said Radda simply. 'I freely offer', she added, turning to Maleg. 'Well? May I?'

'This is madness!' declared Reena aghast. 'If they find you are gone!'

'I doubt they ever will', said Maleg, regarding Stilli calmly. 'Our Headman is a fellow called Durban. I was there to bring him into this world, and I dandled him on my knee when he was an infant. There are many here who hate him for being the lickspittle lackey of you Vhanakhori, but he knows better than to cross *me*. You may go, with my blessing, daughter'.

'There are some who think Mother has uncanny powers', added Radda with a wry smile, having embraced the old woman.

'Maybe I have', chuckled Maleg, 'and maybe I don't, but I know there are a few who hesitate to murmur against me, for fear they may be struck blind or have their livestock die about them. Durban may hear you have gone, but I doubt he will remember it when the Steward comes calling. He would not dare, the dog!'

She gestured upward, to where various bundles hung suspended amongst the thatch.

'Here. You shall have dried meats, dried fruit and as much oats as you can carry for porridge. Will that suffice?'

'And we shall need the means to carry it, and also wet-weather clothes', added Radda, looking askance upon Stilli and Tye's clothing.

'Indeed you shall', agreed Maleg, reaching for a basket. 'Your friend seems a sturdy young man. Surely, he can bear a goodly burden'.

'Well, yes', nodded Stilli with a glance for Tye, reflecting that, in this one respect at least, his presence might be to her advantage.

'I shall bear what I must bear', agreed Tye, beaming about him. 'And bear it with a glad heart'.

'Let us see how glad your heart is when your fellows tear it from your breast', muttered Reena darkly. 'I doubt anyone standing in the way of the vengeful Hierarchy will die an easy death'.

This prospect was in Stilli's mind, too, as she sought for sleep uneasily on a straw pallet, next to the thin wattle partition that separated goat from human habitation. It was quite dark outside, and they must necessarily remain in this house until the first grey outriders of dawn made it possible to pick their way southeast into the hills and forests. Each had a waxed cloak, proof against the season's rains and a rolled blanket, containing provisions, that might be secured diagonally over shoulders and across chest and back, secured at the waist on one side. Tye, at his own insistence, carried as much as Radda and Stilli's load combined.

I must sleep, Stilli told herself. *My body will need to be strong and refreshed tomorrow.*

But sleep would not come. Her body was fatigued through sharing the burden of her racing mind, but her mind would not rest at all. Already, her pursuers must be planning the broadening of their search on the morrow. They would surely calculate that an unaccompanied young girl could not travel far undetected. It would take them some time to make a thorough search of the village. Perhaps, upon visiting the Marcuzio household, they would hear that Tye was likewise missing and conclude that their fugitive was no longer alone. Perhaps they would search the temple, a place Stilli was known to be familiar with, perhaps even the bone acre. It was surely only a matter of time before the search broadened to include the adjacent valley of the Drumogari. But how much time? A little of the night sky showed in the slender gap between the shutters in the wall next to the door. It was this tiny slice of darkness that she watched with obsessive, gritty-eyed attention, hour after hour, for sign that the light was returning.

This was surely the longest night of her life.

'We have the woman', reported the corporal, making his salute.
'We do?' grunted Azimandro, looking up from his inspection of Smeeton's terrified face and relinquishing his vice-like grip on the man's jaw.
'But I'm afraid that she is dead, sir'.
'God's breath!' snapped the general, whipping round. 'What about the girl?'
'No sign, sir'.
The soldier's countenance blenched in face of his superior's sudden fury. Azimandro pushed Smeeton hard against the wall, so forcibly that he slumped gasping to his haunches.
'Where is the woman?'
Azimandro and his troop of cavalry had lost no time in riding from Tazman, once Taradon had discovered where Rosania and her daughter had made their home. With plenty of remounts, the party had made good progress, reaching their destination within two days of their departure. Taradon, to his dismay, had been required to travel with them. Although familiar enough with riding in his youth, his usual practice, in recent years, had been to travel in a light carriage. Accordingly, the journey had left him exhausted, quite apart from a baleful ache in the lower regions of his body. He now helped a trembling Smeeton to his feet and regarded the furious general with alarm. The man exuded a debilitating terror from every pore of his body.
'In a study, to the rear, sir', stammered the soldier with a nod of his head in that direction.
Taradon followed after the soldiers, to see where a handsome woman of middling years lay sprawled upon a rug, her face stretched in a rictus of pain, her sightless eyes staring past them. Two soldiers were gingerly trying to coax a small black snake into the basket they

had placed on its side, next to it. The snake tasted the air with its tongue and regarded them malevolently. A fire asp – the creature sacred to Yuzanid.

'It seems she pressed the thing to her breast, sir', explained the corporal apologetically, as though he accepted personal blame for the manner of her death.

'I can see that, you idiot', snarled Azimandro, his face dark with anger. 'I'm not blind, am I? I suppose it was her husband's, damn her!'

'The daughter cannot be far', suggested Taradon cautiously, having no wish to attract further ire from the general.

'Yes, you're right', agreed Azimandro in more normal tones, having taken a deep breath and clenched his fists at his side.

He spared Taradon a curt nod and strode from the room with the corporal at his heels.

'Bandical, find Sergeant Rocan and tell him I want a house-to-house search, radiating from this location with outposts set at the perimeter, at the access roads and on the high ground to either side'.

'Yes, sir', saluted the corporal, hurrying off towards the front door.

'We shall certainly need more men, if we are to broaden the search', suggested Taradon as Azimandro seized a terrified servant by the arm, shook her vigorously by this limb and demanded that she bring them food. 'And perhaps some dogs', he added, wishing that he had the courage to ask the general to calm down. 'I don't doubt that we can find some of the girl's clothing, that they might take a scent from'.

In an upstairs room, the room that they were told was the girl's, they found a scatter of feminine attire on a bed.

'That smell...' mused Taradon, sniffing the air. 'Can you smell it?'

A fire burnt low in the grate. Taradon stooped painfully to pick a few dark strands of long hair from where they lay on the hearth.
'Hair, general. Burnt hair. What do you make of that?'
'Nothing, why should I?' demanded Azimandro, turning his fierce gaze upon the cleric.
Taradon brandished a pair of scissors that had been lying on the desk.
'The woman cut the girl's hair', he said, snipping the air with the scissors. 'And here we have a complete set of girls' clothing, if I am any judge, replaced by those of a boy, no doubt'.
'Then we are looking for a girl dressed as a boy', agreed Azimandro with a nod and a glance that might be thought to signal approval. 'Is that it?'
'I believe we are'.
When the general strode out, barking orders to various of his subordinate officers, Taradon made his way downstairs to the study once more, where the fire asp was now confined to its basket, this set in a corner by the book case. The woman who had occupied his thoughts so thoroughly for what seemed so long a time continued to lie where she had fallen. Taradon stopped Smeeton in the corridor to establish that the village's priest had been summoned to deal with the body and to request that a cup of tea might be brought for him to the study. There would undoubtedly be papers here that might shed light on family connections and friendships, clues as to where the girl might run to if some emergency threatened. He must go through these patiently, whilst the terrifying Azimandro dealt with the practical side of things. But first, Taradon pulled out a chair and regarded the dead woman sadly. Even in the grip of such an agonising death, he could tell that she had once been beautiful. He had expected to feel triumph upon finding her, but instead he felt only numbness of the spirit and

a debilitating fatigue of mind and body. Surely, he would be rewarded in Tazman for his investigation, but the prospect left him feeling strangely unmoved. It was likely that the girl would soon be found, but this, likewise, failed to stimulate any excitement in his breast. He sought refuge in the familiar patterns of prayer, although the confines of the study and the proximity of the corpse made lying face down upon the floor in the usual manner impractical. Instead, he leaned forward across the woman's desk and pressed the side of his face to the hard oak, muttering the familiar words that brought him nearer to his god.

Did he sense exultation there, Yuzanid's fierce joy in this act of restitution? He did not. There was no sense of the presence of the divine. His soul remained cold and torpid within him, lying quiet as the prayers murmured upon his lips.

Chapter Eleven

Dawn brought with it rain, and Maleg expressed the view that it was set in for the forenoon at least. They should welcome it, she told them, as they passed out into a world where it was yet barely possible to distinguish the land from the sky, because it would make their pursuers' task more difficult.

'And if they have dogs', she added. 'The creatures will struggle to find your scent'.

In truth, despite this notional advantage, Stilli found it hard to derive much satisfaction from the squally rain that blew so persistently into her face. She still felt in the grip of a deep shock, unable to properly process the circumstances that the world presented to her, living moment to moment, as though somehow distanced from her surroundings. There had been many tears and embraces at the door as they made their farewells, for the likelihood was that Radda would never see home again. Now the Drumagaros set that face to the vague shape of the ridge where the forest began and trudged upward along the muddy goat path with Stilli and Tye picking their way cautiously behind her.

'I don't know how you can remember the route. I greatly admire your memory, I do declare', grunted Stilli from behind her.

Her words were uttered mechanically, more from a sense that she must say something to challenge the aching void within her, but the void remained, and with it a chill constriction of her heart that numbed her to consideration of her mother's likely fate and the world that she had lost, at least for now.

'Do not admire it yet', laughed Radda. 'I give you leave to celebrate it when we walk into Mull's camp'.

The wilderness of wooded hills that lay to the southeast of Stilli and Radda's homes offered few compelling options for their salvation. It had not been hard to conclude that they must seek out the encampment of the charcoal-burners, because if any knew the paths amongst the wooded shoulders of those hills and the high mountains beyond, it was those people. There were no roads in those remote regions, and the writ of Hierarchy rule barely reached there. There were tribes in the high mountain massifs who acknowledged no master but their own chiefs, it was said, and who worshipped carved idols in woodland glades, as they had since time immemorial. But the charcoal-burners never stayed in any one place for long, and it had been some time since they had seen their young friend. It was quite likely that the camp had moved on and that Mull had travelled with them.

The rain eventually ceased. As the light strengthened and a watery sun edged above the hills, the trail led them ever upwards, to a place where young saplings had clearly been cut from amongst the forest on either side. These had then been dragged through the brush beneath the sparse canopy spread by the larger oaks, passet firs and screw pines that grew there.

'Look!' cried Radda as they emerged onto a more open slope, from where a vague column of woodsmoke could momentarily be seen against the low grey clouds. 'There, we have it!'

Within a few minutes, the track brought them to a clearing amongst the trees, where a round wattle house with a turf roof stood amongst the various low earthen mounds from which the smoke had risen.

A startled child ran yelling into the house as they approached, and after a few moments, several of his clan came out to meet them. To their great relief, Mull was amongst them.

'Hello, Mull', said Stilli cautiously, noting that the man who stood at the boy's side bore a bow with an arrow nocked to the string.

'It's alright, they're friends', assured Mull after taking a moment to recognise Stilli in her unfamiliar garb. 'Mostly...' he added with a suspicious glance for Tye as the man released the tension in his bow and, more generally, in the air between them.

'This is Tye', said Radda, walking forward to take her place at the front of their small party. 'He is no threat to you'.

'Why are you dressed in that manner, Stilli?' asked Mull, his brow knitted. 'You are not a boy'.

'No, but the people in pursuit of me are looking for a girl', sighed Stilli, setting down her burden. 'It seemed a necessary subterfuge'.

'Who is in pursuit of you?' grunted the man.

During this exchange a number of others had emerged from the hut, including children of various ages, regarding the newcomers with undisguised interest and no small degree of suspicion.

'We are unaccustomed to visitors', observed a woman. 'What is this?'

'I shall explain', said Radda, whose longer acquaintance with Mull suggested that it should be her to take the initiative in this matter.

Stilli's story was not one that could be told in a few sentences. Since it had begun to rain once more, the man who appeared to be the elder of the group led them into the dwelling. This was yet more primitive than Radda's house and lit only by the smoky fire at its centre.

It took some moments for their eyes to adjust to the gloom within. Whilst rain pattered above them, a circle of ruddily lit faces listened curiously as Stilli told her story. This took some time, since some of the elders in the community were evidently quite deaf, and others required amplification or explanation of various points during its course. There were eleven of them, varying in age from a toddling snot-faced child, wholly uninterested in Stilli's explanation, to a woman of evidently advanced age with her arm supported in a sling.

When the story was over and all supplementary questions had been asked and answered, their hosts fell to whispering amongst themselves, occasionally directing curious glances at their visitors. It was clear that the crucial moment approached, the moment in which they must be required to move on or be offered assistance. Stilli sat on the hard earth, one leg tucked under her, lamenting her fatigue and the soreness of her feet in this unfamiliar footwear. How she missed the soft light slippers that were her usual wear. An icy drop of rain fell through the roof and trickled down the back of her neck. She felt hungry, thirsty and filled with a growing sense of resignation. These people evidently held her fate in their hands. They could detain her here if they chose to and send to notify the Hierarchy that they held the precious fugitive captive. Doubtless, they would be well-rewarded. The sword at her side had already attracted interested glances. Would she even be able to employ it, should this be necessary, with all these bodies crowded around her in this dim, humid confinement? Would she even dare, having only ever wielded the blade in sport? How her material circumstances had changed in a few hours! From a lady of leisure in a fine house, albeit a house less commodious than the one she loved, she had become a fugitive from a vengeful state, hunched in a smoky hut where people shared their accommodation with bleating goats and at least one small pig.

'Are these connected with the other one?' asked a young woman of the man, who was perhaps her husband and was called Dran, it appeared.

'You, Stilli, if that is indeed your name', he grunted. 'Do you know one called Axilo?'

'*I* do', interjected Radda. 'He is from *my* community. Why? Do you have him here?'

'Hey, stranger', grunted Dran, peering over his shoulder.

After a moment, a tall young man in his late teens edged his way through the press, from where he had been hidden in the profound shadows at the rear of the house.

'My name is Axilo', he announced in a clear, confident voice, glancing amongst the charcoal-burners and then at Stilli and her friends.

'I know what your name is. Do you recognise these folks?' asked Dran.

'I know Radda', agreed Axilo with a nod. 'She is of my people. As for the others, well they are Vhanakhori, and I do not. I know what they represent, though', he added darkly. 'And it is not good'.

'We shall be the judge of that', replied Dran curtly. 'Your peoples can set aside their wars when they are amongst us. We have no quarrel with the Hierarchy, or the Empire. Our worlds barely adjoin. We stay away from such folks'.

'Nevertheless, those folks may come to us', objected the woman, 'bringing fire and sword with them. The priest people, at least', she added, having considered that the Empire was unlikely to trouble their counsels at this remove. 'We should move these folks on without delay'.

'Perhaps we should', agreed Dran, before turning to confer with his clan.

A low murmuring began, in what was evidently a continuation of their earlier debate, shared by all except for the small child, the goats and the pig, which snuffled busily amongst their feet.

'I like this pig', whispered Tye, nudging Stilli and receiving an impatient glance in response.

Whilst her fate was being decided, Stilli looked curiously upon Axilo and found that he was subjecting her to a dark-eyed scrutiny of his own. This was undoubtedly the youth who had fled the Drumogari village and so condemned his mother to a painful death. He was tall, to judge from the slight stoop his position in the house enforced upon him, with a broad brow and a strong chin that jutted forward now in a manner suggestive of defiant pride. The knitting of his brow and the hostile glint in his eye made plain his conviction that she was his ancestral foe and that she deserved to die accordingly.

'I should like to punch him on that chin', murmured Tye at her side, perhaps divining her thoughts.

'I will go with them', announced Mull when it seemed that no decision might ever be expected from his people.

'Why would you?' asked Dran, reasonably enough. 'What have you to gain? These are not your folk'.

'He likes to go a-wandering', observed the young woman with a shrewd glance at her husband. 'I never saw a lad so footloose. We don't need the hands. The load's near ready now, and the carter fellows will be here inside this moon'.

'True enough', grunted the man. 'We move at new moon. You know that, son. Will you join us at Crags Foot?'

'I may', said Mull. 'I may not, but I know the paths as well as any in these woods'.

'Then go with our blessing', answered Dran after a low sigh and a moment of thought. 'We shall see you when we shall see you'.

Once this decision had been made, wooden cups were brought out and these filled with what might have been mead, in order that Mull's forthcoming journey might be toasted and the newcomers welcomed. The rain had stopped by this time, so the group emerged to sit on logs and on oilcloths set upon the ground, where Stilli and her friends could be subjected to further earnest enquiries and where the path that they must tread might be considered.

'I don't suppose you have a map of these regions?' asked Stilli of Dran, repeating this question several times until he could be brought to understand it.

When he had grasped the concept of geographic knowledge committed to paper, or to parchment, he threw his head back and guffawed.

'This is where my map is, my dear', he laughed. 'Between these here ears. From these mountains to that sea out yonder to the north, it's all in there, and it's all I ever need'.

'I see', said Stilli cautiously. 'And I suppose Mull is equipped likewise'.

'That he is', agreed Dran, 'although you might say his *map* is not as fair as mine, not as complete in every detail. I've been marking down my map for a long time, see'.

He took up a slender stick and cleared an area of earth between the cloths on which they sat.

'Here are the mountains, reaching away down south for many days', he continued, making marks with his stick. 'And here the forests, where we make our living on their shoulders and in the hills at their feet. Here are the streams. The trader people come up there in their boats, to buy our wares from us, at the moons when we have agreed with them, and here, just yonder, is the sea', he indicated, drawing a wavy line. 'Not that we know of it. Our folk don't have no doing with the sea, nor the places close to it'.

'There will be ports and villages on that coast, though', observed Axilo, who had moved close during this explanation and was now sat at Stilli's side, rather too close for her comfort.

'Are you telling or asking?' enquired Dran, casting him a sidelong glance.

'Well, there will, won't there?'

'I suppose, although I don't know it', conceded Dran. 'The woods are what we know'.

'I shall come with you', asserted Axilo simply, regarding Stilli and her friends as though challenging them to contradict him.

'I'm amazed that you should wish to associate yourself with us', laughed Stilli scornfully, edging away from him.

'It is Radda I wish to associate myself with', he replied superciliously, 'as she is of my people, but sometimes we must tolerate uncongenial travelling companions, I suppose, for the good of all'.

'Anyone would take you for a seasoned traveller', snorted Radda. 'Whereas I know for a fact you never set foot outside of our valley'.

'I travelled far in books', objected Axilo, frowning. 'Or at least in one book, I should say. My mother had one, Mirad's *Geographia Toxandriacum*, before these people found it under the floor and burned it last year,' he noted dryly, accompanying this accusation with a broad gesture of his hand toward Stilli. 'She taught me my letters with it', he continued. 'And because of it, I know of many places throughout this island and the word beyond. The Empire, the whole of Toxandria, I have travelled in that book. But now it is ashes'.

He now regarded Stilli venomously. She shrugged and glared back at him.

'I did not burn your book' she countered. 'And if we are to speak of burning, well my own people would dearly love to burn me, too. Do not speak to me of burning'.

'Well', said Axilo, casting his eyes down in face of the ferocity of hers. 'I suppose we shall set that aside for now. But we shall make a stronger party together, and I have a sword – a proper sword', he added with a disparaging glance for Stilli's.

'And where might you be coming by a sword?' demanded Radda incredulously whilst Stilli groped for some appropriate response to Axilo's slight on hers.

'I took it from one of the steward's men, when I made good my escape', answered Axilo proudly. 'Here, I shall show you'.

'When you ran away!' taunted Radda as he stooped to enter the dwelling.

'We all have run away, however we may wish to phrase it', said Axilo a few moments later, returning with a bundle of oil cloth from which he presently drew a sword. 'See? A sword', he said complacently.

'May I try it, please?' asked Tye eagerly. 'Stilli will not let me lay hands on hers'.

'No, you certainly may not, insolent youth!' snapped Axilo, twitching the weapon away from him. 'It is done with filthy Vhanakhori hands now. It desires only their blood'.

It was a perfectly ordinary sword, one of the cheaper sort that might be issued to hired soldiery, notched in a few places on the blade and with evidence of mending upon the hilt, where wire wrappings of different colours were to be seen. Axilo brandished it proudly, nevertheless, swishing it in the air around him in a manner that caused the charcoal-burners to step back and regard him warily.

'This is a true battle sword', he declared, resting the blade in his open left hand once more, 'and I shall not rest until I have placed it in a Vhanakhori throat'.

'Well it shall not be mine', growled Stilli, feeling a hot prickle of anger rise within.

'Nor mine', said Tye, getting to his feet. 'And I shall see to it that you do Stilli no harm'.

'Will you now?' scoffed Axilo. 'Will you? We shall see... Oh, do sit down, you oaf!' he added, having already formed a shrewd opinion of Tye's capabilities. 'Naturally, I do not include present company. I'm surprised that I should have to say it. Are we to go, then? Am I to join you?'

'Well, you have surely charmed us with your honeyed tongue', laughed Radda, breaking the sudden tension.

'How could we not be moved by such a persuasive address?' added Stilli with a grateful nod for her friend.

'Well', blushed Axilo, toying awkwardly with the sword now, seeing that he had over-reached himself. 'I think it better that we put our strength together, that's all'.

The anger drained from Stilli as she looked upon him, standing suddenly vulnerable in the face of their larger party. She exchanged glances with Mull and with Radda, who nodded, although with no evident conviction.

'He called me an oaf', complained Tye when her eye met his.

'He will offer you his apology', said Stilli, turning to Axilo, stern-faced. 'And then he may join us'.

It was a party of five that set out southward along the forest trails later that day. At their head walked Mull, whose valuable knowledge of those parts meant that they had some sense of their immediate route, if not of their ultimate destination. Like his family, he knew nothing of the sea but longed to set eyes upon it, and he was by nature an adventurous boy, glad to take the opportunity to leave his mundane life behind, at least for a while. He carried a bow like his father's upon his back, and next to it a quiver of arrows fletched with grey goose feathers. The way was familiar to him, the paths ones he had known since his earliest childhood, and he recognised the overgrown sites of encampments where his family had stayed in times past. His step was light, his eye wary, for there were many deer in the woods, and with the wind in their faces as it was, it was not impossible that they might come across some such unwary creature dozing and incautious in the unseasonably warm afternoon sun.

What am I thinking, he asked himself with a half-smile. *With these noisy fellows at my heels, talking merrily amongst themselves and tramping through the undergrowth like cattle, the deer would need to be surpassingly deaf, blind and stupid not to be spooked within a mile of them.*

'Do not whistle', he admonished Tye, turning to him and pressing his finger to his own lips.

'Yes, do not', agreed Stilli, ashamed that preoccupation with her own thoughts had rendered her oblivious to her friend's incaution. 'There may be others on our trail'.

Tye frowned and looked about him with exaggerated care, one hand shading his eyes.

'I do not see them', he said. 'But certainly I shall curb my whistling, if it offends you. I was happy, you see. It is such a splendid day now, and these woods are delightful, are they not? How I shall enjoy telling Tolly and Mother of our adventures'.

'What is it?' asked Radda, coming up with Axilo to join them. 'Is anything amiss?'

'Nothing', answered Mull with a despairing glance for Tye. 'I suppose we may rest for a while here. There is a convenient place where we may camp up ahead, but that is some hours distant. We should eat here, but away from this path'.

'Down there, perhaps?' suggested Axilo, pointing amongst the trees to where a sun-dappled clearing could be discerned.

'If you like', laughed Mull, reaching for his water skin. 'But then if I had bloody vengeance on my heels, I'd head up there, where I can look down on the path and see anyone coming along it'.

He indicated a rocky outcrop that jutted amongst the trees some way up the slope of the ridge they were traversing.

Stilli heard little of the conversation between Axilo and Mull as she clambered through the tumbled moss-grown rocks towards that eminence, occupied as she was with thoughts of her inconvenient companion. Truly, Tye was a lovely young man with not an ounce of malice in his body. He was, however, a liability, and she wondered how he might be induced to make his way safely home, if the opportunity occurred. He evidently had no sense that his presence at her side was anything more momentous than an afternoon stroll in the village, or that he might be mistreated, or worse, if found guilty of abetting a fugitive from justice. Sure, those who knew him would confirm that he was quite simple, quite incapable of making such a distinction, but she suspected that this might not be enough to save him. In addition, it was likely enough that the amusement her companions felt with regard to Tye might soon turn to something less congenial – to hatred and contempt, perhaps. Axilo's impatience with him was already quite apparent.

Her thoughts turned to the Drumogaros as she sat with Radda, alternatively taking bites from a crust of stale bread and tearing mouthfuls from a piece of dried sausage. He was a strikingly handsome youth, she conceded, glancing across to where he was laughing with Mull and Tye a few yards away across the low rocky platform that was their refuge, looking down upon the trail.

'He is proud, that one', said Radda, following her gaze and gesturing with her own crust. 'A cut above the rest of us, since his mother was a noble back in the old country, so they say. His father was with her when they were brought here, but he didn't last long, once he had placed his seed in her. He was proud, too, far too proud to submit to the insolence of the steward and his men. He paid for it with his life, of course. We exiles must cultivate humility, you see'.

'It seems that Axilo's efforts have not been rewarded with success', scoffed Stilli as Tye came towards her, brow furrowed.

'Axilo proposes a contest, Stilli, since you are a boy', he said. 'I wish I did not have to mention this to you, but he insists'.

Stilli glanced across to where Axilo and Mull could both be seen smirking.

'Go on', she said suspiciously.

'Well, I hesitate to describe it to you, since it involves making water... and that tree... and a contest to see how high...' Tye stuttered, blushing furiously. 'I do not think you would prosper in it', he added, leaning close. 'My advice to you is to decline this challenge'.

'Is it?' asked Stilli deadpan whilst Radda shook with inadequately contained mirth at her side. 'Is it really? Do please go and tell Axilo that I would be glad if he would go away and boil his head'.

She said this loud enough for Axilo to hear without the need for Tye's services as an intermediary, accompanying it with a glare of particular ferocity.

Axilo and Mull did their best to erase the levity from their faces, although it was quite certain that they would enjoy it later in private discussion.
'That one surely needs putting in his place', laughed Radda when she could speak once more.
'Certainly he does', agreed Stilli heavily. 'And I shall be the one to do it. You will see'.

Quite how this lofty ambition might be achieved was less than clear in Stilli's mind, but she set it aside for further consideration as the party set off once more after their break. In truth, it was advantageous to wear male garb in this situation, except in those circumstances that Axilo had alluded to, where rather more flesh than was comfortable must be exposed and suitable concealment sought. However, stockings and breeches were more practical when pushing through narrow trails amongst prickly undergrowth, and indeed Radda's skirts were already ragged at the hem. As the shadows lengthened, Stilli found that fatigue made it impossible to respond to her friend's conversation with more than the occasional shake or nod of her head. Girls of her station were unused to sustained physical exertion, and she had slept little the previous night. Her shoes hurt her abominably and her back ached from carrying the blanket bundle that she must necessarily bear. She did not complain, however, since to do this would certainly add further to Axilo's low opinion of her. She must continue to place one foot after another, fixing her gaze upon Mull in front of her, and pray that darkness would soon descend upon the woods to enforce further rest upon them all. Accordingly, she could do little more than throw herself upon a mossy bank when Mull called halt.
She lay flat on her back, looking up to where the first stars were dimly to be seen amongst scudding clouds

above. The bodily heat of their exercise soon dissipated as the chill of a November night tightened its grip upon them. Recovering a little, looking around at the party, Stilli was pleased to note that Tye had not thought to recommend a blazing fire to keep the cold at bay. Perhaps the possibility of close pursuit sharpened even his dull mind.

'I have never slept quite like this', he murmured when they had partaken of cold food and drunk of icy water from a nearby stream. 'And I could wish that the provisions were...' he frowned, '... little less resistant to the tooth. But it is good to be here with you, and I think I shall sleep well, regardless. This moss is quite comfortable, I find, if a little damp... and cold'.

'How far do you suppose we have travelled?' asked Axilo of Mull a little later, when Stilli was drifting to sleep.

'Far enough', answered Mull, throwing a wizened apple core high into the brush.

'I suppose we would have gone further without...'

Stilli sensed, rather than saw, his nod in her direction and felt herself stiffen. Presumably, he thought her to be already asleep.

'She did well enough', chided Mull softly. 'I never heard a word of complaint from her. Did you?'

'No, I did not', conceded Axilo. 'But I don't doubt we would be better off without her. The likes of her know nothing of endurance, nothing of bearing the supervisor's lash across their shoulders when they're fit to drop. I expect she will fade tomorrow – and that will be an end to it'.

Stilli felt hot tears start behind her eyes as anger competed with despair for mastery of her. She could not deny the truth of what he had said, but neither could she help the circumstances of her birth and of her upbringing. Of course she had never known what it was like to labour in the fields from dawn to dusk, as the

Drumogari did, and of course her body was soft and weak as a consequence. However, she passed into an exhausted slumber, determined that her spirit must accomplish what her body could not, that her spirit must drive that body relentlessly onward in order that Axilo might be obliged to eat his words at last.

Stilli slept, tight-curled, nestled in her blankets... and dreamed.
The lion came to her again. The lion did not speak. Perhaps it never did, and the shape of it was shrouded in a darkness in which the ghostly shape of its furled wings could only vaguely be glimpsed. It padded away from her into that deeper gloom, and it paused and turned its great head to look back at her. An invitation. She followed. Now she saw through her mother's eyes, and the fear and the panic the woman had felt as she met her end resonated in her daughter's mind. Mother hurried up the staircase to Stilli's bedroom, heart pounding, swept up those severed locks in her hands and, after a moment's hesitation, a moment to glance about her, threw them upon the fire. Then, hearing loud voices on the main staircase, she made her way down the servants' narrow stair and along the corridor to her study, closing the door quickly behind her, locking it, stepping back, fists clenched at her side. Through those ears, Stilli could hear the sound of splintering wood as soldiers hammered and kicked at the door. Through that heart, Stilli felt Mother's despair. This was the end of all things, and death leaned up to embrace her. Through those eyes, Stilli saw Mother's gaze shift to the basket in the corner where the fire asp dwelt. The fire asp. And the fire asp was in her hand and then at her bosom as she pulled her dress aside. She squeezed hard. Her heart pulsed with one last aching burst of love for her daughter, leavened with guilt, tinged with regret.

The fire asp, enraged, sank its fangs into her soft flesh and hot pain blossomed to overwhelm her consciousness. She died.

Stilli's eyes sprang open, but there was only cold darkness around her and the crack of a twig as Mull shifted his stance. He was keeping watch over them.

'Sleep', he whispered from darkness so profound she could barely discern his outline against the night. 'You will have need of it'.

Chapter Twelve

'She came here often, it seems', observed Taradon, picking up the handkerchief that Tye had dropped the previous evening. 'Or at least regularly enough for servants to know where to go in search of her, according to those I spoke to at the priest house'.

He turned the soggy handkerchief in his hand, as though it might be persuaded to give up its secrets.

'I wonder if this is the boy's; if they were together?'

'The idiot?' asked Azimandro, looking down pensively from astride his great black mare.

'Indeed. His mother confirmed that he was missing from their home from around noon and never returned'.

'I know this', snapped the general irritably. 'I read the same report, did I not?'

'You did', agreed Taradon mildly, taking his own mount's reins and climbing aboard it awkwardly, grimacing as various parts of his body registered their complaints.

Wind tugged at the grass around them, and rain continued to fall, driven into his face momentarily by a mischievous gust.

'Then where do you suppose they went from here, if came here they did?' asked Azimandro in a more emollient tone.

He was aware that the cleric's flabby body contained a sharp mind, that the man was too well connected to risk thoroughly alienating.

'Where would *you* go?' asked Taradon, turning in his saddle to survey the view on all sides, wiping rain from his eye. 'We can surely rule out the village and its immediate environs. We are left with the Drumogari settlement out yonder or the skirts of the woods higher up. It seems unlikely she would seek refuge amongst *those* people, a girl of her class...'

'But they might have run into the woods', finished Azimandro, frowning.

'They might', agreed Taradon.

'They wouldn't get far, I should think', grunted the general, peering up along the slope to where the isolated oaks and pines gave way to increasingly dense woodland as the hill rose higher to the south.

'I agree', nodded Taradon. 'I don't suppose there was time to obtain provisions. But it may be wise to engage the services of the local huntsmen who know these parts', he noted, holding up his hands amongst the raindrops and squinting skyward. 'I doubt if dogs will find our quarry's scent in this, but their masters will surely know the ways amongst the woods. There will be signs, perhaps, that skilled men might detect'.

'You are right', agreed Azimandro, spurring his horse away now with a sudden thunder of hoofbeats, adding over his shoulder in a shout, 'And there is no time to be lost'.

'You cried out last night', observed Radda to Stilli the next morning as they readied their packs and stretched aching limbs in preparation for the new day's exertions. It was cold, but the sky was clear and a gentle east wind stirred the branches of the pines above them.

'I did?' Stilli asked. 'I am sorry if I woke you. I had a strange dream'.

'They say dreams are places where our world and that of the divine approach most nearly', noted her friend when Stilli had described it to her. 'And the wall between those worlds may be thinner in such places. I am sorry that you saw what you saw... with your mother.

Small wonder you cried out. However, I suppose your inner mind wished to picture what happened to her after you left. But the lion... the winged lion, that is...'

A distant look came into Radda's eye.

'And you say you have seen this before?' she enquired further.

'Yes, just once', agreed Stilli, looking up from where she had been examining various thorn pricks on her shin. 'Do you consider it significant?'

'And your religion has taught you nothing of your own god's twin, he with whom the whole world is contested, in a battle that may last as long as the word endures? You know nothing of that?'

'I know very well', answered Stilli. 'I saw Tio. We are taught that he is evil, a seducer of weak minds, a speaker of honeyed words and the sure path to perdition if we are tempted to follow him. His name I know, but we do not speak of him'.

'Then follow him you did, in that dream, for Tio's symbol is the winged lion'.

'We must take it in turns to stand guard duty tonight', Axilo instructed Stilli coldly when they were moving once more.

He strode next to her, where the way broadened, and regarded her in a manner that challenged her to deny it. 'I took turns with Mull last night,' he continued, 'but we cannot sustain it indefinitely. It is not fair. Even your idiot friend must take his turn', he added with a nod for Tye, who walked behind them, whistling very softly to himself. 'Although Tio knows I shall not trust to *his* vigilance'.

'You are right', agreed Stilli, feeling a surge of irritation. 'And I shall take my turn, no doubt. I do not expect to be treated differently because of my... status'.

'Because you are a fine lady of the race that oppresses my own?' sneered Axilo.

'Because I am Stilitha', snapped Stilli, regarding him with narrowed eyes. 'I am not a race personified, not a concept nor a graven image on which you may focus your spite'.

'Are you not?' laughed Axilo bitterly. 'Then perhaps you would see things a little differently were we to exchange places. Perhaps if your own mother was cruelly...'

'Do not speak to me of mothers', retorted Stilli. 'I too know what it is like to see my mother die because of the Hierarchy. I hear that *you* ran away, abandoning yours to her grisly fate. It was little different in my own case'.

'I would have died, had I stayed!' cried Axilo, his face darkening.

'And so would I', replied Stilli. 'In that we are equal'.

'We will never be equal', snorted Axilo, striding ahead to where Mull awaited them at the top of a rise.

'He is an angry fellow, that one', said Tye from at her shoulder. 'I don't doubt that I shall have to fight him one day, in order to preserve your honour'.

'You are very kind', murmured Stilli, 'and I thank you for your consideration, but perhaps you will allow me to be the judge of that. It may not necessarily be to my advantage, or indeed to yours'.

She had called herself Stilitha, in that brief heated exchange.

That involuntary act, borne of instinct rather than deliberation, caused her to reflect on her identity as the hours passed and the sun rose higher in the sky beyond the interminable forest. At Radda's home and upon their arrival with the charcoal-burners, Stilli had been required to state her name, but on those occasions it had been entirely automatic. She had stood before them as the embodiment of a story that she must tell, in order to beg their indulgence and their assistance in her flight. Besides, Radda and Mull already knew her as Stilli. It would have been strange to have introduced herself otherwise. On this occasion, though, it had been different. Axilo already knew that story. She might very easily have said *because I am Aramantha*, but she had not done so. She might *be* that doomed child, but the name would never be more than one truth amongst many within her, a pebble on the beach of her existence. The name would never shoulder its way to the forefront of her mind and make that mind its own. She remained Stilitha, moulded and formed by the thirteen years that she had borne that name, even though it was that of the other, the child who had gone to the flames in her stead. She feared, as she trudged onward, that there would need to be a reckoning between her and Axilo before long. For this group to survive, it must surely depend on perfect amity amongst them, perfect unity of purpose; otherwise, they would fall victim to those who so earnestly sought them. Axilo's evident dislike for Stilli, and her own reciprocation in this regard, surely endangered all of them. It was not long before the crisis came upon them.

'I suppose we shall fight our enemies, if we must fight', Axilo had stated in reply to a comment made by Radda. 'Mull has his bow and I have my sword. Stilli likewise has her sword', he added with a scornful glance for her. The party had paused for their first halt of the day, to rest aching legs and to eat more of their cold provisions. There could be no fire, of course, and thus no warming porridge could be made from the oats that they all carried. Stilli had begun to long for a taste of it, even though a week ago she would have turned her face from such meagre peasant fare.

'And she is trained in its use, unlike me', she heard whilst stirring from her torpor.

'Huh?' she muttered, turning to him.

'Perhaps Stilli would care to share with me the benefit of her training', Axilo continued, his voice superficially friendly but bearing within it a harder note, a menace that he could not conceal.

He pulled out his sword from where it necessarily hung, wrapped in oilskin across his back, given that he possessed neither belt, baldric nor scabbard.

'I'm sure I could learn much at the feet of the master, or the mistress, one might say'.

He had the bright blade exposed now, and he cut the air before him meaningfully.

'Do oblige me, Stilitha', he continued. 'Or perhaps you prefer not to demonstrate this... skill... of yours. I'm sure we would all draw our own conclusions from that', he added with a scornful laugh.

'As you wish', she grumbled resignedly, drawing her own blade from its scabbard.

It seemed that the only way to lance the boil of the resentment that had arisen between them was to settle matters in this way. Axilo evidently assumed that he would thereby instil in her a proper sense of her own physical and moral inferiority, given that his opponent was demonstrably smaller and physically weaker than he. Stilli could not discount the possibility that these factors might prove her undoing, but a seething anger enlivened her movements as she turned to face him – and Bondorin's lessons would surely offer her some advantage. She had been a good student, a talented student, he had said. Now she advanced, tight-lipped, to put this to the test.

In truth, Axilo was much in need of instruction. Having never previously wielded such a weapon, he had no clear sense of how it should be employed, other than what his fancy told him. Evidently, one could swipe it around oneself in a showy way, and likewise it was obvious that broad cutting movements could be attempted, in the hope of injuring or otherwise incapacitating one's opponent. Alternatively, the sharp point of the blade might be employed in a vigorous stabbing movement, aimed at the throat and torso.

Of course, Axilo was strong and quick in his movements, but once Stilli had mastered her initial apprehension, she perceived that the advantage lay with her. Naturally, she must be wary lest a stumble place her at his mercy, but thanks to Bondorin's instruction she knew how each scything or lunging attack must be opposed. In many cases, the solution lay in stepping backwards, sideways or simply ducking to avoid the approaching steel. Where the weight or the direction of the blow warranted it, she could intercept his blade and use its own impetus to turn it aside. For now, she made no attacks of her own, except for an occasional feint to test her opponent's reactions. The glade rang with the clash of steel on steel and with Axilo's loud curses as he strove to pierce her defence. The others in the party looked on in dismay, having had their urgent pleas for the combatants to desist ignored. Axilo and Stilli existed now in a web of flashing, clashing metal, in which any misjudgement might bring death or injury to the other. Despite the superiority of her technique, Stilli felt the strength draining from her, and her sword was now becoming heavier in her hand. She must end it – and end it soon. With this realisation came another, that she must reach for that strange power to slow time that lay within her. It had come to her uninvited, unexpected, in the past, but she knew where to find it, where in her mind she must reach. She reached, she summoned, and in that moment her vision was fringed with the curious yellow tinge that signalled her success.

Axilo's blade swung with unnatural slowness now. It was simplicity itself to dodge aside, watch it glide past, reach its apogee and come down once more with no greater success. She smiled to see Axilo's features distorted with the fury of frustration as his heaving, darting, lunging sword moved impotently around her like a gentle metallic ballet. But she was tiring. The yellow at the edges of her vision began to flicker, whilst time, accordingly, stuttered in its progress. She saw that the moment was ripe to draw a line under this exercise. Axilo's blade, thrust with a determination borne of rage, quested for her throat. Engaging her own blade with his, she eased it aside and made a thrust of her own. The yellow tinge vanished, the world continued in its usual motions and Axilo toppled forward with a cry, his sword falling from his hand.

'What have you done?!' gasped Radda in shocked astonishment, rushing to kneel at his side. 'Have you killed him?'

Axilo groaned as she and Mull gently turned him over, to find that her blade had scored his ribs beneath his left arm. The fabric of his tunic and shirt was sliced cleanly and there was a great deal of blood.

'Here, help me strip this off', instructed Radda, turning to Mull, having cautiously probed the wound. 'He will live, I think. I have needle and thread, but I do not have the sort with which flesh might be mended. It is not too deep, however. It may well knit without'.

'Careful, careful!' gasped Axilo as the two eased the bloodied garment over his head.

'I'm sorry', cried Stilli, sinking to her own knees before him. 'I did not wish...'

Axilo could find no words, it appeared. His face was tightly contorted with pain. He did not meet her eye.

'We will need some *widow's fingers* and some *mallow-wort*', Radda instructed Mull, tearing a strip from her underskirt. 'Herbs; ones that may staunch the wound and prevent corruption from setting in. They generally grow about streams. Is there one nearby, do you think?'
'We passed one a little way back', replied Mull with a wondering sidelong glance for Stilli.

If Stilli had expected that she might feel jubilant in her victory over Axilo, she was to be disappointed. The sour taste of shame was in her mouth. In truth, he had been pitifully easy to vanquish, and she regretted that pride had induced her to rise to his challenge. She saw now that the "celerity," as she had come to think of it, was an advantage of real significance. It was quite obvious that there was something quite different about her, something that set her apart from her fellow man, and this filled her with a sense of foreboding. What did it mean? What purpose did it serve, and whose purpose? She began to wonder whether this curious ability and the manifestation of Tio's lion in her dream were in some way connected.
The bout had left her utterly drained of energy and a fierce pain had seized her limbs, occasioned, she supposed, by the necessity of her muscles moving with such unnatural speed. She felt as though those in her calves had been torn, rubbing these distractedly now to ease their cramps as she watched Mull and Tye tend to her defeated opponent. Meeting her eyes, Mull shook his head.
Foolish, his glance seemed to say. *Foolish*.
Stilli could not deny it. She could only sit upon the damp earth, regarding events dully as Radda returned from her quest, took out a wooden bowl from her pack and began making a crushed pap of the small dark

leaves she had brought, grinding them with the back of a spoon and adding a little water from her flask.

''Bleeding's eased off a little', observed Mull, pulling aside the makeshift bandages to inspect the wound. 'I suppose it will knit. It's not as bad as it looks'.

'It had better', grunted Radda. 'Since I have not the means to stitch it'.

Whilst Axilo lay back on a mossy bank, propped on blanket packs, Radda gently covered the exposed wound with the poultice she had made, dabbing it with the unbloodied parts of his shirt and finally binding it once more with fresh cloth.

'I had not taken you for a physician', said Mull as she stepped back to wipe her hands on her skirt. 'Although, I suppose your mother will have taught you. That will work, do you think?'

'It works on my goats', murmured Radda with a grim smile. 'But he will need to rest whilst the wound knits, and neither should he move, perhaps, until tomorrow'.

'Oh'.

Mull scratched his head glumly and looked back along the trail they had travelled.

There was nothing to do but wait. Axilo remained mute, his face pale with pain as Radda's poultice did its work. Mull stationed himself some way away from the party along the track, from where he could keep watch for any signs of pursuit. Tye sat next to Axilo and chewed on a piece of dried goat meat, speaking cheerfully about trivial wounds he had known, until a sharp word from Radda enjoined silence upon him. Radda, having seen Axilo fall into an uneasy sleep, settled herself at Stilli's side.

'What was that?' she asked, regarding Stilli seriously. 'What did I see? No one can move with such speed. No one!' she said, shaking her head incredulously.

'You are mistaken', mumbled Stilli, lifting her head wearily. 'It is nothing, a momentary inattention of yours in the shock of the action, that is all'.
'Momentary inattention?! It was more than that, I swear. It was uncanny!'
'Uncanny?'
'Aye. You know what I mean', Radda replied, fixing her with a piercing gaze. 'What *are* you, Stilitha?'

The charcoal-burners' encampment was empty when Azimandro and his troops trudged into it. There were twelve of them along with four huntsmen from the environs of the village and a number of other local volunteers.
'I have never heard speak of this place', announced Middo, who was amongst these volunteers.
'These camps are never occupied for more than a few months', observed one of the huntsmen, tipping back his broad hat. 'Then they move on'.
Taradon, leading his horse next to Azimandro's, regarded Middo curiously. It was surprising to see such evident zeal for Stilitha's capture in this person, given that she was his own half-sister. He must be aware that he sought to assist in her destruction. Surely, his faith must be strong, to set aside all considerations of fraternal affection. Surely, it could not be that he strove to recommend himself to his superiors and so advance his own interests through contributing to his own sibling's belated sacrifice. Or could it? Perhaps, there had been enmity between them. He found himself regarding the youth curiously as Middo told Azimandro of his contempt for these primitive forest dwellers.
'They were here until a few minutes ago', declared one of the huntsmen, emerging from the roundhouse. 'The fire's still well alight,' he noted, glancing about at the

surrounding forest. 'I daresay they are watching us from out there'.

Azimandro scowled and ran a hand over his bald pate.

'Do you propose to pursue them?' asked Taradon mildly.

'I do not', answered Azimandro, slapping his mount's neck. 'They are not our quarry, and time, as I believe you have mentioned, is of the essence'.

He turned to the sergeant who stood at his side, indicating the dwelling.

'You may put a torch to this, though, and perhaps they will be less shy in future when their betters come calling'.

Nothing could be more certain than that burning down their house would only serve further to increase the "shyness" of these people, reflected Taradon, as flaming torches were applied to the walls, quite apart from causing them to nourish an abiding resentment in their hearts. He sniffed and beckoned towards Middo, who stepped forward eagerly.

'Tell me more of your sister... step-sister', he corrected himself, upon noting the gathering frown in the youth's countenance.

He supposed a step-sister might more readily be condemned to a fiery death than a person with whom he shared full consanguinity.

'Yes, Your Worship', said Middo as the party moved off in a direction indicated by a huntsman at the edge of the clearing. 'She always struck me as in some way out of place in my family, although naturally I had no idea that her mere existence was an offence in the eyes of God. How could I?'

'I'm sure no blame attaches to you personally', Taradon assured him wearily. 'And doubtless your... diligence will be rewarded in due course'.

The next morning dawned grey and cold with clouds massing heavy in the north. Radda, having inspected Axilo's wound, announced that he should be able to move on. He was eager to do this, as he was much improved in spirits after Radda's poultice had worked upon the wound. Nevertheless, he was stiff in his movements, and it would be necessary for the others in the party to share the weight of his burden.

'Do you still believe we are being pursued?' asked Mull of Stilli as they gathered their belongings together.

'I do not know', admitted Stilli. 'My head and my heart have nothing to say. Perhaps they will have lost our trail long ago. Perhaps they are going from house to house throughout the province'.

'Well, I think we should risk a small fire, just for a little while', said Mull. 'It would do us all good to get a little warm porridge inside of us, and we would walk the better for it, I don't doubt'.

All agreed, seduced by the prospect of warm food, and Mull showed them where the driest sticks might be found, under deep thickets and in the sheltered places beneath fallen trees. Before long, Radda had her tinderbox out and a good blaze alight, above which a kettle of water could be suspended from a cradle of longer sticks. Stilli found saliva gathering in her mouth in anticipation as she stirred hot water into her bowl to form a glutinous paste, adding dried fruit and a little of the sweet, crumbled root of *bankfarrow* that Radda had found amongst the tangled roots of the oldest oaks.

'This is really very good', smiled Tye, looking about him happily. 'I swear I never tasted better porridge'.

For once, his remarks brought neither censure nor harsh glances. Warm food filled bellies and hearts with a general benevolence and optimism. Even Axilo, who bore his pain bravely, murmured agreement with him.

The fire made little smoke, and the making of their breakfast took less than an hour, all told. Stilli came across to where Axilo sat, whilst Mull scouted the route ahead and Radda busied herself with cleaning the pots at the nearby stream. Tye had been induced to assist her. By common, unspoken agreement, Stilli was left behind with Axilo, in order that they might compose their differences.

'I am sorry that I hurt you', she said cautiously, averting her eyes from his.

'Nor do *I* rejoice in it', he told her, and then, after a moment, in a softer voice. 'Nor blame *you*'.

She raised her eyes to his, to find that he looked upon her calmly and with no hint of resentment. His mouth twitched upward in one corner as he suppressed a wry smile.

'Nevertheless', she said, 'I am sorry for it'.

'I heard the others say that there is something uncanny about the speed in which you move', replied Axilo, stretching his shoulder cautiously. 'As though you were in the grip of some magic. Indeed, I could barely follow your movements. You were a blur, like the wings of a hummingbird'.

Stilli perceived that this was an attempt to salvage something from the wreck of his self-esteem, having been vanquished by a mere girl, and derived some private enjoyment accordingly. She did not allow this to show in her countenance, though, merely nodding and continuing to regard him watchfully.

'I do not understand what happens to me', she said. 'It has occurred on a few occasions now, and my tutor, Bondorin, taught me to embrace it and turn it to my advantage'.

'He taught you well', acknowledged Axilo, 'and I warrant many a finer swordsman than I might fall to your blade'.

'It is not something I aspire to', said Stilli, thinking that worse swordsmen than Axilo must be a very small category. 'I aspire only to escape from this land and find my way to the Empire at last. In that we are united, I think'.

'We are', conceded Axilo. 'And I was a fool not to see it. Your continued existence is a standing rebuke to Yuzanid and a calamity for his followers'.

'Well, yes', agreed Stilli with a half-smile, 'although I prefer not to be thought merely an instrument of high politics or religion. You will forgive me for claiming a more personal motivation'.

He laughed then, showing his even white teeth and his dark eyes, the latter of which glinted mischievously. It was though a different person sat before her now to the one that had thrust his steel at her throat so murderously.

'Certainly, I will', he agreed. 'And perhaps in a more congenial context, you will teach me a little of your swordsmanship, when you are at leisure to oblige me. No one knows my deficiency better than you, and there is no shame in submitting to the instruction of one whose arm is guided by the divine, perhaps'.

'It will be my pleasure', smiled Stilli in return, and she realised with a sudden warmth in her breast that this was true.

Chapter Thirteen

The party moved on, ever south-eastward, along the wooded skirts of the high mountains that formed the rocky spine of Eudora. The lands to the immediate east were unrewarding to agriculture and peopled only by scattered communities of poor herdsman. The writ of the Hierarchs barely ran there. The potential yields from those lands had never justified the cost of subjecting the people who dwelt there to Yuzanid's yoke. Mull did not know the broken lands, nor indeed the temper of the dwellers within, but he knew the woods and where they approached closest to the sea. It was this place that was their destination, where a stream curled through dismal marshes to where traders came with barges to buy charcoal from Mull's people and to bring them grain, textiles and metal goods in return. Homondril it was called, which meant Rivermead in the ancient language that was still spoken in parts of those regions.
'Three days, perhaps', surmised Mull when Stilli asked him how far they were from this place.
They had emerged onto a slope where the trees were thinner, and the great bowl of the sky could be seen in its entirety, from the mountains to the dim horizon haze where the distant sea must lie. A dark wall of encroaching cloud, surmounted by towering thunderheads, could be seen moving ominously towards them, casting the land into shadow beneath.
'It seems that we shall soon need the rain cloaks once more', predicted Stilli with an anxious skyward glance.
'I'm sure that you are right', agreed Mull. 'And the forest ahead is very dense, quite trackless for some leagues.

We may be best to sit it out until the light permits us to find our way'.

'No', replied Stilli, feeling a curious sensation of impending doom that owed nothing to the evidence of her eyes or ears. 'I think we should push on. I *know* that we should push on', she added, eyes shining with sincerity.

'Very well', replied Mull, regarding her curiously.

He found himself unwilling to contradict a person who appeared to possess supernatural powers.

'There is a long escarpment that crosses our path some way south of here with a cleft on the higher ground up yonder, which we must find in order to pass through it. I trust we shall find it', he added with a skyward glance. 'The light is fading fast'.

The diminishing of that light coincided not only with the thinning of the trees, but also the thickening of the undergrowth beneath them. No path could be discerned there, and so the party must be guided by Mull's experience and instinct alone. Their progress slowed as the rain began and a fierce wind sprang up, blowing into their faces so that the hoods of their cloaks had to be held in place by one hand as they forced their way painfully through mountain gorse and thorn.

'It is not too far ahead, I think', shouted Mull above the sound of the wind, the whip and woody clatter of the low branches of the trees and the fast encroaching roll of thunder.

'What?' roared Axilo, wincing as lightning flashed around them and they stood momentarily starkly exposed.

'The escarpm... the cliffs', bawled Mull, pointing through the trees. 'A mile. Maybe less'.

His subsequent words about the shelter they might find in its lee were entirely swallowed up in a massive thunderclap.

'Here, my Lords', said one of the huntsmen, passing a fragment of torn fabric to Azimandro. 'I think they are not far ahead'.

The horses had been left miles behind now, as the ground conditions had worsened, so the pursuing force necessarily moved on foot.

'What would you say?' asked the general, passing it to Taradon. 'A piece of the hem of a skirt, do you suppose, or shirt, perhaps?'

'Conceivably, but this is certainly freshly torn', agreed Taradon, peering at the fibres along its edge.

He glanced at the darkening sky.

'And perhaps they will encamp now as this storm approaches'.

'Then we shall not', growled the general. 'We shall certainly not'.

'The light is fading', warned the huntsman as thunder rumbled over the hills. 'And there is no clear track ahead. We may blunder past them in the dark'.

The general glared into the growing gloom amongst the trees. Then, having made his decision, he turned to the long file of men behind him.

'We will split into pairs across this broad slope!', he roared. 'Each within hailing range of the next. In that way we shall cover a greater distance. These shall be the dispositions...'

'Are you sure this is wise?' Taradon asked, plucking at the huge man's sleeve. 'Dispersing in this way...'

'Do you choose to question my authority?' bellowed Azimandro, turning a belligerent glare upon him.

Taradon did not, and any detailed objections he might have advanced perished on his lips as Azimandro gave his instructions.

Initially, these dispositions appeared sound enough, as each pair could be seen by their neighbours at intervals through the branches of the intervening trees. The chief of the huntsman continued to walk with Azimandro, Taradon and their servants. Should they need to concentrate their force once more, a series of blasts on the huntsman's great horn would announce this order. However, this arrangement soon proved itself impracticable when the storm descended upon them, bringing with it almost impenetrable gloom and a howling wind so fierce that any ordinary conversation became impossible, entirely extinguishing any hope of further communication with neighbouring pairs of searchers.

'This is hopeless!' growled Azimandro some indeterminable time later, having edged sideways through a dense thicket.

His furious rain-wet face was intermittently lit by thunderbolts amongst the dark skies.

Taradon, panting at his side, could only bite his lip and keep his remarks about having counselled otherwise to himself.

'We shall all be split up, hopelessly lost', he whispered to himself quite inaudibly. 'Disastrous!'

Stilli was adjusting her soaking clothing, having attended to nature's call, when two dark figures emerged from the howling darkness before her. The rest of the party awaited her a little way ahead, and so she was momentarily quite alone. The strangers perceived her standing there at the same time and cried out, although their voices were almost inaudible amongst the din of rain, wind and thunder. Stilli had her sword drawn and was stumbling backward even as they came crashing through the undergrowth towards her. Lightning flashed.

'Middo!' gasped Stilli as her brother was momentarily brilliantly lit.

'Stilitha!' he cried in the same instant, bringing out his sword. 'I have you!'

A great many thoughts came jostling into Stilli's brain as the two men now warily approached her. Foremost amongst them was shock and resentment that her own brother, albeit half-brother, should seek to compass her destruction. There had never been any affection between them, but even so this violated a great many unwritten laws of fraternal duty. Stilli's mind reeled before the force of it. How appalled would her parents be, could they witness it? A cold fury settled in her.

'You do not', Stilli retorted fiercely, her words whipped away by the wind and the rain.

No further words were necessary. Middo's face was filled with a jubilant determination as he beat away the first swing of her sword blade and stepped closer, his left hand reaching for her, the other man attempting to circle around through the undergrowth to her side.

'Oh, you wish to fight, then?' Middo laughed, his words quite lost to her, but his intention clear enough. 'I suppose they will not mind a wounded captive, although I shall have to be careful not to kill you. Tazman and Draganach await that pleasure'.

A gesture to his companion, one of the steward's men, bade him hold still whilst Middo moved forward to attack his sibling.

Steel clashed on steel, lightning flashing on their blades, as they fenced furiously in the small clearing amongst trees and bushes. There was no sparing of effort on either side, no consideration of their familial connection. Stilli saw quite clearly that every blow she must dodge or turn aside was in deadly earnest and that her brother had every intention of disarming or disabling her. There was no prospect of escape, unless through victory over him. She judged that Middo was less expert than herself, but he was strong and his reach was greater than hers. Surely, she must search her mind for the "celerity" once more, in order that speed of movement might supply what mere strength and endurance could not. She reached there but hesitated, even as she turned another questing blow aside, one that had almost found her throat. To use that power had left her aching and exhausted, as her muscles had made clear their objection to such ill use. Would she find herself prostrate, unable to flee further with her companions? She had resolved, after having deflected a series of furious attacks, that there was no choice but to use it when that choice was taken from her.

Stepping back once more, her heel struck a sturdy root and she stumbled. Middo was upon her in an instant, heaving her onto her back as her sword dropped from her hand.

He then stood above her, his grim face lit suddenly with triumph and his dark eyes gleaming with jubilation as he placed his sword point to her breast.

'You are an offence in the eyes of God and I should kill you now!' he roared. 'But I will not, because the belly of Draganach cries out for you'.

He laughed, but the laugh turned to a whimper of shock, and he glanced down to find that the shaft of an arrow projected from his side. He clutched at it with one hand and then collapsed groaning to his knees, his gaze suddenly vacant. Stilli whipped round to find that Mull stood amongst the bushes behind her, another arrow already nocked to his bowstring. Middo's companion fled, the arrow hissing through the air by his ear.

'Come on!' yelled Mull, reaching for one of her hands, even as the other groped for her fallen sword.

Having rejoined the others, they ran pell-mell after Mull as he led them down a treacherous rain-lashed slope, through a succession of thickets and low trees, until a

great black cliff loomed high above them, girt with creepers and grown with tenacious trees that thrust their roots into any convenient cleft on its sheer flanks.
'Which way?' demanded Axilo as Mull hesitated, peering into the gloom.
'This way, uphill!' he shouted, pointing away along the base of the cliff.
At that moment, a sudden flash of lightning, accompanied by a deafening thunderclap, disclosed a momentary glimpse of running figures, not fifty yards away. It was unclear whether they themselves had been seen.
'In here', gasped Mull, taking Stilli's shoulder and pushing her into the dense thicket of young trees, creepers and bushes that obscured the base of the cliff at this point.
Oblivious to the twigs and prickles that plucked at her face in such profusion, almost blind in the darkness, Stilli pushed madly through the resisting mass until her progress was suddenly arrested by cold stone. At her side, Radda stumbled and then fell, cursing as she did so. Axilo and Tye were somewhere close. Another flash of lightning penetrated the prickly growth and a million sparks of dancing light flickered momentarily on the tumbled stone.
'A cave!' cried Radda, half-standing now by Stilli's feet, pointing at her own. 'Look, there's a cave! Here!'
She quickly dipped and wriggled out of sight. Stilli, after a glance at the others, who were panting at her side by now, stooped, plunged to all fours on the hard earth and squirmed after her friend into total darkness. Within moments, before she could even begin to form impressions of her circumstances, her friends were grunting and scrambling in pursuit of her. It was quite dark; Stilli could not see her hand before her face, but it

was dry beneath her, and the sound of the wind and the thunder was more distant now.

'How big?' asked Mull simply, gauging the size of the space they had entered by the echoes, groping around himself for enclosing walls and running his hand over rough stone where ancient roots were interwoven.

'Feel around you', instructed Axilo, taking his cue from Mull. 'Find the edges'.

'I think we're safe now', suggested Radda, reaching around her. 'I doubt they will find us here. We barely found it ourselves'.

'Well, yes', agreed Mull. 'But let us hope we aren't sharing it with one of the mountain lions that dwell in these parts'.

It was likely, however, that any resident lion would already have made clear its objection to their intrusion into its home. Accordingly, after a moment, the sudden tension subsided.

'Radda's right', agreed Stilli.

A dull flash of lightning from the world outside showed that the entrance was low and long, barely large enough for a person to crawl through. Amongst the dense vegetation outside it was almost miraculous that they had stumbled upon it.

'We must have light', she added, effortful grunting suggesting she was unshouldering her blanket pack. 'I have a small lamp in here and my tinderbox. Tye, you have a little bottle of olive oil in yours, if you'd care to look'.

There was no light at all, apart from the occasional dim flicker from the entrance, so it was by feel alone that those objects were eventually located. By this time, the invisible cave floor about them was thickly strewn with the contents of their packs. At last, the sound of Radda's cursing and of metal being struck repeatedly on flint was succeeded by stifled cries of triumph as sparks took hold on the tow she held ready. A momentary cheerful glow flared in her hands as she hastened to press the flaming tow to the wick in her lamp, filled with oil now, although much had doubtless found its way to the floor. 'There!' she announced triumphantly as the flame steadied in the little lamp, and she held it up before her. The light fell unevenly upon the faces of the fugitives, much relieved faces, and pressed back the darkness beyond. They were in a low part of the cave, a confusion of toppled stone. It was with surprise that they noted that some showed clear evidence of the mason's hand. This became still more apparent as, within a short distance, the space opened into a large chamber. Radda's lamp picked out smooth walls, very evidently carved from the living rock, with engaged columns and pilasters set at intervals. Above, high above, at the furthest edge of the light's reach, a barrel vault could dimly be made out, from which water occasionally dripped about them.

'What is this place?' mused Axilo, glancing upward while squeezing water from his sleeves.

They were in a dry place, but their clothes were nevertheless soaked, and each stood shivering as the little lamp, held here and there, gradually revealed to them the circumstances of their refuge.

'Could it be a temple of some sort?' asked Stilli. 'Do the dwellers in these parts build such things, Mull?'

'They build nothing that they cannot take apart within an hour, when they wish to shift camp', murmured Mull. 'And they are very few. I cannot imagine that they, or even their ancestors, made such a thing'.

It became clear that the structure had collapsed at the entrance side, with the ruin of great slabs and shattered columns blocking all but the narrow space they had scrambled through. The roots of the trees that grew amongst the fallen stone above were intermingled with the confusion of it all.

'And here we have a passage', announced Radda, holding her lamp to the furthest wall of the chamber, where a narrow space of darkness suggested a further space beyond.
Her lamp flickered as she held it out before her to investigate its dimensions.
'There is moving air in there', grunted Axilo. 'I feel it on my face'.
'Indeed', agreed Stilli. 'Perhaps we may find another point of entry, or of exit'.
'We may', concurred Mull, 'but I am wary of such places. I think we should stay here and wait out the storm. It must be full night by now. By dawn, things may look different out there'.
'Surely we should explore it', insisted Tye with his usual cheerful insouciance. 'It will be an adventure'.
It was clear that Mull and Radda were uneasy. However fortunate their discovery of this place had been, it may well be that it harboured evil spirits, perhaps the vengeful shades of the ancient dead.
'Adventure or not, I think we should see where it leads', insisted Axilo after Mull had made plain his superstitious dread.
Radda had kept her silence, but it was quite clear that she shared his anxiety.
'As Stilli suggests,' she began, 'we may find another way out, possibly one that issues forth on the other side of this escarpment. How then would we have frustrated our pursuers? If I understand you clearly, Mull, finding that pass you mentioned and climbing up through this escarpment involves making a considerable detour'.
'It does, too', conceded Mull. 'But I still don't like it. I don't like it one bit'.

'Well, we can't split up', observed Stilli. 'We have only one lamp. We either all stay or we all go'.

'Then we go', decided Axilo. 'We all go'.

There was no further argument, since the logic was clear enough, and even Mull and Radda knew that their unreasoning fear must submit to it. With a shrug and a hard swallow, Mull joined the others in groping for their belongings and restowing their packs as best they could manage in the small pool of light cast by the lamp. Then, with Axilo at their head, they stepped cautiously into the passage, their feet splashing here and there in shallow puddles, from which reflected sparks of light danced on the walls. He held the lamp high in front of him whilst Stilli advanced at his shoulder, sword at the ready, in case they should suddenly be assailed by beasts of this world – or of others that their fevered imaginations proposed.

Upon turning a corner, Radda suddenly cried out.

'See! There is light ahead'.

It was true. Axilo shielded the precious lamp with his hand for a moment, and it could be seen that a cool, dim light penetrated into the passage from some way ahead, where another turn hid the way from them.

'We should go back', counselled Mull. 'I don't like this. What is this strange light? It is unnatural'.

Unnatural it evidently was, and turning that final corner brought the party into another high chamber, clearly disclosed to them by the cold and eerie radiance that the walls of the place emitted. The space was hexagonal in shape, with tall columns set at the angles and a domed, corbelled ceiling with carved rosettes set in the recesses. It was extraordinary to find such architectural sophistication in such a place, but all eyes were drawn immediately to the stepped dais at the centre and to the massive stone tomb that stood there. At some time, a section of the ceiling had fallen away and collapsed upon the tomb, so that its lid was shattered and the space within half exposed. A great carved winged lion had once surmounted the lid, but falling stone had broken it and cast it to the floor, where large fragments of head and wings could be made out amongst the wreckage.

'Tio', breathed Radda and Axilo simultaneously, bowing their heads reverently and making his sign in the air before them.

Mull was asking the pair if Tio's kingdom had extended once to these regions, but Stilli, feeling a strange and irresistible compulsion, picked her way carefully amongst the rubble to the far side of the tomb, where the broken lid and a fallen section of the side exposed the interior to view.

'Stilli!' cried Radda when her cautious advance drew their attention. 'Don't!'

She grabbed at Tye's arm as he made to pursue her.

'It's alright', called Stilli in a strained voice, from where she now stood at the far side of the tomb. 'Come see'.

Stilli remained, as though frozen to the spot, as the others approached reluctantly to stand at her side and to see what she beheld. Within the tomb lay a skeleton, its grinning skull turned to them, its ribs smashed by a large splinter of stone.

'Tio's breath', gasped Radda, turning her own head aside. 'We should not be here. Really, we should not'.

'We should', disagreed Stilli, a strange calmness coming upon her, and with it a sense that her consciousness was expanding to fill this serene space.

She felt her mind open up like a flower on a spring morn to embrace what light – what truth – would come.

'He has a sword exactly like yours', Tye pointed out. 'Look'.

It was true. On the skeleton's further side lay a sword that matched Stilli's, with its plain basket hilt and the decayed remains of what once had been a scabbard.
'It's Bondorin', breathed Stilli. 'I know it is'.
'That's impossible', objected Radda, venturing a cautious glimpse at the skull. 'How can it be? This must be hundreds of years old'.
'I care not. This is he', stated Stilli, reaching down to place a finger on the smooth dome of the skull. 'He who taught me'.
'What was his full name?' asked Axilo, who had now once more made his way round to the front of the tomb.
'Why?' Stilli asked, narrowing her eyes, although the great mass of the tomb came between them.
'Just tell me'.
'Ariniall Bondorin', she replied.
'Then we are faced either with a strange coincidence or... a miracle. Behold!'
The party reassembled next to Axilo, to stare at where he had swept the dust of ages from a simple inscription on the front face of the tomb.
ARINIALL BONDORIN, they read.
'That is... uncanny', gasped Radda.
'He wants me to have it', said Stilli, whose eyes now seemed focused on the middle distance.
'Have what, Stilli?' asked Tye. 'The sword?'
'No, the necklace', she breathed, placing a hand on the cold stone surface of the tomb, to steady herself, and stepping around to the open side once more. 'That necklace', she said, pointing at the skeleton.
'Are you sure?' asked Radda dubiously. 'This doesn't feel right. You can't rob from a tomb. It is unlucky. You may awake the avenging spirit of the dead, whoever that may be'.

'It is *my* Bondorin', Stilli assured her whilst the others looked anxiously amongst themselves. 'And I know this is what he wants'.

It was true. She had never felt any more certain of anything. It was as though Bondorin's spirit stood at her side and he smiled that well-remembered wry smile of his, urging her to pick the necklace from amongst the scattered ribs and vertebrae. The beads therein were dull and dusty, but a tiny image of the winged lion glinted at the skeleton's breast. She reached for it reverently, drawing it from amongst the bones and cautiously blowing dust from it. The larger beads were of a clear yellow amber, the smaller, black, like seeds. She recalled now how Bondorin's shirt had once fallen open at the breast to reveal what was surely this same necklace hanging there.

'What is that golden object I spy there?' she had asked at the time.

'Nothing, child, it is only a trinket', he had answered with a twinkle in his eye, before turning their conversation elsewhere.

'And what about this here gold?' asked Axilo, who had overcome his initial reticence and was poking about where the skeleton's waist had once been. 'I'm guessing this was once his purse. Do you suppose your friend would wish you to have this, too?'

Stilli smiled and placed the necklace over her head.

'Do you know, I believe he would', she said.

Chapter Fourteen

Axilo's hopes proved to be well-founded. A second passage, on the far side of the mausoleum, led tortuously upward with many turns and narrow stairs, finally emerging in a chamber very similar to the first they had entered. Here, likewise, the ceiling had collapsed but a narrow space allowed the party to squeeze through wind-blown bushes and stunted trees onto an open hillside.

The storm had passed on into the south by now, leaving only its ragged skirts racing high above. To their great surprise, it was clear daylight when they stumbled from the tomb, whereas their discovery of it had taken place as night was falling, albeit within the faux night of the storm. Could it really be that they had passed the whole of the night within that place? Was there something about it that altered perceptions of the passage of time? All were pleased to feel the light of open sky upon their faces once more. Most had felt some degree of fear in that strange place, and Radda and Mull had evidently felt terror clutch at their hearts. Only Stilli had seemed immune. She knew in her heart that she had found Bondorin, just as he had once found her. She felt a strange serenity in his tomb, an inner peace that dissipated only slowly in the hours after her departure from his resting place.

To their rear, as they emerged, the escarpment sloped gently upward to where the sheer cliffs began. To their front lay more scattered and open woodland amongst the foothills of the high mountains. It was easy enough to see where their path lay in this more tractable landscape, and by the next day they had reached the broad navigable stream that found its way down to the sea at last. Here, about the water meadows on the skirts of the forest, the charcoal-burners were accustomed to sell their wares to the bargemen, and here a little of Bondorin's gold bought them passage downstream, amongst sacks of charcoal that another clan of Mull's people had recently taken there.

'Let them find us now', laughed Axilo as the barge, managed with long poles, nosed out into the slow current.
Stilli nodded, looking back across the riverside mead to where the forest and the hills gave way to the high mountains at last. Could it really be that they had eluded their pursuers? She expected, at any moment, to see riders emerge from amongst the trees and gallop down to the reed-bound banks of the stream.
'They'll never follow us this way', observed Mull, as though reading her thoughts. 'Not unless they have a boat of their own. It's a trackless waste out there. No paths, dense bush. Nary a soul 'cept the few fisher folk with their traps and nets'.
'And where does this great river take us, pray?' asked Tye, perched comfortably on a sack. 'To the ocean, I suppose. How I long to gaze upon the ocean!'
'You shall', laughed Mull. 'And at Shangharad, too. That's the town at the mouth of this river'.
'Do tell me of it', pressed Tye excitedly.
'I would if I could', admitted Mull. 'But I have never travelled this far'.
Stilli nodded. Mull had assured her that the writ of Tazman did not extend there, but her eyes clouded nevertheless. It would be a disappointment to have made this great odyssey, only to find herself arrested upon arrival there. She found that her companions had

begun to regard her with a kind of superstitious awe since her demonstration of the "celerity" and her strange behaviour in the tomb. She could hardly blame them for such an alteration in their relationship, since she had become almost a stranger to herself. The sensations she had felt, the thoughts that had come into her mind since her departure from her native village, had caused her to feel a curious distance from the world that she must necessarily inhabit. It was as though she walked in a dream, albeit the dream intersected with the real world around her.

After the great urgency of their earlier travels, it was wonderful to lie amongst the cargo and watch as the flat wetland landscape passed slowly by on either side. Their clothing stood in clear need of repair, after having being assailed by thorns and prickles of every kind in their passage through the woods. Of necessity, Radda, Mull and Stilli took turns to ply Radda's needle busily as the hours passed. Tye was naturally excluded from this task through his incompetence, as was Axilo, who set himself instead to washing and drying their few garments in the stream, hanging them to dry amongst the rigging of the barge.

'I suppose we shall need to conceal these baubles', observed Stilli, looking up from where she had been counting out the remaining coins.

'I don't doubt it', agreed Radda, threading her needle once more. 'And I don't doubt that you will wish to add to your wardrobe when we arrive at Shangharad', she added, a wry smile accompanying this remark, since Stilli was wearing only an arrangement of empty sacks, and most of her garments blew briskly on the shroud behind her.

A bargeman came clomping past to adjust the great white sail that was hoisted when the wind permitted, and Stilli closed her hands over the coins warily. When he was gone, she held one up to examine it, as she had already done on many occasions.

The coins were quite fascinating. All identical, each a thumb's breadth wide with a finely rendered image of Tio's lion on one side and that of a crowned figure on the other, bearing a sword and a sceptre. The encircling inscription included the word "Niallo" amongst other characters, which meant nothing to her or to her companions.

'I never saw a finer thing', Radda told her. 'Nor did these fellows', she noted, a twitch of her head indicating the crew, 'if their gaping mouths were anything to go by. It's as well you showed them only two. They will be asking themselves how raggedy folks such as us came by them'.

'You're right', agreed Axilo, coming to sit beside them. 'There will be plenty who may wish to part you from them. You should hide them'.

'Hide them where?' asked Radda, head tilted to one side.

'Somewhere no one will look and which we may always have with us', suggested Axilo pensively.

His eye fell upon Stilli, who had noticed that his glance lingered upon her form more than mere chance might explain. She tucked a bare calf and foot out of sight beneath a fold of sacking, feeling a warm flush in her cheeks that was not unpleasurable. She found that she did not resent it – to the contrary, in fact. Likewise, she had found her own gaze drawn to his broad, pale shoulders as he scrubbed at their garments, to the strong curve of his jaw and the wavy dark hair that curled about his brow.

Radda sighed in resignation, having considered Axilo's conundrum, and proposed that the remaining nine coins might be sewn into the waistband of her skirt.

'They'll be safe enough there', she chuckled. 'It's been a while since anyone showed any sign of wishing to discover anything in those regions'.

'Oh, Radda!' laughed Stilli in shock whilst the others looked upon her unlovely form with varying degrees of awkwardness.

'Unless we're a-sailing to the kingdom of the blind!' giggled Radda, making a pretence of reaching blindly about her.

It took two days for the barge to make its way along the meandering course of the river to the sea. On occasion, the vessel had required to be poled or floating off, when the shifting of sandbanks, consequent upon the recent tempest, caused it to lodge upon unseen shallows. Despite having being required to assist the crew on these occasions, it had been a time of rest for the party after days of walking. It was a time during which Stilli celebrated her eighteenth name day, officially coming of age, although it passed by quite unremarked. How she would have marvelled a year ago, if she had been able to see into the future to this day and to the circumstances of her spending it. The weather, although cold, remained dry. Stilli was often lost in her thoughts during this time, inattentive to the chatter of her companions or to the landscape that drifted slowly by on either side. Her mind, having been oppressed with a succession of unexpected terrors in the past days, valued the time to digest these experiences and to subject them to a more leisurely scrutiny. She must mourn for her mother, of course, and the life that she had lost, the life that must necessarily be placed irrecoverably behind her. In addition, she must adjust herself to the notion that her own sibling had sought to destroy her. Their relationship had never been marked by affection, but it was still deeply shocking to know that his enmity towards her approached such intensity. It was possible that he was dead now, of course. Not knowing this added further to her disquiet.

'I hope he is', grunted Mull when Stilli discussed it with him. 'The wicked dog cost me two of my best goose-fletched arrows'.
Dead or not, it was hard not to feel some vestigial regret at the loss of what little family remained to her.

And then there was the necklace. Secreted in her bundle, in order that it may not excite the envy of the crew, Stilli had nevertheless brought it out on many occasions to examine it. Once cleaned of the dust that had dulled it, the clear yellow beads seemed to be made of some kind of glass, adorned with tiny specks of air trapped within. There were just eight of these but many more black ones – much smaller, perfectly round and about the size of a dried pea. The golden-winged lion that hung at the necklace's lowest point was only the size of a fingernail but rendered with the same exquisite attention to detail as those images on the coins. Stilli had only to hold it in her hands to feel a sense of calm reassurance come upon her. Her mind dwelt often on Bondorin and the times she had spent with him. What did it mean, this strange relationship with the living manifestation of a man who had clearly died many centuries previously? Had he been a ghost? He had seemed solid enough.
'It doesn't make sense', Axilo told her when she discussed this matter with him, 'and it makes my head hurt to think of it. My advice to you is not to think of it. It will only cause your rational mind to be uneasy'.
'I think it is Tio's work', Tye suggested. 'I have always been taught that I must revere Yuzanid, but I cannot bring myself to believe that you, dear Stilli, must die to please him'.
'What are you saying?' teased Stilli. 'Are you saying that you have transferred your allegiance from Yuzanid to Tio?'

'Well, no', replied Tye sadly, shaking his head. 'Because that must surely damn my soul to perdition in all eternity. But I find that my mind is oppressed with confusion. The future is obscure to me'.

'Never mind', soothed Stilli, squeezing his hand. 'It is to us all. At least you shall live to see the ocean'.

'That is true', agreed Tye, brightening at the thought. 'And I shall see it at your side'.

They all saw the ocean the following day, when the slow current brought them around a bend in the broad stream and the measureless sparkling expanse of the sea opened before them. The taste of salt was on their lips and in their nostrils, the sound of gulls in their ears.

'It is certainly very large', breathed Tye, causing all to smile around him.

'It is', agreed Axilo, 'and it is the way that will carry us home at last'.

In order to travel that way, it was certain that they would need to secure passage on an ocean-going vessel. The port stronghold of Shangharad soon loomed up to their left, beyond sandbars, and it was from there that such a ship must be sought. The town itself was situated on a rocky spur that rose abruptly from the salt marshes at the mouth of the river. The shifting sandbars, known only to its inhabitants, made it secure from attack from the sea, except by a narrow channel, guarded by great guns housed in emplacements at its seaward end. To approach from the landward side, one must necessarily traverse a narrow isthmus of dry land, on which a strong wall had been built. Surely, a large and determined army with ample provisions might hope to capture the place, but no such legion had ever made the attempt. Nor would one ever, if its shrewd ruler, Count Gradivin, had his way. He usually did.

'Gradivin, aye, he's a fair terrifying prospect', laughed the chief of the barge-traders when questioned on this point. 'With his hair all waxed and starched around him and his eye-sockets painted black as pitch. He may not be a devil from the pit, but he surely does cultivate a resemblance'.

'Likes to put the fear of hell into everyone around him', observed his mate, spitting over the side and fixing his gaze on the still-distant settlement.

'Anyone but a fool fears him', nodded the chief. 'And there's always a few wretches' bones and skulls hung about the walls to serve as reminders, in case you're forgettin''.

'I see', murmured Axilo, doing his best to sound undaunted. 'And I suppose he welcomes visitors?'

The bargeman's mate only laughed and spat over the gunwale once more.

There was no difficulty in gaining entrance to the port of Shangharad, since the river wharves were busy with traders and others whose livelihoods depended on commerce. Tye stood at the edge of the wharf and looked out past the swaying masts of fishing vessels to the palm-fringed shores beyond.

'It is astonishing', he gasped wide-eyed, and then to a startled passer-by. 'How fortunate you are to dwell in such a place, sir'.

The man, bearing a basket of fish on his shoulder, showed little sign of being convinced of his good fortune. He only turned to fix Tye with a wondering stare.

'Where do travellers stay?' asked Stilli of a fellow seated upon an upturned barrel, mending a net. 'Is there an inn you can recommend?'

There were various places within the walls that rose up behind the wharves, it appeared, and before the gates various market stalls had been set up, together with the benches used by moneylenders and changers. Here, they found a trader willing to exchange one of their gold coins for a quantity of others more suitable for securing accommodation or for other small purchases. The man first looked upon it with narrowed eyes, bit it speculatively and showed it to a group of his colleagues, before demanding to know where they had come across it.

'Found it', Radda told him with a defiant glare. 'Although I don't suppose it's any of your business. Do you want it or not?'

He did want it. He was very keen to acquire it, in fact, having never seen such an extraordinary coin, and he was eventually persuaded to part with a handful of silver and copper currency in exchange.

'Surely, now we will be able to charter one of these fine vessels and sail away to Erenor', declared Tye, looking upon these and then at the various flimsy or dilapidated fishing boats tied up or anchored in the harbour.

'I don't know much about the sea', admitted Axilo, 'but I doubt any of these are fit for an ocean voyage. We shall have to ask about such things'.

'I'm sure we must', agreed Stilli, looking up from where she had been poking amongst the strange miscellany of foreign coins that nestled in Radda's palm. 'But I'm sure we must find somewhere to stay first'.

'I don't care for the way that money-changer's talking behind his hand to that ill-looking fellow with the yellow teeth', observed Mull, looking over his shoulder as they walked away. 'He asked if we had any more of those gold pieces, and no doubt he's thinking there is something very odd about us'.

'Well there is, I suppose', agreed Stilli as they approached the town gate. 'None odder. And it seems that we must pay a toll to enter'.

An official, sitting at a bench guarded by two bored soldiers, held out his hand to them and accepted the two brass coins that Radda had seen others part with in return for their entrance. Stilli felt the man's eyes settle upon her curiously as she hastened past, but any questions he might have thought to pose were stifled as a fellow with a mule began loudly contesting the unreasonable price charged for his beast's entry, pointing out that another official had waived the charge altogether only a week ago.

The soldiers stirred from their torpor in order to grin at their superior's discomfiture as the mule-owner's voice rose an octave and an interested queue formed slowly behind him.

It was hard to understand the strange accents of the people they spoke to in the streets, and indeed Vhanakhori was only one of a score of tongues spoken there. However, sign language and loud repetition served its purpose, and eventually they were directed to a lodging house that opened onto one of the narrow side streets on either side of the main thoroughfare. Here, they were unenthusiastically greeted by an ancient crone, bearing a single tooth in her lower jaw, and shown to an upstairs room where various straw pallets lay about the floor. Having parted with more coins and been warned about their conduct whilst staying there, more pallets were provided until there was one for each of them. A bowl and a jug of water stood on a shelf in one corner, whilst a number of hooks in the wall provided for the hanging of their clothes. There was a strong smell of stale cooking and unwashed bodies.

'It has a fine view of the street', announced Tye, opening the shutter. 'And a most interesting aroma. Is that the harbour I discern, between the tower and the... place of execution?'

The party set down their burdens and sprawled upon their pallets, considering the last mentioned of these features.

In the space between the walls and the first houses, they had passed a gallows on which hung a dozen or so corpses in various states of decay. Each of the party, with the possible exception of Mull, was well-used to the sight of dead bodies, but, nevertheless, it was sobering to be confronted with them in such casual profusion. Neither did the passers-by in the street spare them a second glance. Stilli wondered what kind of people dwelt there, whether the remaining gold would be sufficient to buy passage on an ocean-going ship. Axilo had agreed with her that the Empire was many miles away, separated from them by the whole of the island of Eudora as well as the broad Sea of Ormaris. A trading vessel heading in that direction could either travel north, on a route that would bring it eventually round Cape Stromengar with its cliffs and lethal tides, or south around Cape Lial. The latter route would take it through The Narrows, the stretch of water that lay between the great city of Nahleen on the mainland and Tazman itself, facing her commercial rival across the water. Naturally, to pass this close to the citadel of their enemies was not something to be contemplated with an easy mind, and so the northerly route was to be preferred, if opportunity allowed. For now, though, the party could think of little but hot food as the gallows receded in their minds.

'Perhaps you would stay here to guard our possessions', said Stilli to Tye, 'whilst we go to spy out the land and see where the market lies. We shall certainly need to buy fabrics to add to our wardrobe, and we shall bring back something to eat from some of those stalls we passed on our way here. I believe the privy is located under the stairs', she added, perceiving this enquiry as his mouth opened.

Although Shangharad was not a large town, it was a veritable metropolis when compared with Zoramanstarn or the Drumogari village. Stilli and her friends must take care not to gawp as they looked around them and thereby mark themselves unmistakeably as visitors. It was for this reason that Stilli had thought it best to leave Tye at their lodgings. He was almost certain to gaze in transparent wonder about him, any kind of subterfuge or self-restraint being foreign to his nature. Besides, he was the most natural creature in the world with his thoughts perfectly plain upon his countenance and in his demeanour. It was decided that Axilo, as the tallest and the eldest in appearance amongst them, should assume the role of their leader in case they should need to explain themselves. Stilli, whose face and deportment raised certain questions about her status as a "boy," had to take care not to draw attention to herself, particularly since she declined to leave her sword with Tye.

'What did he mean, *what's brought in*?' asked Mull when they had questioned a number of what they took to be mariners outside an inn by the wharves.
'Were you not attending on the barge?' asked Axilo with a laugh. 'This place is a notorious nest of pirates. He means what ships the pirates have captured out there on the ocean. This place sits aside a trade route between Toxandria and the lands to the north and east'.
'Of course', nodded Mull. 'That makes sense. But where are their ships now?'
'We must presume they are out at sea, preying like wolves upon peaceful commerce', smiled Stilli, glancing out to where a decayed mast-less hulk could be seen

lying on its side, half sunk in sand on the far side of the harbour.

Beyond that, a low grey fort was no more than a silhouette amongst distant palms as the sun settled towards the purpling horizon.

By the time they returned to their room, it was already almost dark and lamps were being lit in the mean houses of the poorer people that crowded in upon the narrow streets. In addition to the various fabrics they had purchased for making garments, they also carried a covered bowl containing stew, from which a delicious aroma arose. This was immediately forgotten, however, when they pushed open the door to find that Tye was not alone.

'Oh, there you are!' he proclaimed while standing up, his face wreathed in smiles. 'Allow me to introduce you to Assistant Secretary Benedil Baradian...' he began, turning to the man next to him. 'I have that right, do I not? Mr Baradian is an important official in this fine city'.

'Delighted to make your acquaintance, I'm sure', said Baradian with a low bow and a knowing smile that filled Stilli with apprehension. 'And my colleagues, Cohil and Stane'.

Two bulky, unsmiling men with an air of readiness to resort to violence about them twitched their heads in response.

'Tye here has told me much of your adventures' continued Baradian.

'Has he?' asked Axilo warily, sparing the last-named a critical glance.

'Oh, yes. It has been a most illuminating discussion, most illuminating indeed'.

Chapter Fifteen

It appeared that they had been followed from the town gates. The magnificent gold coin that Stilli had exchanged for small change had excited suspicion as much as wonder. Now, Baradian was keen to discover if they had any more such coins and interested to hear the story of their journey.

'Your friend here tells me that you came across an ancient tomb in the hills to the west of here', said Baradian. 'He also tells us that you are refugees from our friends the Hierarchs beyond the mountains and the woods. We receive so few visitors from that quarter, and so I'm sure my master, Count Gradivin, would be delighted to make your acquaintance'.

Stilli, whose stomach had twisted within her to see these newcomers with Tye, swallowed hard, a sour taste in her mouth. What more might Tye have disclosed to these men in his innocence?

'Certainly we have a few more such coins', agreed Axilo, stepping forward when it seemed that all others in his party were entirely nonplussed by this unlooked-for development. 'And we would be delighted to present them as a gift to the count, in return for his hospitality. All have heard of his benevolence and his justice, even in my own remote village'.

For a moment, Stilli felt alarm at this rash disposal of their funds, sensing a similar disquiet amongst Radda and Mull as they stood at her shoulder. But only for a moment. She quickly saw that Axilo was correct. They were at the mercy of Baradian and these men. They might readily be beaten or tortured unless the man felt confident that he had their full cooperation. But first it must be established that these fellows were true representatives of the count and not merely opportunists claiming to act in his name.

'But it would be fitting if we were to make this gift in person', added Stilli, having quickly considered these things. 'If the good count will be so gracious as to grant us an audience', she added, at the same time allowing her hand to move slowly across her belly, where it lay within reach of her sword hilt.

A twitch of Baradian's eye showed that he recognised this declaration of intent.

'He may well favour you with one', said Baradian, a man of medium stature with a squarish face and a neatly trimmed black beard. 'Particularly, when he hears that you are such a prodigious master of swordplay. Yes', he added with a smile. 'Tye has told us much of your skill'. He stepped towards her and looked her up and down in a manner that caused Stilli to feel a blush rise in her cheeks.

'You choose to dress in male attire and yet the subterfuge is wholly ineffectual. You are absurdly beautiful for a boy, and were you genuinely of that sex you would certainly excite a general admiration amongst those in this place unpersuaded by female charms'.

Stilli felt her initial blush intensify at this lewd hint and also because she had never heard herself described as beautiful before, except by Tye, whose opinions she naturally tended to discount. The words she had intended to say about "exaggeration" died on her tongue as a consequence and she looked aside, finding her gaze engaged by Axilo's. Now it was his turn to cast his eyes down awkwardly.

Baradian laughed to see her confusion and clapped his hands.

'Very well, then. We shall convey you to the count, and perhaps he may call upon you to demonstrate your skill in due course. Do not fear for your bellies', he added, indicating the bowl that Radda held. 'You may set that down here. I feel sure that the count's kitchens can find you better fare'.

Any hope they may have entertained of overcoming these strangers and making good their escape was extinguished when they emerged from the boarding house to find a file of spearmen waiting outside. There was no alternative but to follow Baradian as he led them through narrow and deep-shadowed streets, always upwards towards the count's castle at the highest point in the town.

'They seem most engaging fellows', murmured Tye to Stilli as they walked. 'But I thought it best not to mention to them that you are the Golden Child. I don't know why, I'm sure I don't. It just seemed to me that such a disclosure might prompt your disapproval'.

'You are right', sighed Stilli, much relieved and squeezing his arm. 'You have done well, dear Tye'.

Having been obliged to surrender their weapons, they were conducted through a gate in a high wall, where torches guttered in sconces, through a courtyard where men were unloading a cart, up several flights of steps and then into a small room. There they were required to wait for what seemed at least an hour beneath the impassive gaze of a number of guards. Tye began to speak and was nudged hard in the back.

'No talk!' roared a guard in a strongly accented voice. 'Talk later'.

Accordingly, an apprehensive silence prevailed amongst the company until they were summoned once more and Baradian reappeared at the door to guide them. Led through various chambers and along echoing dark corridors, they emerged at last in a large hall lit by candles and by a roaring fire in a broad grate. Here, whilst more armed guards stood in the shadows around the walls, a huge man sat at a table and ate from the leg of some fowl. He looked up and fixed them with a piercing stare as Baradian brought Stilli and her party before him.

'Here they are, my lord, in obedience to your wishes', said Baradian simply, making a low bow and stepping back.

'Good', grunted what was evidently Count Gradivin.

He set down the leg on a pewter plate before him, wiping hands and beard on a napkin before pushing back his chair and disclosing his full stature to his guests. The bargeman had evidently been in awe of the man who ruled this place, and it was not hard to see why, given that he was well over six feet tall and powerfully built. His face was framed by waxed and oiled hair that radiated on all sides in stiff black curls. The flickering candles on the table glinted upon them in a manner that made it seem as though they writhed like snakes. Deep-set eyes that blinked but infrequently glared from within black painted sockets with a brooding malevolence sufficient to loosen the most steadfast bowel.

'I suppose you know who I am', he growled with a nod of dismissal for Baradian. 'And I don't stand on ceremony in my house, so we keep the honorifics', he gestured in the air with one huge hand, 'the bowing and scraping, to the bare minimum. You may call me "Count," that is all. I know there are some who would like to mention that I'm lord of this and lord of that and Master of the Pirsid Seas, and other such fanciful nonsense, but I don't hold with any of that. All you need to know is that I'm master of this place and every living creature in it. Which includes you', he added with a significant glance.

This was a statement that admitted of no obvious response, and all in the party cast their eyes down humbly. Stilli was all too conscious of the emptiness at her hip where she had become used to feeling the weight of her sword. She felt naked and vulnerable before the count's imperious gaze.

'I am an honest man', continued their alarming host. 'Which you may think odd coming from a man of my profession, whose wealth depends on the plundering of the trade of nations. But all men take from others what they deem to be theirs, do they not? Or else where would kings find their taxes and all the great and lesser nobles in their turn? I ask only my share. If merchants in their plump trading vessels submit to my reasonable demands, they may sail on their way, a little lighter in the hold, no doubt, but with their fat skins intact. That is my bargain, and it is one that all know who sail these seas. But if they choose to fight or run, well that is when my law decrees their death. All may readily understand this. Those who accept my law are those I trust. Those whom I do not trust, I slay'.

Stilli swallowed hard as his eye fell upon her once more. 'Let us be truthful with one another, for there is the sure basis of trust'.

He picked up one of Stilli's gold coins from the table at his side and held it up before him. It was presumably the one they had traded at the wharves.

'This is a remarkable bauble, is it not? I have never seen one like it – and many, many gold coins have passed through these hands. I am told that you have a gift for me', he prompted, tilting his great head to one side and regarding them expectantly.

'If I may borrow a small knife?' murmured Radda.

The Count beckoned and a guard stepped forward to furnish her with his own. Using just the tip of this formidable blade, grimacing with the effort, Radda slit her waistband in various places, in order that Axilo could withdraw the coins concealed there. At last, Axilo stepped forward to place these in the count's open hand.
'Here are the remaining nine', he said. 'You have the tenth and two more are with the bargemen who brought us here. There were twelve when we found them, and now you have all that we can give you. That is my honest account'.
The count nodded slowly and considered the coins in his hand.
'I judge that you tell me the truth', he said, 'now that you understand the consequences of behaving otherwise. To win my trust is to live, to earn my enmity is to die. I am not a man with an active conscience and, if I am minded to end your existence, I shall kill you with no more remorse than I step on an ant'.
Once more, there was no response from Stilli and her friends except for from Tye.
'Well, that seems fair enough', he said with an approving nod.
'It is', agreed the count, singling him out for attention now, so that Tye, regretting his intervention, edged himself behind Stilli. 'It really is'.
There was a silence, during which the count stroked his beard and Stilli felt a pressing need to visit the privy, wherever that might be.
'My servant, Baradian, has given me some inkling of your business here', he said at length. 'But I should like to hear it from you directly. Perhaps you would begin', he said, nodding at Axilo. 'If I am to assume that you are the leader of this group'.

Once more, Axilo was obliged to give an account of their journey, although naturally he omitted to mention that Stilli, or at least Stilli's capture, was the focus of the Hierarchy's most earnest attention. Stilli wondered with some trepidation whether the count might insist that they conduct him to Bondorin's tomb in order that he might ransack the place in search of more gold. He did not, however. Instead, he asked that Stilli should step forward and then subjected her to a long, considering stare.

'You', he said eventually. 'Stilitha. You are one of the priest people, are you not? You are one of the Vhanakhori race who consider this island to be their own and who cower before a god that demands of them the blood of their own children. Why would you wish to run away to the Empire? Surely, you could simply have taken ship from Tazman, if you are a member of their ruling class, as I judge you are. There remains a truce between those nations, and the usual trade between their cities continues. You are holding something back'.

'I am accused of witchcraft', answered Stilli upon a sudden inspiration. 'My reactions are unnaturally fast, as you have heard. It excited the jealously of the Hierarchs, who would have burned me had I not made good my escape'.

'Uh-huh', mused the Count, who continued to direct his fierce gaze upon her, causing her to feel that her legs must surely give way, so debilitating was her anxiety. 'Well, we must surely put your *powers* to the test in due course, in order that we may understand the reasons for your condemnation'.

He stepped into the shadows beside the fireplace and returned, bearing Stilli's sword with its scabbard and belt.

'This is your sword, yes? Although it is a strange object, indeed. I have heard that Skagaari nobles fight their duels with such objects, but it seems an insubstantial thing for the battlefield. Hardly any weight to it', he added, passing it into Stilli's hands.

'I find it convenient', she replied, mastering her voice with difficulty.

'Convenient!' he laughed, a white grin suddenly splitting his dark beard. 'We shall see how convenient it is tomorrow'.

It appeared that this was the end of their interview with the count, and a very disturbing one at that. Having been deprived of her sword once more, Stilli followed her friends as the party was led to a chamber that adjoined the great hall. They were brought food, as Baradian had promised, but the presence of armed attendants meant that no unguarded speech was possible. There was a little stilted discussion of the food and of the security of their bundles that had necessarily been left behind in their lodgings, but in general they ate in glum silence, apprehensive about what was to come. Stilli, in particular, found that she had little appetite for the vegetable stew and the coarse bread that was placed before her. The word "convenient," aligned with the count's huge grin, continued to hang ominously at the forefront of her mind. It continued to resonate there later, when the party were led to their accommodation, a room each for males and females, furnished with wooden beds and decent mattresses.

'Do you think he will give us leave to take ship from here?' asked Radda when the candles were put out. 'Not that we can pay for it now!' she added with a hollow laugh.

'I do not know', admitted Stilli, pulling the blankets up to her chin. 'But I fear that the count wishes to test my powers on the morrow'.

'I believe you are right', agreed Radda.

'But what form that test might take is unclear, is it not?'
'It is', came the answer, the creaking of bed and mattress suggesting that Radda had risen on her elbow to peer at her friend in the darkness. 'But no doubt you will rise to it'.
'No doubt', agreed Stilli, albeit with a hesitancy that spoke of her fear.

The morning brought with it another sombre meal, whilst attendants stood by to overhear any conversation between them. Washed, dressed in their travel-worn garments and filled with trepidation for the day ahead, they were ushered along a corridor and into a chamber furnished with bookshelves and a desk. At this desk sat a man who was presently introduced to them as Kyresios, the count's secretary. Having greeted them cheerfully, Kyresios set down his spectacles and advanced around his desk to shake each of their hands, speaking all the time of his regret at their inconvenience and at the peremptory manner in which they had been gathered up from their lodgings in the town. This approach contrasted sharply with their reception the previous evening and so caused his guests to relax a little and to feel somewhat less apprehensive for their immediate future.
'Do please take a chair', insisted their host, directing a servant to distribute them. 'And perhaps some refreshments would be in order'.
More words with an elderly servant preceded the latter's dispatch to the kitchens.
After he had gone, Kyresios re-established himself behind his desk and told them of the burdensome nature of his work, the dishonesty and indolence of contractors, the interminable delay in securing provisions, until his guests wondered if he would ever come to discuss their own presence there.

'But you must be wondering why I have brought you here', he said at last, regarding them over his spectacles. He spoke Vhanakhori elegantly, but with an unfamiliar accent.

'Yes', agreed Axilo with a glance for his friends. 'We are. And we thank you for your hospitality'.

Kyresios, in striking contrast to his employer, was a very small man, dressed in a great many garments to keep out the cold, although a cheerful fire burned in the grate. He was almost completely bald, retaining only a fringe of grey hair around his age-mottled pate. Stilli judged that he must be well past the Sixty; not that the Sixty counted in this region.

'The count has given me an account of the broad outlines of your story', began Kyresios. 'I am a curious man, you see, and he drew my attention to this', he said, reaching within his clothing and drawing out one of the now familiar gold coins. 'I wondered what you knew of it? The count is not short of gold, since his occupation provides him with great quantities of it, but his description of where it was said to have been found piqued my interest. I am an antiquarian, you see, and an Erenori in exile like two of you here, if my understanding is correct'.

He wagged a finger at Radda and Axilo. Stilli noted that he was missing the little finger from his left hand. His accent was that of the Empire, then, and he was a living link to the place she yearned to reach.

'We were not born in Erenor, although our parents were', said Axilo with a glance for Radda. 'However, we earnestly wish to return there. It is our spiritual home, you might say'.

Kyresios nodded.

'And what of you?' he asked Mull. 'You are native to these lands, I think'.

'I am', agreed Mull, shuffling his feet awkwardly. 'But I wish to look upon wider horizons than the woods in which I have always lived'.

'A laudable ambition, no doubt', said Kyresios with a smile, now turning his attention to Tye.

'And what of you, young man?'

'I only wish to go where Stilli goes', answered Tye simply. 'I admire her greatly and I have made it my task to protect her'.

'Have you really?' asked Kyresios, considering the boy with a keen eye and doubtless drawing conclusions about his mental powers.

'And do you *need* anyone to protect you?' asked Kyresios, looking at Stilli now, his hands cradled before him, his elbows on the desktop. 'I have heard that you are a prodigious proponent of the sword despite your sex, contrary to one's usual expectations. The count was most intrigued to hear of it, as I suppose you know'.

He frowned, as though privately considering some unfortunate consequence of stimulating the count's interest. Stilli's heart fluttered within her.

'Like my friends, I wish to make my way to the Empire', she answered cautiously. 'As I don't doubt you have heard, there are those in my country who wish to destroy me, because they believe me to have unnatural powers'.

'I see', mused Kyresios. 'And you believe that the citizens of the Empire will be more accepting of such things?'

'I do', nodded Stilli, although in truth she had never considered whether her curious ability would see her condemned there. However, it was likely enough that a simple avoidance of swordplay would be sufficient to spare her from censure.

"Well, perhaps you are right', said Kyresios after a moment's thought. 'But perhaps you would oblige me with an account of your travels and of your story in general', he continued, favouring her with a smile. 'I am a very curious man; it is my business to be so. The count told me the bare outlines of your adventures, but it seemed to me that much remained untold, and you strike me as being a particularly interesting person. Let us begin with your family, home and education, shall we? Spare no detail. I have a thirst for facts'.

Stilli found herself obliged to answer innumerable questions relating to her life and upbringing, right up to the present day. As he had admitted, the secretary had an insatiable appetite for information, often raising a hand to quell her flow and requiring her to supply further detail. It was as much as she could do to conceal from him the terrible circumstances of her last conversation with her mother and the grim truths that she had learned.

At last, when the better part of an hour had passed, he leaned back in his chair and regarded her steadily for some moments. It was quite unclear whether he believed her stated reasons for her flight, but Stilli earnestly hoped that her face and her eyes had not betrayed her. In addition, she had found herself spilling out the story of her visions of Tio and her consequent surprising realisation that she was no longer a follower of Yuzanid. It helped to explain why she was there, namely a place where Yuzanid's word was ignored, but it was perhaps an unwise disclosure. She had blushed to feel her friends' eyes upon her as those words had tumbled out.

'But, if I may return to this coin', said Kyresios when he had satisfied his curiosity on all other matters. 'I wonder if you have any idea what you have stumbled upon?'
<u>He held it up before him.</u>
All shook their heads, except for Stilli.

'It is the coin of an Erenori emperor', she suggested. 'I read the name, Niall'.
'You are correct', agreed Kyresios, placing the coin carefully on his desk. 'Niall the Tall was, according to legend, the first of the emperors of Erenor. During his reign, nearly three hundred years of it, if we are to believe the legend, the whole of the great continent of Toxandria submitted to his rule. These other words you see', he said, indicating the text that encircled the emperor's image, 'say *Emperor by grace of Tio*, in Cantrophene, the ancient tongue of the Empire, although it is now the preserve only of antiquarians, I'm afraid'.
'I see', said Axilo frowning. 'I'm sure that is very interesting, but how is it relevant to us?'
'It is relevant, young man, because Niall is reputed to have had twelve paladins, twelve great heroes who sat at his table and fought beside him in his wars. We read that when they fell they were buried in tombs befitting their status, in order that their spirits should guard the extremities of the Empire for all time. One of those paladins was called Arriniall and he was buried at a place quite close to here, which was called "Ashaneel" in Cantrophene, or "Cragsfoot" in the common speech of this island'.
Stilli found that Kyresios was regarding her with a particular intensity during the latter part of this discourse and felt a cold prickle track across her forehead.
'Bondorin', she breathed, wonder and sudden realisation driving caution from her mind. 'My own tutor; the one I told you of. He was this same Arriniall you mention, was he not? Is that what you are saying?'
'I do not assert it as an incontestable fact, but yes, I believe it may have been', said Kyresios, regarding her

over his steepled fingers. 'Which means that you must be a person of the first importance'.

Stilli found that all were regarding her with interest now.

'I must?' she gasped, swallowing hard.

It was far from clear that this might be a positive development.

'Yes', nodded Kyresios. 'You have told me that you have had visions of Tio, one of the reasons for your necessary removal from the bosom of your countrymen. You have become a heretic, it appears – an apostate. The mere fact of such a person's continued existence brings Yuzanid's rage upon his people, and naturally they would seek earnestly to destroy you in order to placate him, were your views and your visions to become known to them. You are undoubtedly a small pawn, or some other piece, pushed hither and thither on their board in the great game of the gods. Tio evidently has a plan for you, should you survive'.

'What do you mean, *should* she survive?' objected Axilo, concerned.

'Oh dear! Did the count not make himself plain last night?' asked Kyresios as Stilli's eyebrows twitched upward and her hands flew to her mouth. 'He wishes to see your prowess with the sword. There is a criminal, condemned to die, who is famed for his skill with that weapon. The count has told him that he may be spared if he kills you. Likewise, he will suffer *you* to live if you kill this man. It is to be this afternoon, after luncheon. I trust you will prevail'.

Stilli found that she had little appetite as the meal was served. Her stomach was a hard knot in her belly, her mouth as dry as parchment. Once more, she felt overwhelmed by the weight of circumstances. To hear that her Bondorin had been the spirit of a long-departed paladin was surprising enough, but to find that she must fight for her life within a few hours was deeply shocking. Her hand trembled as she held it up before her.

'I shall fail; I know I shall', she whispered. 'This hand will not preserve me'.

'You will *not* fail', Axilo assured her, placing his own hand on her arm in a way that was at once familiar, reassuring and at the same time oddly exciting. 'You will recall that you have already triumphed twice in such bouts'.

It was, of course, impossible to say that vanquishing Axilo had been child's play. And only Mull's well-directed arrow had spared her from capture in her skirmish with Middo. She nodded, nevertheless, and managed a weak smile for Axilo and her friends.

'Certainly you must win', added Tye. 'We all have faith in you, as did that distinguished skeleton in the tomb, he whose name escapes me now. I doubt that your opponent will have such support. Surely his spirit will stand at your back'.

Radda and Mull echoed support as her eyes met theirs. She recalled Kyresios' final words to them upon parting. The man had coughed awkwardly as they stood from their chairs.

'I should say that each of your lives, each of your survivals, is contingent upon Stilitha's success this afternoon. The count has made it clear that he will have *all* of you killed, should Stilli be put to the sword. He is a tidy-minded fellow, you see, and to do so would draw a neat line beneath this event, at least in his mind. Your own minds may revolt against the idea, I make no doubt', he added with an apologetic shrug. 'But there we are. It is the count's way'.

All had stared at him aghast. And then, one by one, Stilli's friends had turned their gaze upon her. Nothing could be more certain than that she had their wholehearted support.

Chapter Sixteen

Baradian led them to the castle's central courtyard, where the cobbles remained slick wet from one of the morning's heavy showers. The skies were gloomy and overcast now, in a way that perfectly matched Stilli's mood as she stepped out into the centre of the space. Count Gradivin greeted her and presented her with her sword, hilt first, before being introduced to her opponent, a wiry young man, perhaps half a head taller than she. He regarded her with wary optimism as guards struck the fetters from his wrists and ankles. The stench and the filth of the dungeon lay upon him, and his shirt and breeches were torn almost to shreds.

'This is Dayan', said Gradivin gravely, stepping back, having required a guard to present the man with a sword of his own. 'He has incurred the death penalty for his crimes, but he may redeem himself, should he slay you'.

Dayan licked his cracked lips and nodded to the count, reaching up to push lank black hair from his brow.

'I killed a few, here and there', he grunted. 'I don't suppose one more will hurt, and this a maid, if I'm any judge, clothing regardless. Let's make it quick, shall we, missy?'

He laughed then and weighed the sword in his hand, testing the balance.

'A little heavy at the point, I'd say, but no doubt it'll do the job'.

Stilli glanced about her. The fringes of the courtyard were crowded with curious onlookers, as was the wall walk on two sides and the wooden stair that led there. All had doubtless been told to expect a diverting spectacle. Amongst the crowd, Stilli saw that her friends were having their hands bound behind them, and she felt fear clutch at her heart. The sword that Bondorin had given her, the sword that the great paladin Arriniall had given her, if Kyresios were to be believed, hung at her side in a hand that trembled.

'I do not wish to kill this man', she managed to say with a voice that seemed barely hers to command.

'Of course you do not', laughed Gradivin, folding his arms with a glance for Dayan who seemed no less amused. 'Nor will you be able to, in all likelihood. But then your own life depends upon it, so I don't doubt you will do your best, once steel meets steel'.

'Fear not that you must kill me, girl', sneered Dayan. 'For it will not be required of you'.

'Very well', said Gradivin, stepping back. 'Let us see who lives and who dies. Let us see who enjoys the favour of the gods. There shall be no quarter'.

'Suits me', grunted Dayan, raising his blade and adopting a stance that showed he was no novice in this business.

Stilli raised her own blade, its tip hovering a hand's breadth from her opponent's, and likewise fell into the fighting stance that Bondorin had instilled in her. She knew that in order that she should have any chance to prevail she must reach for the "celerity." At the same time, she sensed that Gradivin and the assembled crowd would not be satisfied to see this bout ended within a few moments of blurred activity. As much as anything, this must be a performance, and she must perform to Gradivin's satisfaction. She found suddenly that she did not fear death. Let fate and Tio determine her course. A calmness and a sense of resignation came upon her as she felt the weapon settle within her grip. She raised its tip to kiss Dayan's.

'Engage!' barked Gradivin.

Before the echoes of that word had reverberated from the walls of the high tower behind her, Dayan's fierce lunge was questing for her throat. He was quick, but she was equal to it, stepping back, guiding her own blade to turn his aside.

He nodded, in a grudging acknowledgment of her reactions, and licked his lips. She made no attack of her own, merely observing his movements carefully as the two slowly circled. She must watch his eyes, the true heralds of intent, and she must be wary that his occasional feints did not develop to the full attack. Here came a swing from high to low, one in deadly earnest, one she must meet with a strong parry, gliding forward with her left foot as the clash of steel jarred her arm. There was an opportunity for a back slash of her own, but he had withdrawn before the attack could be delivered, easily knocking her blade aside, countering with another thrust of his own.

He was fast... and he was desperate. There was a glint of deadly earnest in Dayan's eyes, but the easy self-confidence faded as the bout continued. Dimly, as though in a dream, Stilli was aware of the shouts and the cries of the crowd, the jeers as she almost lost her footing, the laughter as a vigorous push in her back thrust her back into the centre of the courtyard when she retreated too far. It was time. It must be time, because Dayan was more skilled, more experienced than she, and he was stronger. She felt her defence gradually lose its measured control as his attacks came closer to finding their mark in her flesh. With her heart in her mouth, fearing that it might not be there, she reached for the "celerity" and felt a leap of joy as it settled upon her.

As she had come to expect, the world slowed around her and the strange yellow tinge appeared upon the periphery of her vision. It was as though her hearing was dulled but all other senses heightened. She could smell the sweat and the stench of stale urine upon her opponent, the mingled scents of food and horses and spices from amongst the crowd. Dayan's blade sliced past, a finger's breadth from her, and she stepped back to await his next move. It was a delicate matter now. She knew that the "celerity" endured only for a few seconds, and she must judge the moment of attack with care.

Dayan's sword tip slid away from her, slowed, changed direction and came back in a darting lunge. He was so much faster than Axilo and Middo, and his withdrawal left no obvious opportunity to exploit. There seemed little danger that he might strike her now, but already she felt the effect of the "celerity" begin to fade. She must urgently seek the opportunity to evade his guard as their blades continued to clash and the slow seconds passed. There it was! His backhand cut left him momentarily exposed beneath the arm as the steel swished past. Having evaded the blow, she thrust forward and felt her sword tip find its mark beneath the ribs on his left side.

He cried out as she drew back her blade, and his sword fell from his hand with a clatter to the cobbles. The power was draining from her, leaving her feeling breathless, unnaturally weak. Dayan staggered, groaned and placed a hand to a wound already weeping blood. He sank to his knees, shaking his head. She became suddenly conscious of the roaring of the crowd as her mind's focus expanded to include her wider surroundings once more.

'Finish him!' barked Gradivin, suddenly at her side. 'Finish him!'

Stilli's victory brought with it its own great burden. She had no wish to take a life, even that of the man who would cheerfully have taken hers.

'Finish him!' roared Gradivin once more, his voice now loud in her ear. 'You must, or I shall finish your friends'. A sidelong glance disclosed that her friends had their heads pulled back and knives held to their naked throats.

She had no choice.

She must do this.

Tears sprang in her eyes. Her father came into her mind, the sacrificial knife raised in his hand to do Yuzanid's bidding. But this was not Yuzanid's bidding. She did not know whose bidding this was, apart from that of the implacable count; she only knew that she had no choice and that she must do what she must do. Resolve settled in her and she raised her bloodied blade.

'Bitch!' gasped Dayan glancing up, panting hard now as the blood pooled on the cobbles around him.

She thrust hard but the weapon lodged in bone and ligament, causing Dayan to cry out once more and sink forward to all fours. Stilli gasped and whimpered, her eyes filmed with tears. She must end it. As her opponent drew himself upward once more, she struck with all her strength and her sword pierced some vital organ, perhaps his heart, emerging at last from his back. He died, slumping to one side whilst Stilli tugged the blade awkwardly free. She stood panting, tears streaming down her cheeks and, obedient to some instinct, holding the gory blade aloft to the cheering crowd.

I am a killer, said a small voice inside her.

Later, much later, or so it seemed, she stood once more before the count in his hall to receive his congratulations. Her calves and thighs ached furiously, as did the muscles of her arms, as though they had been stretched beyond endurance. Her tears had dried now but the memory of the glad embrace of her friends was warm within her, driving from her mind the horror of the kill. It would return. She knew it would, and it would haunt her, but now she found the composure to look steadily at her host as he examined her sword more closely. The weapon had been taken from her immediately after her victory, and now it seemed that the count wished to discuss it with her.

'The blade is very keen', he observed. 'I trust you must sharpen it often'.

'I have never sharpened it', she replied, shaking her head. 'I doubt I would know how'.

'And there is not a speck of rust upon it', mused the count. 'And yet Kyresios tells me it is thousands of years old. A pretty heirloom indeed'.

'It is'.

He set it down on the table that lay between them and indicated with a curt nod that she might retrieve it.

'Here, I suppose you will wish to practise with it'.

'Thank you', she said, reaching forward to enfold the familiar grip in her hand.

It was quite cold as she held it before her, but quite comforting, too, as though to have been parted from it had required the surrender of a part of her. The thought occurred to her that she could easily thrust it through the man, should she find the resolve. She judged that to do such a thing now that she had crossed the threshold of killing would require no great imposition upon her conscience. It was as though the notion registered upon her countenance.

'Cast out that thought', said the count with a sudden wry smile. 'Even were you to slay me, you would condemn your friends to death. I would not allow you to stand armed before me unless I had first made it clear to all here that my own death must immediately bring about theirs. Besides...' he said, glancing upward.

Stilli followed his gaze to see that two guards had crossbows directed at her from amongst the shadows in the high gallery that passed along one side of the hall and was perhaps usually employed by musicians.

'It would certainly be your last act upon this earth', he continued. 'These fellows are very deadly with those things'.

'I don't doubt it', said Stilli, standing more easily now, feeling that the balance of their relationship had changed in some subtle way. 'But I am neither a fool nor particularly prone to suicidal impulses'.

'I rejoice to hear it,' he noted, smiling that wry smile once more and stroking the tangled waxed strands of his beard. 'You are indeed a strange one. Perhaps the strangest I ever met'.

He clapped his hands, and a woman appeared from the shadows behind Stilli, moving swiftly to stand at his side.

'This is Emeni', he announced, placing his arm around her shoulder and shaking her in a manner that might have set her teeth to rattle. 'She is my foremost wife'.

Stilli blushed and cast her eyes down, making the dip that instinct and habit prompted in her.

'Delighted, I'm sure', she heard herself say in a polite manner that would have pleased her poor mother.

'Emeni suggests that I may employ you for our sport', Gradivin continued. 'The coming week brings with it the closed season for hunting, if you will. My ships will soon find their way home, and the next three months will see their laying down for careening and refitting. The winter is a long one, but it may be enlivened if we may witness some contests of skill such as we witnessed today from time to time'.

Stilli felt her throat tighten with alarm. Raising her gaze she met that of Emeni, a strikingly handsome woman in her middle thirties with raven black hair and a look of hardness in her face. She was dressed in a splendid green gown, embroidered with pearls. A magnificent gold and bejewelled necklace enlivened her decolletage. She did not smile. Rather, she regarded Stilli in a supercilious manner, looking her up and down as though she were a pony she was considering purchasing.

'But sir!' protested Stilli aghast.

'Let us have no debate!' snapped Emeni, an imperious glint in her eye. 'My husband does not care for it. And let us make no delay in arraying you as a champion should be arrayed. These rags will never do. Husband, will you permit me to clothe her as I please?' she asked with a glance over her shoulder.

'Certainly, you may', agreed the count with a nod.

He turned his gaze upon Stilli.

'There are seven ships out there upon the high seas at present, but soon they will find their way here, and each must furnish a champion to test their skills against yours. Seven'.

'And what if I am victorious?' asked Stilli, seeing that there was nothing to be gained from opposing his will, conceding that she might only seek to gain some reward from her obedience to it. 'Will you then allow us to depart freely from here?'

'It is surpassingly uncommon for people in my realm to attempt to place terms upon me', said the count icily.

'But there is a story there, I think', conceded Emeni, regarding Stilli with a certain amusement now. 'And doubtless it would burnish your legend in the minds of the world'.

'Perhaps you are right', acknowledged the count after a moment in which he merely furrowed his brows. 'Perhaps you are right. You, Stilitha', he said, turning suddenly upon her, bringing his terrifying gaze within a hand's breadth of her face.

She could feel his hot breath on her face, causing her instinctively to flinch and jerk her head back.

'Hear this, for this is my judgement' he continued. 'If you defeat my champions during the course of this winter, I shall set you free in the spring – you and your friends. Damn it, I shall even spare you some vessel to carry you away!' he laughed. 'There! Do you like my bargain?'

'I do, my Lord', murmured Stilli, given that there was no alternative.

'But mind this', the count warned, wagging a big finger at her. 'Your fate is bound up with that of your friends. If you die, so do they all'.

'We are to dwell in this castle', Stilli told her friends when she returned to their quarters. 'The count has decreed that we shall be fed and clothed', she said, opening her hand. 'See? He has given me money in recognition of my victory. We shall spend the winter here, and in the spring he will furnish us with safe passage to the Empire'.

All rushed to embrace and congratulate her, but there was a coldness, a reserve in her response, that quickly caused them to step back.

'And what else?' demanded Radda, taking Stilli by the shoulders and looking her in the eye.

'What else, Stilli?'

'I must fight seven more of the count's champions, one from each of his ships, and if I lose, we shall all die'.

The words were bitter in her mouth and she cast her gaze downward, unable to meet those of her friends.

'I am sorry', was all she could manage to say.

'Are we to be imprisoned here?' asked Axilo after a moment of shocked silence.

'No, we are at leisure, providing that we do not leave the castle, the town and its environs. One of us must always remain here, to serve as surety for our good behaviour.

I imagine they would be killed if the remainder of us were to attempt to escape from this place'.

'Well', said Mull, scratching his head. 'I suppose we must all cheer you on and pray that pirates aren't too handy with a sword'.

'Do not feel guilty on *our* behalf', Axilo told her after Tye had mentioned how confident he was of her victories. 'The fault is not yours. Besides, after what we saw today, the likelihood is that none shall vanquish you. It was uncanny, quite uncanny'.

'It was', agreed Stilli with a shudder. 'And it was something that will scar my soul as long as I shall live'.

No one knew for certain when the ships would return to port, bringing with them the plunder of the seas, but it was certain that they must do this before the advent of those December gales that habitually scoured the coast. It was not unlikely that some might have been lost in the great storm of the previous week, so all in the town scanned the horizon for the first flecks of white that might be approaching sails. Such arrivals must necessarily bring with them more contests for Stilli. For this compelling reason, her own scrutiny of the distant horizon was with apprehension rather than with hope.

Still, her party was largely left to their own devices, brought food from the castle kitchens and allowed to pass in and out of the encircling town unmolested. The next few days brought with them much mending of clothes and the making of new ones as Stilli and Radda's needles worked busily once more. Mull, with Axilo and Tye at his heels, ventured out with his bow into the surrounding marshes, where he hoped to add fowl to the grain, dried sausage and root vegetables that was their standard fare. Only the count and his retainers regularly dined on fresh meat, although the poor might hope to enjoy this privilege on the high days of each season. It seemed ironic that the town was awash with gold, spices, rich fabrics and skilfully wrought metalwork but luxurious foodstuffs were scarce. The country thereabouts provided little livestock except for a few sheep and goats.

'As I have mentioned before, I would be glad if you would teach me a little of what you have learned with regard to swordsmanship', said Axilo one fine bright day, when breakfast was being cleared away. 'And unlike the occasion of my first approach, I come to you in humble spirit'.

'Gladly', laughed Stilli. 'Everyone regards me as some prodigy, but in truth Bondorin spent no more than a few weeks with me in imparting those skills. I have no right to claim the mastery that folk credit me with'.

'And you have that "celerity" magic you do', added Radda, passing a jug to the servant that had been assigned to them. 'Let us not forget that'.

'Nor do *I*', said Stilli, 'but the effect lasts only a short time, and I fear to rely upon it. Besides, Bondorin warned me that I might use it only on a limited number of occasions. How many, I do not know. I fear for what might befall me if it does not answer my call some day'.

'With or without it, you fence with uncommon mastery of the art', observed Axilo. 'If an ancient paladin can step out of legend and present you with an enchanted blade, I don't doubt he could likewise plant in you a little of his own skill, even over the short period you mention'.

'Perhaps', agreed Stilli, who had privately wondered if this might be the case.

It was certainly true that the motions of the art came very naturally to her. Perhaps what Axilo had suggested might be a magic sword imparted some of its original owner's skill to its new user.

'But I think that we should do what we can to increase your physical endurance', continued Axilo with a half-

smile. 'Your muscles are not well-conditioned. The life of a lady has done nothing to prepare you for arduous activity of this kind, whereas all of us are well used to it'.
'I'm sure you are right,' agreed Stilli, blushing to recall the privileged status she had once enjoyed. 'What have you in mind, may I ask?'

What Axilo had in mind was a very unladylike programme of running in the terrain around the castle, whenever the ground conditions would allow, and of arduous strengthening exercises that left her red-faced and breathless.
'And you are sure this is of benefit to me?' she asked ruefully one day, having completed a large number of what Axilo described as "press-ups" and "sit-ups." 'Because I can assure you that my muscles beg to differ'.
'Perhaps, but they will be larger and more resilient for it, regardless of their opinion', laughed Axilo, barely out of breath having completed the same routine, whereas Stilli lay prostrate beside him, mopping her brow with a sleeve.
It was necessary that Axilo should watch her closely under these circumstances, but she found that she did not object to it, far from it, nor did she mind when he placed his hand upon arm or shoulder to correct her technique. The same was true when they were practising swordplay and she must hold his hand to adjust his grip, or his leg to improve his stance. There was no recoil from the connection on either side. Instead, the touch of flesh on flesh brought an electric thrill to each. Her eye dwelt languorously upon the taut muscles of his shoulders as he practised his own exercises or lifted the stones that he asserted would strengthen his arms. There were many occasions when this regime brought them close to each other as the days passed, and it began to seem to Stilli that she would like

him to kiss her. The whole of her upbringing, the vast difference in their ranks and prospects, opposed this notion with implacable force, but the idea nevertheless haunted her dreams and there were other – more immediate – considerations that gradually undermined the foundations of such reserve.

These conservative notions were of her past, but the persuasive voices of present circumstance could not forever be ignored. After all, what did it matter that he was a mere Drumogaros and she a Vhanakhori lady, when they lived together in this place and may never return home? Surely they were simply man and woman now, and nothing could be more natural than that they should be attracted to each other.

And it was certain that her feelings were reciprocated in the object of her affection. One had only to observe the flush in his cheeks when she caught him looking at her, the very frank admiration to be seen in his eyes when she walked past him. Regardless of their situation, she found that she took unusual care in her posture and in the sway of her hips when he looked upon her and they walked together. Her hair was growing longer and she often combined a warm smile for him with what Mother might have described as a "coquettish" flick of her dark locks. In short, everything was in place for a kiss to pass from daydream to reality, and in due course it did.

It was a cold but sunny day when their run took them around the periphery of the marsh that encompassed the town on the southerly side. Radda had no truck with running, Mull was out hunting and Tye had been persuaded to go with him. Consequently, they found themselves blissfully unaccompanied as the sun rose to its full height, sparkling on the pale distant sea beyond the sedge. Having passed various curious townsfolk or wandering herdsmen, their pace faltered to a brisk walk and they found themselves amongst some of the low wind-bowed trees that dotted the marsh. They were out of sight from the walls of the town and momentarily quite alone. A brief scan of the marsh-girt horizon, empty except for the remote passage of a flock of small birds, assured Stilli that they were unobserved. Hands on hips, she calmed her breathing and spared a sidelong glance for her companion. Placing his own hand upon the branch of one of the stunted trees, he likewise looked around him before returning his attention to Stilli.

'Well', he said awkwardly. 'You ran well earlier. I swear that you are more eager than yesterday'.

'Oh yes', she agreed, heart pounding in a manner that owed nothing to recent exercise as he drew nearer to her. 'I am... very willing'.

'You are?' he asked, swallowing hard, and a flush came to his cheeks as his resolution faltered.

'Uh-huh', she agreed, meeting his eyes and holding his gaze as he approached hesitantly once more, after another darting glance for their environs.

This was surely it.

Surely, he must summon up his resolve and make real what she had seen so clearly in his eyes.

He did.

After a long moment of agonising indecision, when she feared that the moment must be consigned to history, to remain only a memory of awkwardness and regret, he did. She tilted her lips up to his and they kissed, in a manner that suffused her with a strange heat and caused her to tremble in every fibre of her being as he drew her to his embrace.

Following on from that first kiss, the next few days found them completely absorbed in each other, much to the amusement and dismay of their friends.

Mull and Radda quickly perceived that they exclusively sought each other's company, drawing their own conclusions from the couple's frequent excursions in the marsh. Tye, slower to recognise the signs but eventually making the necessary connection, was utterly downcast and spent long hours on his bed, staring gloomily at the ceiling above.

'Have you lain with each other yet?' Radda asked Stilli one night as they lay in their own beds and the candle was put out.

'Nooo!' answered Stilli vehemently in a hoarse whisper, although the mere voicing of this possibility, the presence of this notion in her mind, filled her with a delicious anticipatory warmth.

'Well, I don't doubt it is in your mind', laughed Radda softly with her usual perspicacity. 'One has only to look at the two of you'.

'What is in my mind is my own to know', objected Stilli primly, provoking only another low chuckle.

She had considered asking Radda about the practicalities of the act that was so often in her mind in recent days but found it too awkward a subject to broach with her. Radda had given birth to a short-lived child, of course, and might be expected to be an informative source on these matters. However, her experience had perhaps not been consensual in nature, and to discuss it might reawaken painful memories.

'Who'd have thought that a fine Vhanakhori maid would be lusting after one of us inferior beings', teased Radda, causing Stilli to curse playfully and throw her pillow violently into the darkness where her friend lay.

There were many more occasions when their journeys into the fringes of the marsh gave Stilli and Axilo opportunity to renew their kisses, and there were other caresses, too, increasingly bold, increasingly explorative as the days passed. Since there was no objection on either side and only the want of opportunity to prevent it, matters might have advanced to their natural conclusion had a sail on the horizon not brought this idyll to a close.

'What is that?' asked Stilli one day, pulling away from Axilo's embrace as her eye was drawn to that ominous fleck of white beyond the low branches of the tree that was their habitual tryst.

'What is what?' asked Axilo, withdrawing his hand reluctantly from within her shirt, where it lay upon her breast. 'Oh, that', he noted, frowning. 'Another fishing vessel, perhaps?'

He made to kiss her once more but she pulled away.

'It is not', she answered, her gaze suddenly distant. 'It is the first of the pirate fleet. I know it'.

Chapter Seventeen

It was. A three-masted vessel of the kind known as a "lazetto" came gliding into port on the evening tide. It had three pole masts, each bearing a much larger yard with a triangular lateen sail. The rails were crowded with a jubilant crew, responding to loud cheers from the throng now assembled upon the wharves. Those more perceptive amongst the onlookers saw that the vessel was low in the water and that the sails were patched in several places. The likelihood was that the ship had seen violent action and was accordingly heavily laden with the plunder of the high seas.

'You should avoid the town tonight', Kyresios told the party, calling upon them as they were preparing to eat their evening meal. 'The crew of yonder ship will descend upon the place like a pack of ravening wolves. The taverns will be full, there will be debauchery beyond my powers to describe and there will be fighting in the streets, perhaps bloodshed. It is always the way when a ship returns home'.

'It all sounds rather splendid', observed Tye with a laugh. 'I regret that we shall miss it. What is *debauchery*, pray?'

Kyresios spared Tye a wondering glance and then beckoned to Stilli.

'Might I have a word in private?'

'You must prepare yourself for another contest', he said when the door to his chamber was shut. 'The count is a man of his word, and he will undoubtedly invite the captain of the *Sea Wolf* – that is the ship that came in today – to furnish a champion to take you on. I cannot say when this will occur; the count has much to do with the assessment and division of proceeds, but I don't doubt that it will be soon'.

He crossed to the window that looked out over the darkened harbour, lit by lamps now, and regarded the unloading of the ship with interest. After a moment, he turned back to regard Stilli as she stood before his desk. 'The count tells me that he has undertaken to convey you to imperial territory, should you be successful in the seven bouts he has in mind for you'.

'He has', agreed Stilli, feeling the weight of this terrifying prospect settle upon her once more. 'And I am told that he is a man of his word'.

'He is', nodded Kyresios.

He held up his hand with its missing finger.

'This is the hand of the Erenori ambassador to Tchikira, an island kingdom on the far side of the Pirsid Sea. Yes, I am an imperial official, whose path crossed that of one of the count's corsairs. I was brought back here together with a large sum of gold and various persons of my suite. The gold, as you might imagine, was received with approval; my secretary and my servants, together with those of the crew of my ship who survived the boarding, were immediately put to death, but I was held here as a hostage. It was judged that a substantial ransom might be sought for my release, and so a message was sent to the emperor in Callisto'.

'Callisto?'

'That is the chief city of Erenor, where the emperor resides'.

'Of course, I have heard of it', nodded Stilli. 'Although I had heard it pronounced otherwise'.

Kyresios indicated the stump of his missing finger.

'The count cut off my finger and the official seal ring I wore upon it, in order to demonstrate proof of my captivity and of his sincerity in doing violence to me,

should the emperor not accede to his demands. I was judged to be a very valuable hostage. This was three years ago'.
'I see. Then why are you yet alive, may I ask?'
'I was lucky that the count's secretary died, of natural causes, shortly after my arrival. As a consequence, the count was in need of someone literate and learned in the ways of the wider world to deal with his correspondence and his record-keeping. As you may imagine, I was very glad to volunteer my services'.
'Of course', agreed Stilli. 'I suppose you were very earnest'.
'I was, and my utility to the count, my indispensability, I should say, has ensured my continued existence to this day. I shudder to think what fate might have befallen me otherwise. The creature had declared his intention of sending parts of me back on a quarterly basis to remind the emperor of my plight'.
'He is a brutal man'.
'He is, although he likes to cloak the pitiless beast that is his nature with a mask of urbanity. It is one of the ways in which he underpins his power. All know that the mask may slip at any time and some unfortunate may feel the full force of his wrath. I never know how I shall find him from day to day. On one day he may appear to me as though he were my best friend, on the next I must face a dangerous storm of disdain and spite. The man is utterly terrifying, which is why he commands the respect and the obedience of all those cruel, pitiless villains in this place. All know that he is even more pitiless and cruel than they'.
'Nothing that you have said eases my mind', murmured Stilli.
'Not is it intended to', said Kyresios, crossing to her and placing a hand on her shoulder. 'You are a strange person and I sense, as our master has sensed, that you

have a certain importance, the nature of which we may not presently divine. I know you would wish to quit this fly-blown dung heap and make your way to the Empire at last. That is also my most earnest desire. There will come a time when another suitably qualified person arrives on this shore, and then I fear that my usefulness, and my life, will be at an end'.

Kyresios was correct in his prediction. A note from his office only an hour later confirmed that Stilli was to face her next opponent on the morrow. Later that night, Stilli received a summons to the count's quarters, where she was met by Emeni, "his foremost wife," in her own dressing chamber. Here, attended by various servants, she had prepared clothing that Stilli would be required to wear during the next day's contest under her husband's eye. Although the quality of the materials and their embellishment was very fine, Stilli was alarmed to see that the clothes were rather small and would surely reveal far more of her flesh than modesty required. Her mother would certainly be shocked to see her so arrayed. Emeni, though, was filled with a child-like enthusiasm that Stilli dared not oppose, although her manner was far from the imperious disdain she had affected on the occasion of their first meeting.

'Your bubs are far from substantial', she said, holding up an ultramarine blue bodice, ornamented with pearls, 'but this contrivance will certainly offer support from beneath and present what you have to their best advantage'.

Stilli had no desire to have her breasts displayed to anyone's advantage, but she only sighed as Emeni bade her to remove her shirt.

'But you have excellent legs, I do declare', cooed Emeni as Stilli stepped out of her breeches. 'And we must certainly ensure that they are properly appreciated.

These boots have a high heel, you see, and they will accentuate their length'.

'Perhaps', conceded Stilli, 'but you will recall that I am to be engaged in a fight to the death, and not to provide some erotic spectacle for the onlooker. Oh, my word! You will surely not tell me that this tasselled object is a skirt!'

'It is a brief garment, I will concede, and you must necessarily wear these briefs beneath it, lest the effect be thought lewd'.

'My lady, this is not serious', protested Stilli. 'It has nothing to do with practicality. My mother would describe this ensemble as designed to titillate, and I cannot, in all honesty, disagree. She would be scandalised were she to see it'.

'Well, she cannot make her views known to us', said Emeni in business-like fashion, passing her the briefs, 'as she is dead, if what I hear of your story is correct, and we need not detain ourselves with her notional opinions'.

Stilli, assisted by various servants, reluctantly donned the garments and presently stood before a large glass that stood in one corner of the chamber.

'If you wish to present me as a spectacle of sexual allure, well doubtless you have achieved your end', grumbled Stilli, surveying herself with dismay. 'But I would remind you of the true purpose of this coming contest. It is to kill or be killed'.

Emeni stood approvingly at Stilli's side, pulling her hair about her head and murmuring to a servant about how it might most attractively be arranged on the morrow.

'Sex and death are two great determinants in human behaviour, are they not?' she observed when this was done. 'Consider the praying mantis. The male of the species consents to his death in order to mate with the female, who snaps off his head when the deed is done, and his corpse continues to couple with her regardless. You shall present an irresistible spectacle, my dear, whether you will it or not. It is *my* will and that of my husband. Of necessity, you must endure or enjoy. The choice is yours. Now, one final thing'.

Emeni beckoned and a servant brought forth a box, from which she raised a glittering necklace of sapphire and gold.

'First, we must remove this dowdy thing', said Emeni, pulling Bondorin's necklace over Stilli's head and placing it in her hand. 'And now we shall array you in this. You will be magnificent!'

There was no denying the truth of Emeni's words. The great river of sparkling blue hung at Stilli's pale breast in a manner that quite caught her breath as she turned here and there to admire it.

'Tomorrow night you will fight', Emeni told her, stepping back. 'You will stand at the brink of death's kingdom, and perhaps you shall defeat him. Enjoy it, I urge you. Embrace the vital spark of life as it flares within you. Life is nowhere sweeter than when death is near'.

These thoughts resonated in Stilli's brain as she tried to sleep that night. She felt that a new Stilitha stood ready to emerge from the quiet, dutiful soul who had once attended drinks parties with her mother, and the sum of whose ambitions was an acceptable husband in a decent house and perhaps children to follow after her.

The new Stilitha was a different creature entirely. Her friends said that she was different, that she was touched by the divine in some way and that the power of god flowed in her veins. Perhaps she *was* invincible. Perhaps she *was* a person who all would now look upon with envy or desire, according to their sex. The figure that looked back at Stilli from the glass had been shockingly unlike the former Stilitha – a new person indeed, a grown woman who radiated sexuality from every fibre of her being and who had the power to command the passions of men.

When she finally slept, when Radda's snoring and the perambulations of her own mind abated, Tio appeared to her in her dream once more. As before, he did not speak. He only stood majestic at the forefront of her mind, starlight reflected on his great furled wings and in the deep pools of his eyes. Even without words, without communication of any kind, Stilli was filled with a deep serenity and calm. She would face the challenge of the new day without fear.

So it had appeared to her in her dream, but when that grey day dawned, and she must face her friends at breakfast, it was more difficult to recapture that serene self-confidence.

'We must treat it as an ordinary day', Radda told them, whilst the rider, *even though it may be our last,* hung unspoken in the air around them. 'I shall go to the market and see if I can find a new pin for my cloak. What of you?' she asked, looking around, daring any of them to murmur of the pointlessness of it all if death awaited them that night.

'Radda is right. Go on. Do what you will', Stilli told them with all the conviction she could muster. 'I shall not let you down. I shall fight for us with all of my heart'.

This much she was sure of, and she was sure also that she must bring matters to their natural conclusion with Axilo. Her experience with Emeni, the story that the mirror told, had caused a rising tide of desire for him to swell within her breast. A sidelong glance was sufficient to assure her that the same resolve shone in his eyes. Accordingly, by unspoken agreement, they set out later that morning for their habitual "run," wearing thick cloaks and carrying more that might be laid on the cold ground beneath them. They walked until the endless sedge of the marsh placed them out of sight of the castle walls and to a favourite haunt of theirs, where a few low trees made something of a bower. There, they laid their cloaks on the ground, unobserved by any but warblers and buntings. They murmured their soft endearments and fell into each other's embrace with quiet desperation, the heat of rising passion driving out the chill of December's sharp air. Now, there was to be no reserve, no caution, no holding back on either side, as death loomed over them with his scythe held ready. They gave themselves up wholly to the heat of the blood in their veins and to the urgings of their flesh, oblivious to all but the joyous sensations of the moment.

When it was done, and they lay in each others' arms beneath those cloaks, Axilo stroked Stilli's hair and gazed into her eyes with an absorption that reflected their shared surrender to the "now" of it. It was as though the world receded around them, remote, irrelevant, and all that existed, all that gave existence meaning, was each other.

'I love you, Stilli', he whispered.

'I love you, too', she replied... and it was true.

That evening, as Emeni and her servants prepared her for her bout, Stilli had time to reflect upon the meaning of her lovemaking with Axilo that morning. She still felt the physical effects of it, and although she had not reached the summit of ecstasy that women were said to achieve, she felt that further exploration might soon show her the path to that summit and was eager to advance along it, should the opportunity present itself. For now, that opportunity stood out of reach, beyond the business of death that she must transact in the coming hour. Nevertheless, despite some little discomfort, there remained a pleasant glow about her as she sat whilst Emeni painted her eyes with kohl and her mouth with carmine red.

The eyes that looked back at her in the mirror held the satisfaction that she had become a woman, that she had crossed a threshold that might never be re-crossed, whatever the next hours brought. Standing at last, to behold her figure in the glass, she saw once more that she was filled with a power that would cause men to desire her. That figure was almost unrecognisable as the Stilli that had walked into this town so recently, and she regretted parting from that mirror when Emeni pronounced herself satisfied and led her from the room.

The great hall was hot and crowded with the crew of the *Sea Wolf*, as well as Count Gradivin's servants, staff and retainers. Stilli saw that Kyresios sat with his master at the great high table at the far end of the hall. Others, on trestles, had been set up around the hall at which the cheerful mariners ate, drank and sang raucously. The hubbub increased remarkably, reverberating amongst the high rafters above, as the gathering remarked Stilli's entry to the broad, clear space between the tables. There was much banging of tankards on timber, much lewd shouted comment as Stilli approached the count and his entourage, her sword swinging at her hip once more. She was very conscious of the nakedness of her thighs above her close-fitting knee boots and of the expanse of bare midriff beneath her bodice.

As she walked with the easy sway that Emeni had prescribed, she glanced to where her friends sat, in order to observe their reactions. She was not disappointed. She had made no mention of Emeni's costume preparations to them, not even to Axilo, and shock was plain upon every countenance. Tye's mouth hung open. Radda and Mull exchanged a wry comment, quite inaudible to her, and Axilo, wide-eyed, regarded her with an emotion that she found impossible to interpret. Her own heart beat heavily within her, but her deportment was as confident as she could make it, and she looked Gradivin resolutely in the eye as he stood to greet her.

'Tio send that I may be strong', were the words that came from her carmine lips as, amongst hoots and cries of delight, the hubbub died away.

'Greetings, Stilitha', laughed Gradivin with a nod to Emeni, who had now taken her place at his side. 'I see that my wife has prepared you well, *very* well!'

A lascivious nod and a leer brought more laughter from the assembled mariners. He raised his eyes from Stilli to address this throng.

'See what entertainment we have prepared for you whilst you gathered in our harvest of gold upon the perilous seas', he continued, glancing about the hall. 'See how you are rewarded! Just as I promised, when first you entered here tonight. This champion of mine, slight as she seems, will take on your finest swordsman in a fight to the finish'.

He leant forward over the table with a broad grin and directed his gaze at Stilli.

'There are doubtless many here who would like to pierce you with their weapons'.

More uproarious laughter proceeded from this, whilst Stilli stood blushing.

'Look at them all', he called to her. 'Eyes starting from their sockets and mouths hanging open'.

Stilli made no response to this comment, could think of none, in fact, and focused simply on controlling her own emotions, the furious beating of her own heart as the mariners drummed their mugs on their tables.

When the noise had died once more, the count summoned the *Sea Wolf*'s designated champion from where he stood at the back of the hall. Tall, long-limbed but with a complexion badly disfigured by smallpox, he advanced amongst loud cheers to stand at Stilli's side, regarding her indulgently. His name, it appeared, was Laric.

'It seems a shame to slay a pretty missy like this', Laric said with a glance for the count. 'I had rather preserve her for another fate'.

'You know my law', snapped Gradivin, his face suddenly serious, the humour dropping away.

His eyes glinted coldly.

'Death or glory'.

He held up a leather purse that clinked heavily with gold.

'You shall fight for this purse, in order that you might combine business with pleasure'.

'Death or glory it is, then', laughed the man, drawing his sword from its scabbard. 'It will be no pleasure, but it is certain that I shall dispatch this maid, if it pleases you. I have slain fairer, I declare, although none that showed any promise of fighting back'.

If Stilli had felt any reluctance in her heart, any disinclination to kill the fellow, this last statement stiffened her resolve very satisfactorily, and her mouth tightened into a line of corresponding hardness.

'Very well', said Gradivin, dropping the purse to the table. 'Let us begin, and we shall see who the gods declare the victor'.

Laric wiped his mouth on his sleeve, sniffed and spat as the two combatants took up their positions in the centre of the hall. Having killed once, Stilli felt no great horror at the prospect. It was another threshold she had crossed that might never be re-crossed. Any reluctance to revisit the experience was dispelled by her readiness to avenge others of her sex who might have fallen victim to this man. It was well known that rapine and murder was the inevitable accompaniment of piracy on the high seas, and she assured herself that one pirate fewer could serve only to contribute to the serenity of commerce. However, as she drew her sword and the two circled warily, she reminded herself that such a resolution meant nothing unless she had the luck and skill to enact it. Would she have either in sufficient measure?

The man's infuriating leer was certainly helpful in enabling her to supply cold anger of her own and to beat down the fear that clutched at her breast. As the tips of their swords kissed, a tense silence fell upon the hall. She told herself that she must not suffer such resentment to cloud her judgement, that she must remain icily calm, the mistress of every nerve and sinew in her body. It was tempting to summon the "celerity" now, if it remained to be found, and skewer this wretch in short order. It was also necessary, however, that she should provide entertainment. That much Emeni had made clear. She had not been arrayed in this titillatory garb unless to provide a theatrical spectacle for the enjoyment of the crowd. They wished to be amused. The count expected that they should be entertained by her, and she must endeavour not to disappoint him. Still, the competing demands of providing a spectacle and of simply remaining alive were not easily to be reconciled.

Stilli knew now that she was swift in her movements, even without the additional supernatural speed with which she had been endowed. Likewise, Bondorin's lessons, the skills that he had instilled in her in so miraculously short a time, enabled her to read the movements of her opponent and oppose them with well-chosen ones of her own. Only in raw power and endurance did he outmatch her. Despite Axilo's strengthening exercises, she was evidently markedly weaker than he, and she dared not take the full force of his blade on her own. Rather, she must use the impetus of that force to guide it away from her. To do that required skill, concentration and a cat-like elegance of movement. It was not unlike a dance, with the two figures advancing and retreating within a deadly mesh of flashing, ringing steel. Yet, it was a dance in deadly earnest, a dance in which one slip or false step might bring destruction with it. Candlelight and firelight sparked from their blades and from their eyes as they wove their lethal dance, accompanied by the cries and whoops of the audience whenever one or the other should attempt some bold stroke or one such endeavour come close to finding its mark.

There were intervals when they paused, taking a breath, stroking hair from brows, gauging their opponent watchfully, before making some new swipe or lunge. Twice, Stilli almost lost her footing in her unfamiliar high boots, twice she twisted and recovered, gliding a questing blade aside.

She sensed that it was time.

She was tiring.

Her movements were becoming less controlled and her margin for error was ebbing away. Laric licked his lips, and the light of anticipated victory glinted in his eye.

It must be now.

Gradivin and his men had had their entertainment. Stilli reached for the "celerity" and found, to her relief, that it was there. Her opponent's dance immediately became a pavane, in which his darting blade crept ponderously towards her side, easily avoided. Now, she must find her own balance and watch for the moment to strike. There were more swings and lunges that she could evade, although his movements were quicker than that of her previous opponent. She dodged and ducked, watching his eyes, in which puzzlement and a growing desperation soon began to manifest themselves. At last! There it was. His arm came up across his body as he prepared a backhand blow, momentarily leaving his armpit and the left side of his ribcage open before her.

She struck with a force that knew no reserve and pierced him between the ribs. The tip of her blade cut through his heart and stopped at his spine. Laric threw his head back, and his mouth stretched in a tight rictus of pain, even as the "celerity" drained from Stilli's body. His sword slipped from a nerveless hand and he fell backward. With a grim flicker of satisfaction in her eye, Stilli tugged her blade free. Laric attempted feebly to raise himself on one arm, fell back once more and died as a pool of dark blood spread on the slabs beneath him. For a moment, there was a stunned silence in the hall and then a huge eruption of cheering, from all present, excepting only the count, who simply nodded, and the man's immediate friends, who looked on appalled. Recovering herself, beating down the rising tide of relief and jubilation in her breast, Stilli stepped forward to wipe her blade on the corpse's shirt and turned to raise it in salute to the count. Cheering, to the accompaniment of mugs beaten on the tables, threatened to raise the rafters. It had been a performance, reflected Stilli as she slid her sword calmly back into its scabbard, and it must be judged a success.

Emeni's approving nod, accompanied by the count's grudging smile as he tossed the purse to her feet, were to live long in her memory, as were the faces of her friends as she strode towards them, her mind still racing with the thrill of victory.

'I have never seen you like this', said Tye when she had received their congratulations. 'You are a girl transformed'.

'Not a girl. She is a woman', observed Radda with a wry smile and a knowing look in her eye. 'If I am any judge – and one that is learning to enjoy it'.

Mull looked upon her, awestruck, as Axilo advanced to enfold her in his embrace. She held out her hand, making clear by gesture and by the look in her eye that this was not the moment for such public tokens of affection.

Many in the hall continued to regard her with a keen interest. Many were calling out to her in their coarse voices and raising their mugs or goblets in salute. She nodded, smiling about her brightly as she made her way through the press around the door, with Axilo close behind. His face when she glanced back was full of uncertainty, but he knew her meaning well enough when she closed the door to his chamber and bade him push his bed against the door.

At last, she fell into his open arms and they kissed, a kiss of fierce relief, jubilation and of something else that she could not at once identify. Desire. For a moment, as she pulled him down to the mattress, alarm sparked in his eyes but then a warm smile spread across his face.

'I never made love to a goddess', he murmured.

'Then now is a good time to begin', she said.

Emeni insisted that Stilli move to a bed chamber adjoining her own in the count's quarters. It was very flattering, a mark of high favour, as Kyresios was quick to point out, but it meant that she could spend less time with her friends. In particular, it meant that she could spend less time with Axilo, a circumstance that she bitterly regretted. She was required instead to attend upon Emeni for much of the day, to serve as her companion.

Stilli learned things about the count's marital relations that filled her with disquiet. It appeared that he had two former wives put to death and had killed another with his own hands when she displeased him. A further incumbent of his bed had avoided either of these two fates by dying during childbirth. Three more wives remained amongst the living but wisely led quiet and retiring lives in order to continue to do so. Emeni, his seventh wife, his *foremost* wife, was a person possessed of great strength of character and an understanding of her terrifying husband that enabled her to maintain cordial relations with him.

'It is like dwelling upon a volcano', she told Stilli with remarkable frankness. 'I know the signs that an eruption is coming, and then I do not stray near the caldera. They say that the soil is exceptionally rich in the vicinity of a volcano, though. I have certainly found that to be the case'.

She laughed and fingered the gold jewellery at her throat ostentatiously.

'I love fine things, you see? It is a weakness of mine'.

It appeared that the count's many legitimate and bastard children were variously employed in the town or on his ships. What might have been termed his "foremost" bastard was presently at sea, commanding the *Waveraker*.

'You have a most stimulating effect upon my husband', said Emeni as they walked together in the small, cloistered garden at the centre of the count's premises.

'I do?' Stilli frowned as the breezes stirred the bare branches of the fig tree at its centre.

'You do. I see it very clearly. He desires you most fervently, but he fears you, too'.

'He fears me?!' Stilli gasped slightly, pausing now and regarding her companion sceptically. 'Why would he fear me?'

'He fears you because he knows that you may slay him where he stands. We have all seen the speed with which you move'.

'He has told me that were I to attempt such a thing, all my friends would likewise be immediately slain'.

'I can see that would be a powerful deterrent', conceded Emeni. 'He knows it to be true, but he is a man with few scruples and fewer true friends. He would not flinch to condemn even those to death, if it advanced his interests. In his black heart he suspects that you might do likewise. Any other woman he desired would shortly find herself obliged to yield to his advances. With you, he dare not. He is at war with himself, because he regards you with superstitious awe, but at the same time he condemns himself for such weak-minded credulity'.

'Did you dress me as you did in order to stimulate his lust?' asked Stilli upon a sudden impulse.

'Perhaps I did', agreed Emeni with a twitch of a smile. 'And *if* I did, it was a most effective ploy. He has not troubled me in the bedchamber for some months now, but last night he was a veritable satyr. He pressed himself upon me most ardently, but I saw the glint of you in his eyes'.

She laughed once more.

'It matters not. We must gather rosebuds where we may, as I believe it is said'.

Chapter Eighteen

Stilli found herself seduced by the presentation of herself that her mentor had created. No longer did she fear the consequences of facing the champions from the returning ships. She had begun to believe, like so many others, that she was touched by the divine and might have been rendered invincible, accordingly. She was intrigued by the sexual allure that Emeni had awoken in her, and she began to savour the raw animal power of it and its capacity to enrapture the men of the town.

Emeni soon added to her wardrobe of figure-hugging clothes in order to assist in the expression of this power. Consequently, her journeys through the streets of the town caused male heads to turn in admiration as she passed, although many a woman rolled their eyes or clucked disapprovingly. She had been a singularly self-effacing adolescent, so it was a joyous discovery for her to break free from dull pedestrian modesty and embrace this new manifestation of her nascent womanhood.

'Is she not a bird of paradise, Kyresios?' Emeni demanded as the secretary passed by her chamber and found the pair of them experimenting with a new ensemble. 'Do these bright feathers not accentuate her form?'

'I'm sure you are right', sniffed Kyresios disapprovingly. 'Although I believe in the case of the birds you mention it is the male of the species whose vanity is expressed in that manner'.

'Vanity', scoffed Emeni when he had gone. 'What does he know, the silly man?'

'Am I vain?' asked Stilli, feeling a sudden pang of disquiet. 'Have I become vain, my lady?'

'Not at all. It is the oldest thing in the world for women to wish to command the desires of men. Tell me, do you wish to lie with every man who lusts after you?'

'I do not, of course I do not, and yet...'

Stilli's eyes clouded.

'And yet what?' Emeni asked, regarding her intently, a half-threaded needle poised before her mouth.

'And yet, I find I wish for them to desire me. It is the strangest thing in my life, I swear'.

'Embrace it, my child', laughed Emeni, 'for soon enough the capacity will pass'.

'She wishes to make of you what once she was', Axilo told her when they walked on the verges of the marshes, hand in hand.

It was the midwinter festival and the remaining six ships of the count's fleet had sailed in during the course of that morning. Accordingly, the town was raucous with drunken celebrations of all kinds. To escape from its environs was a relief.

'I'm not sure what you mean', replied Stilli, swinging his hand cheerfully.

'Can you not see it? She was very beautiful once, but that beauty has faded with the passing of the years, and now she wishes to relive it vicariously through you'.

'Do you think so? Really?' Stilli frowned.

'I do. We worry for you', Axilo said, pausing and turning upon her earnestly. 'You have become someone who is not the Stilli we know'.

'But that is not true', Stilli assured him, pulling on his arm gently to stop him, turning him to her. 'It is a role I must adopt to preserve you; to preserve us all'.

Axilo's face wore its own frown now.

'Of course. I understand that. It is the burden that you bear for us, and we are grateful, but there are murmurings that you bear it all too gladly, that by placing yourself within the count's household as you have, you increase the danger that he poses to us'.

'I do not see that', said Stilli, letting go of his hand and stepping away.

'I do not criticise you', protested Axilo.

'Then who does?' demanded Stilli, eyes narrowed, feeling a rising outrage in her breast. 'I don't suppose that Tye would think to'.

'Radda and Mull, of course', said Axilo, pressing on. 'They feel helpless, vulnerable, their fate entirely in your hands. Mull has found an old boat abandoned in the marsh. He thinks we may escape in it if things go awry'.

'Oh no, Axilo!' gasped Stilli, outrage giving way to horror. 'That would never do. They would surely catch us and kill us then'.

'I do not say I agree with them', protested Axilo earnestly. 'You know my feelings, I hope. But where there was unity amongst us once, I fear mutual suspicion grows now. And we have barely seen you this week, since you are wholly bound up with your new life with the lady of this place'.

'It is not my new life!' objected Stilli.

'Is it not? Then tell that to Radda and to Mull. It appears differently when seen from our quarters'.

'Will you teach me to shoot with your bow?' Tye asked Mull at about the time of Axilo's conversation with Stilli.

'After the last time?' asked Mull, turning from where he was looking out of the window in their quarters and regarding Tye incredulously. 'You lost me my best arrow'.

'Well, yes', admitted Tye awkwardly. 'I cannot deny it, but that was because I am unversed in the way of the bow, and my fingers are not as nimble as I could wish. It was kind of you to let me make the attempt, but I feel that with a little patient instruction, I might yet grasp the essentials'.

'That old fellow in the skiff...' murmured Mull, scratching the back of his head doubtfully.

'I know, he looked most surprised', agreed Tye, reddening.

'Indignant, I'd say. Furious even, and who can blame him?' Mull noted dryly.

'Oh come, Mull. I missed him by a hand's breadth at least', persisted Tye. 'He accepted our apologies in a most handsome manner in the end, I thought. All things considering...'

Radda, who had been mending a sock by the fire, looked up from her work and regarded Mull with a humorous glint in her eye.

'There's little enough to do round here', she said. 'I don't suppose you lack the time. There are plenty of places out there where you could practice, and I daresay Tye would be an eager pupil'.

'Oh, I would, I would', agreed Tye, looking eagerly from face to face.

Radda smiled. Sometimes, it was hard to believe that this tall young man was a grown adult.

'Then I suppose I could ask you to go down to the farrier in the outer court', said Mull, conceding defeat. 'He's been fitting broad points to a dozen arrows for me. Perhaps you would collect them?'

'I should be delighted', cried Tye, hurrying off on this errand.

A silence prevailed in the room for some moments after Tye had left, ended when Mull settled himself on the chair that faced Radda's.

'It's not right, is it?' he observed.

'What's not right?' she asked, setting down the sock.

'You know well enough what I mean', continued Mull, 'and I know you feel it, too. I'm fond enough of Stilli, as you know...'

'But...' interjected Radda, cocking her head on one side and fixing him with a steely glare. 'There's always a *but* coming after a statement like that'.

'But I'm not sure how much more of this situation I can put up with', answered Mull, leaning forward in his chair and rubbing the back of his head. 'We're barely more than hostages here, and our lives hang by a thread. If Stilli fails, that's it for us'.

He looked up to meet Radda's eye now and drew a meaningful finger across his throat.

'We die with her. Doesn't that upset you? Our fate is in her hands. Whether we live or die hangs on the cut or thrust of her sword'.

'You've seen her', said Radda with a frown. 'Don't you think Tio works through her?'

'Tio is not my god!' snapped Mull with a venom that caused Radda to recoil. 'And I do not trust in his notional benevolence in the way that you do. My people have our own god, who dwells with us in our woods. He is far from me and I regret ever leaving my clan. I have seen the ocean now. I have used up my curiosity. I have seen enough of the world to last me a lifetime. I wish only to return to my home. Stilli stands in the way of that'.

There was an angry glint in Mull's eye that Radda had never seen there before.

'So, you mean to take to that boat you found, do you?' asked Radda in a soft voice. 'And what do you suppose would happen to you if you were caught?'

'I would die; you would die, but the end result would be the same. At least my fate would then be in my own hands'.

'I know this is frustrating', conceded Radda, leaning forward to squeeze his hand in hers and receiving a contemptuous snort in response.

He suffered her hand to remain on his, though.

'Frustrating is the least of it', he said after a moment. 'In the woods, I am my own man, in a place that I know as I know myself. Here, I am… nothing', he finished with a shrug.

'If we flee from here, we must all flee together', Radda told him. 'You know that. Our fates are entwined like this here strand of wool. See, look at its fibres'.

She held her wool before his eyes.

'Each strand is weak on its own, but when they are twisted together they are strong. You must see that'.

'And Stilli is the one strand that binds us together', replied Mull in a low voice. 'If she breaks, so do we all. I do not like it, Radda, and I don't know how much longer I can stand it'.

'You must, Mull. You must', begged Radda, squeezing his hand once more.

'I will try', conceded Mull, but Radda's heart sank as her eye met his, and that gaze shifted awkwardly away.

With all the ships back in harbour, ready for the various works that would be done to them during the winter, it could not be long before Stilli was required to demonstrate her skills once more. The prospect of taking a life continued to appal her, but as before, she could at least console herself with the thought that it was the life of one of the vermin of the seas, someone who thoroughly deserved to be dispatched to the judgment of their god.

There was some delay in arranging the details of the bout, however.

Emeni told her, with some amusement, that the eight hundred or so assorted scoundrels who were now crowded into the town had already come to hear of Stilli's prowess with the sword. In addition, the semi-mystical awe in which was held by the inhabitants had come to their ears. It was not surprising, then, that volunteers to fight her to the death were slow to come forward. It required the provision of a purse containing a thousand pieces of gold to break down the reluctance of the crew of the *Raven* and prompt them to nominate one of their fellows.

Their choice, a notorious drunkard and braggart, was a head taller than Stilli and at least twice her weight. Having heard of her skill with the rapier, he came armed with a two-handed sword and an attitude of belligerent ferocity that frightened her almost as much. Nor was he in any way distracted by her charms, since his preference lay with his own sex, the younger the better. Hearing of the man's conduct with pre-pubescent boys, before their inevitable death at his hands, dispelled any remaining reluctance she may have felt to harm him. More than that, it imbued Stilli with an icy resolve to kill him.

It seemed, however, that her opponent had no intention of submitting to this fate.

As ever, on the night of the contest, the count's great hall was packed with diners, drinkers and interested observers of all kinds, and it was as much as his hall stewards could do to keep a clear space of the requisite size in its centre. Having said her farewells to her friends and received a hug from Emeni, Stilli advanced to the foot of the dais, where the count's table stood, to salute and acknowledge the master of her immediate fate. In her mind as she stepped forward was the pressure of Axilo's lips on her own, his firm hand on her upper arm as she withdrew from him.

'You can do this', he had whispered, shaking her arm gently. 'You know you can'.

And it was true. The prospect of violent death remained at the back of her mind, but it did not dominate her consciousness in the way it had done at the outset of her first fight. On the contrary, as she stood beside her opponent, she was filled with a serene certainty that her power would be sufficient to dispatch this man to hell. It was true that the weapon he balanced at his side was almost as long as she was tall, but she knew that the "celerity" was there at her command, when she should summon it, and that this would give her mastery.

So much gold, she thought to herself. *Am I such a prize, indeed*? She asked as the count opened a wooden chest and tilted it to show the assembly the gold coins it contained.

He was speaking now, talking of life and death, of skill and courage to be admired by all. Stilli barely heard him. Tio's lion had come to her in her dreams once more in the previous night, and the power of him still tingled at her fingertips.

She glanced around at the faces of the crowd, male for the most part, presenting varying degrees of age, varying degrees of unsightliness ranging from moderate ugliness to hideous disfigurement occasioned by injury, disease or the inexpert attentions of the tattooist. There were even a few who might be considered good-looking, should one be able to separate their persons from their predatory inclinations. Their faces, as Stilli and her opponent moved to take up their starting positions, held expressions of keen anticipation amongst awe, plain hostility or lascivious intent. There were lewd cries as she strode to her place, and a hand plucked at her arm, quickly knocked away by another. Silence fell, though, as the combatants brought their weapons to the ready and settled their gaze upon one another with steely concentration.

'Are you ready to die, bitch?' snarled Lorid, he who she must kill.

'You are not the first to ask that question,' she replied through clenched teeth, to a delighted murmur running through the crowd. 'Or to feel the bite of my reply'.

Then he was upon her, the great sword swinging, and she was alarmed and appalled by the ferocity of his attack. He left her no space, no time, to evade, and even her most determined parries and blocks were beaten down by the weight and the power of his blade.

This could not last, nor could it end well with her.

Already, pain lanced through her, where the very tip of his sword had sliced her thigh, causing blood to trickle down into her boot. A gasp had gone up from the crowd. She was well aware that she was required to provide a spectacle, to contribute to a drama in which the final act was death. But the only impending death was hers, and it loomed up to face her as she dodged or narrowly swept aside another flurry of furious blows, without managing a single effective riposte of her own.

She stepped back, found a precious fraction of a second to focus her mind and summoned the "celerity". It came, bringing with it its characteristic yellow-tinged vision, the dulling of her hearing as all other senses were heightened.

Lorid's sword swept down towards her with implacable force, in a great glinting arc that must surely cut down between her head and her shoulder, should it connect.

It would not.

She twisted and stepped aside easily, watching the blade slide gracefully past. She brought up her sword tip, poised ready as a determined thrust came hunting for her heart, ducked beneath it, placed her free hand to the floor and rolled aside, leaping to her feet once more as the next slicing cut came questing for her. Frustration and fear glinted in Lorid's eyes. He saw that he was too slow, that his attempt had failed and that now he must pay the price. As the inevitable opening appeared, Stilli lunged forward, perfectly balanced, to slide her steel through Lorid's throat.

He gurgled, gasped and blood spurted balletically as he tumbled slowly sideways and the great sword span to the floor, bouncing once, twice.

The "celerity" faded from her flesh. Lorid died.

The bout had lasted barely thirty seconds. For a few moments, there was a stunned silence in the hall and then a low, awed murmuring began. There was no applause, no congratulation, no ribald remarks. Stilli's thigh began to remind her that she was wounded, a pain that grew with startling urgency and caused her to grit her teeth as she raised her bloody sword tip to the count in salute. He grunted, nodded and closed the lid of the gold chest with a decisive thud.

'It's yours', he said. 'When you wish to collect it'.

Then he sat, reached for his wine goblet and stared at her until she had withdrawn from the hall, doing her best not to limp. There were many expressions of concern from her friends as they hurried her to Radda's chamber.

Radda was dabbing at the wound and clucking anxiously when a knock came at the door.

'The lady Emeni sends her compliments and begs me to tend to your wound', said the elderly physician they presently admitted, opening a case of instruments whilst an assistant stood at hand with bandages. 'I doubt that scratch will require stitching. It looks much worse than it is with all this effusion of blood'.

'My husband does not know what to do with you', Emeni told her the following day. 'Although you will perhaps be glad to hear that he does not propose to require you to fight any more volunteers from amongst his crews, at least for the present. I doubt he could persuade any to step forward, now that word of your... prowess has reached all corners of his realm'.

Stilli's leg was heavily bound and hurt abominably, but the doctor that Emeni had sent had assured her that the wound would heal well in a few days.

'Oh dear', replied Stilli. 'I trust that doesn't mean he has forgotten his bargain with me'.

'I doubt that he has', observed Emeni, handing her a dried fig and taking one for herself. 'But he may seek some devious way to invalidate it and thereby salve his own conscience. His conscience is a flaccid organ where the lives of others are concerned, but his own image is very dear to him and he would not wish to see it tarnished.

'This is a dead time. The ships are all in and the winter storms rage out at sea. We must all endure the next few months as we may and await the coming of the spring. I think you must learn to be self-effacing once more, my dear, and not draw yourself to the count's attention'.

In practical terms this meant that Stilli must forego the garments she had enjoyed wearing in recent times, in order not to attract the eye of others when walking in the town. Instead, Emeni provided her with various loose-fitting clothes designed for the male of the species, intended to enable her to bear and use her sword if circumstances required it. Make-up designed to increase her allure was abandoned, and her hair was simply pulled back behind her head and secured with a fillet.

'You will forgive me for saying that I am much happier to see you thus arrayed', Tye told her as they walked on the verges of the marsh one day. 'I gather that some of the men here might have entertained some very wild ideas about how they might behave towards you in your former presentation. I have learned what "debauchery" is, and I would not wish you to be associated with it in any way'.

In truth, although Stilli regretted the suppression of the image of herself she had so delightedly and so briefly embraced, that regret was not long-lived, and the evident relief in her friends caused her to wonder if she had not fallen victim to some temporary madness.

'I share Tye's relief', Axilo said with a broad grin, after Tye had been summoned to see an unfamiliar dead seabird that Mull had found. 'When first we met, I was proud – as I am ashamed to admit. I thought myself better than you, because you were of the race that oppressed my own. I am glad to say that you were soon able to persuade me of the error of my ways. I feared, in recent days, that you were also becoming proud, full of a sense of your own power and importance in a way that set us at a distance. I am glad that you seem to have stepped back from that and are once more...' he swallowed hard, and a moistness came into his eyes. 'The Stilli that I have come to love', he finished.

They were walking on the edge of a reed-fringed salt lagoon now, scoured by a brisk northerly wind, the bare branches of the scattered trees stirring around them.

Stilli looked around. Away to their right, Mull and Tye were lifting the dead bird by one wing and exclaiming about its long red beak. The dark walls of the town, where Radda sat in their quarters mending socks, loomed across the marshes to their rear.

Moving to embrace him, Stilli made her own soft declarations to Axilo, cooing in his ear, brushing his lips with hers and drinking in the perfection of him through eyes that thirsted to fix such moments in her mind for all time. As Emeni had suggested, the intoxicating joy of life was almost unbearable, almost overwhelming, on the brink of death – and death could reach out his hand for them at any time.

The love that they had found in each other hung by the thread of Count Gradivin's whim, and it was rendered all the more intense because of it. Neither had known these sensations before in their short lives, neither had surrendered or even imagined surrendering their perceptions and their understanding of the world around them to this all-consuming focus on each other. It was like a fever that burned within them and united them with a bond that only death might sever. And death stood at their shoulder.

'My mother would have liked you', he said, flicking away a wisp of hair that had blown before her eyes. 'If only our backgrounds and our upbringings could be stripped away'.

Pain showed in his eyes, and she perceived that he thought of the grim fate that his escape from his village had imposed on her.

'That's what she wanted', she told him. 'She made that sacrifice because of her love for you. She wanted to give you this chance. Surely it is right that you honour her memory, but you must not torture yourself because of it. Believe me, my own people know all about sacrifices'.

There were things that she could confide in Axilo that she would not confide in Radda and dared not in Emeni. Their lovemaking, whenever circumstances allowed it, was as passionate as she had ever dreamed it might be, although always, in her mind, was the fear that a child, a most inconvenient child, might come of it. She took his hands in hers, brought one up to kiss it, glanced to where Mull was casting the bird out into the marsh and kissed Axilo on the lips. He kissed her back, but when they drew apart she saw that sorrow continued to dwell in his eyes.

'What do you fear?' she asked.

'I fear that we may be parted', he answered. 'That the count's malice shall condemn us all and this...' he squeezed her hand, 'shall be at an end. I fear that you will grow away from me as Tio moves within you to bend you to his will, or that you will cast me aside in obedience to some urge to make of yourself something else. It matters not. I shall love you wherever, whatever and whenever you are. All these "evers" shall be yours'.

If Axilo and Stilli were glad to explore the glorious potential of their love together, many of Axilo's waking hours were spent in exploring another love – the love of books.

Kyresios, recognising his evident intelligence and hearing him talk of the one book he had known with such enthusiasm, admitted him to his private library one day. Axilo, who had been discoursing cheerfully about Mull's woodcraft, was reduced to awed silence as he stood before the ranks of dark wood bookshelves, each crammed with volumes of all shapes and sizes.

'The count prizes gold, but this is the plunder of the seas that I most value', said Kyresios with an indulgent smile. 'I have an arrangement with the captains of his vessels. If they find books upon captured vessels, they bring them to me'.

'There are so many', breathed Axilo, running his finger along a dusty row of them.

'There are, and some very ancient and valuable editions, too, many of them in Cantrophene. Would you like to read them?'

'I would, indeed!' cried Axilo, eyes shining. 'But I doubt that I have the skill'.

'I may assist you, perhaps', smiled Kyresios, who had conceived a strong liking for the young man and whose heart was warmed by his evident admiration for his collection. 'Can you write?'

'I can form my own name as my mother showed me, but anything else is beyond me, I fear. The Hierarchs do not encourage it in their Drumogari'.

'Then I shall teach you. Perhaps, in time, you may be my assistant. The fellow who presently serves that function is a lazy, insolent wretch'.

Axilo's eyes clouded as he looked around the fine, well-proportioned space.

'I should be delighted, and yet the future is uncertain', he said with a frown.

'I do not disagree. We are all dependent on the caprices of my master', observed Kyresios. 'Until spring, when the ships sail once more, he need not decide whether he must honour his bargain. Likewise, your friend Stilitha has not slain the seven champions that she must, in order to complete her side of it. Until then, until he reminds himself of your existence, we must take each day as it comes and find what pleasure we may'.

Axilo was interested to reflect, as those days passed, that Kyresios had appeared to associate himself with Stilitha and her party in a way that seemed to go further than simple fellow-feeling might explain.

When Stilli could be spared from attendance upon Emeni, she joined Axilo with Kyresios in his library, and there, whilst a cheerful fire drove out the winter chill, they spent many hours discussing history, geography and poetry, and many other things besides.

The days passed into weeks and then months, and still the count did not bestir himself from his torpor to command Stilli complete the challenge he had set for her, or to simply command her death. It was as though the count and the world at large had forgotten them as the gales of winter scoured the bleak marshes and made moan about the castle walls.

Chapter Nineteen

'They cannot simply have disappeared', observed the Supreme Hierarch.
His chamber was cold on this dank December morning, and the newly laid fire had yet to drive the chill from the air or from his bones. He pulled his robe more closely around him and glanced sidelong at his nephew, whose manner of dress proclaimed a serene indifference to extremes of heat or cold. His cloak, however, hung dripping on the back of a chair, showing at least some small concession to the elements.
'I'm sure you are right', agreed Azimandro, looking up from his scrutiny of the large map of Eudora that occupied most of the table before them. 'But nevertheless, they appear to have done so. I suppose that escarpment edge I mentioned would be about here', he noted, indicating an area on the north-eastern fringes of the mountains that lay between Crane and Racine. 'But when we passed through there and emerged on the far side, there was no sign of them. Our trackers were at a loss'.
'I suppose you will have enquired of the local residents, visited villages and such places? A little gold is known to loosen the reluctant tongue and stimulate memory, I have heard it said. Someone must have seen them pass by'.
'I have other ways of loosening reluctant tongues', chuckled Azimandro grimly. 'But your question reveals your ignorance of this obscure corner of your realm. It is a wasteland of marsh, bleak moor and uncleared forest, undisturbed since Niall's time. There are no villages. The few wandering herdsman who live in that

region acknowledge your rule only when the sword's point obliges them to'.

'Simple economics', grunted Zanidas, reflecting wearily that no other living creature dared to speak to him in this manner but was quite impotent in face of it. 'The kind of garrison that might remind those people of their obligations would cost far more to maintain than we could ever hope to receive in taxes or resources. It was always thus, in many of the remoter parts of Yuzanid's kingdom'.

He frowned.

'But do you suggest that our fugitive has gone to ground amongst the scattered hovels of these people?'

'I do not', answered Azimandro, stroking his chin. 'Where would you go, if you sought to avoid the fiery embrace of our Lord?'

Zanidas crossed the room to poke a little more life into the fire and to give himself a moment to think. At length, he turned to his nephew, poker dangling from his hand like a sword, causing Azimandro's mouth to twitch into a mocking half-smile, quickly suppressed. The flabby old man, bundled ridiculously in silks and woollens, made an unlikely warrior.

'I suppose she might attempt to find her way to where that devil Tio's rule holds sway', he said, pressing a handkerchief to his red-rimmed nostrils.

'To the Empire', agreed Azimandro with a nod. 'That is my thought and that of Taradon. She may seek to flee to the Empire'.

'Surely she won't come here, to Tazman, then', said Zanidas, eyes clouding. 'That would be folly'.

'It would', agreed Azimandro. 'She has not placed herself this close to the north-eastern edge of our realm merely to return this way once more. She would be required to cross through hundreds of miles of closely watched territory in order to reach the wharves of this place. No. She must seek ship closer to hand, and I can think of only one place that might serve her needs'.

'Where?' Zanidas asked earnestly, setting down the poker and walking over to peer at the map, where his nephew's large finger now lay.

The Supreme Hierarch drew his spectacles from an inner pocket, placed them on his nose, and looked closer.

'Where?' he asked again. 'I see nothing here'.

Azimandro laughed.

'Sure, it does not feature on this map, or on any other, to my knowledge, but somewhere here', he indicated, stabbing his finger at the map. 'Amongst these dismal marshes, at the mouth of a river, lies a town, a notorious nest of pirates – and that is where I think we may find her. The place is called Shangharad'.

'Shangharad! Yes! I have heard of it', mused Zanidas, looking up at Azimandro with rheumy eyes, curiously magnified by the lenses. 'A thorn in the side of our commerce, I understand. Well, I suppose you will be making arrangements to go there'.

'If only it were that easy, uncle', sighed Azimandro, straightening up and stretching himself languorously. 'But as we have discussed, it is very remote and surrounded by swamps that would be quite impassable to any but the most determined force. Likewise, the sea approaches are said to be very treacherous and difficult with many a lethal sandbar ready to snap the masts out of any unwary ship that encounters them. It is for that reason that the wretched place has remained inviolate so long'.

'I know', sniffed Zanidas. 'I have had several delegations of merchants complain to me of the depredations of those corsairs'.

Azimandro nodded in agreement.

'But it would be very costly, perhaps very hazardous, to attempt to stamp out this nest of snakes, and for these reasons the attempt has not been made. It is a nuisance to us and to our trade, but the nuisance has not become acute enough to merit determined action'.

'Until now', said Zanidas.

'Until now', concurred Azimandro.

'Who rules this place?'

'A fellow who styles himself Count Gradivin', answered Azimandro, flexing his knuckles and yawning in a manner that no other inhabitant of the realm might think appropriate in this context.

'Then he must certainly be notified that he must give her up forthwith, if he has her', snapped Zanidas, bristling once more at his nephew's insolence.

'Perhaps he should', agreed Azimandro with a half-smile and a glance that harboured an unspoken taunt.

It was clear enough to Zanidas that he despised his uncle, but that uncle felt powerless to oppose him. The spirit of Yuzanid moved within him to some degree. He saw it, saw the dangerous elemental power in the man and, despite himself, despite his disgust at his own weakness, he was in thrall to it.

'And, in addition, a demonstration of force must be made', continued Zanidas, setting these thoughts aside, sweeping off his spectacles and crossing to peer out of the window.

Beyond the rain-streaked window panes, the city lay hunched beneath weeping clouds as far as the vague grey line where the heavens embraced the land.

'This army of yours', he said, waving a hand vaguely. 'Clogging up the city. Take it out to Racine. Advance northward to the fringes of those stinking marshes and let it take up quarters there, ready for a determined progress to the walls of this accursed place when the weather allows. Let this Count Gradivin fellow know that we are in deadly earnest'.

'But what about our plans to chastise the Empire?' asked the general. 'The truce ends soon enough and we intended to make our attack shortly thereafter. You know this'.

'I do know this', sighed Zanidas, turning back to his nephew. 'I know it very well, but I also know that our endeavours are doomed to failure unless we first fulfil our sacred duty to our Lord. The Golden Child is our absolute priority. We must secure her person – and your army is required to demonstrate the sincerity of our intent'.

'Very well', grunted Azimandro, rolling up the map. 'But when one draws back the bowstring to let fly an arrow, one cannot long hold it back'.

'You will get your war', assured Zanidas, placing his hand on Azimandro's shoulder and looking into his eyes. 'I promise you. But first Yuzanid must have his due'.

Azimandro nodded, although resentment smouldered in his countenance.

'And in the meantime', continued Zanidas, 'we shall send emissaries by sea'.

It was late January and there had been days of snow in Callisto, the place that was called, simply, The City. The Empire of Erenor's capital, that busy hub of commerce and governance, was almost stifled beneath a chilling blanket of snowfall, continually renewed whenever attempts should be made to clear the streets.

Paril Tyverios, Admiral of the Fleet, made his way cautiously across the slippery cobbles of the outer ward of the emperor's palace with his staff following equally cautiously in his wake, their breath silver amongst the drifting snowflakes. They skirted the base of Brodon's

Column, but the great statue of the long dead emperor himself, on his marble charger, was lost high above amidst the grey murk of snowfall.

'I trust there will be a warm welcome for us within', suggested Paril's assistant, Garrant, at his side as a servant bearing a snow-clearing broom, stepped aside to let them pass, his face pinched and blueish with the cold.

'No doubt the temperature will be warm enough', grunted Paril, pulling the hood of his cloak further down over his face as they approached the famous Leonine Doors, where Tio's bronze image glared down forbiddingly upon them from the plinth above the portal. 'Whether we shall bask in the warmth of His Majesty's approval, though, is another matter entirely', he added grimly.

The temperature within those portals was hardly less icy, given the impracticability of heating the vast and labyrinthine sequence of halls and corridors that encompassed this wing of the palace. However, there was no snow to blow into their eyes, and the chilly air was at least free of the piercing wind that blew the snow into high drifts in the streets beyond. Paril could throw back his hood, respond courteously to the greetings of heavily wrapped functionaries in the corridors and prepare himself for his meeting with the emperor with some composure.

In truth, it would have taken a tempest of truly titanic dimensions to distract him from the task at hand, given that this coming interview had occupied his thoughts for the best part of the previous week.

He found himself clenching and unclenching his fists anxiously as he approached the silver doors of the emperor's lesser audience chamber. Here, he must pause beneath the impassive gaze of the splendidly liveried guardsmen who stood there and submit to the questioning of the official who sat at the desk to their side. This official was well-known to Paril, offered him a vague smile, indeed, but must necessarily consult with his notes as though he did not, before vanishing along a corridor that gave access to the side of the chamber through a more ordinary door. Whilst the official notified the emperor of Paril's arrival, the admiral had leisure to inspect the beautifully wrought carvings on the doors between the guards.

In twenty-four panels, amongst ornate foliate scrolls, ancient artists had depicted scenes from myth and legend, beginning with the creation of the universe and finishing with Niall's stepping out onto the shore of Toxandria almost four millennia previous. It was at moments like this, as it was intended to do, that the vast weight of history seemed to bear down upon him with irresistible force. Of course, it was necessary to stand in silence in this revered space whilst a few stray snowflakes drifted down from the windows below the high cupola with its mosaics, far above his head.

At last, the silver doors drew smoothly open and Paril was admitted into the imperial presence by the High Chamberlain and his assistants, bowing low as Paril advanced into the chamber. Garrant and the others must wait outside, where benches around the outer walls were placed for the accommodation of supplicants.

Inside, the glazed windows were shuttered against the cold but the place was aglow with candle light from great chandeliers that cast a warm light upon the Emperor of Erenor.

'Your Grace', murmured Paril, settling himself to one knee before the living embodiment of Tio's earthly realm.

'Tyverios', grunted Emperor Gelon from his place on the raised dais at the rear of the chamber.

The chair he occupied there was not the imperial state throne from the Aulophagynt, where the emperor sat in glory amongst the highest in the land on formal occasions. This one, although encrusted here and there with gold ornament, was a more ordinary chair, and doubtless more comfortable for it.

'I hear you come with a proposal', continued Gelon, stifling a yawn and getting to his feet in order to approach his subject. 'You may stand'.

He indicated a perfectly ordinary table with chairs next to one of the glowing braziers that rendered the space habitable. Maps were strewn upon the table, as were ink horns and writing materials.

'And then you may sit', added Gelon with a wry smile, indicating one of the seats. 'I am aware of the purpose of your visit, and I suppose we must look at your plan in detail. This will be the one that your superior is so anxious about, I take it'.

'Indeed', agreed Tyverios. 'The same. But he authorised me to refer it to you nevertheless'.

'You have evidently driven the Lord High Admiral to distraction and he wishes to rid himself of your importunings', laughed the Emperor, pulling out a chair for Paril and gesturing towards it in a way that might not be declined.

Paril sat, albeit awkwardly.

Gelon was very different to his late unlamented elder brother Stireon, with whom he had shared the throne for the better part of four years. Stireon, in the absence of virtues that would command the respect of others, had insisted on every courtesy and dignity that his exalted status allowed. Lesser mortals were never permitted to sit in his presence, and given that he was half a head shorter than his younger brother, arrangements had of necessity been made to ensure that this head was always raised above all others in any official gathering.

But now Stireon had been gathered to the embrace of Tio, and Gelon ruled alone – at last. Energetic, intelligent and possessed of a powerful charisma, Gelon commanded the respect of all, without recourse to archaic ceremony.

Paril glanced around as he ordered his thoughts, no small task in those intimidating circumstances. It was almost possible to believe that he was alone with his emperor, although a secretary behind a carved and pierced ivory screen would undoubtedly be taking notes, and various guards stood in shadowed niches around the chamber.

'You are aware that the Vhanakhori are preparing a great armament?' asked Paril.

Gelon, seated on the opposite side of the table, inclined his head gravely.

'So I am told. They have perhaps recovered from the ignominy of Stromengar'.

'It would appear that they have and that they wish to renew the naval war with us when the truce ends'.

'Which is rather fewer than three months away', observed Gelon, regarding Paril shrewdly. 'And I am told that their ships outnumber ours by a fair margin'.

'They do', agreed Paril, wondering how to point out that the Imperial Navy was at a low ebb in a way that did not imply criticism of his host. 'Our brave mariners would doubtless perform prodigies of heroic endeavour in defence of the realm, but numbers bring with them their own inevitable logic and...'

The emperor raised a hand to stem his subject's flow.

'The Duke of Caneloon, your superior, my Lord High Admiral, Nestorides, judges that our fleet may not be risked on the high seas against such odds, because its loss may not be countenanced, whereas its continued existence obliges our enemy to practice caution with regard to making any amphibious descent upon our coasts', the emperor noted, smiling mischievously and stroking his small, precisely cut beard. 'And you consider this approach folly? Many would consider it prudent'.

'They might', conceded Paril, pleased that Gelon had not explicitly associated himself with the latter position. 'But I consider it excessively cautious'.

'You do?' Gelon enquired, nodding slowly. 'I have heard that you are a bold fellow. Then what course do you propose?'

'This', said Paril, leaning forward over the map.

He drew from his pocket a small, carved wooden model of a galley, no larger than the tip of his finger, and placed it over the tiny painting of the great port of Caneloon, where it lay at the base of its marsh girt gulf.

'Do go on', urged Gelon. 'Unless you wish me to believe that you agree with Nestorides, namely that the fleet should remain at anchor there. He is a master of inaction, is he not?'

'Not at all', said Paril, suppressing a smile. 'For the purposes of this illustration, Your Grace may wish to imagine that the date is the twelfth day of February...'

'The eve of the expiry of the truce', observed the emperor, nodding thoughtfully.

'Just so, and the fleet sails here...' indicated Paril, moving his model smoothly out of the gulf of Caneloon and into the Sea of Ormaris that lay between the mainland and the island of Eudora, '... and descends upon the enemy fleet in Tazman here as it lies unmanned and at anchor. We burn the ships, capture as many as we may, sack the warehouses on the wharves there and sail away crammed to the gunwales with the riches of one of the wealthiest cities in the world'.

Paril looked up from the map to find that Gelon was regarding him steadily, one fine aristocratic eyebrow raised in a quizzical manner.

'And Nestorides is not enamoured of this utterly foolproof plan, this flawless scheme by which we might encompass the downfall of our enemies? Is he blind? Is he unmoved by its obvious merits, its transparent brilliance?'

Gelon picked up the galley and regarded it pensively for a moment, before throwing it onto a nearby brazier, where it quickly burst into flames, a perfect metaphor for Paril's plan.

Paril found himself blushing, unable to respond to the emperor's caustic irony.

'Naturally, he perceives that some might raise practical objections'.

'He is right to perceive them. He would be blind not to. Perhaps you can assure me that he is wrong... that everyone is wrong but you'.

'I shall try', said Paril, swallowing hard.

'But you succeeded?' asked Mirona Tyverios, Paril's wife, when they spoke several hours later. 'You persuaded His Grace of the virtues of the course you propose?'

Paril ran a hand through his thinning hair and strode to the window of Mirona's chamber, which offered a view of the city rooftops as dusk settled upon the city behind shifting curtains of snow. Mulled spiced wine, in a fine goblet, nestled in his other hand and he took a deep draught of this comforting concoction before turning to his wife.

'I did not, I think', he admitted. 'But I persuaded him that it was not utter folly, so at least I may count it a qualified success'.

His wife, who was well-accustomed to speaking her mind to him, and whose mind was as sharp as any in the realm, affected what she conceived to be the bluff voice of their emperor.

'It is a scheme of such wild-eyed idiocy', she began, 'that only a madman could have conceived of it, and accordingly our enemies will be deceived, unprepared, when our mighty fleet descends upon them'.

She reverted to her ordinary voice.

'That, as I understand it, is what you were attempting to convey to His Grace'.

Mirona came up at his side, held his arm gently and smiled that half-mocking grin at him that always awoke one of his own. They had been married nearly twenty years, and the union had been a strong one, combining political expediency with genuine affection.

'Nestorides will not see it', laughed Paril. 'Although he certainly thinks me a lunatic. Much depends on the wind, of course'.

'On Tio's will, then', nodded Mirona, taking the goblet from Paril's hand and raising it to her own lips.

She was a handsome woman in her mid-forties, with high cheekbones and dark hair that swept to her shoulders, shot through with more than a few strands of sliver.

'Surely we must pray to Tio with unusual fervency', she added, her full red lips twitching into a smile once more

'Yes, we require that the wind should be in the west', agreed her husband. 'But that is the prevailing wind in that season, and Tio need not depart from his usual practice on our behalf. I explained that the wind will carry us down the straits to Tazman and that swift vessels will scour the seas before us, to ensure that no word is carried to our enemy in advance of our descent. The final stages will be under cover of darkness, so that the breaking of dawn will see us sail into the inner roads of the great harbour there. And then we shall see that devil Yuzanid bow before the fury of his divine brother'. Paril pressed his lips together firmly and an expression of inflexible determination settled in his features as he uttered these final words.

'It is quite certain, I declare', said Mirona, stepping back from him, her own face serious, now. 'I have seen it written in your countenance, as though by Tio's hand'.

'Admittedly we will need a goodly parcel of fortune and some exceptional skill amongst the scout ships, but I am quite sure of their mettle. I have trained them myself'.

'And I suppose the harbour of Tazman will be undefended?' ventured Mirona. 'I suppose the custodians of the fortresses at the harbour mouth will cheerfully salute you, will look upon you indulgently as you sail past with your brave fleet to destroy their countrymen?'

'You sound alarmingly like His Grace', chuckled Paril, playfully pinching her cheek. 'And as I did to him, I shall assure you that my marines, set ashore under cover of darkness, will fall upon those fortresses like a thunderbolt, even as the first light of dawn streaks the sky. Their guns will be silent as we pass them'.

'Well, it all sounds perfectly straightforward, husband. I cannot see any way in which circumstances may conspire to frustrate you. You have thought of everything. I take it that your next task is to convince Nestorides of the virtues of your plan'.

'It is, my dear, and it is for that reason that I may not tarry here. I must be away to Caneloon once more tomorrow. Garrant is even now arranging for the carriage'.

'Always such haste, such importunate urgency', clucked Mirona. 'What is it with you military men that time oppresses you in such a manner? And you a hundred miles away and more'.

'Well', replied Paril, crossing to a table where a pitcher stood and refilling his goblet. 'If you wished to dwell in a landlocked city, three days from the coast, and you wished to remain close to your husband, it was perhaps not wise of you to marry a sailor'.

'You have me', she conceded, 'although you are far from being a horny-handed tar, I declare. Admiral has a fairer sound, and I don't doubt you will add more laurels to your brow when spring comes. Our daughter will be disappointed to hear that you must away so soon'.

'I must go to her', nodded Paril. 'Is Cortesia parading herself once more before the love-struck youth of the city?'

'She is not', answered Mirona disapprovingly. 'At least not just now. She is in the library'.

'Of course. The library – amongst her true and favourite sweethearts, for books will never disappoint her'.

In Kyresios' library, more than five hundred miles away, a discussion on eagles, vultures and other raptors native to the western regions of the Vertebraean Alps was interrupted by the arrival of a servant, who delivered a message that Kyresios read with apparent concern. He made his apologies and left, leaving Axilo and Stilli to converse alone.

'We should perhaps practise with the swords again after lunch', observed Stilli, crossing to look out of the window. 'The snow appears to be abating'.

'With pleasure', smiled Axilo. 'After all your patient tutelage, I feel that I may be able to best the average five-year-old'.

'Nonsense!' laughed Stilli. 'You are coming along very well'.

She was reassuring him of this with kisses when Kyresios' return obliged them to pull awkwardly apart.

'Do not blush on my behalf, please', urged Kyresios with a vague wave of his hand, returning to his chair and looking strangely flustered.

'Is something amiss?' asked Axilo, having exchanged a wondering glance with Stilli.

'There is', admitted Kyresios. 'Very much there is. News has come across the marsh. It appears that a large force of the Hierarch's army has encamped on the further edge of that region and is said to be bringing in supplies in large quantities'.

'Do they mean to attack this place by coming through the marsh?' asked Stilli, eyes wide, a prickle of fear traversing her scalp.

'It would be wholly impractical during winter', replied Kyresios, waving this notion away. 'But it is not impossible they might attempt it in the spring. It is certainly intended as a threat, at the very least. My master will be concerned. I ask myself why the Hierarchs are suddenly so interested in us', he continued, suddenly piercing Stilli with his bright blue eye. 'It as not as though our activities have been any more predatory than usual this last year. Gradivin is careful to ensure that his presence here never becomes more than an irritant. If trade were to suffer too grievously from his predations, the Hierarchs or even the Empire might finally be stirred from their torpor to eradicate him. It is a fine calculation, but one he has managed successfully, until now'.

'I see', managed Stilli, swallowing hard as her host continued to regard her with interest.

'I wonder what might have changed?' continued Kyresios. 'And there is another thing. During the most recent of these tempests, a ship was dashed upon the sandbars to the south of this place and some poor wretch was cast up on the shore clinging to a spar of wreckage. He soon died, but before breathing his last, he claimed that his ship bore an embassy from Tazman that was attempting to reach this place. I ask myself why the Hierarchs should risk sending an embassy to this obscure place, amidst this season of storms, when no sensible mariner ventures forth from his harbour'.

'Oh', said Stilli, casting her eyes down into her lap.

'I ask myself if there is something that you have not told me?' continued Kyresios smoothly. 'And I urge you to come forward with it before I convey this intelligence to my master – as I must'.

Stilli exchanged an anxious glance with Axilo before deciding that she must place her trust in this man. There was no alternative.

'I am the Golden Child', she said bluntly.

Chapter Twenty

It was already growing dark when Stilli had begun her story. Kyresios sent for lamps as the meagre winter light failed and, in the yellow glow of these, Stilli hesitantly admitted the truth of her significance to her pursuers. It was a lengthy tale, but Kyresios attended closely, nodding his head or pursing his lips from time to time. At last, he leaned back in his seat and uttered a deep sigh, running a hand over his bald pate.
'Tio's breath', he murmured. 'This is not good news'.
'No', agreed Stilli. 'But what does it mean?'
'It means, in all likelihood, that your chances of departing from this place are utterly destroyed', said Kyresios. 'I am sorry to tell you this, but it is true. If the count hears of it, he will do one of two things, if I am any judge. If he fears that the Hierarchs may send a significant force against this place in spring, he may think it politic to surrender you to them in order to avoid future difficulty. On the other hand, Gradivin may see you as an opportunity to enrich himself enormously. He has an insatiable thirst for gold. He may propose to sell you to them for some huge sum of his own invention. In either case, I'm afraid the future looks bleak for you, my dear. For you and your companions', he added with a glance for Axilo, who sat glumly, looking from face to face.
'Then why are you telling us this?' asked Stilli after a few moments in which her thoughts were not hers to command. 'Why are you already not whispering this into your master's ear? Why are we not already on the way to confinement in some dungeon beneath this castle to await his pleasure?'

Kyresios nodded slowly.

'It appears that you are a person of great importance', he said at last. 'As has become increasingly apparent. Your curious status as Yuzanid's thwarted prize would make you a vital commodity in the eyes of those who worship and those who abhor him alike. Oh, how the emperor would love to deliver you to safety, should he ever learn of your existence! That would surely be to spit in Yuzanid's eye and to confound his followers. We must look for an opportunity to spirit you away from here at the earliest opportunity'.

'We?' Stilli gasped, her heart leaping within her at his use of this word.

'I say *we* advisedly', cautioned Kyresios. 'My deputy Baradian has been remarkably obsequious to the count in recent times, and I fear that he claims to be able to replace me. Naturally, should the count come to give credence to this, my life would hang by a thread. The Empire has seen fit to ignore my plight – so far. He may choose simply to send them my head in order to underline his sincerity in any future dealings.

'No, this new development has forced a decision upon me at last', announced the secretary, waving away Axilo and Stilli's declarations of shock. 'I shall come with you'.

'You will?' asked Axilo and Stilli in unison.

'Indeed', agreed Kyresios, nodding gravely. 'It seems certain that the Hierarchs have attempted to communicate with the count through that first doomed embassy, although their attempt perished upon that fatal storm-lashed sandbar. They will try again, no doubt, but first they must await the outcome of the first, and it may be some time before they realise it was lost. They may attempt to send a party through the trackless marsh, but I rather doubt it at this time of year. I think their dignity will be better served by making another attempt by sea. And we shall be ready for them', he added with an enigmatic smile.

'You will not mention any of this to the count?' asked Stilli, hardly able to believe her good fortune.

'I will not. At least for the present, I am the chief conduit by which intelligence of this kind reaches his ears. It is my contacts who have imparted this news to me, and there is no reason why they should choose to inform others lower down the chain of intelligence, if you take my meaning. We are very fortunate that Baradian is nursing a head cold and has been languishing in his quarters these last few days, or he might have been the first to hear the news. For the moment, the count need not know of the movements of the Hierarchy's forces or of the destruction of its embassy – nay, even its existence – but word may still reach him by other means. We have contacts in Tazman and further afield, and although I would usually hope to see correspondence from them before it passes his desk, I cannot be certain of it. I'm afraid that we face a very uncertain future'.

'I believe we already did', laughed Axilo, 'with Stilli's life and those of her friends' hanging on the thread of your master's whim. Could we not steal a vessel from yonder harbour and sail it away?'

'If you have some miraculous way of furnishing it with a skilled and willing crew of mariners, prepared to sail out into the teeth of these gales and face the deadly wrath of the count, then certainly we may', said Kyresios regretfully. 'But I fear that we may not be so fortunate'.

'What about the marsh?' asked Stilli. 'Mull has found an old boat'.

'If it comes to it, we may need to adopt that expedient option', sighed Kyresios. 'But I fear we would soon be caught. None living out there would wish to annoy the count, and many would be delighted to gather the reward for your capture. Besides, it is vast and trackless waste and we would remain within the dominion of your enemies even should we, by some miracle, gain the far side of it. No, I think we must await the coming of a second embassy', he said, placing his hand on Stilli's, where it lay on the table between them. 'And then we may have our ship'.

Azimandro was sharpening and polishing his sword when the vision came. He might easily have entrusted the task to some servant, but he felt a particular affection for this blade and would not countenance anyone to touch it but he. He had been invested with the weapon by the Supreme Hierarch himself, at a great ceremony beneath Yuzanid's gaze, and it was easy to believe that the god had placed some of his power within it. Despite the circumstances of his having received it, the sword was no decorative, ornamental weapon to be borne aloft in arcane ceremonies. On the contrary, it was a plain, practical sword, perfectly weighted and adapted to its owner's huge stature. It had drunk deep of the blood of Yuzanid's foes, and only Azimandro's hand would bring its bright steel to the finest of razor edges. He felt that it was almost a living thing, an extension of his being. In battle, he felt that it embodied the white-hot rage of Yuzanid, enabling god, man and steel to move as a single, invincible entity. He was reflecting upon this circumstance, as he often did, when Yuzanid entered his mind, appearing before him as a vague, shimmering form in the corner of his chamber.
'Master', murmured Azimandro in astonishment, falling upon his face before this apparition.
'Sinew of my hand, light of my fury', rumbled Yuzanid's voice within his head. 'For long the wall between the worlds has hindered communication with my subjects but now that wall is breached, at last. How fare my ungrateful servants in their attendance to their duty'.

'You know that this one is faithful and true', answered Azimandro, his lips almost brushing the hard tiles of the floor. 'My people are humble, they are penitent and they strive to repair the bargain that was broken'.

'But you fail', snapped Yuzanid. 'You continue to fail, and your realm continues to suffer my displeasure because of it. Where is my Golden Child that you have promised me? I thirst for her spirit as I have thirsted these thirteen long years. I have sent my people signs, but for the first time, I break the wall between the worlds to assure you of this with my own voice. I sense that a crisis approaches, and my thirst is great. Unless our sacred bargain is repaired, I shall not aid you. You know this'.

'I do – as do I thirst to deliver her unto you', replied Azimandro. 'With all my heart I desire it. And I shall slake that thirst before long. We believe we know where she lies'.

'That knowledge is mine also', agreed Yuzanid. 'My brother has done what he may to frustrate my perceptions of this corner of my realm, but nevertheless I have seen through the veils that cleave my world from yours. There is a small town on the fringes of Eudora that lies beyond the remit of your power. The ruler of this place is a minor irritant, a thorn in the side of Erenor, Vhanakhor and other kingdoms besides'.

'Shangharad', muttered Azimandro. 'We had drawn that conclusion. We have sent an embassy to demand that she is given up to us, so that we may fulfil our side of the bargain at last'.

Yuzanid uttered a bitter laugh.

'You will never hear any result from your mission, because that embassy was lost, shipwrecked in a tempest. I tell you this that you may send another. I know that your plans require my consent and my approval. You should know that I shall frustrate all of

your ambitions, I shall raise not a finger to sway the course of destiny until what is mine is mine once more. Hear me, for you are dear to me, the vessel of my earthly power. None shall stand before you when our bargain is restored'.
'I shall restore it, Lord', cried Azimandro, tensing the muscles in his arms and back, his face rising from the floor. 'I promise you'.

It was the end of January before Stilli entered the count's thoughts once more, after a long period during which it seemed he had forgotten her.
She had become thoroughly used to a quiet life amongst her friends, barely venturing into the streets of the town for fear of exciting comment, and spending much time amongst the wintry wastes about its walls, watching for any sign of a second embassy from Tazman. It was not to last, however, as was disclosed to Stilli by Emeni one afternoon.
'I'm sorry to say that he has remembered you', she said as they walked together in the little garden courtyard, wreathed in their own breath whilst glinting frost encrusted the delicate branches of the little trees and shrubs.
'He has?'
Stilli stopped abruptly in her progress at Emeni's side, so that she must swivel to look back at her. She found that her heart was suddenly racing and a hotness came into her brow despite the chill of the air.
'Yes', confirmed Emeni, approaching her now and placing a cold hand to her cheek. 'I thought I should tell you. For long it has suited him to pretend to have forgotten you, since he does not understand you. He may even fear you in some deep crevice of his dark mind. But last night, in the hall, one of his captains drew

you to his attention, and he could ignore you no longer. He proposes another *entertainment*'.

'But my lady', objected Stilli. 'I had thought that no others in his ranks could be induced to fight me, given that my reactions are, well... as they are'.

'I doubt that circumstance has changed', answered Emeni, her hand falling away and a wry smile twitching at her lips. 'But he has something in mind for you, nevertheless. I cannot tell you what to prepare for, because I do not know. However, I am to tell you that your presence is required, you and your friends, in the hall tonight'.

It was with the severest trepidation that Stilli answered the count's summons that night. As ever, the hall was hot and crowded with a jostling mass of mariners at the tables set up there. Lamps and candles glinted on chins and cheeks made greasy by the roasted flesh of swine and fowl. The clink of jugs and goblets, where the count's wine sloshed, was almost lost in the cheerful hubbub of a company that had eaten and drunk well, awaiting only the entertainment that had been promised them.

Stilli, that entertainment personified, found herself arrayed once more in what she thought were her "provocative" garments and required to stride into the hall with her sword at her left hip in the manner that had preceded her previous victory. Whereas once, for a while, the short skirt and the tight bodice had filled her with a sense of delicious power, she now felt only vulnerable and exposed as she advanced to stand before the count at his high table. The nick on her thigh was long healed, but she was conscious of its fine white line on her flesh and wondered whether that flesh would face fresh injury as the count and his lieutenants looked upon her. There was laughter amongst them and an anticipatory glint in their eyes as the count stood and the hall fell silent.

'Stilitha', he roared in a voice adapted to carrying to the furthest reaches of the hall, stirring the dust in the rafters above. 'Did you think I had forgotten you?'

'I have awaited your pleasure', she answered as confidently as she could muster but feeling the blood drain from her cheeks. 'And I have been ever at your command, should you seek to summon me'.

She spread her arms wide, bands and bangles sparking in the candlelight.

'That is a pretty bauble', grunted Gradivin, gesturing at the sapphire necklace. 'Remove it now, for I would not see it broken'.

Servants stepped forward to unfasten it behind her neck and carry it to the count's table, where Emeni spared Stilli an anxious glance. What did this mean? He had never commented on the jewellery at the outset of her previous bouts.

'We mean to place another ornament in your breast', laughed one of the men at Gradivin's side, an ugly rogue with a straggly beard. He brandished a knife.

Gradivin held up a leather purse that clinked with gold. 'I have decided to offer a prize to any who can pierce you with a knife or blade of any kind. It will be a test of skill on both sides, and I wager that there will be no shortage of volunteers to try their luck. You are fast. You are fast indeed, but we shall see if you may evade flying steel'.

Stilli swallowed hard. This was an entirely new form of challenge. She could see now that one wall of the hall had been cleared, leaving a space where she might take up her position facing the leering villains of the crowd, who now stepped out from their tables to watch this test of her skill.

With Gradivin to guide her, his big hand upon her bare shoulder, she was pushed roughly into place, whilst some of the bolder brutes urged him to caress other parts of her. She turned her back to the wall, settled her stance, took a deep breath and watched carefully as the fat man took up his position twenty paces from her, where a line had been marked on the tiles. He weighed the knife in his hand and narrowed his eyes. A throwing knife. She had heard of them but never seen one. Now, it appeared she might see many.

She must summon the "celerity" straight away. She did. It came.

The world slowed around her as she had come to expect, even as the man's hand crept back, moved forward and the spinning steel came arcing towards her with balletic grace. It was directed at her breast, where the necklace had so recently nestled, but it was easy to step aside and watch the knife collide harmlessly against the wall behind her, rebounding to the floor, where a servant snatched it up in ludicrous slow motion. A low murmur of approval, weirdly distorted, spread amongst the crowd as another of the count's lieutenants stepped forward to try his luck. Having easily evaded this first deadly missile, Stilli felt confident she could survive such a challenge. Once more, a knife glinted in the air as it glided towards her. The blade had been thrown with deadly accuracy. On this occasion, she watched its spin and trajectory with the closest attention, moving her hand to grasp its handle, snatching it from the air.

There was a great slow cry in the crowd, whoops of absurdly low-pitched croaking delight as she brandished the knife triumphantly before her. Had she the skill, she could have thrown the weapon back to its owner and had the satisfaction of seeing it buried in his throat. But she did not have the skill, and she feared the consequences of such retaliation. Accordingly, she merely dropped it to her side and prepared herself for the next.

It came, more came, and soon several were thrown at once, obliging her to dodge, seize or divert a constant stream of steel, amongst a slow cacophony of distorted whoops and cheers. It was certain that the "celerity" must fade, and fade it did, so that several knives came agonisingly close to finding their mark in her flesh.

Now a fellow came forth with a crossbow, placed a quarrel to the string and raised the blunt nose to aim. She had feared that the "celerity" would not serve her once more in such close proximity to her previous summons, but come it did and Stilli felt a warm tide of relief race through her as its fresh force transformed her reactions for a second time.

The crossbow twitched in its user's grip, and the quarrel sailed towards her amongst more knives, a pewter jug and an incongruous flying chamber pot that some excited pirate had snatched up. Stilli seized the jug and used it to turn aside the quarrel. Its deflected course caused it to lodge in one of the textile hangings with which the wall was enlivened. The flow of weapons briefly halted as raucous laughter rocked the hall. The quarrel had pierced the belly of one of the various naked female figures that were embroidered there, a nymph or a goddess no doubt. Certainly, it pleased the count's men but before long the steel rain of missiles began and Stilli was obliged to call upon the "celerity" again and again.

At last it ended. The count raised his hand and the steel tempest ceased. Glancing around, Stilli found that she was surrounded by knives, quarrels, goblets, pitchers and the chamber-pot, which thankfully had been empty. All had missed their mark in a deluge that seemed to Stilli to have lasted hours but was almost certainly only a few minutes.

'Very good', nodded the count with what seemed only grudging approval. 'I declare that you have passed this test. We must find something more to push at the limits of your powers'.

This ominous declaration rang in Stilli's ears as she limped painfully from the hall, joined by Axilo and her friends. She barely heard their anxious voices, barely felt Axilo's strong arms about her shoulders as her legs gave way beneath her. Four times, she had summoned the "celerity," and her limbs ached cruelly with the protest of muscles and tendons forced supply such violent and unnatural movement. It was too much, too much, and the tears sprang in her eyes, even as her friends looked on aghast.

'Get her up! Ger her up!' she heard on the edge of consciousness as the great hall doors slammed shut behind her.

'Mind her head. Here. Here. Let me'.

Any further words were lost to her as darkness descended to snuff out her consciousness like a candle flame.

Stilli awoke to find that it was daylight and that Axilo was looking upon her anxiously from a chair at her bedside.

'How are you, dear Stilli?' he asked softly as her eyes eased open.

She tried to lift herself on her pillow but the pain of protesting muscles seared through her and she sank back with a gasp.

'Do not move', urged Axilo, placing a cool hand to her cheek, leaning forward to kiss her brow. 'You must rest. You have survived another of the count's challenges and spared us all once again. But it has cost you, my dear', he added, his brow furrowed. 'And I wonder how long it will be before he brings about your destruction. What new devilry will he conceive of?'

'Where am I?' Stilli asked, her eyes taking in the unfamiliar ceiling and walls.

'Lady Emeni thought it wise that you were removed from her apartments', answered Axilo. 'In order to lessen the chance that her husband will be reminded of your continued existence, or come to resent your association with her'.

The latter was the more likely explanation, Stilli reflected. It was clear that she already occupied the forefront of her terrifying host's mind once more. Emeni knew her husband very well, and some change in his mood had made it seem prudent to disengage from a person the count had evidently decided to destroy.

'Tye came to watch over you these last two nights as you slept', informed Axilo. 'We assured him that you needed only rest, as the doctor made clear, but he would not accept it. I sent him away not an hour ago when he was nodding at your side. He will be mortified to hear that it was I who saw you awake'.

'Dear Tye. He is such a sweetheart', murmured Stilli, and then, her eyes widening. 'We must get away from this place, Axilo! Surely we must. I don't know how much longer I can rise to these perverse challenges'.

'Then you will not rejoice to see this', sighed Axilo, reaching to the table at her bedside and holding up the necklace that she had taken from Bondorin's tomb.

Stilli saw at once that there was something different about it. Almost all the beads were small and black. Where once there had been eight of them, now there was only a single yellow one, dangling close to Tio's golden lion pendant.

'How?!' Stilli gasped in exasperation, jerking upwards once more and sinking back with a groan.

'Please do not bestir yourself', soothed Axilo. 'But tell me, when was the last time you saw this?'

'Lady Emeni took it from me', answered Stilli. 'When I was required to dwell with her. I watched her put it away in a box, for safe keeping, she said. She thought it a dowdy thing, which I suppose it is. I wondered then if I had miscounted the yellow beads, since only seven remained, but how? How?' she repeated, her eyes widening in confusion as they fell upon the single yellow bead. 'I don't understand'.

'Lady Emeni brought this back to you as you slept', said Axilo. 'She too noticed the difference, the absence of those yellow beads, and was perplexed by it. I think I have the explanation'.

'You have?'

Stilli tried once more to sit up, cried out and sank back upon her pillow.

'Pray, do not agitate yourself, Stilli. It is this', he continued, fingering the beads pensively. 'When you call upon what your refer to as the "celerity", these beads are transformed from one state to the other. The yellow ones shrink and lose their lustre as they give up their power to you. They become the small, shrunken black ones we see here. This necklace is the source of magic for your extraordinary speed. It must be. I can think of no other explanation. Ask yourself on how many occasions you summoned that power since you acquired this necklace. I have no doubt you will find it has been seven times, the number of yellow beads that have vanished'.

'Then what..?' Stilli asked, swallowing hard.

'What if they all become exhausted?' supplied Axilo. 'Yes. I have been asking myself the same question, and the answer that comes to me is not one that I care to dwell on'.

'I might die, might I not?' Stilli forced herself to say.

'You might', agreed Axilo grimly. 'We all might'.

Chapter Twenty-One

'This boat of yours, where does it lie?' asked Stilli when she had recovered sufficiently to raise herself from her bed the following day.

She felt extraordinarily stiff, but the necessity for urgent action drove out all thoughts of a properly restful recovery.

'It is hidden among the reeds in a place I know', answered Mull, regarding her warily. 'Perhaps twenty minutes from here'.

The party sat, or stood, in Stilli's new room, from which a window offered a view across the marshes to which Mull referred. The window was glazed but a cold draught penetrated around the frame and all were wrapped warmly against the chill.

'Are you suggesting we should make use of it?' asked Radda. 'Are you thinking you may not wish to face any more of the count's challenges?'

'Stilli will rise to any challenge!' protested Tye loyally.

'No, Tye', said Stilli patiently, waving his protest aside. 'Radda is right. It is because of this'.

She drew out the necklace from its box and held it up so that her friends could examine it, turning then to Axilo in order that he could explain his theory about its function as the source of Stilli's power, the likelihood of its imminent exhaustion.

'It was put away for safety when Lady Emeni gave me the sapphire necklace, and I gave no further thought to it', sighed Stilli, whilst all pondered this news gravely. 'I expect that I would have noticed the substitution of the yellow for the black after each of those fights if I had thought to look'.

'Then you surely daren't fight again', observed Radda. 'You might find that one is not enough. It would surely be fatal if that power wasn't there for you'.

Stilli nodded, and the party exchanged anxious glances.

'We should be away', urged Mull at last. 'We must begin to assemble provisions for the boat'.

'I shall go to the market', declared Radda. 'And buy dry food'.

'Only a little', warned Axilo. 'Perhaps you should buy a little over several days. We must be careful not to attract attention or invite suspicion. We shall certainly be destroyed if the count hears of it. Could the provisions be stored in the boat?'

There was much practical discussion, of what kind of provisions they might need, of whether a compass might be procured and when they should set out, if that decision was indeed to be forced upon them.

'No word of this', Mull told Tye, finger raised. 'Do you hear me? No word. Our lives depend upon it'.

'I detect mistrust', complained Tye, wounded by the accusation. 'Am I not the soul of discretion in all matters?'

Stilli placed her hand on Tye's forearm and his expression softened.

'You have made friends amongst the servants here, Tye. You must say nothing to them. No farewells, no hints about great adventures to come, no earnest enquiries about the extent of the marsh. You do understand, don't you?'

'Of course, Stilli. You may rely on me', asserted Tye with a peevish glance for the others.

It appeared that Tye had eventually recognised Stilli's evident attachment to Axilo and understood its true meaning. She had come across him one day, shortly after her first lovemaking with the object of her

affections, finding him sitting alone in his room, whittling a stick. A scatter of shavings surrounded his chair and a piece of torn rag was tied around his thumb.
'Oh Tye, you have cut yourself', she remarked, seeing that blood seeped through the rag. 'Let me see'.
She approached to take his hand and unwind the rag, in order to inspect the wound.
'It is only a small cut', she observed as he held his thumb patiently in position for her. 'But did you wash it before you bound it? That knife is not the cleanest, I think'.
Tye shook his head, setting down the knife.
'Then we had best wash it, had we not? Is there water in that jug?'
The boy sat quietly whilst Stilli washed the wound and bound it once more, using a strip of clean handkerchief.
'There', she said at last. 'I daresay Radda would have done that for you, if she hadn't been in town'.
'I'm glad it was you that did it', smiled Tye sheepishly. 'I liked it. You noticed me'.
'I always notice you, Tye', objected Stilli, letting go of his hand and frowning. 'Of course, I do'.
'Not so much', sniffed Tye, inspecting his bandaged thumb and then regarding her sidelong. 'Not nowadays. You notice Axilo much more than me. You and he are...'
Words appeared to fail him, and he shook his head awkwardly.
'We are very close, yes', agreed Stilli.
'You love him, don't you?' said Tye in a small, sad voice.
She shuffled a little closer to him on the edge of the bed they now sat on, placing a consoling hand on his shoulder.
'I do', she agreed, looking earnestly into his eyes. 'I really do. I never thought I could love anyone in the way I love Axilo. But I love you, too, Tye'.
She opened her arms to embrace him and, after a moment, he began to cry.

'No, Tye, don't be like this', she soothed, stroking his hair. 'I know you'll always be there for me'.
'Not like that, not like man and wife', he sobbed into her shoulder, which was now damp with his tears. 'I wanted to marry you'.
'You know that can never happen', she told him. 'Not in this life. I am Axilo's, and one day perhaps I shall have a ring on my finger to declare it. The love you and I have is of a different kind, Tye, you must see that, but it's just as precious'.
It took many protestations of this kind before Tye could be, in some small way, consoled and his shoulders ceased to heave. She handed him the remainder of the handkerchief so that he could dab at eyes and nose.
'There's surely some lovely girl out there for you', she told him, squeezing his arm. 'Someone just like you, perhaps'.
'Another idiot?' he laughed bitterly, scrunching the handkerchief in his fist. 'That's what I am, isn't it? An idiot. I hear it all the time from folks when they think I'm not listening, and sometimes when they just don't care. I'm not like everyone else, am I? I'm like some lesser creature, some lesser vessel of the gods, wherein my brain was never quite finished. I still love you, though, and it aches within me when I see... when I see...'
'I know you do', comforted Stilli, feeling a surge of pity in her breast that almost robbed her of speech. 'I couldn't wish for a better friend. And I love you, too, just as I said. I have a very special love for you, a very special place in my heart'.
'Then I shall treasure it', he said, straightening his back and mastering himself. 'You know this. And I shall adore you 'til my dying day'.

The dying day that all of them must face seemed palpably closer when the date of the count's next feast was announced, and that within four days.

Emeni approached Stilli to warn her, regretfully, that her husband had already mentioned a fresh idea for her employment as "entertainment." It appeared that rather than preserving her own skin from flying missiles, she would be required to preserve those of her friends. They were to be secured to a wall and subjected to a rain of knives and other projectiles that Stilli must knock aside or pluck from the air.

'I am very sorry to have had to tell you this', said Emeni, having outlined this horrifying scenario.

'Then I will surely die', said Stilli. 'We will all die'.

'You doubt your powers?' asked Emeni, eyebrow raised.

'Certainly, I do', agreed Stilli, leaning on a table for support.

She felt suddenly sick to the stomach, her mind whirling vertiginously. She dare not disclose to Emeni that only a single yellow bead, a single burst of superhuman speed, remained to her.

'Then I don't know what to say to you', said Emeni grimly, placing a light hand to her shoulder. 'You must prepare yourself as you will, for what...'

It appeared that Emeni could not complete this sentence, although its burden showed clearly enough in her eyes.

'To die. I must prepare myself to die', supplied Stilli, but the thought did not find its way to utterance, and after a moment, when Stilli made no reply or gave no reaction, Emeni quietly withdrew.

It appeared that their only slender hope of salvation was Mull's hidden boat, and all agreed when Stilli had told them of the count's intentions that they must make use of it at the earliest opportunity.

However, as it transpired, there was no need to assemble provisions and barely any opportunity for Tye to unwittingly disclose their plans to others. Even as the company assembled glumly for their midday meal the next day, Kyresios entered their chamber looking unusually flustered. He was unattended and closed the door firmly behind him, having first glanced back to see that the corridor was empty. By this time, he had everyone's undivided attention and various items of food were poised between plate and mouth.

'The crisis is upon us', he announced, 'and we must make our decision'.

'What decision?' asked Radda, reasonably enough.

'At this very moment, a ship from Tazman, the *Storm Petrel*, a very weatherly brig bearing a flag of truce, is at anchor in the harbour, having been brought in by the pilot. The captain of the guard has notified me and begs that I may inform my master'.

'Then they have come for me', cried Stilli, her face suddenly ashen, letting fall her spoon. 'The Hierarchs have reached out their hand for me. What are we to do?'

'Do not despair', soothed Kyresios. 'At least not yet. Gradivin is out hunting on the fringes of the marsh to the south of here. He will not return 'til dusk. We have until then to act'.

'Act? How? How should we act?' demanded Axilo, wide-eyed.

'By responding to this demand', said Kyresios, holding aloft a letter in one hand. 'This is an official demand from the Hierarchs that Count Gradivin should relinquish one Stilitha Zandravo into the custody of the Vhanakhori envoy on this ship, or face the implacable fury of the Hierarchs. It threatens invasion by land and by sea, should the count choose to refuse their demands'.

'He will, won't he?' gasped Tye. 'The count will surrender Stilli to them'.

'He will if he is *able* to surrender her', replied Kyresios with a wry smile. 'I don't doubt it for a minute. But he may not do so if she is already surrendered'.

'What do you mean?' demanded Stilli, brow clouded. 'You are talking in riddles'.

'Hear me!' cried Kyresios, raising both hands to quell further protests of this kind. 'Hear me out. I have the authority, in Gradivin's absence, to convey you across the harbour to this ship with your friends, who will pose as my servants. Stilli must submit to be bound at the wrists in order that this subterfuge may succeed. There must be no farewells to any here, and we must go immediately. There is no alternative. I shall go now to set arrangements in place, and I shall be back within the hour. You must pack what things you can carry in a few bags and be ready. Do you understand?'

He glared about him with great intensity.

'But dear Kyresios', objected Stilli after a few moments of stunned silence. 'Shall we not then find ourselves upon a ship bound for Tazman, where my enemies await me?'

'We shall', agreed Kyresios with a nod and a tight smile. 'But then I have heard that gold speaks very eloquently to the men of the sea'.

A little more than an hour later, a launch, rowed by two of Kyresios' servants, made its way across the still waters of the harbour to the brig that was anchored there whilst a crowd of interested onlookers observed from the quayside. The crew of this vessel, some of whom darted anxious glances to the forts on the harbour's seaward side, stood ready to receive their visitors whilst the envoy from Tazman looked on anxiously from the quarterdeck, the brig's captain at his side. The pirates of this place had an evil reputation, and cutters crowded with armed men stood to in case the encounter should end unsatisfactorily.

'You will let me manage the negotiation', instructed Kyresios curtly as the launch came alongside.

'Why are you all looking at me like that', grumbled Tye as the party stood awkwardly in the swaying boat ready to face the climb up the brig's steep side to the quarterdeck.

Stilli, with Axilo at her side to steady her, was particularly hard-pressed to maintain her balance, since her hands were bound behind her, this to create the illusion that she was being transferred as an unwilling prisoner. Nevertheless, with a great many considerations weighing on her mind, it was not hard to maintain an expression of sullen discontent as sailors looked down upon her curiously from the gunwale above. With no means of holding on to anything for support, she was roughly bundled up the side with mariners above and below to impel her, arriving panting and dishevelled on the deck, where she found herself on her knees, regarded in wonder by the Vhanakhori envoy.

'And this is she?' she heard him ask Kyresios as the others in her party arrived around her.

'It is', agreed the secretary. 'The count has directed that she be given up. You will be aware that he seeks to give no offence to your nation'.

'Other than through relentless piracy and brigandage on the high seas', scoffed the envoy, whose name, it appeared, was Dannad.

'The count is aware that ships claiming to be acting in his name may inadvertently have given offence in the past', said Kyresios. 'For that reason, he offers your masters a token of his esteem, which may be found in the chest even now being brought aboard'.

Dannad and he turned to observe as a heavy wooden chest was effortfully brought over the side by perspiring crew members and placed at their feet. Stilli, remaining on her knees, recognised it as a larger version of the one that Gradivin had awarded her upon her most recent victory. Once opened, Dannad's eyes showed a very marked gleam of venality as they beheld the glittering cargo within. Gold coins of many sizes and denominations lay within, a fortune in any realm on earth.

'Handsome, handsome. I'm sure that will be received in the manner it was intended', he concluded, licking his lips.

'There are other negotiations that my master has authorised me to conduct with your superiors upon our arrival in Tazman', continued Kyresios smoothly. 'I feel sure that you will convey me and my suite', he said, a gesture encompassing Stilli's friends. 'We make no great claims in terms of accommodation, and doubtless you will be congratulated for furthering the cause of diplomacy'.

'Absolutely, very welcome, I'm sure', said Dannad, his eyes still fixed upon the gold until Kyresios closed the lid with a firm click.

'And here is a gift for you, in consideration of your generous offer to accommodate us', added Kyresios, withdrawing a leather purse from within his garments and pressing it into Dannad's hand. 'I trust you will show us to your accommodation'.

'Of course', agreed Dannad, taking the purse gratefully. He exchanged a few words with his captain, whose own eyes were lit with a very perceptible yearning for the chest's contents. The man went to seize Stilli roughly by the shoulders, prompting Tye to step forward anxiously, until Axilo's hand on his arm forestalled him.

'The prisoner need not be confined or ill-treated', instructed Kyresios. 'You will be aware that they are a person that the Hierarchy would wish to see delivered unto them in the best of health and treated with the respect that their unusual significance merits. Nor need she remain bound, unless you fear that she may plunge into the open ocean and swim away like a dolphin. I shall vouch for her good behaviour until our arrival in Tazman. No doubt you will wish to raise anchor immediately', he said, directing a meaningful glance at the nearest cutter with its crew of scowling pirates. 'These fellows are by nature inclined to resent the intrusion of strangers into their realm – and not all are as obedient to the wishes of my master as might be desired'.

'Well yes', agreed Dannad with a nod to the captain. 'Give the word, if you will, Captain Mariant. It seems that we have transacted our business here, and I believe you mentioned something about the tide, some urgency?'

Nothing could have improved the alacrity with which the crew set themselves to the capstan and their other stations to win the anchor, which rose dripping from the waters. Within minutes, jibs and topsails were set and sheeted home, by which the vessel might be urged out into the open water, assisted by the swiftly ebbing tide. The heavy chest was stowed away below decks, under Dannad's personal supervision, and locked within his cabin. Whilst accommodation was prepared for them, Kyresios stood on deck with Stilli and the others as the ship nosed out past the grim forts at the harbour mouth. The ominous blunt noses of cannon there threatened bloody ruin but now kept their silence. Soon, the pilot cutter that Kyresios had summoned was guiding them through the channels that led between treacherous sandbars and reefs towards the line of choppy waters which marked the boundary of the open ocean. There was a stiff breeze now, and the ship heeled as more flapping white sails were hoisted and let fall from her yards.

'When may we expect to see Tazman?' asked Kyresios of the brig's captain, once he was observed to have leisure from instructing his crew.

'That would depend, sir', answered the captain, a broad, short red-faced fellow, cramming a blue woollen hat onto his head. 'With these winds we should make Cape Lial in two days, but then there's The Narrows to pass and we'll be beating up against the Westerlies that blow this time of year. Maybe five days, all told', he added with a nod. 'Gods willing'.

'Gods willing', repeated Kyresios with interest. 'You are not a follower of Yuzanid, or indeed a Vhanakhori, I gather?'

'Not me, sir, nor any of us', laughed the captain, pushing his hat back on his head. 'The ship's a chartered vessel out of Dendera. We've a reputation, well-earned I might say, for being the most weatherly vessel on this coast, and we were in Tazman at the right time when they needed someone to hurry along their envoy'.

A downward glance, one of disgust, indicated the present location of this person.

'Seeing as how their last one came to grief, if what I hear is true', he added.

'I believe you are right', agreed Kyresios with a significant nod for Stilli. 'Do you know, Captain Mariant, I don't doubt that this will be a most stimulating voyage'.

Stilli, once freed from the cords that had bound her wrists, rubbed her sore flesh ruefully and blinked in the gloom as she was led down a steep ladder into the interior of the ship. There, various officers of the crew had been obliged to quit their tiny, cramped cabins and seek alternative accommodation, in order that their guests might avail themselves of them. Kyresios was soon engaged in fresh conversation with the envoy and his secretary, so she found herself alone, locked in a dark cubicle barely long enough to stretch out in and equipped with a swinging cot suspended from the beam overhead. A horn lantern hung from a hook on the bulkhead, and a pot with a cloth over it had been provided for her comfort. There was little other provision for her comfort, unless a thin blanket upon an equally thin, discoloured mattress could be described as such. After the quarters she had become used to, it seemed impossibly cramped. To add to this imposition, the lurching deck beneath her had already begun to cause a growing nausea to gnaw at her belly. Perhaps she was not a natural mariner. She could hear Tye and Axilo moving about beyond the thin oaken panels of the cabin's wall, but she did not call out to them. She had been told that she must disclose no acquaintance with them. Alone, isolated, her mind moved restlessly between fear and confusion.

Did Kyresios really intend to deliver her up to the Hierarchs? He had seemed a friend, a valued companion in recent weeks, but now they sailed for Tazman where she faced a fatal appointment with Draganach's bronze belly. To be sure, she had escaped from the count and whatever challenges he might have conceived of to bring about her death, but now she sailed upon a vessel in an enterprise that might readily bring about the same end. She climbed with difficulty into her cot and lay there, regarding the timbers of the ceiling above her morosely, fingering Bondorin's necklace where it lay at her throat once more. Even in the gloom she could easily find the single remaining bead by touch and caressed this absently as the wind rose to a sustained roar outside and the cot swung wildly with the vessel's heave and pitch.

Stilli's friends huddled in the small space described to them as the "ward room," where benches, a hanging table and numerous fragments of food suggested this served as the ship's officers' dining room. There were no portholes, or "scuttles" as the crew described them, and the company sat in the dim yellow light shed by a couple of swaying horn lanterns that swung from the low ceiling beams.

'I had always wanted to see the sea', Mull groaned, his face pale as the deck lurched and swayed beneath them. 'But I had not thought it would be like this'.

'Certainly it is a vigorous, stimulating motion, is it not?' chuckled Tye, beaming about him, apparently unaffected except in terms of the amusement it brought him. 'I swear I have never felt anything like it. Tell me, sir,' he added, plucking at the sleeve of a mariner who came hurrying through, 'do you suppose this tempest will soon abate?'

'What tempest?' demanded the man, before vanishing up a ladder.

'I fear the sea conditions are no more than might be expected at this time of year', observed Axilo. 'That is why the pirates remain in Shangharad during these months, no doubt'.

'Well, we must hope we don't share the fate of the last embassy from the Hierarchs', muttered Radda darkly as an empty pewter mug and plate came sliding across the table towards her.

'Do we even trust Kyresios?' demanded Mull in a strained whisper, having first glanced over his shoulder. 'Sure, he has escaped from the count, but at our cost, it seems to me. A Erenori diplomat like him, a clever fellow, is bound to find his way back to the Empire eventually, but what about us?'

He looked pointedly at Axilo and Radda.

'I'm thinking about us stepping ashore in Tazman', he suggested. 'Nobody much cares about we forest folk, I reckon, but you two can look forward to an appointment with the hangman, I should have thought, running from your valley as you have'.

'Burning and hanging yield pretty much the same result', observed Radda resignedly. 'And one murder should not be judged more heinous than another if it snuffs out a life'.

'And what about Stilli?' demanded Tye, after the others had lapsed into a reflective silence. 'She will burn in Draganach's belly. My faith argues that this is Yuzanid's due, but my soul rebels against the notion. How may we preserve her?'

'Let us not talk about death and the snuffing out of lives', cautioned Kyresios, emerging into the space and holding on to the walls for support. 'At least not prematurely. And let us keep our voices down, for Tio's sake. Nothing leaks more grievously at sea than secrets, I have heard, with all these fellows sealed up together in such close proximity and barely a finger's breadth of timber between mouths and ears'.

He shuffled himself onto a bench as Axilo and Tye made way for him.

'You are asking yourselves whether I have betrayed you, in order to save my own skin', he surmised, looking from face to suspicious face. 'And it is a fair question'.

'Perhaps you may set our minds at ease, then', suggested Radda. 'For we face certain death in Tazman, all except Tye and Mull here, and even they might be condemned for conspiring to assist Stilli in her escape'.

'For such contingencies to occur, we must first reach Tazman, must we not?' said Kyresios, leaning forward and speaking in a voice barely audible above the wind, the creak of timbers and the cries of the crew going about their duties above. 'And that is by no means a certainty. This is a chartered vessel. I received intelligence that this might be the case, after the destruction of their previous embassy. The crew of this vessel owe the Hierarchs no loyalty other than what their gold has purchased...'

'And a pound of gold may drive out an ounce', interjected Axilo. 'Is that what you're saying?'

'You are very astute', agreed Kyresios. 'And all set eyes upon the vast quantity of gold that my chest contained. This vessel has a crew of twenty-three, with four officers amongst them. Doubtless, their minds will be working upon the potential division of that sum amongst them, should this ship sail past Tazman and find some other refuge instead. There is enough in that chest to purchase a dozen ships such as this, or set each of them up for a lifetime of comfort and leisure'.

Kyresios smiled now, looking upon faces in which new hope was kindled.

'But I don't doubt they are honest men. They will look on approvingly with smiling indulgence whilst the envoy conveys this vast sum of glittering gold into the grateful hands of the Hierarchs'.

'So you seek to corrupt them?' asked Tye, whose eyes betrayed some glimmer of understanding. 'Is that what you're saying? Do you suppose that they may be persuaded to renege upon their contract?'

'Let none say that you are a dullard', laughed Mull, slapping him on the shoulder. 'How many are there in the envoy's party?'

'Only four', nodded Kyresios. 'He has his own secretary, a servant and a big brute who serves as a bodyguard of sorts. This was meant to be in the nature of an exploratory contact. The count's violence, greed and intractability are well known. I doubt anyone in Tazman imagined he would give up his prize without demur. I expect they thought a much greater degree of threat and coercion would be required in due course and that a powerful squadron would be sent nosing around this coast once these winter storms abate. I envisage a great army would begin finding its way across those marshes to threaten his walls'.

'Four, you say?' mused Axilo, whose face now wore an expression of cautious optimism. 'I suppose the crew could deal with them handily, if the captain directed them to'.

'I think you are right', nodded Kyresios, a mischievous glint in his eye.

Chapter Twenty-Two

'The captain is a moderately honest fellow', Kyresios told Stilli later when he visited her in her cabin.

They sat upon three-legged stools set in the narrow space next to her cot and rested their backs against the partition wall. Outside, Axilo and Tye patrolled the corridor to ensure that no eavesdroppers were at hand.

'Moderately?' repeated Stilli, whose seasickness had diminished somewhat but whose stomach nursed a sullen resentment of its situation.

'Indeed, but it would take a paragon of virtue, a shining saint of incorruptibility, not to be unmoved by that goodly portion of the count's treasury I was able to spirit away. We are very fortunate that the arrival of this ship and the count's absence from the town coincided so neatly, thank Tio!'

Kyresios cast his eyes upward and made a sign before his breast that Stilli had come to recognise as a token of piety. Her own hands twitched instinctively to mimic it. How far she had come from Yuzanid's grip.

'I have represented to Captain Mariant that he might have that chest for his own enjoyment, he and his crew, if only he could deliver us safely to a port in imperial territory, Garabdor, for preference, but really any cluster of seaside hovels owing allegiance to Callisto would do perfectly well. He has agreed', he added, forestalling Stilli's enquiry.

'Tio be praised!' gasped Stilli, prompting Kyresios to press a cautionary finger to his lips. 'And when might I expect to be released from this captivity?' she asked, looking around pointedly at the cramped cabin that enclosed them.

'He wishes to round Cape Lial, which, as you know, forms the south-easterly tip of Eudora, and then, when the intervening land mass takes the brunt of the northerly gales, he may have leisure to spare time from the management of sails, masts, cordage and the many other preoccupations of the mariner'.
'But soon?' pressed Stilli urgently.
'Soon', agreed Kyresios with a smile.

Soon, indeed, but not soon enough to relieve Stilli of the tedium of her solitary confinement, the deprivation of the company of Axilo and her friends. During the voyage towards the storm-bound cape, Stilli often had the unwelcome company of the envoy, who called in to see that she was safely secured despite the evident impossibility of her escaping his clutches. He invariably enquired politely of her health and looked upon her with a complacent smile, quite sure that her delivery unto the appropriate authorities in Tazman would have a salutary effect upon his career prospects. In addition, the burly bodyguard, although frequently incapacitated by seasickness, was sometimes to be found maintaining a watch outside her cabin.

Matters came to a head during the fifth day of their voyage when the *Storm Petrel* was working its way westward through The Narrows, the stretch of water where the shores of Eudora most nearly approached those of the mainland, no more than twenty miles wide at some points. The skies were quite clear at this point and the wind had died to a whisper, barely sufficient to fill the sails the mariners described as "topgallants and royals," high above the deck. Further sails, called "studdings," had been set up on either side of these, to gain every ounce of thrust from the fitful gusts. Consequently, in the bright morning sunlight, a towering white pyramid of sail presented a most impressive spectacle to those passengers standing on deck.

'I suppose we will see Tazman soon', supposed Dannad the envoy, peering away at the distant green-grey headlands that marked the Eudoran shore. 'Although, I must say, we appear to be closer to the mainland then we were on our outward journey. No doubt that is a temporary condition, brought about by your necessary manoeuvring to make best use of the winds', he added with a smile for the captain.

The envoy was in good spirits. It was likely that the evening tide would see him in Tazman once more with a valuable prize to present, not to mention a sizeable sum of gold. He was perplexed, therefore, to see an expression of discomfort settle in the captain's round, weather-beaten features as a group of the larger crew members gathered around him.

'Is there anything wrong?' he asked, his smile fading.

'I'm afraid there is, sir', replied the captain regretfully. 'I'm afraid... the fact it is... we won't be calling in at Tazman at all, beggin' your pardon'.

'What?! You must!' objected Dannad, his mouth falling open. 'Your contract...'

'Circumstances alter, do they not?' observed the captain. 'And the likelihood is, I'll soon be retiring from this seafaring lark, me and all the boys', he added with a nod for his grim-faced officers.

'This is outrageous! What can you mean by it?' demanded the envoy, whose face had assumed an alarming shade of crimson. 'You will convey me to Tazman at once – as your contract requires of you'.

'I will not', said the captain, shaking his head. 'We'll set you ashore on this side, tomorrow some time, and you can find your own way home, no doubt'.

'Stayn...' the envoy began, turning to his bodyguard for support.

His mouth began to form the words *arrest this man*, but Stayn's impassive features, the knitting of his narrow brow, showed that he well-appreciated the futility of it. He shrugged resignedly as three of the burlier members of the crew stared meaningfully at him.

'I think it better if you remain in your cabin', advised the captain in a low voice. 'We don't want any trouble here. Any awkwardness from you and it will be the hold, where you can sit in the dark and make the acquaintance of the rats. I trust we understand each other'.

Still protesting feebly, shrugging off the captain's hand on the shoulder, the envoy was led below deck where, to add to his misery, he was to find that the great chest of riches had been removed from his cabin.

'Allow me to congratulate you', murmured Kyresios, regarding the envoy's bowed shoulders with satisfaction as he was led off to his confinement. 'I do declare you managed that very well, Captain Mariant'.

'I deserve no congratulation', said the captain with a frown, rubbing his chin. 'For to break a contract in this manner does sorely try my conscience'.

'Doubtless you will have the wealth and the leisure to reflect upon it in comfort', observed Kyresios with a nod. 'You may attend to the mending of your conscience with my blessing and gratitude once you have delivered us safely to imperial shores'.

'I could, or I could simply knock you on your heads and drop you over the side, you and the envoy both', declared the captain, regarding him sidelong. 'Fear not, though', he added with a chuckle, seeing the sudden dismay in Kyresios' face. 'That conscience you mention has more than enough to be going at'.

'I suppose we may release Stilli from her cabin now', said the secretary with a weak smile and an involuntary exhalation of relief.

'I suppose we may', agreed the captain with a critical glance for the set of the topsails.

Soon, a blinking Stilli was standing with her friends on the quarterdeck, giving and receiving hugs and congratulations on their good fortune. Kyresios basked in their approval, nodding and smiling as the bay of Tazman opened slowly to their right and the gentle winds wafted them slowly past as the sun ascended the heavens.

'By nightfall we should have you out of these waters', the captain told Stilli. 'And we'll make straight for Marabdorin, that bein' the closest sizeable port to the border, if this wind holds'.

But the wind did not hold. What little breath of wind there was completely died and the *Storm Petrel* found herself becalmed in a sea like a polished mirror with barely a ripple to mar its smooth surface. The sails hung slack from their yards and the bright pennants dangled limply from the mastheads. Given that this was a busy shipping lane, even at this time of year, the surrounding sea was dotted with other becalmed vessels of various sizes and descriptions.

'This will never do', muttered Stilli anxiously, squeezing Axilo's hand as they stood at the rail together, their breath vapouring the chill air around them.

Their eyes strayed from the western horizon, where salvation lay, to the ominous grey and white mass of the city behind them.

'I am no mariner', admitted Axilo, shielding his eyes. 'But I swear we seem closer now. We can't be going backward, can we?'

'I'm afraid we can and we are', said Kyresios grimly, joining them at the rail. 'A westerly current flows through this channel and we're drifting back towards Tazman upon it. The wind may pick up soon enough, however', he continued, perceiving the dismay in their faces. 'I suggest that we pray that Tio may send us a favourable wind'.

Stilli required no encouragement to do this, given that Draganach's grim temple could already be discerned in the higher part of that distant city, beyond various intervening towers and domes.

It seemed, however, that Tio was deaf to their prayers, or else Yuzanid's power overmatched his in this place so close to the heart of his dominions. An occasional zephyr was observed to trouble the waters here or there in the broad channel, but the *Storm Petrel* remained in a glassy calm. The captain sent out his launch and his best oarsmen ahead, to bring the brig's head round and tow her onward, but it was clear that their efforts would be in vain when an ominous low vessel appeared from behind one of the low islands that sealed the bay.

'Mother of gods!' declared the captain grimly, spitting over the side. 'Now we're for it'.

'Why? What is it?' demanded Tye, glancing back from where he was leaning on the foremast shrouds.

'That, son, is a guard ship from Tazman', informed the captain, observing the newcomer through narrowed eyes. 'And she's a galley'.

'She moves with a purposeful air, does she not, with all those oars rising and falling?' observed Tye, speaking for all of them. 'And quite independently of the fickle winds, I suppose. Where does she go, do you think?'

'Too close to us for comfort, that's for sure', grumbled the captain, and then to his lieutenant. 'Stand ready with the signals'.

'Those are the flags by which vessels communicate with each other at a distance', explained Kyresios as Stilli and Axilo looked on, blank-faced. 'They hoist them to the masthead or to other places about the ship. The captain may be required to announce the ship's identity and her business'.

For now, thankfully, this was not necessary because the galley appeared to show no interest in them, altering course in a manner that would cause it to pass close astern of them, even as the first breath of a fresh wind plumped the *Storm Petrel*'s sails. It was a grim, low-sided vessel, painted in red and black with a long bronze ram cutting the water at its bow, a ram that could all too easily stove in the side of a vessel such as theirs, if directed with sufficient force and speed. It was said that dozens of such ships crowded the military harbour in that city, ready for renewed war with the Empire.

'Gods be praised', murmured Captain Mariant, glancing up at the sails of his own vessel.

Stilli's heart, which had laboured to an increasingly anxious beat as the galley drew near, looked over the rail to see that water was running smoothly past the sides once more, albeit agonisingly slowly. A gull's discarded feather crept past, inch by tortuous inch. But they were moving. At last they were moving!

'Perhaps we shall be spared yet, my dear', said Axilo softly at her side, divining the content of her mind.

He squeezed her hand, and once more hope sprang in her breast. During her confinement in that dark cabin below, her mind had moved to a fanciful consideration of the future they might enjoy together, should they reach the Empire at last. She had imagined a modest house in the famed city of Callisto itself, a small garden and a job for Axilo in the employment of Kyresios, once restored to his position in the emperor's service. In her wildest, most optimistic imaginings, ones almost lost in a golden haze, she had seen herself at Axilo's side as a priest sealed their partnership in marriage. And then there had been children – a boy and a girl, growing strong in a safe household with bright futures to embrace.

She turned, tears rimming her eyes, and nestled close to Axilo, squeezing his hand in hers. His wistful expression, his slow nod, suggested that such thoughts were in his own mind, too.

The galley was almost directly astern now. The faces of the crew and the ranks of the labouring oarsmen were clearly to be discerned. Some were busy beneath its stubby mast, hoisting the single triangular lateen sail that might assist its progress when the winds allowed. Some shouted cheerful greetings to those of the *Storm Petrel*'s crew whose duties placed them on the poop deck, receiving strained and awkward replies in return. Any suspicions that the galley's officers might have entertained regarding the business of the brig were enormously magnified when a slight young man jumped from her forecastle, landed with a huge splash and began striking out urgently towards the galley.

'What happened? What happened?' demanded Radda, crossing from the other side of the deck with Mull.

'Dannad's servant', moaned Kyresios, watching appalled as the galley hove to amidst a sudden confusion of cries and barked orders, attended by much frantic backing of oars until the swimmer could be dragged from the water.

'What?!' Radda cried, her eyes suddenly wide.

'The envoy, his bodyguard and his secretary were confined to the hold', explained Axilo, aghast. 'But that little fellow seemed no risk to us and was suffered to remain on deck'.

'And now he will be explaining all to the captain of yonder galley', cried Stilli, bringing her hands to her face. 'Surely he will. Surely!'

'And yet we are pulling away', observed Mull dryly, glancing upward to where the sails were drawing now.
'We are, but see, he turns to pursue!' gasped Radda, pointing away astern of them to where the oars of the galley were rising and falling purposefully as her bow turned towards them. They were beyond hailing range by now, but various signal flags were rising to the peak of the galley's mast.
'Heave to. Prepare to be boarded', interpreted the captain, shading his eyes. 'Curse them! Curse this fickle breeze!'
'They will catch us, won't they?' demanded Stilli despairingly, tugging at Kyresios' sleeve. Her golden dreams had already vanished like those ephemeral wisps of mists on the placid waters around them.
Kyresios said nothing, although his lips moved wordlessly, glaring astern at the galley as though mere implacable force of will could delay its progress. It was no use. Despite the crew's frantic activity, despite their assiduous attention to the set of sails, the galley gained steadily upon them.
'Can you not fire your guns?' asked Stilli as the captain hurried past, indicating the cannon that stood about the deck in the waist of the ship, two on either side.
'Those are no use in a chase', Kyresios told her with an ironic laugh. 'Since they can be directed only to the sides. I doubt he has the men to man them, anyway. Besides, we should need to turn to present our broadside to them, and then we should surely be lost. This is not a warship. There must be a hundred men on that galley, oarsmen and marines. We should be overwhelmed in an instant'.
'Do they have cannon, too?' Mull asked, but his enquiry was answered for him as a puff of smoke preceded a loud report and then the whirring passage of a

cannonball that skipped along the ruffled water to the side of the brig and then sank amidst a splash.

'Tio's breath! He'll have our range in an instant!' cried the captain, whose face was red with passion and who seemed close to tears of rage and frustration. 'Damn him, the dog!'

The consequences of his actions, of his greed and his folly, were all too obviously to be discerned in his eyes, together with a sudden furious impatience with his guests.

'Damn you, too!' he added, glaring about him at Stilli and her friends. 'This is your doing!'

Whatever protest Stilli and Kyresios might have mustered was lost in the cries of the crew, attendant upon another cannonball passing through the main and foremast topsails, this accompanied by a great tearing sound, the parting of numerous ropes and the dull clatter of wooden blocks to the deck.

The galley was clearly gaining upon them rapidly now, and the two cannon, one on either side of the wicked bronze ram in its bow, were firing busily. Another ball clipped the end from a yard, leaving the white sail flapping wildly, and another with a crunch that juddered throughout the whole ship smashed into the stem, carrying away timbers that arced lazily through the air behind them.

'Shall we start the water?' demanded the first lieutenant, grim-faced.

'What?' Stilli asked, recovering her balance after this impact and staring urgently at Kyresios.

'He means should they pump her water over the side to lessen the ship's weight and thus increase her speed', explained Kyresios. 'It'll be the cannon next'.

'It won't do', cried the captain, turning to them. 'It really won't do. We've had it'.

'No!' cried Stilli and her friends despairingly as a ball passed close enough to ruffle her hair.

'Put up the helm', instructed Mariant resignedly, throwing his hat to the deck.

Within moments, the *Storm Petrel* was hove to, sails flapping impotently, the way coming rapidly off her, gliding to a halt. Her masts swayed gently as the galley came alongside.

'We must certainly fight', grunted Axilo, reaching for a cutlass that one of the sullen mariners had set down.

'It is no use', sighed Kyresios, placing his own hand on Axilo's to forestall him. 'I'm afraid that Yuzanid is too strong here. Observe'.

He drew his attention to the galley's deck, where a dozen or more marines had arquebuses aimed at them, the smouldering match already acrid in their nostrils as the breeze carried it aboard. Stilli's own hand fell away from the hilt of her sword and she pressed herself against Axilo, resting her tear-wet face upon his shoulder.

'We are lost, my dear. Surely, we are lost!'

Chapter Twenty-Three

'I trust everything is in place', sighed Nestorides, the Lord High Admiral of the Empire of Erenor, taking a sip from the cup of herbal tea that stood on his desk before him. 'For this great adventure of yours'.

'I believe it is, my lord', nodded Paril Tyverios, reflecting that were his adventure to succeed, his superior would be glad enough to use the word "ours," would be happy to claim all credit for it, in fact. Were it to fail, however... well, the blame would then surely fall squarely upon Tyverios. It had always been that way, since, in the dawn of time, the first man to assume any form of command had appointed a deputy.

'The fleet is fully provisioned', he answered. 'The marines are going aboard, even as we speak, and the scout ships are already at sea'.

Nestorides set down his cup with exaggerated care and wiped his lips with a crisp white handkerchief. He was an elderly man, a tall man, but age had not bowed his back and he had a fine mane of white hair that fell to his shoulders. His eyes, deep set on either side of a long, purple-veined nose, regarded Paril unblinkingly. Paril saw the deepest apprehension there, a tenuous resolve that must not be allowed to falter.

'The die is cast', he added, to make it quite clear that Nestorides could not abort the operation at this late stage through sheer fright and mistrust.

'Is it?' asked Nestorides after a lengthy silence, during which he twice swallowed hard. 'Is it now? Good. Good'. He nodded and flexed his hands slowly, laying them flat upon the desk once more.

The upper part of the Lord High Admiral's face gave an impression of power and authority, one that was vigorously contradicted by the small mouth and the weak chin beneath. The lowest of his chins shelved gently to his neck amongst various folds and wrinkles of grey flesh. Beneath this, stringy tendons could be seen at work, alternately tensing and relaxing as his mouth worked upon its next contribution.

'And I suppose the weather is deemed favourable?' he asked. 'All your preparations may come to nothing if Tio sends us an easterly gale'.

'Those who know these things tell me the wind is set fair in the west and will continue so as far ahead as they can tell', answered Paril evenly.

'I doubt anyone can claim to know these things for sure', observed Nestorides, pushing back his chair and crossing to the window of his quarters, which offered a fine view of the harbour beyond.

Paril came to stand at his shoulder, regarding the military port with its serried ranks of warships lying at anchor there, a forest of masts and rigging. There were forty-six warships of various sizes, ranging from the *Swiftsure* of 250 tons to the *Avenger*, his own flagship, of 1,250 tons. Gathered beneath his gaze and that of his companion was virtually the entire naval strength of the Empire, apart from those swift sailing frigates and corvettes that he had sent ahead to clear the way. It was an impressive sight. He knew, because his agents had assured him of it, that the equivalent of this port in Tazman was likewise congested with the vast fleet that the Hierarchs had prepared for this coming spring, when they would certainly descend upon the Empire's coasts like wolves upon a flock.

'And our intelligencers?' continued Nestorides, stroking his vestigial chin. 'Their work proceeds alongside, I trust. I'm sure success depends upon them as much as it does upon our brave mariners'.

'Surely it does', agreed Paril. 'And I concluded my final meeting with Zarion only this morning'.

Zarion, the Vhanakhori consul in Caneloon, was on as friendly terms with Paril Tyverios as any citizens of hostile states could be in time of truce. He was, of course, the main conduit of information regarding the imperial fleet to interested ears in Tazman, but he was also a cultured and gentlemanly fellow, a convivial companion, if you could forget his compatriots' notorious addiction to human sacrifice and to other evils besides. Paril had known him for some years and felt confident of having developed a fair understanding of the fellow. He was moderately clever, ambitious and unshakeably confident in his own abilities – a combination that naturally opened him to the potential for error. Paril's own observations were regularly supplemented by those of his own agents amongst Zarion's domestic staff. Any information Zarion sent onward to his masters in Tazman was sure to be privy also to imperial intelligence and to pass across Paril's desk shortly thereafter.

'I am quite certain that he has swallowed our story', informed Paril, to forestall the Lord High Admiral's next enquiry.

The man's lips worked wordlessly for a moment.

'You are?' he enquired simply.

'Indeed'.

'And they assume that the fleet sets forth to smite the pirate nest?'

'They do'.

Paril and his staff had done everything in their power to create this impression. It was well known that he who styled himself "Count Gradivin" had abducted a high-ranking imperial emissary some time ago and grievously insulted his imperial majesty by sending back the man's official ring of office, complete with the finger that had worn it. Kyresios had been the emissary's name, and his kidnapping was a challenge that the Empire could not leave unanswered for long. The Hierarchs well understood this. In addition, the merchants of Caneloon and of other commercial cities had suffered gravely from the depredations of Gradivin's corsairs during the course of the previous year, driving insurance rates to ruinous heights. Surely it would be a gamble to venture around the storm-bound coasts of Eudora in this season, but the Hierarchs, and their consul, would certainly understand the motivation that underlay such a perilous venture. Besides, the pirate fleet was likely to be hull-down for careening or other seasonal maintenance in port. To catch them unawares with a force of this strength would surely lead to their utter destruction. The best of it was that the Hierarchs would also rejoice to see the extirpation of this irritant. An imperial descent upon Shangharad very much suited their interests, and if the emperor's fleet came to grief in a storm, which was a not unlikely contingency, then all the better.

'You take a great risk', Zarion had warned as their last meeting drew to its conclusion.

'The emperor's honour is at stake', Paril had replied. 'Lesser nations may justly wonder at our inaction if we do not soon smite Gradivin. I trust your masters will not resent this incursion upon a coast they may regard as their own preserve'.

'I think not', laughed Zarion, who was a large, bulky man with a beard that spread across his ample chest. 'If I may be candid with you…'

'I'm sure you always are', smiled Paril, interjecting and raising his glass.

'Ha-ha! Then doubtless they pray for your fleet's destruction, its dashing to pieces upon that fatal shore, but upon its journey homeward, of course, having first destroyed Shangharad'.

'We shall certainly do our best to oblige them, at least in the second article. As to the other, then our rival gods must doubtless wrestle to bring the winds within their power'.

'Praise be to Yuzanid!' cried Bozarian with a grin, clinking his wine glass against Paril's.

'And to Tio. And death and destruction to our enemies', added Paril, draining his glass in a single draught. 'Now I believe that I must leave you. I have an expedition to prepare'.

Stilli had known some misery in the last few months of her life, but there had been no previous lowness of spirit to compare with that she endured as the galley conveyed her to the port of Tazman. The vessel had no hold sufficient to accommodate captives, and so she found herself confined in the officers' quarters at the stern of the vessel, bound hand and foot together with her friends. She lay face down on the hard boards with her cheek pressed against the cold oak. Between her and Axilo stood the gold chest, and upon this sat the envoy's bodyguard, eating from a large pie and humming a cheerful tune to himself. The envoy was in equally good spirits, as well he might be, and could be heard outside conversing with the captain of the galley in animated tones.

'Certainly you must share a claim of the credit', asserted the envoy with a laugh. 'The arrival of your vessel was most providential.

'And your servant showed admirable presence of mind', pointed out the captain.

'He did! He did! And he shall be richly rewarded for it!' cried the envoy, clapping his hands. 'It has occurred to me that I may free him from his servitude, for by his action he has spared me from ignominy'.

'And condemned me to death', reflected Stilli glumly as these words carried to her ears.

'Stilli?' murmured Axilo from his place beyond the chest.

'You, shut up!' snapped the bodyguard, poking Axilo with his toe.

Stilli exchanged glances with Radda, who lay next to her, and found only bleak acceptance in her face. Surely it would soon be over.

As the galley came alongside the wharves in the military port, amongst a great cacophony of barked orders, running feet and the creaking of timbers, Stilli resolved that there was little left for her but to face her impending death with whatever dignity she could muster. This task was rendered more difficult by the red, tear-streaked presentation of her countenance, and by the broad dark stain on her breeches, where her bladder had eventually surrendered its burden. Having had the painful bonds at her ankles released, she found herself roughly manhandled to the dockside, during which various impertinent mariners' hands took the opportunity to caress her person. Blushing, blinking, she stood at Axilo's side whilst an interested crowd gathered to observe the arrivals. Various earnest conversations took place with those in officialdom, before they were led to a grim single-storey building with thick walls and pushed within. A heavy door slammed and a key turned in the lock.

'What now?' asked Tye in a small whisper. 'It appears that our fortunes have sunk very low. To think that the day began with such promise! I swear I never felt so profoundly low in my spirits'.

'It is not necessary to whisper, I think', Axilo told him glumly. 'And I'm sure we all share your sentiments'.

'Are you alright, Stilitha?' asked Kyresios, from where he had applied his eye to a crack in the door.

The only light in the cell came from a small window, high in the wall.

'As well as might be expected', she answered sullenly. 'I am cold, but then I shall soon be warm enough, no doubt'.

The prospect of Draganach's fiery belly came into all their minds, as she had intended that it should, and a silence fell amongst them. Stilli immediately felt a pang of guilt, regret that self-pity had induced her to forget the grim fate that must also await Axilo and Radda at least. Tye, exculpated by his evident stupidity, may yet find his way home, but in all likelihood Mull would be condemned by association with them and face the gallows in his turn. She glanced at Kyresios, who had now slumped to the cold tiles of the floor, his back to the wall. Would his diplomatic status spare him? Perhaps. Even in times of war, the Empire and the Hierarchy preserved the niceties of polite diplomacy.

The light was fading by the time a key grated in the lock and the door swung open once more to reveal the heavily stubbled face of their gaoler and a file of liveried guardsmen. The leader of these demanded that they should get to their feet, and soon they were being conducted through the crowded streets of the city, where lights were already being kindled in windows, shopfronts and on the tall metal columns that stood along the major thoroughfares. Stilli had never been to Tazman, and under more auspicious circumstances she might have marvelled at the fine public buildings, the perfectly proportioned squares and the ornate temples of her nation's capital city. With the others, she found herself tied with rope at the waist. Her party were thus connected inextricably together, and so escape was rendered wholly impracticable unless as one united body, a most unlikely contingency. Besides, the proximity of Kyresios' back, inconveniently close in front of her, made it impossible to spare much attention for her surroundings. Her thoughts were turned inward to a grim consideration of the pain of burning, to the likely duration of that torment before her body should give up her spirit at last.

It was quite dark before they were led into a torchlit courtyard and through a succession of dim passages, emerging at last in a brightly lit entrance hall before a pair of ornate, bronze-bound doors. Various uniformed guards stood there, guards of superior status, it appeared, and those who had escorted them were dismissed with no great ceremony or consideration.

'Untie this one', grunted what was evidently an official with a curt nod for Stilli. 'She's the one we want. Just her. Take the others to the Portway prison'.

There were loud protests, a brief scuffle and then Stilli found herself separated from her friends, the rope that connected them severed in a way that seemed as much symbolic as physical.

As she writhed, protesting, in the arms of her captors, Axilo's anguished face receded along the corridor away from her, intermittently visible between burly military bodies. This was it, then, the final, inevitable parting that sundered her from her love forever.

'Shut up!' snarled one of the three guards who secured her, his gloved hand on her mouth stifling her cries, smothering Axilo's name on her lips.

She ceased her struggle, hanging suddenly limp between them, tears coursing over her cheeks and her mouth tensed in a rictus of despair, quite at variance with the impression of quiet dignity she had resolved to convey.

Plumbing the unfathomable depth of misery, Stilli stood sobbing quietly as the doors opened to reveal a vestibule in which several elderly priestesses, robed in all their red finery, stood ready. These bowed gravely and accompanied the guard as he led Stilli, stifling her sobs now, along a short corridor and to a large chamber with a cheerful fire at one end. Here, a number of blue-robed servants stood by, gathered around a bronze bathtub from which fragrant steam arose.

'You will be made ready for your audience', said the guard, indicating the tub and various items of feminine attire laid across a table. 'I trust you will cooperate. I'll be right outside if there's any trouble', he added, this with a deferential nod for what might have been the chief of the priestesses, to judge from her high-piled grey hair and her supercilious air.

Then he was gone, and the door closed softly behind him.

'Perhaps you would undress', said an attendant, a tall, willowy girl with long dark hair in plaits. 'You are very dirty'.

It was indeed a great relief to remove her filthy garments and enter the warm water of the tub, although the attention of the servants in washing her back and her hair was a strange and unfamiliar one. Nor was it entirely without ominous overtones. The quiet chanting of two priestesses who stood back from her, their reference to a book upon a lectern, made it clear that this was in the nature of a ritual cleansing. The likelihood was that this would be her last bath in this life, and consciousness of this made it hard to surrender herself entirely to the soothing pleasure. She remembered burning her forearm upon the edge of a kitchen skillet once, the searing pain of it as her flesh recoiled. What would it be like to consumed by flame, her tender skin shrivelling and blackening from the bone? The smell of burning hair was familiar enough to her from misadventures with candles over the years. The imagined stench of her own burning flesh came vividly into her mind as the servants bade her stand and wrapped her in soft towels.

'Do you know who I am?' she called out to the priestess at the lectern, but the woman's voice continued without hesitation.

'We know', murmured the servant who towelled her hair at her ear. 'We know very well. You are late, very late'.

When Stilli was dry, her hair had been brushed and she had been arrayed in clean white clothing, she was led along a corridor to a chamber where a smallish, thinnish man stood warming himself next to a fire. He turned as she was shown in, exchanged a few pleasantries with the priestesses and then closed the door as they withdrew. He had thus far avoided more than a fleeting glance for her, as though he wished to enjoy a full scrutiny of her alone. Now she stood upon a broad rug embroidered with blue serpents and awaited his greeting with grim resignation.

'Then *you* are Stilitha Zandravo', he said at last, having considered her to his satisfaction, having walked about her, in fact.

His dark eyes glittered in the firelight, lending him an air of menace otherwise unsupported by his physique.

'What an unexpected pleasure' he continued. 'I have looked forward to this moment for what feels like many months, although the facts are otherwise, of course. My name is Preceptor Taradon, and I was placed in charge of securing your person'.

'Which you have done', she answered tersely. 'Congratulations'.

'Which I have done', he agreed. 'Although you have proved irksome in your resistance to the fate that God has decreed for you. It is a strange thing that you have now been delivered unto us in this unlooked-for manner. There will be many who will rejoice to hear it, my esteemed colleague, Marshall of the Faith, General Azimandro, amongst them. It was with him that I was charged with bringing you to this place. He is presently in the army camp beyond the city walls, but I have sent for him, in order that he may share my pleasure in meeting you at last. We had anticipated some difficulty in extricating you from that pirate lair you had taken refuge in, but here you are. Yuzanid smiles upon us. You cannot possibly imagine the lengths we have gone to, in order to track you down. Still, all obstacles are set aside now and we may proceed as was originally intended all those years ago'.

He rubbed his hands gleefully together and favoured her with a tight smile, one that could not seem anything other than malicious in the circumstances.

'What happened to my mother?' asked Stilli bluntly, giving voice to a question that had nagged at her ever since her abrupt departure from Zoramanstarn.

In her heart she knew the answer to this question, but her ears desired confirmation of it.

'She took her own life upon our arrival to apprehend you both. Your father's asp', he added, anticipating her next question.

'Of course', she nodded.

She had known; she had always known that her mother was dead, and this confirmation caused her no renewed surge of grief.

'I suppose you would have murdered her anyway'.

'She would have faced justice', agreed Taradon with a frown. 'Appropriate to her crime, and that would certainly have incurred the death penalty'.

'Imposed with fiendish cruelty, no doubt', shrugged Stilli.

'We are not here to discuss your mother', countered Taradon after a momentary pause. 'We are to prepare you to meet your maker, we are...'

'He is *not* my maker, he who you propose to despatch me to', scoffed Stilli.

'So you are become a heretic', observed Taradon evenly, his eye narrowing.

'A follower of Tio, certainly', replied Stilli, feeling a certain pleasure in the discomfiting effect that mentioning His name had upon her host in these circumstances.

Taradon twitched, and his face became suddenly pale.

'And I pray that he will embrace my soul when you have killed me', she continued. 'For what is the price of heresy but death? And I believe you propose to burn me'.

'Certainly we do', said Taradon, regarding her coldly. 'And when we have destroyed your flesh, you may be sure that Yuzanid will torment your soul in all eternity for such a betrayal of your birthright, such a treacherous denunciation of your faith'.

'It was never my faith', spat Stilli, warming to her theme. 'Although I was obliged throughout my life to participate in the empty rituals of it, to observe its inhuman cruelty. But now I am free of it, and I go to my death without its dismal chains. One thing I *have* learned from your faith – life must be surrendered with an easy mind when the time comes that we must relinquish it. I shall not submit to *grifdenzail*. I shall go to my death with a glad heart – a glad heart, I tell you – and in the certainty that Tio shall snatch up my immortal soul even as my body succumbs to the flames'.

Taradon looked upon her, taking in the fierce glint in her eyes and the proud tilt of her chin, and he was oppressed by a strange doubt, one that contrasted bleakly with her own evident certainty. The image of a little girl, the little girl that Stilli had once been all those years ago, came into his mind. He could see her standing before him, her small body clothed in the same white but wearing an elaborate headdress and bearing a posy of flowers in her hand, as Yuzanid had always intended that she should.

'And what of my friends?' the child asked.

Taradon blinked, shook his head and the vision vanished. He looked up, met the young woman's eyes and shuddered.

'They will face trial, of course', he answered.

'And then they will die'.

'In all likelihood, yes', he agreed.

She nodded, her mouth set in a grim line.

'And what now?'

'We await the dawn', Taradon answered, mastering himself. 'There is a chamber where you may sleep or pray, the choice is yours. Priestesses of my order will attend upon you and see to your needs, both physical and spiritual...'

'Ha!' she scoffed.

'...if you have any'.

He pulled a cord on the wall and the door opened behind Stilli. Two priestesses advanced to stand at her side.

'Goodbye, Stilitha', Taradon said with a grave nod of his head.

'Goodbye, Preceptor Taradon', said Stilli coldly. 'May you burn in your own hell'.

Stilli barely slept during what was surely her last night alive. Her family came into her mind: her father who had given his life in dutiful service to that cruel god, her brother who had drunk deep from the well of wickedness and her mother, her mother, who had given everything to preserve her from the fate decreed for her. To what end? To purchase thirteen more years of life for her? Had it been worth it? She had found love at last, but that love was not to endure, it appeared. Axilo's face came into her mind, his dear face, and she imagined his arms enfolded around her as the hours and minutes of her life ebbed away.

Taradon's sleep was hardly any better than that of the coming dawn's sacrifice. He found himself curiously disturbed in his spirits, at a moment when he should have felt nothing but jubilation. He had succeeded. He had traced the girl to her hiding place, and various unforeseeable circumstances had brought her to this place, to face the inevitable sacrifice. All would congratulate him, perhaps his career would be advanced by it, and yet he found that his spirit lay cold within him. A wholly unexpected emotion troubled him. Envy. He found that he envied the girl the unshakeable certainty that he had seen in her eyes. She was quite sure that her god would embrace her immortal spirit. He had nothing to console him except the dead words of the scriptures, the words he knew so well but that had no power to stir his spirit. Even the complex rituals of his faith brought him no consolation, only a further numbing of the soul. He cried out to his god in his prayers, invoked him and beseeched him, but to no effect. The heavens were deaf to his entreaties.

Taradon wondered if he possessed a soul at all, if the frail, fleshly frame he inhabited was all that he had. He was, in short, in the midst of despair when a servant touched his shoulder to tell him that the time was upon him, that dawn approached and that he should attend to his robing.

He was engaged in the third ritual cleansing of his hands when a loud bang caused him to drop the soap, a detonation that reverberated around the city and rattled the shutters at the window. At the same time, a sudden light flickered on the wall at his side, painting a momentarily vivid image of those shutters. The chamber he stood in adjoined the sacred terrace of the temple of Draganach, and he was halfway through the door when a wide-eyed servant cannoned into him.
'We are under attack!' he gasped. 'Look!'
Taradon hastened after the servant onto the broad terrace beyond, to see that the low clouds over the city were lit ruddily by the flames that now issued from one of the two great fortresses that guarded the entrance to the harbour. As he watched, dumbstruck, there was a second great explosion from its sister fortress across the intervening channel and an eruption of flame that sent fragments of stonework soaring high over the city.
The shipping in the harbour, the serried ranks of galleys and other warships, were eerily lit with a flickering orange light that reflected in the oily waters around them. Already, crews were setting out for them in myriad small boats and launches, the harbourside a scene of frantic confusion, like a broken anthill with distant figures hurrying hither and thither.
'What is *that*?' demanded the servant, all social distinctions set aside, pointing out between the shattered fortresses where more flames could be seen, gliding inward towards the port.

'Fireships', replied Taradon bleakly, pressing the knuckles of one hand to his lips. 'Spare us, Lord! Spare us! Fireships!'

He seized the servant by the arm and shook him.

'Summon General Azimandro. Get him here without delay!'

It was the thirteenth day of February, and the truce with the Empire had expired.

Chapter Twenty-Four

Paril Tyverios limped as he hurried through the dark streets of a city already awake, already thoroughly alarmed as the two fortresses burned furiously behind him. He had barked his shin painfully against some unseen obstacle in the pitch darkness beyond the postern gate that his agents had flung open in the city walls. They were through this crucial obstacle and passed into the maze of streets behind, even as the first sleepy defenders of the garrison stumbled out onto the fighting platforms. Too late! At his back were three hundred picked marines, many of whom were intimately familiar with this harbourside quarter of the city. Those who were not so were at least thoroughly used to the scale model of the place that Paril had had made in Caneloon. In the preceding month, as the plan for the assault had taken shape, they had been required to plot routes from temple to temple, warehouse to warehouse, barracks to barracks and commit these indelibly to memory.

Citizens, crying out urgently, were spilling out into the streets to see what ailed their stricken city. Others, more sensible of imminent danger, were gathering their valuables and taking steps to hide themselves away in cellars or attics, for war was notoriously cruel to cities and to their inhabitants once the walls were breached. Paril and his men ignored these irrelevances, pushing through them purposefully as they threaded their way towards their objective. There was no need for organised violence yet, no armed resistance gathered before them, although doubtless it would soon be encountered, once the city's authorities imposed some order amongst the prevailing panic, once the city's trained bands could be hastily mustered and arrayed. For now, though, for these precious few minutes, they had the initiative and the power to strike wherever they would.

'Get up, man!' he called, as behind him a marine tripped and fell.

With a comrade, he had been carrying a barrel of gunpowder on a stretcher. This toppled and began to roll, stopped and reinstated by various strong hands as the soldier was raised to his feet once more.

'Come on!' roared Paril as the party surged onward once more. 'We're nearly there'.

In front of the largest of the city's barracks, this where the galley slaves dwelt, there was a brief skirmish with soldiers of the garrison, but they were not numerous and quickly scattered, leaving a few of their number slain or groaning and bleeding out their lives on blood-slick cobbles. It was the work of moments to break down the door of the barracks and liberate hundreds of cheering, rejoicing slaves onto the streets, freed from their shackles and with a world of hatred for their masters to express. Here, in a dark corridor, Paril was taken by surprise, tripped, pushed and momentarily sent reeling helpless to the floor whilst a cursing guard loomed over him. Rendered heavy and clumsy by cuirass and mail, the admiral found himself momentarily at a disadvantage. His assailant was big and his hand was at Paril's throat, squeezing the life from him whilst he squirmed desperately in his grip. A knife came up, sparked in the half-light, poised to strike. Paril gasped, looked death full in the face, and then a sturdy, three-legged stool, swung with huge force, connected with his assailant's skull with a sickening crack. Paril, eyes wide, still sprawling, found himself looking up into the face of a towering black man, his powerful torso gleaming with sweat. Eyes glinted white in the darkness. A slave.

'Thank you', grunted Paril, accepting the great hand that descended to haul him to his feet. 'Thank you, sir'.

The man only grunted and nodded. Within a moment, there were expressions of dismay and concern as his officers and men arrived belatedly from other corridors to assist.

'Are they all out?' demanded Paril, brushing himself off, exuding authority once more. 'Yes? Then it's the temple next. Let's go!'

Emerging into the street, lamplit in this more central region of the city, Paril glanced down to the harbour where an astonishing scene opened to his gaze.

Fireships, gliding ominously into the harbour, had engaged with the crowded ranks of Vhanakhori warships, and the fire was leaping from deck to deck, mast to mast. Distantly, panicked mariners were jumping into the water, some as human torches, swathed in writhing sheets of flame. At the same time, Paril's largest and strongest vessels were following majestically in their wake, firing broadsides from both sides into the packed shipping. There was a constant crackle of arquebus fire punctuated by the deep, rippling boom of cannon as these stately gods of war dealt fiery ruin about them. Paril only took a deep breath and a moment to impress this glorious image immovably upon his memory, before running onward, his force now swelled by eager volunteers amongst the slaves. At his shoulder ran the fellow who had saved him.

'What is your name, man?' demanded Paril, laughing jubilantly between laboured breaths.

'He'll never answer you', panted a smaller slave, a white man with long, plaited blonde hair. 'Ohk, we call him, but he ain't got no tongue, see?! Ain't that right, Ohk?'

Paril had no breath to devote to further comment. He only nodded and spared his saviour a grin. His force had emerged into the square before the great temple of Draganach, and here there was a formed body of the city guard to oppose them, perhaps a hundred strong. No matter. There was a ragged ripple of arquebus fire and a few arrows sped towards them. Several amongst Paril's force fell, but the impetus of their charge was unstoppable and the defending force was quickly scattered or beaten down amidst a furious storm of violence. Behind him, medical orderlies stooped amongst the huddled bodies of the wounded, but Paril barely noticed. His attention was fixed on the huge bronze doors of the temple precinct, swung shut now with a ponderous clang.

He stood at the threshold of Draganach's shrine, the chief of the city's temples, a place where unspeakable crimes were committed in their cruel god's name. A glance behind revealed that the Erenori force had possession of this broad square, at least for a while. To one side, a mob of gleeful slaves had brought ropes and were attempting to topple one of the equestrian statues that stood at its centre. More were running in and out of buildings, laughing and shouting, agents of vengeful chaos. There were screams, the crackle of flames, death cries, abruptly cut short. Beyond, around the square's periphery, various buildings were already ablaze, bathing the invaders in a ruddy, flickering light.

'Bring up one of the smaller barrels', Paril instructed his lieutenant, indicating the base of the temple doors. 'Let's have this open'.

'What's happening?' demanded Axilo, sitting suddenly upright as sleep fell away. 'Did you hear that?'
'How could I not?' mumbled Mull, rubbing his head ruefully and picking filthy straw from his hair.

There had been a huge reverberating detonation that seemed to shake the building around them, causing particles of dust to fall from the ceiling beams above. It was still dark, but enough light penetrated from the corridor beyond their cell for the captives to make out each other's pale, wondering faces.

'The city is under attack', cried Kyresios, pressing himself against the door and peering through the tiny iron-barred window.

There were more explosions, the growing sound of fighting outside, shouting, cries of pain or panic and, finally, that of running feet in the corridor beyond.

'Let them out', someone was calling in a huge voice. 'Let them all out!'

A key grated in the lock, and suddenly light from a brandished torch shone in their faces, borne by one of a party of joyful, freely perspiring galley slaves, spattered with the blood of their oppressors.

'Come on! What are you waiting for?' demanded one as the party moved off along the corridor to open more doors. 'You're free! We're all free!'

'We've got to get to the temple precinct', cried Axilo, seizing Kyresios' arm. 'Stilli will be there, won't she? They might...'

What they might do to Stilli was in everyone's minds but found no immediate utterance as her friends hurried out and found their way to the entrance of their gaol.

In the guardroom by the entrance, Radda found their coats, taken from them when they came in the previous evening, as well as Stilli and Axilo's swords, which had been confiscated at the moment of their capture. Snatching these up, pushing through the remains of a shattered door, they emerged blinking in the sudden light of burning buildings. They found themselves in the square before the lower walled enclosure of the temple, a place of noble refinement and elegance, of ancient buildings famed throughout the realm.

Everywhere, chaos now reigned. War brought fiery ruin with it. Parties of running men, shrieking women and slaves with torches were everywhere to be seen, breaking down doors and setting fire within. Outlined against these flames, an organised group of soldiers was formed up before the main gates of the temple whilst officers barked orders and sergeants pushed men urgently into their ranks. Two engineers were carrying what was evidently a small but heavy barrel towards the tall temple doors.

'I know that man!' gasped Kyresios, indicating what might have been the leader of this regiment. 'Tyverios, hey! Tyverios!' he called, running out across the square with an urgency that belied his age.

Various officers attempted to stand in his way, but their chief knocked a questing blade aside and advanced to meet him.

'Kyresios! Is that you?' laughed Paril, slapping him on the shoulder. 'I hardly believe it! This is no small coincidence'.

'What are you doing here?!' cried Kyresios, momentarily overcome by joy, momentarily with his wits astray.

'I'm surprised that you should ask,' chuckled Paril, pointing to where his men had set their burden to the base of the gates and were stooping to light a fuse with the smouldering match from an arquebus.

There was no time for discussion, no time for the sharing of stories as the fuse sparked into fizzing life. Already, another party of armed defenders was entering the further side of the square and Paril's marines were wheeling to face them, swords and axes at the ready.

'There's a girl inside there. She must be freed!' Kyresios shouted urgently into the admiral's ear, even as he instructed his officers.

'Not now. Not the time!' replied Paril as the huge slave at his shoulder took up a discarded war hammer, a toy in his great hand.

He hefted it experimentally and grinned.

'No, Listen!' Kyresios implored, snatching at the admiral's sleeve. 'She's the Golden Child. They will sacrifice her, and then Yuzanid will aid them once more in all their endeavours'.

Both men instinctively twitched and shrank down as a deafening explosion rent the air and a shockwave plucked at their clothing and hair. A shower of debris fell around them.

Paril blinked, momentarily deafened. Understanding seemed to dawn in his eyes, but there was no time to act upon it. A new battle had begun, and he must direct its motions as the two forces clashed. He turned away, drawing his own sword, leaving Kyresios staring helplessly at his back.

'The gates!' roared Axilo into Kyresios' still-ringing ear. 'Look!'

One of the doors to the temple enclosure had seemingly been completely shattered and the remains of its twin hung, swaying drunkenly from a single hinge.

There was no plan, no discussion of options, only an unspoken unanimity of purpose. Stilli's friends pelted through the gates. Mull, a grim smile on his face, picked up a bow and a quiver of arrows from where they lay beside the sprawled corpse of an archer. Kyresios took up a discarded sword and passed one to Tye, who hefted it purposefully in his hand, an angry gleam in his eye. Even Radda picked up a knife and hurried after her friends as they charged across the broad open space of the temple temenos, amongst running groups of startled clerics and servants.

'There, the basement entrance', called Kyresios, who had fallen behind and was limping badly now. 'There, see!'

He pointed with a trembling sword tip towards the huge bulk of the great bronze serpent that occupied the centre of the space. From its massive coils the neck and head thrust up high towards the sacrificial platform on the upper level. It was from this platform that victims were pushed, to fall into the serpent's gaping jaws. Ominously, flames already issued from these jaws, casting a flickering orange glow onto the parapet of the platform above. Agitated figures were gathered there, looking down upon them and gesturing wildly.

Marines came running into the enclosure with an officer at their head, calling out to their fellows, who were bringing more barrels of gunpowder. Clutching his sides, panting, cursing the indignities of age, Kyresios staggered to a halt, even as Axilo and the others vanished within the temple.

'Help them!' croaked Kyresios to the newcomers, waving his sword feebly, but the marines ran past him, intent upon their task.

'What do you mean, *unable to get here*?' demanded Taradon, his face contorted with rage, holding a trembling servant by the lapels of his jacket. 'He is absolutely required to be here!' he hollered.

At this most vital of times, the High Patriarch had been outside the city conferring his blessings upon Azimandro's army in one of the minor festivals of the year. Various human sacrifices had been conducted there in order to secure Yuzanid's approval for the coming campaign. Such things were entirely irrelevant now. It was essential that Zanidas should be brought to the temple and there induced to perform this one vital sacrifice with all possible dispatch. Exultant messages had been exchanged the previous night in which Taradon had described the details of the girl's surprising capture and stressed the urgency of the High Patriarch's return to the city.

'The streets are full of enemy soldiers and it seems that his carriage was overturned in the confusion', croaked the servant. 'No one knows where he is'.

'What?!'

Taradon's mind reeled beneath the onslaught of events. He gave the servant another vigorous shake but the poor man only quailed, his eyes wide with terror. For a long moment, the two men merely glared helplessly at each other whilst resolution gathered in Taradon's breast.

A glance at the burning city, the blazing vessels in the harbour, was sufficient to confirm that there was no time for the High Patriarch to be located, rescued and conveyed thence. The sacrifice must be conducted regardless.

'Fetch the girl!' he barked, letting go of the servant. 'Have her brought to the terrace. Well?! What are you waiting for? Quickly, man!'

The ferocity of his countenance, the awful gleam in his eye, caused the servant to turn and run whimpering for the door.

The man had no sooner vanished than another figure strode purposefully into Taradon's room – Azimandro. His face was dark with anger and he was wearing only his arming doublet, having had no time to don his full array of armour. Mail clinked about him as he moved, and his great sword swung at his side.

'We must do this ourselves', Taradon told him after he had explained the High Patriarch's present travails. 'I am the most senior cleric on hand. My master, the Hierarch of Nahleen, left only yesterday and the other Lords Spiritual are doubtless attending to their own

security, the security of their own temples, there must be...'
'Shut up, man!' snapped Azimandro. 'You're babbling!'
'Have you brought troops?' demanded Taradon after a moment in which he recovered his composure.
'Only my retainers and the girl's brother, there was not time', replied Azimandro, crossing to the window to regard the chaotic scene bleakly. 'Although doubtless they will be on their way by now'.
'It is the thirteenth', observed Taradon.
'I know what the date is', spat Azimandro. 'They have caught us with our breeches down'.
'They have', agreed Taradon, running his hand over his head. 'I have sent for the girl'.
'Good', nodded Azimandro. 'If anything is to be salvaged from this wreck, we must dispatch her to our Lord without delay'.

Stilli was awakened from a shallow sleep by cries from beyond her room and the sounds of running feet in the corridor. It was clear that something was happening in the city beyond this temple, but it was some time before it became clear to her that the place must be under some form of attack. She could hear dull detonations, which might be cannon fire, and the distant sounds of voices raised in passion.
The two priestesses who watched over her were exchanging urgent whispers when the door flew open to reveal the chief of her captors, Taradon, and a giant of a man whose tattoos and garments proclaimed his status as a high-ranking warrior. This must be the general of whom Taradon had spoken. Taradon seemed markedly less self-assured than in their previous meeting. Whatever he might have been about to say was cut off, his mouth half open as the soldier strode towards her, his countenance dark with subdued rage.

'We're taking her now', he grunted to the priestesses, who stood aghast, hands raised to their faces.
'But the robing. What about the robing?' asked one in pleading tones, indicating white garments and a headdress laid out on a table.
'Never mind the robing', snapped the warrior.
Leaning forward, he seized Stilli painfully by the wrist and hauled her from the bed on which she still sat.
'Our Lord will have to take her as she comes', he added.
'We must set aside protocol on this occasion', Taradon assured the priestesses apologetically. 'There is no time'.
He had barely uttered these words than Azimandro was through the door, once more, half-dragging, half-lifting a panting, protesting Stilli.
'Enough!' cried Azimandro as they emerged into the corridor, slapping her face with his free hand in a manner that caused her momentarily to see a constellation of prickling stars.
She gasped and yelped, groping for consciousness as the man's huge hand on her back urged her forcefully towards a staircase. Impressions crowded in on her: Taradon's pale, anxious face glimpsed at her shoulder, the sound of clashing steel – distantly and then closer – panicked servants stumbling down the staircase, faces filled with dismay, even as her roaring, cursing captor shouldered through them. Cries, many cries, the dull report of a distant explosion, firelight flickering distantly in the harbour as a broad space opened around her and a chill dawn breeze plucked at her hair.

'That way! Up yonder staircase!' cried Kyresios between laboured breaths, pointing away towards the end of the broad hall they had entered.
Leaving him gasping in their wake, the remaining members of the party hurried in the direction he had

indicated, through a space made busy with running servants, clerics and functionaries.

A group of armed men appeared, perhaps temple guards, but their attention was apparently focused on reaching the courtyard outside, and they passed by without so much as a sidelong glance for Stilli's friends, who, taking the stairs two at a time until reaching the first landing, found themselves confronted with a familiar figure. It was Middo, sent by Azimandro to investigate the disturbance in the lower temenos.

'Ha!' cried Axilo, hurling himself instinctively upon the hated adversary, sword swinging but finding himself repelled by Middo's own swiftly drawn blade.

There was a passage of desperate swordplay, during which it became apparent that Middo was more skilled than Axilo and, moreover, perfectly recovered from the injury that Mull had inflicted on him previously. Amongst much grunting and cursing, amongst the cries and imprecations of others on the stairs, Axilo found himself pushed back, almost tumbling when his heel found the edge of the step, recovering, taking a step down and then attempting to thrust upward beneath his opponent's guard.

'They're going to kill Stilli! You know that!' called Radda, stepping back as a fat cleric tumbled past her and went sprawling helplessly on the stair.

She stooped to pick up Stilli's sword in its scabbard, which Axilo had necessarily let fall.

'God wills it!' snarled Middo. 'Die, Drumogari vermin!' he continued, making a darting thrust at Axilo's breast.

Axilo, pierced below the rib cage, staggered and toppled sideways. He would certainly have received his death blow right there as Middo, eyes gleaming, jubilantly drew back his bloodied sword to strike again, but Mull, finally presented with a clear shot after what felt like minutes of futile dodging to and fro, raised his bow, let fly and sent an arrow cleanly through Middo's throat.

Middo coughed, gasped, dropped his sword and groped at the shaft, but the wound was a mortal one and he sank to his knees, shock driving out that momentary glint of triumph.

'No mistake this time', grunted Mull, placing another thrumming arrow in the stricken body, even as Middo sank to his knees and toppled forward to lie twitching on the stair.

'Are you alright?' gasped Radda, looking to where Axilo was struggling to his feet, a great wet patch of blood upon his tunic.

A hand came groping round, fumbled amongst the gore and came up before his face so that his astonished, anguished eyes could gaze upon it.

'Yes', he answered, wiping the bloodied hand on his breeches.

He glanced up the staircase to the next turn, where Tye, calling Stilli's name urgently, was already out of sight.

'Come on!' Axilo cried, rallying his friends with renewed vigour.

He snatched Stilli's sword from Radda's grip and stepped over Middo's motionless form, from which blood was dribbling steadily from step to step. With Mull and Radda in his wake, pushing past two horrified priestesses, Axilo forced his body upward towards the temple terrace with every ounce of his declining strength, with every fibre of his being, every fierce impulse of his spirit.

The terrace, a broad space that could accommodate hundreds on holy days, was empty except for a few horrified onlookers when Azimandro strode out on to it, heaving and pushing his captive before him. Two teenage girls, temple acolytes, fled the balustrade, from where they had been observing the city's devastation as the general approached the *break*. There, the balustrade ceased and the terrace jutted out like the spout of a jug above the gaping jaws of Draganch's great serpent.

'There shall be no ceremony', snarled Azimandro, casting Stilli to his feet and looming over her like death himself. 'Nor need there be. But My Lord shall take his due. He shall take at last what your mother once denied him!'

Stilli sprawled helplessly in the narrowest part of the "spout," hemmed in by the huge bulk of Yuzanid's avenging angel. Heat, rising from the serpent's mouth, pressed upon her back and curling wisps of acrid smoke rose about her.

He reached down to grasp her arm once more, but at that moment, with a great cry of anguish, Tye came charging out onto the terrace with Axilo close on his heels. Tye had a sword clenched in his fist, his face distorted with rage, and he raised the weapon high as he closed with the general.

'Noooo! Stilliii!' he cried.

Azimandro cursed, turning to face this new threat, and his great sword came zinging from its scabbard. One step was all it took to take up his stance, one second in which to bring up that sword to deflect Tye's clumsy blow. Within the span of that same second, he raised it high and swung it in a powerful arc that struck Tye between neck and shoulder, scything down through flesh, clavicle and ribs with brutal force.

The youth, with his cry of desperate fury changing abruptly to one of sudden pain and dismay, staggered sideways and collapsed. The unfamiliar weapon he had snatched up on the stairs skittered away across the smooth marble slabs.

One second.

In the same vital second that Tye's sacrifice had purchased for her, Axilo, only a few lurching, gasping strides behind him, threw Stilli's sword.
The weapon, freed from its scabbard, arced spinning through the air, even as Azimandro tugged his weapon free from Tye's flesh. He flinched instinctively, snapping his body into a curve as the glinting blade flew past.

With realisation flashing in her brain, Stilli reached desperately for the "celerity", even as Axilo's arm came back to throw. One bead remained. One single bead, and when that gave up its miraculous power, so would Stilli be forced to give up her life. But there it was. The world slowed to a crawl around her. There was poor Tye, slumped in his own blood, there Axilo, hunched, half-collapsed to his knees now, caught in the moment of his fall, the scabbard dropping to his side. His eyes. His eyes. A glimpse of death was there, and of other things besides – love, despair, desperation.
But now she must snatch her own gaze away and direct it to the sword. To the sword! She heard her own breath gasp in her throat, as though in another's throat, as that blessed blade span gracefully through the air towards her, past Azimandro's slowly turning shoulder. She was already halfway to her feet when the grip nestled into her hand and she plucked it from the air.
Azimandro was half-turned towards her now, his frown intensifying, his mouth tensed in a grimace of fury. He changed his stance, so slowly that it appeared he was performing some graceful movement of dance, and his arm rose once more as his bloodied sword swung towards her, droplets of poor Tye's blood flying from it in a vivid red constellation. Even in this slowed world, there was a speed and determination about the

impending blow that promised her certain destruction, should it find its mark.

She must fire sinews and synapses into urgent action.

Pressing forward within the encompassing arc of his steel, she drew back her arm and turned away his blow, even though the crushing weight of it jarred her arm and shoulder painfully. She darted a thrust of her own, but it seemed his motions were almost as quick as hers, and his blade swept across to deflect it from his throat.

Even with the "celerity" in her frame, the contest was unequal. Azimandro was more than twice her weight and a head taller. Her initial attack had won her a little space as her opponent had necessarily stepped back, but still the fiery gulf yawned at her heel, and any stumble, any false step, might yet see her plunge to her destruction. There was a glint of pure hatred, such malice in Azimandro's eyes as they fought that Stilli realised with a thrill of cold horror that she beheld Yuzanid there, that his implacable fury shone through this earthly vessel's eyes. Perhaps the god had overreached himself. Perhaps his insatiable thirst for Stilli's death, his impatience to possess her, overrode the skill and training of his servant.

Azimandro lunged forward, one arm reaching to grasp her, the other bringing back his blade, ready to drive it through her torso with every atom of the god's insensate rage. His hand reached for her sword arm as he surged upon her, and his shadow – the god's shadow – fell upon her soul. But she twitched aside to evade the approaching hand, brought her sword arm back and the broad expanse of his chest opened before her. Clenching her teeth, she stabbed upward and forward with all her strength. The tip of her sword momentarily sparked reflected fire, before it drove through the tight fabric and felt of his arming doublet, punching between ribs and into the general's lung and heart. Azimandro's head jolted back and his jaws opened wide, strands and globules of spittle flying in the air around him.

He slumped towards her, his vast weight bearing her down, towards the edge of the terrace. He was going over, impelled by his own momentum, but he was taking her with him. She yelped as one leg slid over the edge, the heat of the flames suddenly upon her. Impressions rushed in upon her, even as the momentary god-given strength faded and she scrambled to redistribute her weight. She gasped and cried out. Her left hand flew instinctively to her throat and to the gold image of Tio that nestled there at the end her necklace, a necklace that now contained not a single yellow bead. Her fingers closed about it and she squeezed, even as her body rolled towards the brink. Her lips and her throat were too slow to form the words of His name, to invoke him, but the name flashed across her brain as the two bodies tumbled.

Time stopped, quite abruptly, and Stilli stood upon the terrace where the grim tableau was frozen like some waxwork display. There was no sound, only the thud of her own heart in her chest and the incredulous gasp in her throat. She was looking at herself, at her own body, half-embraced by Azimandro's as the two of them teetered on the precipice. Her own sword tip projected a hand's breadth from the general's back, and his face, tilted backward, was contorted with sudden searing pain.

'I am here, child', said a voice at her side, and she swung round to find that Tio himself stood there in all his glory and his brilliance, wide white wings folded at his back.

Light poured from him so that she shaded her eyes, and his voice was like warm honey. Tears sprang in her eyes.

'This is the end, then. I am dead', she said when she could find her own voice at last.

'It is not quite the last moment of your life; not quite, but yes, it approaches', agreed the god's voice regretfully. 'A few more moments will see you perish in the fire, and that creature with you, although his heart may beat its last before the flames embrace him'.

'Then how can I see this?' asked Stilli, dragging her eyes from this compelling spectacle and turning to Tio.

She wanted to step forward to run her hand through the soft curls of his glorious mane, but reverence and awe froze her into immobility, and after a moment she cast down her gaze.

'I have caused your spirit to step out of your mortal frame', replied Tio, 'and I have momentarily stilled the wheel of time, in order that I may speak with you'.

'What will happen to me?' asked Stilli, glancing down and seeing that she was dressed as her physical self was dressed.

'Long, long ago, thousands of your years ago, there was a time when we gods strode forth more boldly upon this earth. The wall between the worlds was weaker then, and there were more places where we could set forth our strength without constraint. It was a time of magic, if you like. At that time, my champion, Niall, came across the sea and he, in his turn, had his champions. You have encountered one such paladin. It was he that gave you the necklace that you bear at your throat. Into this necklace I breathed a little of my power at that time, and by invoking me, in extremis, by squeezing the image that was wrought in gold, you have summoned me and have drawn upon that power'.

'Those beads, they likewise enabled me to draw upon your power, did they not?' surmised Stilli.

'They did', agreed Tio, inclining his noble head.

'And what may I now call upon you to do?' asked Stilli, glancing about. 'If a mortal may be so bold'.

Tio followed her gaze and the two of them looked upon the burning buildings in the city beneath them, the blazing vessels in the distant harbour. Tio laughed, a bass rumble, and flexed his great wings so that whirling motes of brilliant light flew from them, like snowflakes in a zephyr.

'We stand at the core of my brother's earthly realm', he said. 'And yet my own people have reached out to injure him here. His attention is wholly absorbed in your destruction, and whilst his gaze was focused upon that end, so has Erenor put forth her strength to smite him in his heartland. He is furious, he is distracted, and so I can exert a fragment of my own power even here. The door between the worlds stands ajar, a very little, and I may preserve your life, if you wish it'.

Stilli regarded him with awe. Gratitude and relief surged in her breast, but then her eye fell upon Tye's crumpled body.

'Quite dead, I'm afraid', said Tio mournfully, following her gaze. 'And beyond salvation'.

Poor, sweet Tye. He had given up his life for his one love. Her eye then turned to Axilo and she ran to him with a cry, settling at his side. Strangely, when she touched his dear face, he was hard as stone, his unseeing eyes fixed upon the two tumbling bodies at the edge of the terrace, his countenance transformed by agony and grief. He was half-raised on one arm. The other reached out to her, the fingers red with blood. More blood spattered the marble slabs beneath him.

'He is gravely injured', Tio informed her.

She turned her head to look up at him once more, and he paced gracefully to stand above her, his great head casting an eerie radiance upon Axilo's waxen features.

'His life ebbs away and it is not within my power to preserve him. We stand in the heart of Yuzanid's dominion...'

'But you could save him', interjected Stilli, oblivious to the lese-majesty of interrupting a god.

'I could', agreed that god, showing no evidence of being offended. 'But then I could not save *you*'.

Stilli's head sank and her tears splashed upon her lover's face, and she caressed those familiar contours which felt so strange, so cold, like that of a carven statue. Her love burned within her breast like the white-hot fire of the forge, so that all earthly considerations fell away and a delightful warmth spread through her.

'It is perfection, what we have', she murmured. 'So pure, so all-encompassing, and I know that should we both live, this fire shall die down and become a red glow of coals as the years pass and, perhaps at last, a bed of cold ashes when we two are old and grey and nod by the fire. I have seen it in others. I have seen it so many times'.

She glanced up at the god, now flexing his wings slowly so that light particles danced about him.

'As have I', he said at last.

'And I know that if I live, my life will be empty, meaningless without him. I cannot find my life's one love and then surrender him to death, surrender that love to death when I have a chance like this'.

'A chance?' Tio tilted his great head.

'I love him more than life itself', she said, summoning resolve. 'And so I beg you to spare him in my place. I shall go into the flames as fate intended. Will you do that for me, my dear Lord?'

'I will', agreed Tio solemnly. 'I see into your heart and I perceive a radiant sincerity there. Yuzanid may have your body, but I shall take your immortal spirit before the flames enfold your flesh, if you will it'.

'You know I will it, Lord, but may I have a moment?' begged Stilli, putting her arms around Axilo's stony shoulders, her own cheek next to his.

She sobbed then, and in her tears was condensed the entirety of their precious short time together and all of the notional years that had lain ahead and may never now be explored.

'Goodbye, Axilo, my cherished, dear love', she said. 'I will always be with you. When the first light of day falls upon your face, I shall kiss you, and when your cheek finds the pillow at night, I shall be there. I shall dwell in your heart for all time'.

'Are you ready?' asked Tio at last, spreading wide his wings and stiffening himself as though some great outpouring of strength gathered within his frame.

'I am ready', she confirmed.

'Then so be it'.

Time suddenly moved on with a lurch, and she was once more in her body, unbalanced, toppling at the brink. She caught a glimpse of Azimandro's turning bulk, falling into the hungry fire between the gaping jaws of the serpent. Impressions crowded in on her – the screams of her friends, one last glimpse of Axilo, her sword falling from her hand. She was going, she was about to tumble helplessly into the fire. She shrieked, one last anguished yell, and in some dark recess of her mind she saw the malevolent Yuzanid reach up for her from beneath, like some spirit of the flame, to seize her spirit, triumph written in his fiery features.

He reached in vain.

At the same time she was conscious of a great noise, a great explosion and an expression of sudden consternation grip the god's exultant face. The colossal bronze serpent shattered into a million shards and Yuzanid's grip upon the world momentarily faltered, even as Tio's increased. Suddenly, there was a firm grip on her arm and on her clothing. She was tugged roughly away from the edge, and glancing up she found herself looking into Mull's eyes, his own face red with exertion.

Epilogue

Paril sighed and set down his pen. After the vast expenditure of nervous and physical energy that the day had imposed upon him, he felt a growing heaviness in his limbs and a corresponding mental fatigue, one that had caused him to puzzle over the wording of his report far longer than would ordinarily have been required.

In truth it was an extraordinary report, one that he had hardly dared to imagine himself writing only a few days previous, and the full extent of his triumph had yet to register itself fully upon his consciousness. He lifted the first page, turned it so that the lamp on his swaying desk best illuminated it and fixed his secretary with a weary stare.

'You will add all the usual honorifics when you make your fair copy, I take it?'

The secretary nodded. The ship made another lurch beneath them as the freshening breeze impelled them homeward. Astern and on either side, a small armada of captured Vhanakhori vessels sailed with them, the Hierarchy's projected invasion strangled at birth. Paril, reminded of this circumstance, allowed himself a small smile and began to read.

'At sea, the thirteenth day of February 3956 AN.

Your Imperial Highness,
I beg humbly to report upon the actions conducted by your fleet under my command since the expiration of the recent divine truce. Our Lord Tio, having favoured us, in his great and merciful benevolence with a

favourable wind, your servant was able to conduct the fleet expeditiously throughout the night of the twelfth/thirteenth, arriving in the bay of Tazman without apparent detection by the forces of our enemy. Your Majesty's marines, under the command of the valiant officers detailed below, were able to execute a most successful descent upon the landward side of the two powerful fortresses there, those that guard the anchorage and protect with their guns the outer and inner harbours. These were swiftly rendered inoperative in a manner highly conducive to the subsequent success of our operation. Following from this, assisted by the actions of agents within the walls, Your Majesty's forces were able to conduct a most destructive combined assault by land and sea. By sea, the introduction of fireships into the military harbour was highly effective in disrupting the enemy's response to our incursion, causing a very satisfactory degree of panic and creating the conditions by which the most powerful vessels in Your Majesty's squadron were able to bring their great guns to bear. Estimates of vessels sunk or disabled, and of those made captive, are detailed below, together with accounts of the actions of officers who particularly distinguished themselves in this action and whose meritorious conduct Your Highness may wish to recognise in due course.

By land, marines descended upon the ropewalks, sail lofts, chandlers stores and ship sheds of the port, freeing several hundred enslaved oarsmen of the enemy fleet, whose own readily comprehensible desire for vengeance upon their erstwhile masters added very satisfactorily to the force at our disposal. As a consequence of your forces' actions in the necessarily short occupation of the port, great quantities of naval stores were destroyed and numerous buildings of a military or naval function burned or otherwise rendered useless. Furthermore, in an action undertaken by your servant and those forces immediately under his command, the great temple of Draganach, in which, over countless years, our impious enemy has caused many poor wretches, both child and adult, to perish in human sacrifice, was razed to the ground. The gigantic effigy of a serpent there, in whose fiery belly uncounted multitudes of victims have been burned over many years, was utterly destroyed with gunpowder, in a manner that will surely dismay our foes and glorify our Lord.

It is a matter of curiosity and coincidence to recount that your servant encountered a member of your diplomatic service, one Beremil Kyresios, whose capture and detention, contrary to all diplomatic norms, by the corsairs of Shangharad has long been a source of grievance to your realm. Your Majesty will be glad to know that, together with a number of other captives, detailed below, this Kyresios has been liberated, brought away and presently sails with your servant'.

'There', said Paril, setting down the page and rubbing his eyes. 'I trust you will apply your official eye to that and correct any infelicities of prose I may have committed to the page before bringing it before me for approval?'

'Indeed', nodded the secretary, who had worked with Paril for many years and could be trusted to ensure that the full report was compiled without delay. 'I note that you have not mentioned the girl, at least not by name. May I ask why?'

Paril ran his hands through his hair and frowned.

Why indeed? She had been the Golden Child, a girl intended for sacrifice, who had escaped that fate rather more than thirteen years ago and who had been on the verge of succumbing to Draganach's flames. The

Hierarchs' greatest general, one Azimandro, had perished in her stead, consigned into the flames, even as the gunpowder barrels placed about the serpent's base had utterly destroyed that infamous abomination. There would be no further sacrifices of that nature, at least not for a while. The girl and her surviving friends had been plucked from the terrace by marines, moments after the great explosion that had shattered the serpent and brought the temple crashing to the ground, both upper and lower precincts with all their columns, treasuries and shrines, all consumed in cleansing flame. Stilitha, the girl was called, and a curious story had emerged concerning her origins. Her mother had been an Erenori maiden, exchanged in the peace of 3943, and had married one of the enemy's leading clerics shortly thereafter. When the lot had claimed her own daughter for sacrifice, the woman had substituted the orphan child of a servant, a girl of similar appearance and age. The subterfuge might deceive the Hierarchy, but their god could not so easily be denied his due. Accordingly, Yuzanid had withdrawn his mandate from them since that time, and all manner of catastrophes had befallen their race as a consequence. Once their grave offence had come to light, the Hierarchs had spared no effort to bring her to that grim place at last. Even as their efforts were crowned with success, the imperial fleet had approached unseen, as though all the efforts of the Hierarchs and their bestial god, all of their attention, had been directed solely to this girl and her destruction. Tio's will, his divine blessing, could certainly be discerned in this turn of fate. Now, together with Axilo, the young man who was her lover, she sailed with him on this vessel – as did two of her friends and the slave whose timely intervention had spared his own life. Tyverios had resolved that this giant of a man should be freed and would be invited to serve in his own household accordingly. This Axilo had been gravely injured in the moments before the destruction of the temple, but the timely intervention of Kyresios and various skilled medics had spared him from death. Kyresios had indicated a desire to look after him, once he had recovered from his injuries, and, together with the girl, he would doubtless be conducted with the diplomat to Callisto in due course. It appeared that he was a talented youth, and Kyresios had spoken of employing him on his staff once he was restored to his office.

But the question of the girl remained unanswered, even to himself. Why had he not mentioned her in his report? She had only recently stood before him in this cabin and recounted the curious events that had brought her to that place. Tio had appeared before her, she had said, in the moment before Azimandro's fall. He had offered to spare her from death. However, Tio had told her then that his power in Yuzanid's heartland was insufficient to spare that of both her lover and herself. She must choose where he should wield that power. In her despair, and in the fullness of her love for the young man, she had begged Tio to consent to her destruction and to spare his life instead. And yet, ultimately, both were spared.

Perhaps even Tio had not foreseen the consequences of the sudden eruption of twenty barrels of the Empire's best gunpowder on those events. She surmised that Yuzanid's power was diminished in that fatal moment and Tio's commensurately increased, thereby enabling him to compass the survival of both young lovers after all. It was a remarkable story but one that he had not set down to paper, maybe because issues of faith and of supernatural occurrences would seem out of place in this bald military summation of events.

He took a sip from the wine goblet that stood before him, and his eyes, unfocused, looked within. He was not a particularly pious man, not one whose lips were habitually in motion with prayer, but there was something about the story of this girl that affected him in a manner that was quite unfamiliar. It was an extraordinary tale and one that under other circumstances he might have dismissed as mere visionary ravings.

And yet he found that he could not discount her story. He would have been loath to have brought it to utterance if any had required it of him, but a certainty grew within his breast that she had indeed been touched by God, as she had maintained, that she stood beneath Tio's personal protection and that the events he had heard described to him on the temple terrace in the moments before the explosion must be viewed in that light.

In a manner quite contrary to the bluff practical quality that formed the core of his character, he found himself wondering whether God had indeed made his presence felt there, and with more than natural force. How else could a slight maiden such as she have run her sword through the Hierarch's greatest champion? A sergeant of marines had witnessed this, a moment before the general fell into the flames and the consequent explosion had torn the bronze serpent apart. He was a practical man, and his account had been laboriously drawn out of him with much awkwardness and hesitation. She had seemed to move with unnatural speed, he had reported, and a supernatural radiance had gleamed momentarily about her.

'What do you mean, supernatural?' Paril had pressed, eyes narrowed.

'Oh, nothing, I suppose', mumbled the sergeant, his craggy features suffused by a sudden blush. 'No more than an illusion, I daresay – a trick of the light, that's all'.

Postscript

The two gods sat side by side on the sandy hummock , where a gentle breeze stirred the long sea grasses. At their feet, drawn with stick in the sand, was a map of the north-eastern parts of Toxandria. There lay the island of Eudora, with its principle cities marked with shells and stones. Tio leaned forward to tease the sand upward into shapes that represented the mountainous spine of that island, placing dried curls of black seaweed to show the smoke that issued from the volcanoes there.

'Your people labour here... and... here,' noted Yuzanid, pointing with a gull's feather. 'Captured and enslaved by my own. In many other places besides. And look yonder,' he said, indicating the coast opposite Eudora. 'Did not this land once belong to your adherents?'

'It did,' agreed Tio calmly. 'And it will do so again, no doubt, in the fullness of time.'

'Oh, so the mists of time have parted for you, have they brother? And you can see along the threads,' laughed Yuzanid scornfully. 'Is that what it is?'

'Not at all,' replied Tio. 'It is just that my people's devotion to me stems from love and not fear. And fear is no great driver of excellence, in my view. My people shall drive out yours one day, I do assure you. Their prayers and devotions rise up to me in a ceaseless, invigorating stream, I find, whereas yours...'

'What of mine, brother?' enquired Yuzanid, his countenance darkening. 'I suppose those souls I gather unto me represent no less an increase to my strength. And there are many,' he added. 'There are very many.'

'Quite so,' agreed Tio, busily placing inverted mussel shells in the undulating space between Eudora and the mainland. 'And they are yielded up from blood-wet altars throughout your realm.'

'They are,' agreed Yuzanid, somewhat mollified. 'Such is their devotion, and I warrant a single soul is worth a thousand thousand prayers.'

'And yet, not all devotions are as you would wish them to be,' countered Tio, continuing patiently with his work whilst his brother glared out towards the sea and the vague horizon at the verge of vision.

'Your meaning?' Yuzanid asked, a suspicious gaze now directed at Tio.

'I think you know my meaning,' laughed Tio.

Glancing down, Yuzanid saw that curls of dry seaweed now emerged from around the green stone that represented the Tazman. The upturned mussel shells were suddenly revealed as a fleet, the seaweed as smoke, pouring from the burning city.

'I do now!' cried Yuzanid furiously, leaping up and scattering the map into a sudden cloud of drifting sand with a few wild swipes of his foot.

'There was a girl, was there not?' asked Tio imperturbably.

'You know there was!' spat Yuzanid, his face red.

'Or rather there *is*,' continued Tio, 'and continues to be so, much to the disgrace of your people, much to your own discomfiture, no doubt.'

Yuzanid frowned and his mouth moved wordlessly as he stood over his divine brother, arms folded.

'There will come a time...' he warned at last, raising a finger.

'Oh yes, there will come a time, alright,' agreed Tio, standing up to stretch himself languorously. 'There is a time for everything, I hear, but this time was mine, I think you must agree.'

'Perhaps, brother,' conceded Yuzanid. 'But there will be another time, and then you shall learn humility.'
'And you acceptance,' smiled Tio.
'Acceptance?'
'That love shall always vanquish fear, brother. That what is freely given is worth more than what is surrendered at the sword point or beneath the lash.'
'We shall see,' sniffed Yuzanid, turning to look out over the measureless grey ocean.
'Oh yes,' agreed Tio. 'We shall see. Because that is what gives our existence meaning, does it not? In that we are agreed.'

Author's Note

Indi Authors often struggle to get their work noticed in a crowded marketplace, so I should like to give my particular thanks to those generous people who kindly undertook to ARC read this book in advance of publication through contact on TikTok. Their commitment is much appreciated and their names are below:

ShannonM @shmould1
Kari T @kari__t
Jamie @sh3l_indulgence
Jaycruzin @jaycruzin
Crab and Bell @crabandbell
Victoriareads @victoriareads0
Bella's Library @bellasbooks_5
Sky @thebookishbrand
Katie @katiecrutchfieldw
Alicia @obsessedwithbooks888
Sara @sarad_morrison
Kelli @kmartvet
Bethany Knight @bemysbookshelf
Christina @chrissygreads
I read books @lifewithkim__
Book Talks With Rosie @rosalies.library
Veronica Gomez Marin @vgomezmarinsbooks
Fantasy Reader @booktok_fantasy
Whit_Sea_Reads @whit_sea_17
J M McQueen @the libraryofimagination
Brie Rose @brie_rose44
Destiny Snyder @lostinliteracy
Kait @kait.booktok

Other Books by Martin Dukes (aka RJ Wheldrake)

That Which The Deep Heart Knows
1st in the Chronicles of Toxandria
Romantic Fantasy

An ancient empire, a prince unexpectedly thrown into the maelstrom of politics - and a tavern girl. Love, loss and a conflict of gods.

Hearts of Ice and Stone
1st in the Britannia Trilogy
Dark gothic fantasy

In Darkharrow, the dead lie slumbering. Some, whose hearts are of stone, must await the last trump for their awakening, but others whose hearts are of ice may be summoned to new life. But to what consequence?

A Moment in Time
1st in the Alex Trueman Chronicles
YA Sci-fi Fantasy

Alex Trueman is trapped in the strange world of Intersticia, a world trapped between moments in time. Follow him in his first adventure, 'A Moment in Time'. (1st of 5)

Worm Winds of Zanzibar
2nd in the Alex Trueman Chronicles
YA Sci-fi Fantasy

Take a journey with Alex to exotic East Africa. Madness, murder and mayhem await him there in his greatest adventure yet.

Printed in Great Britain
by Amazon